Williams, Thomas.

    Leah, New Hampshire.

LEAH, NEW HAMPSHIRE

The Collected Stories of
Thomas Williams

WILLIAM MORROW AND COMPANY, INC.
NEW YORK

"The Fisherman Who Got Away" was first published in *Seasons of the Angler* in 1988 by Weidenfeld & Nicholson, edited by David Seybold.

"The Orphan's Wife" was originally published in somewhat different form under the title "Another Country, Another Time," *Saturday Evening Post*, May 25, 1963. The lines quoted in "The Orphan's Wife" from "The Hollow Men" by T. S. Eliot are reprinted from *Collected Poems of T. S. Eliot* by permission of the publisher, Harcourt, Brace & World, Inc.

These stories originally appeared in the following publications: "The Snows of Minnesota," *The New Yorker*, February 12, 1966; "Paranoia," *Esquire*, November 1970; "Goose Pond," *Esquire*, November 1957; "Certainties," *Esquire*, December 1965; "The Survivors," *The New Yorker*, August 21, 1965; "The Skier's Progress," *The New Yorker*, February 2, 1963; "Horned Pout Are Evil," *Esquire*, December 1966; "The Old Dancers," *Saturday Evening Post*, November 14, 1964; "All Trades, Their Tackle and Trim," *Esquire*, November 1965; "The Buck in Trotevale's," *Esquire*, August 1958. Copyright © 1957, 1958, 1963, 1964, 1965, 1966, 1970, 1989 by Thomas Williams.

It is the policy of William Morrow and Company, Inc., and its imprints and affiliates, recognizing the importance of preserving what has been written, to print the books we publish on acid-free paper, and we exert our best efforts to that end.

Library of Congress Cataloging-in-Publication Data

Williams, Thomas.
    Leah, New Hampshire : the collected stories of Thomas Williams.
        p.   cm.
    ISBN 0-688-11544-6
    1. New Hampshire—Fiction.   I. Title.
PS3573.I456L4   1992
813'.54—dc20   91-40940
                                                                                     CIP

Printed in the United States of America

First Edition

1   2   3   4   5   6   7   8   9   10

BOOK DESIGN BY LYNN DONOFRIO DESIGNS

Contents

Introduction by John Irving	7
Author's Note	15
Goose Pond	21
The Skier's Progress	35
The Survivors	61
Horned Pout Are Evil	79
The Snows of Minnesota	87
Paranoia	107
The Buck in Trotevale's	121
The Orphan's Wife	145
All Trades, Their Tackle and Trim	181
Voices	187
The Fisherman Who Got Away	213
The Old Dancers	225
Ancient Furies	245
The Voyage of the *Cosmogon*	257
Certainties	281

Introduction

by John Irving

THOMAS WILLIAMS was born in Duluth, Minnesota, in 1926; at age ten, he went with his divorced mother to New York City, where he attended Staten Island Academy, the Little Red School House on Bleecker Street and the High School of Music and Art; at fourteen, he moved to New Hampshire, where he died of cancer in 1991. Except for Army service in Japan and university studies in Chicago, Iowa City and Paris, Mr. Williams was very much a New Hampshire man, as his Author's Note to this collection attests. (Leah, New Hampshire, is a fictional town; its denizens—old-timers, newcomers and tourists—and its enduring landscape are the common ingredients these stories share.) Although I was born in New Hampshire and didn't move away from the so-called Granite State for twenty years, and I have since lived in Vermont for twenty more, I would never profess to understand New Englanders as Tom Williams understood us.

He was an outdoorsman, a sportsman, a hunter and a fisherman, a conservationist and an environmentalist—and a man who built his impressive house of wood and stone with his own hands (and with the help of his wife). He was a college professor, too—my personal favorite at the University of New Hampshire. But if he would correct you when your language was vague, he was also instructive during a walk in the woods: he knew what sort of moss or fern you were standing on, and the name of the tree you were leaning against; he knew the birds and the animals, and—astonishingly—he was also one of those men who understood how mechanical things work. He knew engines, he knew tools, he knew guns.

He was contemptuous of those of us who drive a car without knowing the first thing about what makes it run; he was outspoken on the subject of people who toy with firearms without knowing enough about how to handle them; he was critical of those would-be athletes who shamelessly sport the newest and best equipment but who cannot control their skis or deliver a second serve with authority. This definitive lore (of all he had taken the trouble to learn, in the most careful and correct detail) is vitally a part of his fiction. But what I admire most in these stories from Leah, New Hampshire—and in Mr. Williams's novels—is how much he knew about human nature, and how much he fathomed psychologically about people. And what Tom Williams knew especially well was what is darkest and most hidden in us; I don't mean only the Conradian fascination with abomination, which Mr. Williams brilliantly explores and consistently exposes under a fresh light, but also those telling revelations of our smaller weaknesses—our unspoken lies to ourselves, our most cleverly concealed embarrassments, the hypocrisies we successfully hide from others. In this sense is Mr. Williams a wonderfully old-fashioned writer: he reveals moral truths about ourselves; he makes discoveries about us, of an often painful nature.

I don't mean to imply that he is a cruel writer, for he writes about what is violent and deceitful in our nature out of the most passionate affection for humanity—even for our darkest side. And he is also old-fashioned as a fiction writer in this sense: real characters populate his stories, and they develop and become known to us—much better understood by us, finally, than are most of the people we actually know. This revelation of character occurs in the context of a narrative that gains momentum; in other words, he is that dinosaur among contemporary writers of fiction, an actual storyteller, and in these stories something of real interest actually happens. In short, these stories are about something. They are not merely exercises of "voice," or other self-conscious displays of the writer's ability with the language. Mr. Williams's ability with the language is considerable, but it is—quite correctly—the content of his writing that impresses; he doesn't need to show off with words because he's interested in showing us bigger things. (Even so, and even in the offhand context of his Author's Note, Thomas Williams shows us how comfortably the language yields to him: "In the fall," he writes simply, "the deer are the color of the spaces between the trees.")

In describing the fictional landscape of Leah, Williams writes: "Around the town, on old asphalt and dirt roads, are tar-paper shacks, and moldy house-trailer slums; in New Hampshire the brush and the trees grow quickly and screen these places from those whose theories, political, economic, and aesthetic, would be damaged by too much ugliness." That human weakness, to hide "ugliness," is a theme with him, and Williams was no fan of "theories"; as for literary theory, he called it "an interesting game in itself, all but separate from the problems a writer tries to solve. Theory can be dangerous to art because theorists have a tendency toward dogma." His work is altogether rational, more pragmatic than theoretical; it is as planned and painstakingly crafted as a good stone wall—the kind without mortar. Williams liked stone walls; upon discovering this evidence of human habitation in woods now reclaimed by brush and trees, he speaks of these walls as "a reminder of mortality, of the dogged energy of the dead."

And this is the quality of his writing to me: lucid, terse, unfancy, which well befits a man who always knew what he meant—Tom Williams was never merely groping for ideas. He writes with inspired common sense.

The oldest of these stories, and surely the most often anthologized, is "Goose Pond," originally published in *Esquire* in 1957; more than half of Williams's stories were published in *Esquire* or *The New Yorker* from the late 1950s through the 1960s. "Goose Pond" is an absolutely perfect short story about a fifty-eight-year-old man trying to come to terms with his wife's death, his sudden loneliness and his awareness of his own eventual death; this is serious stuff, but written with an exquisitely light touch.

Robert Hurley's children think that their father needs to be rescued from his loneliness and grief, but it is not the company of his children or his grandchildren that Hurley needs or seeks; he wants to be more alone, to reassure himself that there is a rightness to this passage from life to death that he has just experienced. On a trek into the woods, Hurley kills a deer with a bow and arrow; then he beds down for the night near a pond where the geese bed down, too. "Each one its own warm life deep in the cold sky, and they called to each other, kept close and on course together, facing with disciplined bravery that impossible journey." Thus Robert Hurley finds the correctness of life's essentially "impossible journey" that he is looking for.

The newest of these stories, and the last short story Tom Williams wrote before he died, is "The Voyage of the *Cosmogon*," which is published for the first time in this collection. The story will remind the reader of an old *New Yorker* story also collected here: "The Snows of Minnesota." In that earlier story, Williams describes the painful relocation of a fifth-grade boy from Minnesota to New Hampshire. His parents are extremely sympathetic characters, but the lonely boy nonetheless feels homeless; following a huge snowstorm, he constructs an elaborate snow fort, a secret network of tunnels under the snow, which his father correctly recognizes as the ten-year-old's attempt to rebuild his life in Minnesota. But in "The Voyage of the *Cosmogon*" the world has darkened; this time the relocated boy is an eighth-grader, and his mother, a single parent, is not sympathetic—she's a woman of sluttish insensitivity engaged in a sordid affair with a married policeman.

The fragility of life is thematic in many of these stories, perhaps best described in a former *Saturday Evening Post* story from the 1960s, "The Old Dancers," in which a shy, elderly couple—a second marriage for both—attempt to cope with the woman's minor illness, requiring only a medical examination and a small surgical operation; she considers both an invasion of her privacy. "Each had lived too long in a house of shouting and tears, and now they were careful of each other, careful about such things as nakedness, and the shutting of doors."

In one of the newer stories, "The Fisherman Who Got Away," this fragility is felt even in the act of catching a fish. "His rod quivered—a snag or a hit. A fish, he knew as he picked it up, because it moved a little to the side, undulant, like a heart-beat, a small spasm of opinion." Even from the fish's point of view, life is fragile. "Beneath the water the cold muscles fought for life against this fragile extension of his touch. How sicken-ing it must be to be pulled by the invisible—like having a fit, epilepsy, a brain spasm. What did the fish think pulled him so hard, and what part of him said no?"

But the reader can never assume that lugubriousness lies at the heart of Williams's thinking; the humor and the irony are broader than that, and often best glimpsed in his precise intro-duction of minor characters. In "Voices," the main character's mother is supporting "a young man she'd met at an Arthur Murray Dance Studio, a dance instructor named Stavros whose arms were raw from the abrading operations necessary to re-move the tattoos he had decorated himself with in an earlier, less classy life. . . . She'd bought Stavros a business he'd been interested in, a series of ancient popcorn vending machines, the kind with a bare light bulb to keep the popcorn warm, in run-down Washington, D.C., movie houses. The problem was crick-ets, which liked popcorn and invaded the machines. It was disconcerting to patrons when they felt the frantic soft bodies of crickets in their hands, or mouths."

In "The Skier's Progress," Williams describes a local ski hero who preys upon unhappily married women and young, inexperienced girls; he writes: "On the back of his electric-blue Bogner stretch pants there can be found a dark circle as big as a dime; a few days ago, at a party, he sat on a fragment of Vienna sausage. He knows the spot is there, and he is a little worried about the direction in which he turns. It seems to him that there is always something he half tries to conceal—his bit-ten fingernails, the little spot on his pants. He has resigned himself to such nagging imperfections, and if he thought too much about them he might realize that they reflect his own opinion of his immortal soul. . . . Like many libertines, he be-lieves in the existence of another race of human beings, so different from himself—the ones who are faithful and honor-able, to whom love and sex are exquisitely the same, who stand immaculate in the sight of heaven. He feels that somehow he has been excluded from this race, and that he could no more enter it than he could grow wings."

In another story, a man who feels guilty for his intention to marry a younger woman contemplates "a past that included some dangerous experiments with ugliness, and too much indifference to the coldness and cruelty of the world"; he marries her anyway, of course—and he continues to feel guilty. (The story, "The Orphan's Wife," although it is as well written as the other stories collected here, is my least favorite; it feels too big and cumbersome to be a short story at all—it reads more like the unfinished business of a novel in progress. But perhaps it stands out to me in this respect only because the other stories are so very fine.)

In a story about a fiction writer, Williams confesses to the familiar fear that writers have of their real-life subjects. "Like those who fear dogs only to excite in all dogs an immediate, aggressive affection, I seem doomed to be the chosen confessor of those who have systematized their delusions. I wonder if they know how much they frighten me." (This story was published in *Esquire* under the title "Paranoia," but it is actually an excerpt from Williams's National Book Award-winning novel, *The Hair of Harold Roux*.) The surprise in the story is that the writer is more to be feared than his subjects. "We use each other, the materials of reality, our experiences, everything at all in our 'encapsulated delusional systems.' Even in my apprehension I sense my kinship with G., and cannot wholly condemn his mad attempt to make his own satisfying order out of chaos. I, too, am driven by a similar *horror vacui*. Though I would call my work by another name, I will use G. and all the rest for my own purposes, use them coldly and without mercy, more coldly than their own warm needful selves could ever understand."

A *New Yorker* story from the 1960s, "The Survivors," is also excerpted from a novel—in this case, *Whipple's Castle*. (When Williams died, he was at work on a novel about David Whipple, the young protagonist of *Whipple's Castle*; David had moved away from Leah. In the unfinished novel, David Whipple is in his sixties; he is moving back to New Hampshire.) "The Survivors" explores "the irrational guilt that all survivors feel." David's best friend was killed in a bicycle accident when they were both schoolboys; now a grown man, David confronts the silence that endures between himself and his best friend's father. "We stood there in a kind of deadlock, looking at each other. Then, with tolerance and complicity, we slid our soft glances apart."

And several stories pursue the justification of hunting, or killing game; it is a subject that Williams worried over all his life. He never picks easy targets; he is not merely creating those knee-jerk Bambi-lovers who see the killing of any wild animal through tear-glazed, Disneyesque eyes. Rather, he picks good arguments against himself; *then* he comes down hard, in favor of the killing. The least impressive of these stories is "All Trades, Their Tackle and Trim," in which Williams seems to be deliberately baiting the anti-hunters among his readers. (In another story, a character says, "I am not a snake-poker"; in this story, Williams is clearly poking a snake.) The best of these arguments-within-a-story is incomparable, although Williams is slightly disparaging of "The Buck in Trotevale's" in his Author's Note, in which he calls the story "not wrong, but slightly odd"; he goes on to say that the story "approaches sentimentality, the death of force." But to me it is from this proximity to sentimentality that the story derives its dangerous ambition, its uncomfortable reality. It is my personal favorite among these stories, and it pokes a lot of snakes by creating a so-called moral certainty and giving it stunning, symbolic expression; then, always subtly, the story undermines the exact same "certainty."

In a story titled "Certainties," Mr. Williams concludes: "There are few dark places left on our maps, and we need that dark, if only to leave behind us all our rigid, belittling geometries, signs, and boundaries—certainties that diminish us, that tell us by the numbers exactly where we are, and that things are merely what they are, not what they can seem." The power of these stories from Leah, New Hampshire, derives from the "dark places" that Thomas Williams so skillfully uncovers; yet we never feel diminished by these stories—instead we feel remarkably whole, completely illuminated. Mr. Williams has shown us more than our ugliness; he has also revealed those passions and misgivings that make us worthy of each other's sympathy.

Author's Note

LEAH IS an imaginary town in the State of New Hampshire, a state that can be cruel, especially to its poor, or sick, or old. In its public, or collective, stance, it can act as a skinflint and a buffoon among its neighbors. Its people, however, like most Americans, can be decent and generous if, for a moment, they forget dogma, forget "conservatism," and sanctimony, and the myths of an imaginary history. To me Leah quite often seems to be a real town in an imaginary state I have to prove over and over again in order to believe in its beauty and its paradoxes. Given the land, the history, the strange politics, the town settles into its valley beside its river and, at least for me, is there.

Right now, at one o'clock in the afternoon, I see the mountain, the lake, the wild brook in the woods, the October light that is nearly level as it crosses the valley. The famous colors have gone, and the old golden ones are going. Then, in a week or so, the hills will be the color of gray branches tinged by purplish winter buds, with green-black pyramids here and there meaning spruce or white pine, balsam fir or hemlock. The names of the trees are still known in Leah. In the fall the deer are the color of the spaces between the trees.

Leah was once mostly field and pasture, but now it is nearly

all woods below its ledgy mountains. In the woods you find
stone walls, always a reminder of mortality, of the dogged energy of the dead. Most New Hampshire towns are large geo-
graphical areas, with a center—a village—somewhere in the
vastness of the township. Some towns haven't any land at all,
like the town of Cascom, which is a small center within the
township of Leah. Or Northlee, which is the county seat in
Saxon County, and is also within the township of Leah. That's
where the two colleges are—Northlee State College, formerly a
teachers college, and Northlee College, which is private, famous, and expensive. Northlee is five miles north of Leah, but
in Leah.

I can't remember when I decided to use Leah for the name
of a town, or exactly why, except that as a child I had the
dangerous Protestant habit of reading the Bible without much
knowledge, without exactly knowing what the Bible was. Jacob
cheated his brother Esau, the hunter, out of his birthright.
Jacob, the smooth one. Jacob was tricked by Laban into mar-
rying Leah, thinking he would get beautiful Rachel. Leah, as
the Lord saw, was hated. As I remember they were all selfish
and vicious, and the Lord's pronouncements didn't make much
ethical sense either. My father, a Midwesterner, looked into his
own heart and found goodness, so his God, like him, was gentle
and fair-minded. My own more Eastern revelation I found in
the tale of the soldier who, with the best of intentions, steadied
the Ark of the Covenant and was struck dead for his presump-
tion.

The motto of Leah is "Don't patronize me."

In the thirty-some years since the earliest story in this collection was written, Leah has changed, but not as much as have
the towns to the south and east. There are a few condominiums
on Cascom Lake, a shop in town called Woks of Life, and an
industrial park containing long metal buildings with signs on
them like *Zeta/Seal, Camtec,* and *Intertone.* The tannery is gone,
its owners having chosen to move rather than stop polluting the
Cascom River. Herbert Woolley's yarn mill is still operating, but
the two red brick woolen mills have become a condo complex
and a discount outlet. There is only one shopping mall, always
with a unit or two empty. The population has grown about a
third, but many hill farms have gone back to the twilight of the

woods, so more people live in the "built-up" town itself. Around the town, on old asphalt and dirt roads, are tar-paper shacks, and moldy house-trailer slums; in New Hampshire the brush and the trees grow quickly and screen these places from those whose theories, political, economic, and aesthetic, would be damaged by too much ugliness.

There are reports of vandalism and theft by young men. Restaurants and stores can't find enough help. Last week a cow moose was seen near the bridge to Wentworth Junction, and a European wild boar, escaped from a private park, was shot on Cascom Mountain—reddish eyes, a hairy face, and tusks like yellow fingers.

The mode of Leah, to which there are disturbing exceptions, is inner, reflecting an outer world governed generally by rational pragmatism, the kind we live with while trying to forget the decrees of the famous, whom power has driven asinine.

Since these stories were written over such a long time, from the fifties to the eighties, they may seem to be by different writers who happen to bear the same name. The person I am now may have changed a word or a punctuation mark here and there in this book, but not anywhere the number my present eye and ear find strange. At sixty-one I don't think I have the right or the temperament to correct that fellow in his twenties who, in "Goose Pond," entered the psyche of what he thought to be an ancient man of fifty-eight. I can correct neither his style nor the conclusions he reached. And there is the stylistic exuberance, or the simple colors, of "The Buck in Trotevale's," a story which seems strange to me now. Not wrong, but slightly odd, and which, perhaps too fecklessly, or bravely, approaches sentimentality, the death of force.

Two of the stories here, in different form, were small parts of novels. I include them because of their separate and balancing views of the town.

I hesitate to say more about the stories themselves because in reading what writers have to say about their own work, I find that they are nearly always wrong. Since many of these are writers I trust and admire, I suspect it is also true of me. The area in which a writer becomes new, and original, is to the practitioner *terra incognita*. Literary theory is an interesting game in itself, all but separate from the problems a writer tries

to solve. Theory can be dangerous to art because theorists have
a tendency toward dogma. A new theory must destroy the old
and all perceived children of the old; there is no fine scientific
or revolutionary purity about evolution, or synthesis. I think I
know what I want to do—to populate an imaginary world with
real people, and to cause the identification with others that is
the best, the life-giving, talent of our race. I want to do this, and
though I, too, am obviously haunted by theory, it is left behind
at the moment when the white page is covered by shadows.

Themes and tendencies, however, may be perceived afterwards. The rational child in the power, benevolent or otherwise, of irrational adults. Captives taken into exile. Loss, the
purest of our emotions, so pure it has a clear, lunar beauty not
subject to rationalization, as are hope, despair, anger, joy, love,
and all the rest, though they have their moments.

A while ago I was driving north on Route 4, and came up
behind a very old couple in an ancient Ford Fairlane with New
Hampshire plates. The old man was driving at thirty miles an
hour in a fifty-mile-per-hour zone, and as I watched he carefully and evenly took an off-ramp the wrong way, toward a new
section of superhighway. If you are going north and you want
to go west, you take a left, up the perfectly geometrical curve
according to some ancient map you have in memory. Only now
do I ask myself why the two old people had to go west, toward
Concord. The Department of Motor Vehicles is there, and perhaps it had to do with the validation of his license demanded
periodically at his age. Somehow, in here, the idea of story
begins. Their old moss-colored Fairlane is not used for long
trips these days, especially not on improved highways. He can
remember when Route 4 turned left to go west, when it sometimes went between houses and barns. If you live into your
eighties you can't have been stupid. Think of all the strategies
against accident and death you've conceived of and acted upon.
Think of the thousands of things you know—practical things,
such as the names and functions of the parts of the engine that
moves you along. Also the names of harnesses, trees, grandchildren, guns, animals, and tools. Think of history, all of it
dangerous and unexpected when it was new, and he and his
wife have survived it all until this moment when he carefully
feeds them into what must seem to him a field of artillery fire,

in which every missile comes toward him, in all lanes, at sixty-five and seventy miles an hour, each one imperiously and stupidly arrogant about the right-of-way. So now, if they survive, he is cursed as a freak and an incompetent. And then there is the business of the renewal of his license.

This seems to be the way a story begins for me—at least this as yet unwritten one. I'm not sure what it will be about, either, but I'm almost certain it will have in it names like pinery hook, crupper, planetary gear, whiffletree, and magneto, and that it will take place in Leah.

Thomas Williams
Durham, New Hampshire
October 1988

Goose Pond

ROBERT HURLEY's wife died in September, and by the middle of October he had more or less settled everything. His son and daughter were both married and lived far away from New York; his son in Los Angeles, his daughter in Toledo. They came east for the funeral and each wanted him to come and visit. "I'm not about to retire. I won't be an old man in a guest room," he told them, knowing the great difference between the man he looked at fifty-eight and the man he felt himself to be. It had taken Mary six months to die, and during the last few of those months he began quietly to assume many of her symptoms. The doctors noticed it and understood, but his children, accustomed to a father who had always been to them a commonsense, rather unimaginative figure, were shocked by his loss of weight, by a listlessness as unlike him, as unsettling to them as if the earth's rotation had begun to slow down.

But he would do no visiting, even though his business did not need him. "I know what visiting is," he wrote to his son. "I don't do it very well. Please don't call so much. You know how to write letters." "Daddy," his daughter said, long-distance. "The children are crazy to have their grandfather come and see them."

And he thought, there is one place I would like to go, and there are no children I know there. "I'm going to New Hampshire, to Leah," he said.

"All by yourself? What for?" She began to get excited, almost hysterical. He could see her biting her lower lip—a habit of her mother's. Afterwards she would be calling Charles in Los Angeles.

"I was born there. Your mother and I lived there before you were born. Do I need any other reason? It's October. Anyway, I'll be back in a couple of weeks."

"But, Daddy, we felt that you shouldn't be alone. . . ."

"I haven't been alone for thirty years," he said. "I want to try it again. Now go back to whatever you were doing. I can hear a baby crying in your house. Go take care of it. I'm going to stay with the Pedersens. Do you remember the old people in the big house on the mountain? If they still take boarders, that's where I'll be." *If they're still alive,* he thought. He wanted to walk in the woods again, but he had other reasons. The sight of his grandchildren, the hundred times a day when their small disasters caused screaming, tears; he couldn't stand it. They were always about to hurt themselves, they nearly fell so many times. They had so many deadly years to make. Automobiles, knives, leukemia, fire. . . . On the afternoon of the funeral he had watched his granddaughter, Ann, and suddenly he saw her having his wife's senseless pain, saw her crying not because of a bumped knee, but at more serious wounds. And the Pedersens? They were so old, they had somehow escaped, and as he remembered them they lived dried-up and careful, in a kind of limbo. He would go to the Pedersens, on Cascom Mountain.

Nana fussed with the Edison lamp, turning the white flame up in the mantle, moving the broad base across the crack made by the table leaf; then with the side of her hand she wiped the shiny surface of the table where it had been. The light shone past the tinted shade, up the glass chimney, and sharpened her old face, made her glasses glint for a second until she moved away, tall and always busy, her small eyes always alert. She rarely sat down, and even then seemed poised, ready for busy duty. The old man settled himself cautiously, as he did now, one piece at a time. Nana had his zither out of its case, the light just right; made sure he had his hearing aid, his pick, an ashtray near. In spite of his age, he smoked cigarettes.

Back in the shadows, between a lacy, drooping vine and the narrow window, Nana's older sister, blue dress and high black shoes, composed and fragile face, sat in a rocker and never spoke. Nana herself was seventy-nine. For forty years she had bossed the seven-mile trek down to Leah in the late fall, back up the mountain again to this high old house in the spring. It was Nana who dealt with the world, who shut the windows when it rained, herded great-grandchildren when the family came in the summer, locked the house for the winter. In a few weeks they would be going down to their small apartment in Leah, to take their chances on another winter.

The old man tuned his zither, humming in a dry, crackly falsetto and turning his wrench as he picked the short strings. Tuned against the windy old voice, the crisp notes of the zither were startling, clear and metallic. There seemed to be no connection between the voice and the sounds of the strings, as if the old man heard other notes, the sounds of memory to check his instrument against.

"German *concert* zither," Nana said proudly, still hovering over the lamp. She rearranged his cigarettes, the coffee cup. She spoke from behind him, "He don't hear so good," nodding vigorously. "But he got the hearing aid." She pointed into his ear, where the pink button shone like a flower against brown freckles. "He don't wear it all the time, like he should." She moved quickly away on some sudden errand, and the old man looked up and winked at Hurley.

"Sometimes it makes too much noise," he said, smiling benevolently at his wife. She began to move the table. "It's all right. It's all right!" he said. In his fifty years in America he had mastered the sounds of English, but the rhythms of his speech were Scandinavian. "I'm going to play first a Norwegian song."

Nana poised herself upon a chair, folded her hands firmly, set herself for a moment, and then began energetically to smooth her apron down her long thighs. The old lady against the wall stopped rocking. It always startled Hurley when, out of her silent effacement, she responded.

The old man bent over his zither, his shiny face as ruddy as a baby's. His mottled, angular fingers worked over the strings;

he swayed back and forth to keep time and snorted, gave little gasps and grunts he evidently did not hear himself, in time with the music. Beneath, occasionally overcoming the sibilant, involuntary breaths, the music was poignantly clear, ordered, cascading, vivid as little knives in the shadowy room. At the end they all applauded, and the old man bowed, very pleased.

That night Hurley climbed the staircase that angled around the central chimney, an oil lamp to light his way, and entered his cold room in moonlight almost as bright as the lamp, but colder, whiter against the lamp's yellow. Two little windows looked down across the old man's garden—"Mostly for the deer," the old man had said of it—then over the one still-mown pasture left to the farm, down the long hills silvery in moonlight to Cascom Lake in the valley, white among black surrounding spruce. Behind, on the other side of the house, he could feel the dark presence of Cascom Mountain.

He wondered if it would be a night for sleep. He was tired enough. In the last few days he had taken many of the familiar trails, especially following those that he remembered led through hardwood. Although the leaves had turned and mostly fallen, here or there one tree flamed late among the bare ones, catching light and casting it in all directions as if it were an orange or soft red sun. He stopped often in the woods, surprised by each molten maple branch, even the smallest bright veins of each leaf golden and precious against a gnarled black trunk or the green twilight of a spruce grove. He walked carefully, resting often, sampling the few cold, sweet apples from the abandoned mountain trees, eating Nana's sandwiches a little at a time. He wanted the day to last as long as possible. At night he thought of his wife.

The high, sloping bed was wide and lonesome as a field of snow. During his wife's illness he could not sleep in their own bed, but slept every night on a studio couch where he could reach the sides, hold himself down, and remember exactly where he was and why she was not beside him. If he woke in the night and for a second forgot, he had to learn over again from the beginning that Mary was going to die. It was always the first time over again, when they had left the doctor (the poor doctor, according to Mary) at the cancer hospital and walked together to Grant's Tomb. Mary finally said, "You know? They should pay a man a thousand dollars a minute for having to say those words."

Then the inevitable sequence of hours came through his mind, one after the other, until the afternoon when she was not so brave anymore and shook her head back and forth as if to throw off the plastic tube that went into her nose and down, jiggling the clamps and bottle on its hanger. Tears rolling from the outside corners of her drowned eyes and she cried pettishly, "Help me, help me."

She had taken pain better than most, was better at taking it by far than her husband or her children. When she'd had the compound fracture of her wrist she had been the calm one, the strong one. And he thought, *My God, how much pain she must have if she is caused to do this—if it is Mary who is caused to do this. . . .*

As they cut nerves, cutting off pain in little bits and pieces, it was as if they cut off her life, too, by shreds—the pain, the possibility of it forever gone; the life forever gone. But new pain took the place of the old. She lived for six months and died almost weightless, ageless, the little lines and wrinkles of her familiar body smoothed as if by a filling pulp. Her arms turned to thin tubes, her forehead waxed as taut, as translucent as a yellow apple. Her eyes, before the final cutting, watched him, blameful as a beaten child's. She whined for help: "What is happening to me?" And being a man only, he could stand, and stand, and stand, helpless at the foot of her crank-operated bed, the simple handle drawing his eyes, mocking, it seemed to him, telling him to crank, to grasp the handle in his strong hands and crank, sweat at it, crank faster and harder, crank until she is well again.

He turned and his hand touched the firm, virginal pillow next to his. The linen smelled country-new, of washdays and clotheslines.

At midnight he heard what he first supposed to be a hundred dogs barking in the distance, and as the barking changed on the wind he suddenly knew, in exactly the same way he had known in his childhood, that it was the Canada geese flying over, low here because of the height of the land, streaming over in the darkness. *Lorlorn, lorlorn, lorlorn,* the geese called to each other as they passed. He ran to the window—remembering an old excitement, feet numb on the cold boards—but the geese did not cross the moon. He remembered them well enough that way: the long wavering files of geese, necks thrust out straight, dark wings arcing tirelessly on their long journey over the guns, through all the deadly traps set for them—the weather, the ice, the hunting animals and the traitor decoys. Each one its own warm life deep in the cold sky, and they called to each other, kept close and on course together, facing with disciplined bravery that impossible journey.

He came awake in the indeterminate time when night was breaking and the small windows were luminous squares upon the wall. He lay on his back and watched the light grow, the corners arrange themselves and moldings darken, wondering at a curved shape above the closet door. As the morning increased (he heard pans banging down in the kitchen, Nana's sharp morning voice) he finally saw that the curved shape was a bow hung on pegs. This room evidently had been a young boy's during the summer: a huge fungus platter hung between the windows and in the back of the closet he had found a fly rod enmeshed in kinky leader. Nana had missed a trout hook crusted with dried worm, stuck high on a curtain.

Before he went downstairs he remembered the bow, took it down, and, wondering at the easy memories of his youth, strung it. He instinctively placed the lower end against the inside of his right foot, and his left hand slid easily up the wood with the string lightly guided by his fingertips. The string vibrated tautly, and he remembered, too, how a bow seemed lighter after being strung, the tense pressure communicating energy to the arm. He estimated the pull at sixty pounds—quite a powerful bow.

"Oh, you found the bow 'n' arrow!" Nana said when he came into the kitchen with it. "You going to shoot? Say, how did you cock it?"

He placed the bow against his foot, pulled with his right hand, and pushed with the heel of his left hand, his fingers working the string out of the notch.

"Nobody could fix it. The children going crazy they couldn't shoot, nobody could cock it," Nana said admiringly.

"Do you have any arrows?"

The old man had decided to listen. "In the umbrella stand is some arrows," he said, and Nana rushed out after them.

After breakfast she insisted they all go out and watch him shoot, and he was surprised at his own excitement when he fitted the nock of one of the warped target arrows to the string. He drew and loosed the arrow across the thirty yards between the driveway and barn. *Whap* as the arrow hit the silvery, unpainted wood of the barn and stuck, quivering. A cloud of swallows streamed out of a sashless window, and shreds of dusty hay fell from between the boards. The old people were impressed.

As he drew his second arrow the bow split apart above the grip. Arrow, string, half the bow fell loosely over his arms.

"Ooooh!" the old people sighed. "The wood was too old," the old man said. "It all dries up and it got no give to it."

"I'll get you another one," Hurley said. They shushed him up, said it wasn't any good, that nobody could cock it anyway. But later when he drove his Drive-Ur-Self Chevrolet down into Leah for groceries and the mail, he stopped in at Follansbee's hardware store.

Old Follansbee remembered him from the times he and Mary had come up to ski, possibly not from the earlier time when Follansbee was a young man working in his father's store and Hurley was a boy.

"Do for you?" Old Follansbee's bald head (once covered with black, bushy hair, parted in the middle) gleamed softly, approximately the same color and texture as his maple rolltop desk.

"I'd like to buy a bow—and some arrows," Hurley added in order to specify what kind of bow he meant. In Leah he had always been constrained to come immediately to the point. The old man led him to the sporting-goods corner where rifles and shotguns, fish poles and outboard motors, knives, rubber boots, decoys, and pistols lay in cases, on counters, or were hung on racks. He remembered this part of the store and the objects he had fallen in love with as a boy. No girl had meant as much to him at fifteen as had the beautifully angular lines of a Winchester Model 06, .22 pump. He even remembered the model number, but from this distance he wondered how a number could have meant so much.

He tried out a few of the pretty, too modern bows until he found one that seemed to have the same pull as the one he had broken.

"That one's glass," Old Follansbee said. "My boy says it don't want to break."

"Glass? It's made of glass?"

"Correct. Strange, ain't it? What they can do these days? You'll want some arrows, did you say?"

He bought two arrows. When he'd pulled the one out of the barn it came apart in his hands, split all the way up the shaft. He decided to replace it with two, even though he knew the New Hampshire way was to resent such prodigality. He bought a leather arm guard and finger tabs; then he saw the hunting arrows. The slim, three-bladed heads suggested Indians and his youth. The target arrows, beside them, seemed to have no character, no honest function. He bought two hunting arrows, and under old Follansbee's suspicious, conventional eye, a bow-hunting license, feeling like a child who had spent his Sunday-school money on a toy.

At the post office he found a joint communiqué from his worried children. "We have decided that it would be best . . ." the words went. He sent two identical telegrams: *Having wonderful time. Tend your business. Love, Dad.* They all believed in the therapy of youth—in this case, grandchildren. He couldn't think of a way to tell them that he loved them all too much.

Nana and the old man walked with him as far as the ledges at the top of the wild orchard, careful in their white tennis shoes. Nana stood splay-footed on the granite, queen of the hill, and surveyed the valley and the advancing forest with a disapproving eye.

"I see Holloways is letting their north pasture go back," she said, shaking her head. She had seen whole hills go back to darkness, and many fine houses fall into their cellar holes. She turned toward Hurley accusingly, he being from the outside and thus responsible for such things. "You got to pay money to have them take the hay!"

"Tell me it's cheaper to buy it off the truck," the old man said. "But I told them it don't grow on trucks." He stood beside his tall wife, in his baggy pants and old mackinaw. His new tennis shoes were startlingly white. "I call this the hill of agony," he said, winking at Hurley.

"You see where the deer come down to eat our garden?"

Nana said, pointing to the deer trails through the apple trees. "We tell the game warden to shoot. Nothing. They hang bangers in the trees. All night, bang, bang! Nobody can sleep."

"Neither could the deer. They stayed up all night and et my lettuce," the old man said. He laughed and whacked his thigh.

"You shoot me a nice young deer," Nana said. "I make mincemeat, roasts, nice sausage for your breakfast."

He had tried to tell them that he didn't want to shoot anything with the bow, just carry it. Could he tell them that it gave a peculiar strength to his arm, that it seemed to be a kind of dynamo? When he was a boy in these same woods he and his friends had not been spectators, but actors. Their bows, fish poles, skis, and rifles had set them apart from the mere hikers, the summer people.

"I won't be back tonight unless the weather changes," he said. The sun was warm on the dry leaves, but the air was crisply cool in the shadows. He said goodbye to the old people, took off his pack, and waited on the ledges to see them safely back to the house below, then unrolled his sleeping bag and rolled it tighter. The night before he had noticed on his geodetic map a small, five-acre pond high in the cleft between Cascom and Gilman mountains. It was called Goose Pond, and he seemed to remember having been there once, long ago, perhaps trout fishing. He remembered being very tired, yet not wanting to leave; he remembered the cattails and alders and a long beaver dam, the pond deep in a little basin. He was sure he could follow the brook that issued from the pond—if he could pick the right one from all the little brooks that came down between Gilman and Cascom.

His pack tightened so that it rode high on his back, he carried his bow and the two hunting arrows in one hand. He soon relearned that arrows pass easily through the brush only if they go points first.

Stopping often to rest, he climbed past the maples into ground juniper and pine, hearing often the soft explosions of partridge, sometimes seeing them as they burst up and whistled through the trees. He passed giant beeches, crossing their noisy leaves, then walked silently through softwood until he came to a granite knob surrounded by stunted, wind-grieved hemlock.

To the northwest he could see the Presidential Range, but Leah, the lake, and the Pedersens' farm were all out of sight. He ate a hard-boiled egg and one of the bittersweet wild apples he had collected on the way. The wind was delightfully cool against his face, but he knew his sweat would soon chill. At two o'clock the sun was fairly low in the hard blue sky—whole valleys were in shadow below.

He took out his map. He had crossed three little brooks, and the one he could hear a short way ahead must be Goose Pond's overflow. By the sound it was a fair-sized brook. When he climbed down through the hemlock and saw it he was sure. White water angled right and left, dropping over boulders into narrow sluices and deep, clear pools. He knelt down, drank, and dipped his head in and out of the icy water. His forehead turned numb, as if it were made of rubber. A water beetle darted to the bottom. A baby trout flashed green and pink beside a stone. It was as if he were looking through a giant lens into an alien world, where life was cold and cruel, and even the light had a quality of darkness about it. Odd little sticks on the bottom were the camouflaged larvae of insects, waiting furtively to hatch or to be eaten. Fish hid in the shadows under stones, their avid little mouths ready to snap. He shuddered and raised his head—a momentary flash of panic, as if some carnivorous animal with a gaping mouth might come darting up to tear his face.

Following the brook, jumping from stone to stone, sometimes having to leave it for the woods in order to get around tangles of blowdown or waterfalls, he came suddenly into the deep silence of the spruce, where the channel was deep. In the moist, cathedral silence of the tall pillars of spruce he realized how deafening the white water had been. The wind stirred the tops of the trees and made the slim trunks move slowly, but could not penetrate the dim, yet luminous greenness of the place.

And he saw the deer. He saw the face of the deer beside a narrow tree, and for a moment there was nothing but the face: a smoky brown eye deep as a tunnel, it seemed, long delicate lashes, a black whisker or two along the white-shaded muzzle. The black nose quivered at each breath, the nostrils rounded. Then he began to follow the light brown line, motionless and so nearly invisible along the back, down along the edge of the white breast. One large ear turned slowly toward him. It was a doe, watching him carefully, perfect in the moment of fine innocence and wonder—a quality he suddenly remembered— the expressionless readiness of the deer. But other instincts had been working in him. He hadn't moved, but breathing slowly, put his weight equally on both legs. The light sharpened as if it had been twilight and the sun had suddenly flashed. Every detail—the convolutions of the bark on the trees, tiny twigs, the fine sheen of light on each hair of the doe, each curved, precious eyelash—became vivid and distinct. Depth grew, color brightened; his hunter's eyes became painfully efficient, as if each needlelike detail pierced him. The world became polarized on the axis of their eyes. He was alone with the doe in a green world that seemed to cry for rich red, and he did not have time to think: it was enough that he sensed the doe's quick decision to leave him. An onyx hoof snapped, her white flag rose, and the doe floated in a slow arc, broadside to him, clear of the trees for an endless second. He watched down the long arrow, three blades moved ahead of the doe, and at the precise moment all tension stopped; his arms, fingers, eyes, and the bow were all one instrument. The arrow sliced through the deer.

Her white flag dropped. Gracefully, in long, splendid leaps, hoofs stabbing the hollow-sounding carpet of needles, the doe flickered beyond the trees. One moment of crashing brush, then silence. A thick excitement rose like fluid into his face; his arms seemed to grow to twice their normal size, become twice as strong. And still his body was governed by the old, learned patterns. He walked silently forward and retrieved his bloody arrow, snapped the feathers alive again. The trail was a vivid line of jewels, brighter than the checkerberries against their shiny green leaves, unmistakable. He rolled the bright blood between his fingers as he slowly moved forward. He must let the doe stop and lie down, let her shock-born strength dissipate in calm bleeding. Watching each step, figuring out whole series of steps, of brush bendings in advance, he picked the silent route around snags and under the blowdown.

In an hour he had gone a hundred yards, still tight and careful, up out of the spruce and onto a small rise covered with birch and poplar saplings. The leaves were loud underfoot, and as he carefully placed one foot, the doe rose in front of him and crashed downhill, obviously weak, staggering against the whippy birch. A fine mist of blood sprayed at each explosion of breath from the holes in her ribs. He ran after her, leaping over brush, running along fallen limbs, sliding under low branches that flicked his cheeks like claws. His bow caught on a branch and jerked him upright. After one impatient pull he left it. He drew his knife. The brown shape ahead had disappeared, and he dove through the brush after it, witch hobble grabbing his legs.

The doe lay against a stump, one leg twitching. He knelt down and put one hard arm around her neck, and not caring for the dangerous hoofs, the spark of life, raised the firm, warm neck against his chest, and sighed as he stabbed carefully into the sticking place. Blood was hot on the knife and on his hand.

He rolled over into the leaves, long breaths bending him, making his back arch. His shirt vibrated over his heart, his body turned heavy and pressed with unbelievable weight into the earth. He let his arms melt into the ground, and a cool, lucid sadness came over his flesh.

He made himself get up. In order to stand he had to fight gravity, to use all his strength—a quick fear for his heart. His joints ached and had begun to stiffen. He must keep moving. Shadows were long and he had much to do before dark. He followed the blood trail back and found his bow and one arrow. He limped going back down the hill; at a certain angle his knees tended to jackknife, as if gears were slipping.

He stood over the clean body of the doe, the white belly snowy against brown leaves. One hind leg he hooked behind a sapling, and he held the other with his knee as he made the first long incision through the hair and skin, careful not to break the peritoneum. He ran the incision from the tail to the breast, then worked the skin back with his fingers before making the second cut through the warm membrane, the sticky blue case for stomach and entrails. He cut, and the steamy innards rolled unbroken and still working out onto the ground. A few neat berries of turd rattled on the leaves. He cut the anus and organs of reproduction clear of the flesh, then found the kidneys and liver and reached arm-deep into the humid chest cavity, the hot smell of blood close to his nostrils, and removed the yellow lungs in handfuls. Then he pulled out the dark red heart. Kidneys, liver, and heart he wrapped carefully in a plastic bag, then he rose and painfully stretched. Goose Pond lay just below; he could see a flicker of water through the skein of branches, and there he would make camp.

With his belt looped around the neck and front hoofs, he slid the doe down toward the pond. It was dusk by the time he found a dry platform of soft needles beneath a hemlock, next to the water. The doe had become stiff enough so that he could hang it in a young beech, head wedged in a fork. He spread his sleeping bag, tried it for roots and stones, and found none. The last high touch of sun on the hill above him had gone; he had even prepared ground for a fire when he realized that he had no energy left, no appetite to eat the liver of the doe.

Darkness had settled in along the ground, but the sky was still bright; one line of cirrus clouds straight overhead still caught orange sunlight. Across the silver water the alder swamp was jet black, and the steep hill rose behind, craggy with spruce. A beaver's nose broke water, and even, slow circles spread across the pond. The dark woods filled with cold, and one of his legs began to jerk uncontrollably. He took off his boots and slid into his sleeping bag.

The doe was monstrous, angular against the sky, her neck stretched awkwardly, head canted to one side. The black hole in her belly gaped empty. He drew his sleeping bag up around his face.

If he were twenty again he would be happy. To have shot a deer with a bow—he'd be a hero, a woodsman, famous in Leah. How it would have impressed Mary! She would have said little about it—she went to great lengths never to flatter him; her compliments had been more tangible, seldom in words. He must think of something else. The world was too empty. The cold woods, the darkening water, were empty. He was too cold, too tired to manipulate his thoughts. And the progression of hours began again. Mary's eyes watched him, deep in sick hollows. How could her flesh turn so brown? Why could he do nothing to stop the pain? She watched him, in torment, her frail body riven, cut beyond endurance. The disease had killed her bravery with pain and left her gruesomely alive, without dignity, whimpering like a spoiled brat, asking for help she should have known did not exist. And he stood by and watched, doing nothing. Nothing. He was not a man to do nothing. *Mary, did I do nothing to help you?*

He heard, far away, the lonely cry of the Canada geese. He was alone, hidden in the blind night, high on the stony mass of Cascom Mountain.

And then they came in, circling, calling to each other above the doubtful ground. Perhaps they had seen the reflected circle of fading sky, or remembered, generations remembering that geese had rested safely in the high pond and found food there. The scouts came whistling on their great wings, searching and listening. They sent their messages back to the flock waiting above, then planed down, braking, smeared the water with wind and came to rest in a flash of spray. The flock circled down after, careless now it was safe, honking gaily, giving the feeding call prematurely, echoing the messages of the leaders and landing masters. "Come in, come down and rest," they seemed to call, until everyone had landed safely. Then the voices grew softer, less excited, and only an occasional word drifted across the water.

Robert Hurley lay in the warm hollow of his sleeping bag, where the hours had stopped. He thought for a moment of the doe's death, and of his knife. The geese spoke softly to each other on the water—a small splash, a flutter of wings, and the resting, contented voices in the deep basin of the pond. As sleep washed over him he seemed to be among them; their sentinels guarded him. When they had rested well they would rise and continue the dangerous journey down the world.

The Skier's Progress

JAPHET VILLARD has installed himself at the Mountain View, a place he has known through so many of its transitions he sometimes has the illusion that he can see right through walls. Wasn't there a window right there, a long time ago, through which one could see the ridge of Splitback Mountain? He sits now in the too artfully rough-textured modern lounge, waiting for his daughter Margaret and his grandson Billy. The fieldstone fireplace is new. Wasn't there a plaster wall right there, with a flue plug big as a dinner plate in it? And painted on the tin was a mountain, in all the primary colors of his youth—an Alp, perhaps, or maybe one of the nearby White Mountains. From this position he is sure he might once have looked straight into the kitchen and caught a glimpse of a deep slate sink.

Now, for all the weathered silver boards someone has taken from old barns, for all the deliberately rustic stone and the hand-hewn beams, a little sign by the door says, "No Skis in Lounge, Please." How would they have greeted the eight-foot langlauf boards upon which he used to travel snow unbroken by anybody but snowshoe rabbits? Those pure wood monsters with their leather bindings would be museum pieces now—they'd have them up over the mantel to smile at. No steel edges, either—did you need them in that high and virgin deep snow?

But he is no pure sentimentalist for the past. Along with the new skis he bought for his grandson, he has for himself a pair of Head Vectors, whose edges are so sharp they'll pare your fingernail. It's been just six weeks since he underwent surgery, though, and he wonders if he will ever be able to use them—if, in fact, he did not simply buy them because they are so beautiful to look at. If he does manage to ski, he'll take the lifts now, and try not to chide Billy for not wanting to break his own trails, crest to crest. Japh has never been a man to bellyache about the changes in the world; his pride has been to compete, to improve himself.

He looks at his wristwatch. It will be an hour before the tows close on Splitback, before the gondola lift is still. He does have a slight pain down there, and he has a creepy vision of the scar. But he will wait until five for the drink that will help him ignore such things. There must be pain, he knows. Without privation, life is bland. Without mountains and freezes, what good feelings can a man get from his good legs and living heat? And Japh has done his work in the world as well as anybody.

He'll be glad to see his daughter, whom he loves, and his grandson, whom he also loves, but who might have been a better man of sixteen if he'd had to follow Japh across Splitback before the bulldozers had banked each trail and cleared out the blowdown. In these days, the weekend sports would break their necks if they had much more than a mogul or two to cope with. Then he chides himself; he's had his clear and beautiful times in the wilderness, in the winter that sometimes froze his cheeks and heels.

A little pain ominously tickles his haunch, and he moves his legs as he looks at the grandfather clock. In the rack next to his chair is a skiing magazine, and on the cover is an Alpine snow-field full of powder as white and pure—in the Kodachrome, at least—as the snow he can remember.

At Splitback Mountain, Margaret Woolley is walking across the hard snow of the parking lot, her skis over her shoulder. She is tall, and her ski boots fit well, so that she strides stiff-ankled, in that odd, somewhat majestic way skiers must. In it there is some awkwardness, yet there is also that strange pre-

diction of grace one sees in a walking swan. Her dark gray
stretch pants fit her long legs well   tightly but not dangerously
so—and even though she is thirty-eight and the mother of two,
one would never know it from her hips, which are neither too
round nor too starved and pelvic. Her face, especially now that
it has been burned by the wind of her last run down an intermediate trail called the Cataract, is blotched here and there
with a deep red, but these marks will fade in the warmth of the
car. Her hair is glossy black, and she has removed her yellow
toque, so that her hair's black thickness will rise and loosen.

She is no more vain than any other good-looking woman;
she knows what she looks like. And today she has seen with her
own eyes (blue, and rather glinty in the freezing air) the young
girls who, in ways she can never recapture, proclaim with every
gesture their fresh youth. To her sixteen-year-old son, who
made his last run down the more dangerous Spout and is idling
the car's engine in order to get the heater going, she feels that
she is not really a woman at all but a force, or, more accurately,
a combination of forces and indications. Does it please him, she
wonders, to have a mother who skis well? She would like to
believe this, but she knows that at his age he wants to appear
older than he is, and will, therefore, in the most natural and
heartless way, condemn her to old age. And yet to have a
mother who wears the correct clothes, who has the leisure to
keep up, even though she hears with half an ear the latest skiing
terminology, might give him some pride in his family's position.
It is this doubtful claim, she is afraid, that she has on him as a
companion. She sadly realizes that the force she will always
retain is made of affection, love, and, most of all, the authority
of motherhood; she is half policewoman, half indentured ser-
vant.

Now she is in the row in which her car is parked, and that
little white dot falling from the vent window is a cigarette butt.
She has a pang of sadness whenever she sees Billy smoke, for it
proves without a doubt that she is an old woman. At that very
moment, the edges of her skis seem to press more heavily into
her shoulder, which has suddenly become bony and vulnerable.

Billy has seen her coming, and he is afraid she may have
noticed the cigarette falling down the black side of the car; he

had been daydreaming, and hadn't seen her quite soon enough. He doesn't want to smoke in her presence, to assume that much equality. Although he has never tested her, he is afraid that in her loneliness she might take too strongly to an offer of companionship. It seems right to him that he have secrets from her. He is not a cruel boy, but he is a boy without a visible father. His father's name is Herbert, and even before his mother and Herbert separated, Herbert had never been too visible, had never been too much of a force in the family councils. Neither Billy nor his sister, who is eighteen and married, even looks much like Herbert. They are tall and dark like their mother. Sometimes Billy thinks of his father as a kind of alien, a grumbly guest who somehow by accident mated with the tall woman in those brownish, historical photographs in the hall desk drawer at home. There is something vaguely unreal about the whole business.

As his mother approaches, he jumps out to take her skis and poles, and expertly clamps her skis into the rack on top of the car. He wants to drive, and he wonders if he should ask or merely get in behind the wheel and pretend that no decision on who shall drive is necessary. There are certain things about this problem he can't understand. For instance, he picked out this car. It is a Pontiac Tempest, and he knows the number of cubic inches in its cylinders, its compression ratio, its valve lift, its turning radius, and the width not only of its spark gap but of its point gap. He has had his driver's license for a month, too, and yet each time he asks to drive he sees his mother hesitate, and think. This gives him much pain, but he will never complain about it.

Finally, he makes up his mind. His mother has to sit on the passenger side in order to remove her ski boots, and he slips in the driver's side, ostensibly to help her put her boots in her boot tree. He knows that she knows, but in this family (except for his father, who always had to explain the already known) communication is always a fine compromise between words and gestures. When the boots and poles have been stowed behind the front seat, Billy sees her thinking, and is pained. But then he is made happy, because the time for her to suggest that on these icy roads perhaps she'd better drive has passed—just barely— and he very carefully eases the car out of the parking place and turns left toward the highway. He loves the feel of driving, and it is wonderful to him that the hood of the Tempest turns and moves at his instigation. He feels that it could never happen that he might drive off the road, or that the car might not obey not only his manual directives but his will. He is young enough, in fact, to feel that it is miraculous not to have to walk.

He is very careful, and though it seems to him just a little dishonest, he drives much more slowly than he ordinarily would. The lodge is five miles down into the valley, and it is his intention that his mother not feel the slightest sense of risk. He has more magic to experience, and sometime within the week, preferably Thursday night, he wants her to let him take the car out alone.

While they drive, they say a few things to each other.

"I saw you on the last run," he says. "Where the Spout crosses the Cataract. You looked pretty good, actually."

"Thank you," she says, but she wonders why that word "actually" disappoints her. She has never pretended to be expert.

"You still rotate a hair too much," he says.

"I know it. It's the Arlberg in me. I can't get rid of it. I learned it too well, too long ago."

He shrugs. It isn't at all sad to him. He doesn't really expect his mother to get any better.

What he really wonders is, will she let him take the car one night? It has been a vacation full of the possibility of miracles, and he has been given the opportunity to fall in love. Gloria Stacey, at home, in high school, is one of those girls one simply never considers. She is made of light gold, and her eyes are dark amber. In his class there are four such goddesses, and Gloria is either No. 1 or No. 2. Carol Eckhardt is another, then Norma Tolman, and then Brenda Fortuna. Gloria is so beautiful and talented and gracious he has never even had the nerve to dance with her, much less engage her in conversation, even though he considers himself no dub at either of these arts. He is afraid that if he put his arm around her slender waist, or if he pressed his chest against hers, he would explode.

Yesterday they met at the bottom of the gondola lift, and they rode together in the enclosed little car (a blue one, No. 79) for twelve and one-half minutes. She is here for a week, with her parents, and she skis fairly well for a girl, but he skied so beautifully before her eyes that she, with a powerful ability to smile and say right out whatever she meant, told him so. She is staying at the Bella Vista Lodge, a mere two miles away from his. Twice more they rode the lift together, first in a red car and then in a yellow one, their shoulders nearly touching. He hoped the cable would stop, as it often did, and leave them for precious minutes suspended fifty feet above the tops of the sleet-covered spruce, a mile above the valley. But the cable never stopped.

Even though he thinks her kind notice of him is simply caused by their both being so far away from home and that perhaps she hasn't yet had time to meet another of the golden people here in the mountains, he feels that if he is given the chance to use all of his talents he may have a chance to win her. If the gods are kind, he will touch her lovely hand; if they are madly generous, he will kiss her beautiful lips.

Now the car hums down the mountain road, and the dark trees rise on each side. There is a small river down to the left, full of rocks encased in ice, but here the salt has cleared the road and even dried white on the asphalt. Billy pretends, carefully staring straight ahead, that it is not his mother who sits beside him but Gloria. The sleek instruments in front of him are friendly and romantic, and the smell of the car is as new and crisp as the treads of the tires, whose grip upon the road is all for him. Beside him is Gloria, and perchance her hand will move along the top of the seat and rest lightly upon his shoulder. The neat legs he can just barely see from the corner of his eye are not clothed in dark gray but in brilliant young green, and they belong to Gloria. He is taking her away.

Margaret turns to look at her son. The one eye she can see is squinted slightly, as though he feels either joy or pain. He loves to drive, and she is happy to see him having so much pleasure, even though it is hard for her to understand why driving can make him so happy. She tells herself to remember that whether she can share them or not, she might still be surrounded by great pleasures.

Soon they will be back at the Mountain View Lodge. The sun has been gone a long time behind the mountains, and now it is dusk. The one discreet little neon sign will be lit, and waiting for them in the lounge will be Japh Villard, her father, who cannot ski this week because he has recently undergone a prostatectomy. He will be standing there by the fire, though, waiting for the stroke of five, his gallant old legs encased in immaculate ski knickers or lederhosen, speaking with some old friend or other of Tuckerman's Ravine and the Headwall, and the peculiar crystalline structure of the corn snow there one April, years ago, or how he helped Sepp Ruschp plan the National. Japh has been staying in the Mountain View since before the old farmhouse that is its basic structure had an inside toilet, and the present owners sometimes feel, during Japh's annual visits, that they are only mortal, that their short period of custodianship will end long before Japh does.

When Margaret and Billy enter the lodge and cross the new Swedish hemp rug toward the big stone fireplace, there is Japh, sneaking a glance at the grandfather clock. He is talking to Bucky Scudder, the ski instructor.

Bucky hasn't waited for five o'clock, however; an awful thing has happened to him that afternoon. At three o'clock he didn't feel like skiing anymore, and canceled three lessons and came back to the lodge. He is forty-two, and he has begun to wonder if he really gets more pleasure from *après ski* than he does from skiing itself. Skiing has been his whole life, and lately he has begun to think too much about his life. Since four o'clock he has nursed a beer, and now it is flat and the bottle is warm in his hand. He likes to talk to Japh, because it is the old man's best talent to make the things he is interested in seem more important than anything else in the world. Bucky has heard Japh's stories before, but somehow they come out again ringing with the enthusiasm that Bucky himself is afraid he might be losing. He is happy to see Margaret and Billy, too, for they admire his skiing. Because he does this one thing so well, he thinks perhaps it really doesn't matter that he is past forty and overweight. He is Bucky Scudder the skier, who flashes across moguls with such control and precision—the flash whom all the other skiers on the slopes stop to watch. The ones who don't know who this is ask the others, and as he schussbooms over a fifteen-foot dip, he hears them yell "Buuuckyyy!" as though they were yelling "Track!" in admiration of his exuberance and daring. But isn't this cry of admiration for the old party boy just a knife's edge away from derision? Down he goes, anyway, his *Wedeln* so crisp he never seems to care at all for the configuration of the snow, or that the slope here is forty-five degrees and that he is now entering an impossible turn. He is out of sight for a moment—but there he is again, ten feet in the air, followed by a veil of snow, triumphantly flying.

If he could not do that . . . He knows he is a man who has some doubtful habits. He has been cruel to women in little ways. He bites his fingernails. On the back of his electric-blue Bogner stretch pants there can be found a dark circle as big as a dime; a few days ago, at a party, he sat on a fragment of Vienna sausage. He knows the spot is there, and he is a little worried about the direction in which he turns. It seems to him that there is always something he half tries to conceal—his bitten fingernails, the little spot on his pants. He has resigned himself to such nagging imperfections, and if he thought too much about them he might realize that they reflect his own opinion of his immortal soul. It is for this reason that he has never thought of trying for Margaret. She is kind, and a lovely woman; she is out of his class. Not only is she unattainable, but he would not know what to do with her if by some miracle he did get her. He is used to small change, and would be confounded by riches. He would love her, and how could he ever reveal his ragged self to such a woman? No, he'll stick to his own kind, the ones in whose eyes he detects his own dishonesty.

Now, Japh declares, it is five o'clock, so they all sit at a bench and table near the fire and wait for the owner's wife to bring them drinks. Billy will have a Coke, and Bucky decides to switch from beer to martinis, which Margaret and Japh are having.

"It was pretty icy on the Spout in places," Billy says. "But not too bad," he quickly adds, glancing diffidently at Bucky.

"Couldn't we use a few inches of fresh powder?" Bucky says, and the others nod dreamily.

"Now, I grew up on powder," Japh says. "We had to make our own trails. We had to *walk* up hills." His lined, shiny old face is still dreamy, and Bucky wonders how they could have liked skiing so much in those days. But he did, too; he has walked up many hills in his time, too. Japh's face turns scornful.

"I mentioned sealskins—could you believe it? And some of these young bunnies didn't even know what I was talking about. They never went up a hill on their own steam."

"I've got a pair," Billy says. He wonders where they are, though; he hasn't seen them for a long time. Then he thinks they'd look pretty good tied around his waist, like a belt. Five points, man! It would look as though he sometimes went up higher than the tow, and came down cross-country. Gloria might ask him what they were!

"Why climb when you've got a ride?" Bucky says. He wants it to come out ironic, but it comes out sad.

Margaret hears that sadness, and looks at him. She has never seen him sad, just as she has never seen him without a deep-red tan. He still has the tan. His big round face is the color of briar, and full of muscle. In the summer he runs a ski school in Chile, and he never leaves the hard winter sun for very long.

Japh says, "Ten inches of new powder," and sighs.

Some college boys have clumped in, and sit themselves at a booth in the back of the room. They have stopped for one expensive beer before going back to their ski dorm and their six-packs. Margaret sees them casting somewhat furtive looks at Bucky, and nodding their heads. "Down hill," she hears one say, and in the context of Bucky's sadness she doesn't realize for a moment that the boy said "downhill," not "down hill." Bucky has been a national champion, and their looks are not derisive. One boy has an unfortunate voice that carries to her ear as if by wire: "When he's showing a class, he never hops. God, he's pretty! But you watch him when he's by himself. He hops. You just watch." Another boy at the booth nudges him; the voice fades. Margaret wonders if Bucky heard. But of course he has, she knows. She has always liked him and felt sorry for him. She has seen him at parties, when a certain brutal look on his face could wipe away his intelligence the way a damp cloth wipes a slate, and what was left was only darkness, unself-loving. Then she would look to see what woman he had decided to cut out of the herd. They looked so much alike, all of Bucky's girls. Girls in their thirties. They always had good figures, and a husband somewhere, and children somewhere, and bright, unhappy, smiling faces. Her heart goes out to them. How pretty they had all once been, and how much they had been taught to expect.

After another drink, dinner is ready, and Japh invites Bucky to eat with them. After dinner, they sit around for a while. Billy has gone to examine his new skis—the present from Japh—to see if that ice on the Spout has marred their bottoms. Bucky almost falls asleep over his brandy and coffee. It is fairly early, but nothing seems to be developing, and they all decide to go to bed. The lifts will open at eight-thirty, and that is what they have come for, isn't it?

For a while Japh tries not to think of the little pains that flicker through his skin. His doctor has told him to take as few of the white pills as possible, and he thought the martinis might suffice for tonight. But the pains are just enough to keep him awake and thinking. They are not much in themselves, and if he hadn't a too vivid idea of the surgery that caused them, and of the greater pain his doctor had predicted to come, he might be able to sleep. Finally, he gets up, and on the way to the bathroom he looks down and sees his ropy old shanks, skinny as ski poles below the jockey shorts he now has to wear. He takes two of the pills, but it is a concession he is not happy to make.

He has to sleep, though, and he must do what will let him sleep. He wants to see the sun rise in the morning, and he wants to be rested then. He wants to eat the early breakfast that has always been his favorite meal, and to feel in the other people there the excitement of anticipation. He may feel it—unfortunately, perhaps—too strongly in himself, because to stand on skis at the top of a mountain is a thrill that time and weakness have never dulled. Sometimes he feels like a character in a fable, whose Midas wish has been wholly granted, and in his old age he must pay tenfold for all the pleasures he has had from all the cold bright days and those lovely, curving descents across the snowfields.

He can say to himself that he has had a good life, that his moderate success in the wool business (yarns) has let him enjoy his hobbies. His twenty-four-foot sloop, *Prometheus,* is snug in its blocks at Great Bay. His son-in-law, Herbert Woolley, seems to have been destined even more than his name might indicate to be successful at running the mill. Herbert—one needn't actually *like* a man to take him into the business, but at least that part has worked out well. That Herbert has left Margaret for that rather dim accountant, Verna Price, does not bother Japh as much as he feels it should. He has always suspected Herbert of being a romantic fool, and he feels that Herbert will come back. Everyone has taken advantage of Margaret's good nature.

He can say to himself that he has led a good life, but this is like saying that his life is over, and he is cursed with a perpetual eagerness. To see the sun rise, to see the first deep snow of the winter, to smell the bay mud at low tide, with the sand eels shooting away in formation beneath the bow of his dory as though swept by a broom—it is almost as though these little visions, these little memories that impinge upon all of his senses, are the only real losses he must suffer. He does love. He does try to protect the people he loves, but has he ever needed them very badly? His wife, who died twenty years ago—a good woman, who loved him, whom he never really disappointed. Margaret, who is so much like her, so generous. He cannot say that he doesn't love, but then it is not a word he cares to define too exactly. What is true is that in his brightest memories, in those memories that make him feel his heart beat in his chest, there is just the one man alone against a beautiful and dangerous world.

Bucky is in bed, but the shower he took beforehand has waked him up. It is still relatively early, and at first he considers getting dressed and going out, maybe to the Bella Vista, to look for a little action. He knows a girl who is there for the week, sans husband. He met her last year when she bought the series of lessons called "The Housewives' Special." She's all right—blond, lean, nervous, all decked out in the very latest stuff advertised in the skiing magazines. But she reminds him so much of all his women, and he wonders if he has become sick of the illicit, sick of the vacation spirit in which there are just two kinds of liaison, one justified by a weirdly out-of-date coyness that later turns false and hysterical: "I love you! God! I love you!" The other is just as false: "You were good, you know?" The sophisticated camaraderie of the adulterers.

He has eaten dinner with Margaret, and she is not like that. He knows that she has never been unfaithful to Herbert Woolley, for instance, and he knows it because this is the kind of thing he knows. He can see her clear blue eyes, and in them he sees no avarice, no larceny. Like many libertines, he believes in the existence of another race of human beings, so different from himself—the ones who are faithful and honorable, to whom love and sex are exquisitely the same, who stand immaculate in the sight of heaven. He feels that somehow he has been excluded from this race, and that he could no more enter it than he could grow wings.

He can't sleep, but he doesn't feel like going out, so he reaches over to the table beside his bed, snaps on the lamp, and takes the new *Skiing* and turns its pages, thoughtfully staring at all the new faces, the kids who are expected to do well at Chamonix, at Snow Valley, at Innsbruck, at Zakopane. Or who did well at the F.I.S. Games. He's seen some of them. Périllat, with this thing called *projection circulaire;* it looks like nothing Toni Sailer didn't do. But it's something; it's an improvement. How would Dick Durrance have utilized the new equipment, the new techniques? Or Torger Tokle (dead in the Italian mountain campaign)? Oh, they were all good, and all brave, the old and the new. There was no Golden Age, even if Japh says so. There is age, though, Buck.

Can he remember himself back there, when the snow was lighter and more powdery? He almost got married once, but then he got the invitation to go out and train for the Harriman, and it seemed too complicated, at the moment, to do both. And after the Harriman, in which he did very well, there was the business of promoting the Bucky Scudder Quick Release Binding. It wasn't a bad binding, either, and while it was in fashion he and its inventor and its backer made some money. The only trouble was that all this was in the West and Lois, who was his fiancée, wanted to graduate from Smith.

She was like Margaret. With this thought, he trembles, surprising himself. Margaret is here in the same lodge, sleeping in a bed similar to his. Lois was like Margaret in that she always seemed to be looking beyond the day or the night, to be seeing something out there more meaningful and complete, like a whole life.

He drops the magazine beside the bed and turns out the lamp. In the dark, he is rigid, his hands on his thighs, which are as hard as iron. He has always had amazingly strong legs. Maybe he's a little overweight, but he's hard, his body is hard. Then he feels his heart pumping in his breast. It seems to be working so fast, so desperately. He doesn't like to be aware of the machinery. He must relax, but the pump can never rest. It is then that he half wills himself into his old dream, the one that frightens him. First, there is the vision of himself rising out of his body. As he rises up and out above the lodge into the night, he can see his body down there on the bed. Smaller and smaller it grows as the mountains rise smoothly up with him. It is silent up here, silent as a gondola, but down there in the little body is the tiny heart. Then he can no longer see the little body at all, and he is somewhere like Chamonix, at the top of the Piste Verte, which falls away below him like a cliff. How can he run it in the moonlight, with the shadows of the dead crags crossing the blue snow? But he must race back down to his body before it is too late. He has never been so afraid, and even more horrible is the knowledge that when he reaches the Alpine town all the windows will be dark, all the chimneys will be cold. No one else will be there at all.

In his room, Billy lies in bed constructing the most elaborate fantasy. The object is to strand himself and Gloria in a gondola—all night long. He is kind, and doesn't want to strand a hundred other people, so he is thinking powerfully to find a way to keep them off the lift. Of course, he then has to invent the most godawful snarl somewhere in the lift mechanism. Everything has to be practical, because if it isn't, some of the fantastic reality of his vision will depart. It's cold, but not too cold up there—just cold enough to make Gloria chilly. Say twenty-nine degrees Fahrenheit. For a while, they sit not touching, side by side in the little two-passenger egg. The moon rises over Splitback and bathes her cheek with soft blue light. She shivers, and the night wind gently sways the cable. He puts his right arm up, up, and she leans softly against his chest. Her golden hair lies along his neck, smooth as soap; it is silver in the moonlight. Her right hand moves across and lies chastely upon his ribs. His parka covers them, and as she breathes he can feel her alive in his arms. All right: let eternity pass.

In her room, Margaret is sound asleep. Her long hands are together beneath her cheek, and if it weren't pitch dark one could see her abundance of soft black hair, the sweet curve of her lips, the softened line of her lower cheek with its almost invisible fuzz. She makes a long shape beneath the blanket, and as she breathes long, steady breaths she exudes warm moisture into the cold air. It is very cold in the room; the air seems as cold as iron. She stirs, and whimpers softly. But it is nothing—no more than any dream in which loneliness and death put on silly disguises and caper about masquerading as birds, or snowflakes, or upside-down houses.

When the phone rings, Margaret comes swimming up from sleep. She doesn't want to. She has at last found a calm place down there, where it is warm and silent. The jangle of the phone pulls her up, up like some underwater creature, and unwillingly she surfaces into the cold air. The phone keeps ringing, and she puts her hand out to see if Herbert has got up to answer it. The sheets are cold, and she realizes that Herbert has not been there at all, that she is at the Mountain View. She takes the phone from the bed table. It is so cold she rubs it in both hands to warm it up.

"Margaret? Margaret?" she hears it say. As she puts it to her ear, the voice grows and becomes Herbert's voice, but she is still half asleep, and it is confusing that Herbert should be calling her by phone while she is in bed.

"Margaret? Are you awake? It's not late. It's not late."

"Yes," she says. Now she is awake. She can see his face, wherever he is—the heavy, worried expression he always wears, the petulance around his mouth.

"Margaret? Did I wake you up?"

If she says that he did, he will be unhappy. He knows he woke her up, of course, but Herbert is always discomfited if one answers his rhetorical questions with the truth.

"No, I was awake," she hears herself say.

"Are you all right?" he asks.

Again she cannot give him the answer he deserves. "I'm fine, Herbert." She cannot make herself ask him about Verna Price, either, because whenever they speak to each other (and not through letters, in which he knows what he wants and says so with authority) she hears in his voice the nervous little child she knows is there. "What do you want, Herbert?" she asks, as kindly as she can.

"I'm at the Bella Vista," he says, and she knows she has

been untactful. She has asked him a question he isn't yet able to answer. "I want to see you, Margaret. Are you sure you're all right?"

Are you happy, Herbert? she wants to ask. But of course that sort of question would disorganize him totally, the way Billy's questions and answers always do.

"I was coming from Montreal, on business," he says. Whenever he lies, there is a very slight change in the register of his voice, as though the diameter of his throat had grown smaller. "I just thought I'd swing over and see how you and Billy were. It's been six months, Margaret."

So he wants to come back, she thinks. He doesn't like Verna Price anymore. She is very sorry for Herbert. Every once in a while, he thinks he has found someone whose admiration for him is unalloyed. If she could only explain to him that he isn't such a bad man after all, that the truth about himself he sees reflected in other people's eyes is not such a horrible truth, that everyone meets with that look.

"I want to see you, Margaret. I want to see you tomorrow morning."

"I have ski lessons tomorrow, Herbert."

"Ski lessons!" he says, and she hears behind his disdain that he is hurt.

"I've paid for them already."

"With that—professional?"

"Bucky Scudder, yes," she says. She is sick of his jealousy, mainly because he will never admit it, and so she adds, knowing that she is being as cruel as she has ever been to him, "He's very good."

Herbert is silent. Finally, he says, "You watch out for him, Margaret. He's no good."

She wants to laugh, but she cannot be that unkind. Neither can she understand why she is so fond of Herbert. "We'll be skiing all morning at Splitback," she says.

"All right, Margaret."

"If you want to see us," she says.

"All right. Good night, Margaret."

"Good night, Herbert."

The room is so cold. She squirms down into the warm place, but the cold has crept in upon her, and she must push her feet into frigid places. She thinks, with a smile, that she could use Herbert right now. Yes, she would like him here beside her. The very resilience of the mattress is wrong; it doesn't slope down toward the warm man. She liked him in his sleep, when she could mold her body to his back. He slept warm, and his skin seemed to glow with smooth warmth. They made love quite often, and then she was happiest, for they never spoke. It was only afterward that he became cold and disapproving, and she knew he thought her a mess. But while it lasted it seemed to her that inside the man there were great bent springs so strong that when they were let go, their wonderful, awful recoil threatened the very bases upon which they were mounted, and in truth they did jar and weaken the whole hulk of the man so that he was for a time afterward sprung, like a broken clock. Sprung and cold, for she was never allowed to comfort him then.

At her window, she hears the ticktick of the beginning snow—those hard little pellets that often come at the start of a snowfall. She will ski tomorrow, but now she wonders how she will want to get up and face that coldness, that singular movement through the cold daylight air. She would like to be deep in warm darkness, with a man to hold her until she descended into sleep.

Bucky wakes up at the first light. He hasn't gone to bed so early in a long time, or after so few drinks, and he feels just good enough to worry about his physical condition. If he doesn't eat a lot, he feels weak, but he's got to lose some weight. He lies in bed and looks around his room. It is his winter room—his Northern Hemisphere winter room; he owns part of the Mountain View. The room is a shambles, as usual. Clothes hanging all over the place. Empty quart beer bottles in the corner. Sue, the owner-manager's wife, comes in once in a while and cleans up—she's awfully nice about it—but why, he asks himself, must he be such a slob? Why must that stick of deodorant be on the windowsill and not in the bathroom cabinet? Why must a damp washcloth be sitting in a ball on top of the bureau? Perhaps this small-boy carelessness was once excusable, even charming, but now he is a big man of forty-two. God! Why doesn't he get his clothes to the laundry more often? He has twenty shirts, and seventeen of them are dirty.

He gets up on his elbows and looks out the window. His room is in the back, and he looks across a field toward a hill gray with hardwood trees. New snow—it's a beautiful day, and the clean snow and blue sky, seen across the room full of his jumbled and soiled possessions, depress him so much he shuts his eyes. Suppose he'd had a heart attack and died in the night, died and ended himself forever here among his grubby artifacts? What has he ever done that could stay bright and clean? Oh, he has plenty of memories of fun and glory, but all that passes. Whatever he's really wanted to do he's done very well, and so he does have those memories, but they keep passing back into the years. He's had good luck with his investments in places like the Mountain View, and if skiing stays popular, and snow continues to fall in the right places, he'll probably do better. He's been a good friend, and a generous one. He has no idea how much money is owed to him, but it must be thousands. Every once in a while, he's surprised by a check for twenty dollars or five hundred dollars from an old friend who did remember some loan or other.

Nobody will hate him when he goes out, probably, except maybe a few husbands, so what the hell? But what's he done in this world except have a pretty good time? It's too late now to worry about it—you're not a young anything at forty-two, except maybe President, and he hasn't been nominated—so why does he worry about it? Maybe it's the idea of dying alone, and having them find his corpse with all its little secrets. He's got to change. Something has to make him change. So he stops biting the cuticle of his little finger.

Enough! He jumps out of bed. He's going to clean up his room, for a start. He takes a shower, shaves carefully, does a few knee bends, applies the deodorant. But he can't find any clean shorts, so that's one strike against him. This is depressing, but he does tear the sheets off his bed and pile all his dirty clothes on them, including the Bogners with that grease spot on the back. He puts on one of his three clean shirts, and an old pair of non-stretch ski pants—they're clean, anyway. He's got a million pairs of socks, and he does find a clean pair of them. He thinks, Now what's dirty about me except my shorts and my personality?

He hoists the large bundle of dirty clothes onto his shoulder and goes down to the kitchen. Sue and her husband, Roger, are preparing for breakfast, and he helps them set out the silverware. There are thirty paying guests, and since they are all skiers, at least twenty-five will make it to breakfast. When he sees that there isn't much more he can do, he sits down at a kitchen table to look at the morning ski reports. Excellent everywhere. Then he looks up and sees Sue and Roger working side by side at the counter. They're young kids, really—in their late twenties. She's shaking up frozen orange juice, and he's running the big toaster. They are in their working clothes and aprons, and her arm touches his accidentally, meaninglessly, and neither of them even notices it. Bucky stares at them, the man and the woman working together as though they weren't man and woman at all. They slept in the same bed last night. And he thinks about how they live together and see each other all the time, naked and dressed, and how they must know all about each other. They must be so honest. Roger happens to turn and see him staring, and to cover his embarrassment Bucky grins at him and shakes the morning ski report. "Good snow!" he says.

"We're doing all right!" Roger says. "A good winter so far. Doing all right, Bucky!"

Bucky has a glass of orange juice and one piece of toast, calls the ski school and arranges to have one of his instructors take over his earliest class, then puts his bundle of clothes in his car and drives down to the village laundry and dry cleaners. On the way back to his car, he is startled to see Herbert Woolley going into the drugstore. What's Herbert Woolley doing around here? He thinks of Margaret as he's seen her on the mountain, skiing alone down the Cataract, tall and graceful even if she is an unreconstructed Arlberger. And there is Herbert Woolley, come nosing around. Bucky knows the whole story—how Herbert left her. He's talked about it with Japh, who seemed, on the whole, pleased that Herbert had gone. But the sight of Herbert in his dark blue overcoat, his city pallor, and his city shoes is a shock to Bucky, and suddenly he realizes that he is jealous, that he has been counting upon Margaret's loneliness, and that his new regimen of cleanliness is an attempt to make himself worthy of her. And the moment he admits this to himself he sees that he must have Margaret—she will improve him; he loves her. She is so valuable he must go to her right away. Has Herbert seen her yet? What if they spent the night together? With this thought comes a stroke of jealousy that is painful. It is in his stomach, in his diaphragm. He has trouble getting a breath. Her lesson with him is in one hour, but can he risk waiting that long? Then he gets his breath. He knows what he wants, and suddenly he feels very strong—what he wants is dangerous, but he can cope with danger.

When he gets to the mountain, it is nine-thirty. He spots Margaret's car in the parking lot. Everything is under control so far, but how is he going to approach her? How is he going to let her know that he is going to change his life? He sees her in one of the T-bar lines. It is a weekday and lines are all short. He half runs to his office in the base of the gondola lift, puts on his boots, and picks out a pair of limber recreational skis. By the time he gets back to the T-bar, she is on her way up, and he puts on his skis, deciding to wait for her. But he's trembling, and he seems to have all kinds of excess energy, so he herringbones a third of the way up the slope to meet her. On her way down she sees him and stops next to him—stemming too much, but her eyes are bright from the wind, her legs are trim and strong, and he has the feeling that he can teach her to ski very well. He knows he has that power.

"Is it time for my lesson?" she asks, surprised.

"No, I just saw you." That seems to him a poor effort, and he tries again. "I just saw you going up the T-bar."

Now she is looking at him queerly, and he doesn't know what to say, so he does a kick turn, jumps off his poles, and does a gigantic *Geländesprung* from the top of a mogul, four wedels and four hop christies, another *Geländesprung*, during which he turns lightly in the air and comes down to a dramatic stop, snow exploding higher than his head. He feels like a bird. In the air he could feel the pressure of the air itself on the bottoms of his skis.

Down she comes, checking a little and flexing her knees. He knows he can teach her how to use reverse shoulder. *Now*, he thinks, as she does a pretty fair parallel christie and gains speed, now put your weight on the downhill ski and face the fall line, *there!* She goes by him quite fast, her skis hissing over the snow, and stops before the last steep grade to wait for him. He feels so good he takes the grade down to her on one ski and jumps high into the air before he turns and stops beside her, light as a feather.

"Beautiful!" she says. "Bucky, you're beautiful!" Tiny points of light glint all over her clothes. Her face shines with admiration for him, and in his triumph it seems that his life has changed already, that from now on his whole life will have a chance to be as beautiful as so many of his days have been.

The last of the skiers have gone to the lifts. Japh has watched them go. He didn't sleep very well. His knees feel weak this morning, so after Margaret and Billy left he took his second cup of coffee into the lounge and watched the skiers decide where to go, who would go in whose car, who was going to be brave and take the Spout. They swung their boot trees and checked to see if they had their wax, their wine, their cigarettes. The women were gaudy and happy in their bright clothes; the men strode around proudly in their trim, varied uniforms. Now they have all gone, and Japh doesn't know what to do with himself. He feels too weak even to skate, and yet his hands are trembling with excitement.

Wryly he considers this gift of his, the gift of excitement that has outlasted his youth. There are two things that have never lost their power: the sea and the mountains. They are all he has ever needed. They have always been there, indestructible, and they have never failed him. The one receives and cannot be filled, the other can never be diminished. Now he would be at the summit of Splitback, putting on the new skis he has never used, letting them slip for the first time through the new powder.

At least he can look at his new gear. He goes to the ski rack in the hall and takes his boots and his new Heads up to his room. This is more or less against the rules, but he is careful not to let his edges touch the walls or the doorframes. He puts the skis down on the rug, where they bounce upon their camber. They are subtly arched and tapered, and look like speed. They haven't received their first scratch, and they are black and silver. He has always liked the look and the feel of gear—a brass turnbuckle for the rigging of his sloop, or a toe release. Both are so spare and pure about what they do. Here are his skis, perfect and ready. His Arlberg straps are threaded to the cables, and now lie slack, waiting to be crossed over his boots.

So he takes his boots out of his boot tree. He admires the boot tree, too. It is made of extruded aluminum, not an ounce heavier than it must be, and as with all fine gear there is not a dimple or bump or a rivet upon it that does not perform some necessary function. And the boots, their leather and lacings, their handsome thick soles. It is a little painful for him to bend and put them on, to pull the inner and outer lacings tight, but he does, and then he fits them to the bindings of his skis, snaps the cables tight, and winds his Arlberg straps around and down through their tension buckles. All this equipment is heavy, and though his legs are bound rigidly to all this weight, he suddenly feels light and agile. He bounces, and unweights his skis. There is some pain, but the camber pushes him up so that for a moment he is weightless. It is the strength of memory in his legs.

Where shall he choose to be, poised for the long downhill run? No choice—it is Tuckerman's Ravine, on the corn snow of late spring; Tuckerman's, because you have to climb those miles to get there. You have to pay for each precious christiania. As you descend, there is the memory of the long climb, like a debt paid in full. There is the Headwall beginning its impossible curve up toward the vertical, all-blinding white. Who schussed it that time? Was it twenty years ago? Names of skiers, and their tough red faces, pass through his memory. Berndt Nadsen? Joe Foss? Pee-Wee Bellavance? Bucky Scudder? Toni Matt? Who was that black dot, no bigger than a spider, he once saw drop down across the snow at the speed of falling?

But it is his own long run he can feel now, the curving, the kernels of ice from his wake hissing and rattling as he unweights and begins his next long turn toward the narrowest part of the Chute, where he will flash through a cleft in the dark granite, his ears popping. The skis, their pressure and their edges, the perfection of control at speed—there is no other thing in the world so prideful and so beautiful.

Herbert Woolley is standing by the base lodge, watching his wife and Bucky Scudder as they come planing over toward him. They are side by side, and it is as if they are dancing or making love, the way they come down so smoothly together.

They don't see him, and he runs over to intercept them. His life cannot go on as it is now; he must get it back in order again. It is too frightening to be as alone as he now is, and he must do something. Already he has been as brave as he has ever been in any situation in which he has not had a perfect right. The very idea of coming here among all these insane people who throw themselves off cliffs and break their legs for fun—these insane people in clothes gaudy as peacocks and parrots—is so dangerous. To see his wife he has come through an environment as alien to him as the most exotic jungle. He has made it here, but over all his thoughts hangs the terrible feeling that he has forgotten something—something he can't quite remember to remember but which is as deadly in its absence as a neglected inoculation. He can usually depend upon his senses to warn him of danger. For that reason he never smokes, he never drinks. Should he deliberately put himself in jeopardy? Should he ever lessen in the slightest his awareness of danger, dull his reflexes and his alertness in this hostile world? But what is it that he has forgotten? As he runs, he is unstable; he feels drunk. His first mistake is that he tries to cross some snow that hasn't been trampled down, and his left leg, in his thin Italian shoe and silk sock, garter, pantleg—everything—goes right down out of sight. There is ice up his pantleg, in his shoe, under his garter. And then—ignominy!—Bucky Scudder is there, grabs him under an armpit, and pulls him out. He can't even feel his left leg, it is so cold. His garter is like a metal band around his calf, and he hops and stamps. "Margaret," he says. There she is, his wife, in all that equipment.

"Are you all right, Herbert?"

"I want to talk to you," he says desperately, for now both she and Bucky Scudder are expertly removing their skis, both of them bent over at once, doing professional little things with snaps and cables.

"But I have a lesson right now, Herbert," she says. Then her face lightens, and he knows that expression—she has found a way to be kind. "Why don't you ride up with me, and we can talk? You can get a round-trip ticket."

He looks over toward the gondola lift, where it ominously hums and bangs. The alternative is to have her go up all that way alone with that big animal, Bucky Scudder. "All right," he says.

He goes ahead with Margaret, feeling barefoot and vulnerable as she and Bucky Scudder clump solidly in their huge boots. He is aware of Scudder following him, the weight of the big man. When he has to pay money for the coming ride, he reflects with near hysteria that it is always the most unpleasant things one has to pay for. Then up the stairs into the groaning machinery. Margaret carries her own skis—he thinks to offer to carry them, but she seems so much stronger than he. They come into a huge room open at one end, and hanging from the ceiling is an engine, whole, eviscerated from some motor vehicle. Why isn't it running? Is it for emergencies? A wheel ten feet in diameter turns too fast for its size, and men stand too close to iron teeth and make mad, meaningless gestures as they push and pat the big metal parts. The gondolas come whirling in, freewheeling, and a madman swings them around on their track so that they bang into each other like battered old oil drums. They are rusty and tinny, their windows are cracked or missing, and the welds that hold these cheap tin spheroids to their stems are as sloppy as wax on the sides of candles. None of this slipshod workmanship escapes Herbert as he crosses to the loading place. But he must follow Margaret. The egg the attendant chooses for the two of them and locks them into is full of slush. The thin round walls of it are dented and wet, and the seat is cold from its long empty trip down from the mountain. He wipes the windshield and looks up to see the towers and the thin cable going up, up. With a terrible shock he realizes that those tiny things hanging out over nothing up there are identical to the very thing that encloses him. Then they are moving forward. There is a bump, and a screech of machinery. Something must have gone wrong, but he is rising anyway. The car is hanging by a hair, by friction; a bump will jar it loose. He doesn't dare look. Why did he wipe the mist from the windshield? There is a little bar he can hold, and he shuts his eyes as tight as he can, rising, swaying, rising. Part of his overcoat is caught in the door, but there is no handle on the inside. He will fall out. The cable will part, and they will snap out into the air like the end of a whip. They will be crushed. They will fall and fall down to the mountain below. He holds on desperately, but what good is it to hold on to a piece of metal when the whole business will surely fall?

*   *   *

Margaret can see Herbert's fear. The cable moves silently and their gondola sways gently as they are lifted up the mountainside. Occasionally there is a series of little bumps as the bar attached to the top of the gondola passes over the pulleys of a tower, and when this happens Herbert shudders. She has wiped the mist from the windows, and the spindly tops of the spruce pass silently below. By turning her head she can see her skis and poles on the rack outside, and the valley sinking below as the tops of the white-and-green mountains rise up higher into the light blue sky.

Herbert's eyes are still shut tight. Shudders pass through his body, and from him comes a small, high sound. His hands are clenched around the little bar beside him, and his head is bent forward as though waiting for a blow.

"Are you all right? Herbert, are you all right?" she asks.

His head, though still bent forward, turns slightly. His eyes open just to slits and clamp shut again. "Margaret," he says in a tiny voice. "Margaret."

"Are you all right, Herbert?"

"Margaret, I'm so scared." His voice is tiny, like a little leak in a pipe. "I want to get down out of here."

"You can't," she says. But she pities him. "We'll be at the top in about ten minutes. There's no danger, Herbert."

"I'm frightened," he declares in his tiny voice. Shudders now pass across his shoulders, and she puts an arm around him to try and comfort him; he is rigid.

"It's all right, Herbert. It's all right now."

"I can't help it," he says. With eyes still tightly closed, he turns toward her like a child and grabs her around the waist, his head against her breast. "My coat's caught in the door. I don't think we're attached right. I think we're going to drop."

"It's all right," she says. She strokes his cheek with her hand, feeling the bristles, the smoother skin around his eye and temple. He has always been afraid of the most unexpected things, and it's not the first time she's had to comfort him. "We'll be at the summit pretty soon," she says.

"But how am I going to get down?" he cries.

She has heard that cry before, from little boys up in trees. "Just stay on and you'll end up back at the base."

"You can't leave me, Margaret!" His arms are locked around her waist. "You can't leave me alone in this thing!"

They are approaching the Summit House. Below them she can see the skiers swooping down, and hear the swift hiss of their skis as they pass across the lift line to whatever trail they've decided to take. She wants very much to get out into that bright air and snow. She wants to put on her skis and feel the snow light and powdery beneath her, to look down the miles into the valley and feel that each foot of altitude is a gift of energy she may expend in any way she chooses. Then their gondola passes into the hollow-sounding darkness of the Summit House.

When the young attendant opens the door of his gondola, Bucky jumps out and receives his skis and poles from another attendant, whose job it is to take them out of the rack.

"Buckyyy!" they say, delighted to see him.

He grins at them and walks out into the snow to find Margaret. Among the few stunted spruce, other skiers are laughing as they lean against the wind and put on their skis. "Which trail this time?" one calls. "I feel brave! Let's take the Spout!" But Margaret isn't there. Bucky jams his skis into the snow and goes back inside, to the observation room. It is empty except for Billy, who is smoking a cigarette and kicking one boot against a splashboard.

"Billy," Bucky says, and Billy turns away from the window. "Have you seen your mother?" Billy shakes his head and starts to speak, but Bucky turns and goes back to the lift line. "Did a man and a woman get off just before me?" he asks the young attendant.

The boy grins and shakes his head. "They didn't want to get off, Bucky. Went back down, skis and all."

Bucky goes back to the observation room. What did he really have in mind, anyway? And now she's gone back down.

Billy stamps his cigarette into the tracked-in water on the floor. He looks listless and unhappy.

"Want a Coke?" Bucky asks, and Billy nods.

"Want a cigarette?" Billy says. Gloria has gone home, and she didn't tell him.

Bucky gets two Cokes out of the machine, accepts a cigarette, and they both stand there in the water kicking their boots against the splashboards. Through the glass they can see the mountains descending, dark green where they are covered with spruce, spiderwebby where tall hardwoods stand leafless, white in the few openings visible, and then, as far down and away as they can see, everything turns blue.

In his room at the Mountain View, Japhet Villard is on his knees on the rug, his elbows on the bed. Even though he has taken four of the white pills, it is the only position he can find in which he is not in excruciating pain. He is angry and at the same time terrified, for some monstrous force has got him down and won't let go. He is very angry, and there are tears on his face; he sees one drop to the bedspread. When he curses out loud, he is repaid by a knife thrust. The doctors told him it might not be pleasant, that from his old tissues he might expect recalcitrance and pain, but he could never really believe that time would betray him. He has always faced up to fear, to any challenge. His image of himself is that of a clean, brave man, eyes squinted against the freezing wind, a great, wild mountain submissive but grand beneath him. His pride has been to out-last hardship and pain. But there are positions in which no dignity is possible, in which one cannot rally one's forces, and here he is, upon his knees at last. He has to grin; a grin, he thinks, is the only intelligent response to this sort of thing.

The Survivors

SOMETIMES WHEN I see old Mr. Caswell pulling his shiny little mail cart up our front walk, I think of his son, Ben, who used to be my best friend. That was twenty years ago, when Ben and I were in high school together. Ben looked a great deal like his father, and now I think there was in both of them a kind of wheyish strength. They were both pale and thin, and they had a metallic hardness in their bodies, as though blood didn't run in their veins at all but some sort of indestructible grayish fluid. I could never think of either one of them getting a tan, or blushing, because the warmth of color never appeared on their faces. They looked so much alike that I sometimes wonder if I don't get the two of them mixed up in my memories—as though Ben, too, has had a chance to grow old.

Mr. Caswell was our mailman then, in 1943, and he still is, though he's near compulsory retirement. He's very slow, so that when he delivers we don't get our mail until five o'clock in the afternoon, when I'm home from work. Sometimes he drops a letter or two along the way, and the kids in the neighborhood call him "Old Butterfingers." My son, Davy, is too young to participate in the business of Mr. Caswell's nickname—and perhaps, with the unexpected tact of children, none of them says it in Mr. Caswell's presence, for he is a kindly man, unobtrusive, tolerated even by the neurotic collies that have overrun our town in recent years. To Davy, Mr. Caswell is "Mr. Caswell," and at our door he greets the old man with a delight that is never diminished. I'm glad Davy likes to greet him, because I find myself hesitant, even a little embarrassed, to say much to him. It's on account of Ben. We've never talked about Ben in all those years. Although Mr. Caswell might like to, I think he may sense my embarrassment, and himself feel hesitant to speak of his son. If there is only a little mail for us, Mr. Caswell promises to bring more tomorrow, then smiles at Davy, nods at me, and walks on carefully, yet lightly for a man of his age. It seems strange to me to see him in the new official uniform with the blue Ike jacket—as though he were a veteran of a war I know he missed.

In 1943, both Ben and I were in love with that war. And suddenly, sitting at home after work today, I remember something that happened to me on a September night of that year. I stood on top of a crude tower made of pine logs. The tower was on top of Pike Hill, which overlooks our town of Leah. I had just turned sixteen, and I was armed, not with the antiaircraft gun I would have chosen but with my Winchester .22 pump. Shells were scarce in those days, and I owned ten of them—just ten—each a little jewel of power. At home in my room, I would play with them, line them up on their primer ends and shake each one at my ear to hear the smokeless powder whisper from inside. Now they were where they belonged, inside my rifle. Identical, anonymous, one in the chamber and nine in the tubular magazine, they gave to my rifle the proper weight of danger. I was alone on the tower. The only light was from above, from the stars, and soft darkness came in on me from the side, as though I stood on a submerged rock in a warm lake. If it hadn't been for the war I might have been a little afraid. What nonhuman creatures might swim, with leathery flippers, out of the darkness to slide against my legs? But the war precluded such complicated, peacetime nightmares. The war was bright and official, like ballistics.

My duties were official, too, and I carried my loaded rifle— half toy, half deadly weapon—because one part of me, at least, could believe in the possibility of an enemy invasion of central

New Hampshire. Witness all that adult effort with huge logs, a ladder and platform of dressed lumber, even a telephone line strung up through the pines and birches of Pike Hill. From eight o'clock until eleven that night, when Ben Caswell would relieve me, I was the Air Raid Watcher. If I saw or heard an airplane, I was to write it down in a little book that hung by the telephone, and describe its course and whatever else I could determine about it. If something really suspicious occurred—a sky full of parachutes, perhaps, or the drone of a hundred black Heinkel transports crossing, as they did in movies, a sky whose stars jerked ominously from side to side—I was to call Mr. Bemis, our Town Clerk, who was also Chief Air Raid Warden.

What did happen that night was just outside the realm of any possibility I might have had in mind, and that may have been why it left me so emotionless. It was a very warm night, and the warmth gave it an odd depth and clarity, as though I could have heard someone talking over in Vermont. The dark pines below me seemed every so often to breathe out wind. I could hear them receiving the wind and moving with it, and then a slow gust would come folding up over me, gentle and warm as bathwater. I leaned against the wooden rail and aimed my rifle at imaginary planes; I saw a meteor, and wished it were a burning Zero or Focke-Wulf. Below me, down the hill where the maples and elms began, the window lights of Leah were slowly going out. Then I must have decided to get the binoculars from the telephone box. I had my rifle in my right hand, and I must have cocked it fully, so that the hammer (it was a Model 62, which had a hammer) wouldn't obscure the rear sight. I must have forgotten to set the hammer back on half cock.

There is a sort of instantaneous precision about accidents, especially accidents with guns. They start and they are over, and there doesn't seem to be any middle part at all. There were sparks—the sky was full of sparks—but where was the explosion? I knew that I had been setting the rifle down, and then the explosion must have come, but it was like no shot I'd ever heard. It was more like one huge peal of a bell, a bell with no resonant aftertones to let me know that I had actually heard it, so that I wasn't quite sure that I had heard it all. And all those sparks. I'd never shot a .22 at night before, and hadn't known how much fire came out with the bullet. I just stood there for a moment, aware that my side itched—in the ribs on my right side. I don't believe it ever occurred to me that I might have been shot, and in fact I wasn't, but when I turned the flashlight on myself I found some interesting things. I say "interesting" because I'm sure it is the only way to describe my attitude then. There was a burned hole about as big as a fifty-cent piece—only elongated somewhat—in my shirt. My undershirt was dark at that place but not burned through, and the slight burn I received on my skin was no more than a vague red spot. I didn't find out until later that night when I was home in my room that the bullet had actually gone beneath the folds of my shirt and come out near the breast pocket. Still, I did not tremble, nor did my pulse increase because of that discovery. In a way, I suppose, it's useless to worry about a spent bullet, because by that time it's got to wherever it was going. I did worry some about my mother's ever missing that shirt and undershirt, which I put in the trash can, but if she did she never said anything about it to me.

When Ben came to relieve me (our DeMolay chapter, a sort of junior Masonic order, had volunteered for this duty), we didn't make much of my accident. I told him about it and showed him the hole in my shirt, but then we looked back at the sky, and soon I left for home. We were acting out bigger and better possibilities, and to have made too much of my little scrape with reality would have been to change the subject.

We knew, both of us, that an airborne invasion of Leah was fairly unlikely. We both had *National Geographic* maps on the walls of our bedrooms, and we followed the war with little glass-headed pins. Sumatra, Java—the Battle of the Java Sea had been a frightening affair, even to us, because the Japanese seemed so invincible—Singapore, Dieppe. Gabriel Heater's voice was as certain as God's, and proclaimed doom to the Axis. We had been worried, but by September of 1943 we had no doubts about winning. We could forget the war for hours at a time, but we didn't want to forget it, because I'm sure we believed that it would be through the war that we would grow up, grow into men who could have the experiences we wanted to have. How could we deserve the lovely girls we wanted until we had been to war and come back, like the heroes in *The Saturday Evening Post*? One had to have in one's eye that virile gleam that looked across a peaceful garden and saw in memory the deaths of comrades. There was no civilian love in those days; "They're either too gray or too grassy green," sang the Andrews Sisters, and we believed what they sang.

We didn't have to man the watchtower; it hadn't been taken seriously for a long time, and I'm sure Mr. Bemis had no desire to be waked up in the middle of the night. But he couldn't say no to our patriotic gesture. He was a Mason, after all, and we were DeMolay. And this was a time when, upon the patriotic whim of the high school principal, the whole school might suddenly, in the middle of any day, have to march all around town behind the band, singing "God Bless America."

There was Eddie Kusacs, too, to remind us all that we should have been at war. Every once in a while—it could be a quiet school afternoon, and we'd be in study hall—there would suddenly appear outside the windows Eddie Kusacs's great blue Marine F4U, its wicked radial engine screaming and blatting in our ears, its inverted gull wings wheeling down between the trees. Then up and back and around he'd come, lower than some of the school windows, as though he were following the cinder driveway that led down around in back to the boiler room. The huge airplane seemed to be going too fast and too slow at the same time—too fast for anything in Leah, too slow for the noise it made. After a few passes, during which I'm sure we never breathed (we drank the sound; we were avid for that real noise), he'd come straight over the athletic field and drop a little yellow parachute about the size of a bushel basket. Then he was gone, flashing over a hill and out of sound, all that power suddenly gone out of the air.

But how real that airplane was, and how we wanted it! We would all be out of our desks and at the windows, and each time it happened we felt that we would never have to go back, that somehow our lives had changed. When that violent machine hung in the air, we knew how inconsequential were the too familiar trees and streets of Leah. After it had gone, everything around us seemed tired; the dust in the sunlight of our brown study hall turned with a golden slowness. Then one of the teachers would go out and get the parachute, and we'd all file into the auditorium to hear what Eddie had written—usually best wishes to Mr. Skelton, the principal, and Miss Dube and some of the other teachers, and come on, boys, join the Marines. We'd all known Eddie. We'd known him when he came to school in a '35 Plymouth coupe, and here he was, godlike in his deadly blue Corsair.

The war was close enough to us; we were sixteen, and you could join the Navy or the Marines at seventeen. But what were we to do in the meantime? At least to me, we were living in a sort of limbo, a place where nothing much mattered, where we couldn't get hurt because we could not believe this limbo to be a place where one was really mortal. And this, I suppose, accounted for my indifference to the tiny bullet that so nearly entered my side. It was only a .22.

If anyone had asked me who was my best friend that year, I would have said Ben Caswell, and yet I wonder how much we actually liked each other. There were friends of mine I think I liked better but didn't see as often. In some ways, Ben and I were too much alike. We were both rather bossy, and so we were always a little irritated by each other. If I wanted to cross the street, or take a shortcut on my bike, chances are Ben wouldn't, and you couldn't make him change his mind. Quite often we would go to the same place by different routes.

Ben was tall and skinny and hard; he could knock a hole in you with his elbow. His face was long and plain and pale—slightly gray, like dishwater—and his hair, the color of gunmetal, was flat and unhealthy-looking. He'd had undulant fever for a long time, back in the third and fourth grades, and I remember him bringing his special milk to school in mason jars. He was strong enough, though. I could get him down, mainly because I was a little more compact, and thus quicker, but I always got bruised in the process, and once I had him pinned I was afraid to let him up. It can be very boring just holding somebody down.

Ben got better marks in school than I did, and I tried to discount the importance of this, feeling I was just "mentally lazy," as Mr. Skelton had once called me. I didn't consider algebra, for instance, to be a discipline that might prove my brain unequal to Ben's. I considered those who were good at it to be slightly mad, and their concentration upon its rigid difficulties rather inhuman. In any case, Ben was very good at this sort of thing; his homework was always done. Most of us didn't care very much about homework, but Ben always did whatever he contracted to do. I considered this a lack of a sense of humor, and the teachers themselves didn't seem to care as much as Ben did. Sometimes we would study our algebra or trigonometry together at my house. These sessions were mostly for my benefit, because, whatever the reason, I could hardly cope with things mathematical. Ben was appalled at the shortness of my span of attention.

"Look," he'd say. "You take the sine minus the cosine . . ." and with his words, so sober and knowledgeable, I would feel a weakness setting in, a strange, highly pleasant weakness in my legs and arms—euphoric, because everything became hilariously funny—and I'd look at an equation made up of things called sines and cosines and see in it elaborate scansions. One, without its pluses and minuses, went, "Sine, cosine, cosine, sine = cosine, cosine, sine, sine." This I sang to the tune of "Yankee Doodle," while Ben looked stern and disgusted. I thought it hysterically funny, and my arms turned so weak from laughter I couldn't even hold a pencil. "Sine *minus* cosine!" Ben said, and I fell out of my chair onto the floor, screaming, "I'll sign! I'll sign anything! Just let me out of here!"

For some reason, I found it impossible to take those steps, those intermediate little steps, toward what I wanted to be. I wanted to be grown-up and powerful right now—to be part of the war, part of the world. Ben took each step as it came, and really mastered it. His head was full of equations and ways to factor them. I never took the time. But I was a little stronger than Ben. Yes, I was; I could take him in a fight. Out on the street, I could take him down, but always I was fearfully aware of the difference between us, and I knew that what I took down to the dirt and held there was somehow more intelligent, more valuable, than I was.

Ben had many ways of being irritating. His bike, for instance, and his loyalty to that monster. It had thirty-inch wheels, and the tires were about as big around as your thumb. These were irreplaceable, of course, and not just because of the war—where could anyone have ever found such oddities? And the rubber, in the few places where it showed through the friction tape, was very old, actually sticky to the touch. The rest of us had balloon tires.

Between the girls' entrance and the boys' entrance to the high school was a cement sidewalk, and frost had heaved up one of the blocks so that it was canted at about a twenty-degree angle. Before school and after school, while the girls stood at their entrance and watched, we'd get on our bikes, head down the walk away from the building, and hit that ramp. Pete Kelly had the record jump—a good fifteen feet, marked in chalk with his name. Mine was nowhere near that, and Ben's was less than mine; his excuse was that crazy giraffe of a bike. I always tried to get him to use mine—it was a prewar Elgin—but he never would. Once, when it was his turn to go, I tried again. "Here, take mine," I said, in a rather unpleasant voice that was an insult to his bike. The other jumpers were standing around impatiently, making airplane noises, and I didn't hear his answer. I reached for his bike and at the same time pushed mine toward him by the handlebars.

With a short, violent move, he shoved my hand away. "Mine!" he said. "I'll use mine!"

"Okay, hammerhead," I said.

Sometimes his loyalty to that bike . . . No, the way he could bring up out of nowhere something that sounded like principle—this would enrage me. At the same time, I had to respect it, and that made it even more irritating. Here he was, with his narrow, washed-out face and lank, washed-out-looking hair, and he could be as recalcitrant as a rock. I kept thinking he should have been more like his father, who looked like him but was a shy, friendly man who had to say hello a thousand times a day on his mail route and still seemed to enjoy it. For a moment I felt like kicking out a few of Ben's spokes, but I didn't, and he went ahead and made his usual short jump. I don't think he really approved of the jumping, but we all had to do it. This was in lieu of being Eddie Kusacs in his Corsair, I suppose.

On the way home that afternoon—it was a Friday—Ben and I ended up fighting, our bikes in a pile on the sidewalk. I had Ben pinned, as usual, but in the process he'd hit me in the nose, and it felt like a wedge driven between my eyes. My poor nose; I couldn't comfort it because I needed both hands and all my strength to hold Ben down. My cheekbones ached, and I seemed to taste the metal fillings in my teeth. I had Ben's head halfway under somebody's barberry hedge, and one of the little thorns had come off its branch and was sticking in his cheek.

"There's a thorn sticking in your cheek," I said. "I can see it sticking right in there."

Convulsive movements on his part. His arm rose, and for the space of an inch it was invincible; I couldn't stop it. But his strength was like a pump working upon my tiny but real center of fear, and this forced strength into me so that I could push him back down again. His bony wrists gave my fingers pain as I leaned on them.

"Sticking right into your flesh," I said. "Must be in a quarter of an inch."

He'd never say a word while we were fighting. For him it was all beyond words, it was all power. He had no need for talk because what he wanted to do to me was clear enough. I had to talk. I was always talking at his face, which was as unforgiving as a bird's. I dreamed of it, that smooth, blank face. I'd talk and talk while he despised my arguments.

"Will you give up? Will you give up? Can't you see I've won? I've got you pinned, you *bastard!* Hey, Ben, will you give up? I'll spit in your eyes, you bastard!"

I felt him waiting, letting his strength return. I was always just barely surprised by his sudden strategies. He tried to butt my face with his forehead, and almost did. When I fought him, it was always to contain, to immobilize him. Though I may have bragged that I was deadly, any blow of his that was really meant to hurt stayed with me for days, frightening yet admirable.

Even when his father came along, I didn't dare let him up.

"What's going on here?" Mr. Caswell said mildly. He was smiling, which shocked me.

I hardly dared look away from Ben, but I had to glance up at Mr. Caswell's thin yet somehow droopy face.

Since Ben wouldn't talk, I had to answer. "We're wrestling," I said.

Mr. Caswell shifted his leather mailbag from one thin shoulder to another, then pulled his lapels straight. He just stood there in his baggy uniform, and it seemed strange to me to see a face so like Ben's yet so mild. "Why don't you come along home?"

"I don't want to let him up," I said.

Mr. Caswell understood why. "Ben," he said, "if David lets you up, will you stop fighting?"

Ben wouldn't answer; he tried to bridge and throw me off. I threw my weight on him hard and flattened him out again. Then he tried to butt me with his forehead, but he'd tried that before.

"You boys are friends," Mr. Caswell said. "Why do you have to fight so much?"

"He wouldn't use my bike!" I said. I was very angry, and sorry for myself, and was even afraid I might cry.

"Ben wouldn't use your bike?"

"He wouldn't use it!"

"My goodness!" Mr. Caswell said, trying to be funny. He was a funny man, actually. One time he told us he had a cold in his elbow, and he said it in such a serious, surprised sort of voice even Ben laughed. "Heavens to Betsy! It's like I tried to give a man five dollars and he wouldn't take it so I hit him!"

Neither Ben nor I felt this was very funny.

"Well, what are you going to do when it comes suppertime? Can we send out some food for you?" Mr. Caswell asked.

"I don't want to keep him down!" I burst out, regretting it immediately, because I saw a flicker of satisfaction on Ben's face. "I wish I had another arm," I said through my teeth. "I'd bash your face in!"

"Well, boys," Mr. Caswell said, "are you going to hurt yourselves?"

"I don't want to hurt him!" I said, still feeling sorry for myself. After all, hadn't I won this fight?

"Ben?" Mr. Caswell said.

Ben wouldn't answer.

"Ben," Mr. Caswell said. I sensed pride and resignation in the word. Mr. Caswell thought for a moment, and then he said, "Well, I'm not going to butt in. Seems you're both old enough so it wouldn't help anyway. I'd stop and chat awhile, but I've got to finish my route."

Before he left us, he reached down and with gentle fingers

brushed the thorn from his son's cheek. It was just in the skin, and Ben's cheek didn't even bleed. Then he was off, ambling along in his casual, mailman's stride, leaving us with our problem.

It was now late in the afternoon. Just perceptibly the light was fading. It was the time when near things still have sharp edges and colors—the barberries of the hedge gleamed orange-red, and the round leaves were dark green still. We seemed to have been prisoners of that small place for hours, and I began to recognize each tuft of grass. A few inches from Ben's white hand was a crushed dandelion stem, split and bent so that I could see the silver inside of it, and I saw it again, with recognition, noting that it hadn't changed. Ben strained against my weight. Each time, I could summon just enough strength to overpower him.

How long were we held in that deadlock? It began to grow dark. Ben's face flickered like a dim light as my eyes moved, and the small twigs faded upward into his hair. I knew he would never give up. Once, he actually spoke, and frightened me. "Will you give up?" he asked. It was like a dream in which logic turns crazy. Was he the one who held me down? Once, he caught me off guard and turned me over, and for a violent moment we scrabbled, sobbing, into the barberry hedge. I fought him back down again, and brought him gasping into the bare dirt alongside the hedge. I hadn't known I had such strength; I'd bent his arms where I had no leverage, where pain alone seemed to be my strength. My fingers seemed to have gone right through his wrists between tendon and bone, and he cursed me in a high, strangely boyish voice, half bawling—one long, little scream. I sobbed my own curses back at him, crying because it was so unfair that my greater strength hadn't won this fight. And then there were long periods of silence, almost of relaxation, and I listened to the cars pass along the street. Then a light came on in a window across the street, and we knew it must be near suppertime.

And somehow our fight ended, not necessarily because of supper and its official demand upon us. Our fights always had to end in some sort of truce, which could be forgotten, so that we could fight again the next day. Neither of us ever won; most fights are not clearly won, and ours never were. On this occasion, I'd have to meet him the next day, Saturday, because we both had Saturday jobs at Milledge & Cunningham, sweeping up bushels of thread and cloth from beneath the cutting and sewing tables. Instead of overalls, they were making field jackets and fatigue clothes for the Army. Where Lucky Strike Green went, we thought. And Sunday night, Ben would be relieving me again on the Air Raid Tower. We couldn't get away from each other if we tried.

When I got home, my soiled clothes were noticed, and I learned that about fourteen people had managed to see the fight, including my sister, Catherine. It was decided (my father abstaining) that after supper and a bath I would go to the Caswells' and apologize. My arguments against doing this are of no matter here; I had to go. I didn't mind facing Ben or his father, but Mrs. Caswell was another thing. She usually affected a richly ironic tone that left me speechless—even, I sometimes felt, armless and legless. I couldn't cope with it. "To what honor do we owe your illustrious presence, Sir David?" That sort of thing. Mr. Caswell was hardly ever in sight. He'd be down in the basement or out in the garage.

I rode my bike the two blocks to Ben's house. I didn't have a light, and there was only one streetlight in between, but we always rode right on through the darkness. Our house was huge—we had rooms we never used at all—but Ben's house was very small. It had enough rooms in it, but they were all in miniature—neat, small rooms crammed full of things. The Atwater Kent radio touched the living-room sofa on one side and the matching chair on the other. You could bump your head if you weren't careful going up the little stairs. Ben was an only child, so they didn't need a lot of room, but to see him stooping around in the halls and in his own narrow, low-ceilinged room made me want to get outside. The place was like a doll's house, and Mrs. Caswell was the doll—she was round and short. The rest of us should have been outside, sticking our hands in through the windows. Nothing inside ever seemed to change, to get used; the lace antimacassars on the sofa arms never got dirty, never were pushed askew.

When I reached the house, I dropped my bike on the grass and went up on the little porch as quietly as I could. Finally I

knocked, and Mrs. Caswell came to the door. Her skin had tiny
striations on it, like a McIntosh apple; in some kinds of light she
looked as though she had a rash all over. She was full of pressure, and she made me nervous.

"David, David, David," she said, sighing with weary tolerance, as though I'd been there too often. Which I certainly
hadn't. She smiled—she always smiled—and I thought it hurt
her to smile, because that constant irony seemed to be the result
of pain.

She put her hand on my arm and drew me inside; she was
always touching me. "Our postman is in his hobby shop," she
said, "and our Good Boy is in his books."

She sat me down, too deeply, into the sofa. I never knew
where to sit on it, in that last moment when there was still a little
choice, because the cushions tilted and shifted. This time I sat
next to an arm, too deep, but I hooked an elbow over the arm
to hold myself up.

"Shouldn't you allow Benjamin to do his homework?" she
asked. "I suppose yours is all done, neat as pie?"

"No," I said. Already I was going into a mild, classroomlike
coma. Nothing that was going to happen was anything I wanted
to happen.

"But David," she said, affecting a reasonable tone, "how
can our Benjamin be valedictorian if we don't let him study?"

This was ridiculous. Nothing in the world could keep Ben
from being valedictorian. Usually a girl was, because they took
easy subjects like home economics or typing, but Ben's only
rival, Joan Warren, had moved to Northlee. Who cared, anyway? I don't think Ben cared; he just had the habit of doing all
his work. You could never pin anything like that on Ben. I
thought, Why is she trying to ruin his reputation? My mother
would have more sense than that.

Ben had heard us, and came stooping down the stairs, no
opinion of my presence visible on his sallow face. Behind him,
the wallpaper was the same sallow color as his face.

"Hi, Dave," he said. His eyes were blank, as though he were
still thinking equations.

It was then that I confessed, lying, and trying to make little
of it. "We were just wrestling," I said.

"Just wrestling," Ben agreed.

"My little boys were wrestling!" Mrs. Caswell said. "My little cubs, trying out their new muscles!"

"Yeah," I said. "Just wrestling a little." I got up to go, and as I turned toward the door she came up to me and took me fiercely by the arm. I looked down into her face.

"Don't you realize that Benjamin is a genius?" she said. There was a lot of hissing in her voice; she really meant it. I didn't really doubt it myself. But she scared me. She scared me by saying such a crazy thing. I jerked my arm away from her hand and ran out of her house.

A few days later, just before school let out, Eddie Kusacs buzzed us all again. He came five times in all, that year, and each time is distinct in my memory. I don't know where he came from, or what he was doing in a Marine Corsair so far from the sea. But there he was, fracturing the blue sky above the high school, fracturing our attention, fracturing the school, the teachers, telling us how we were the prisoners of our little town. Then he was gone.

The bicycle jumping that afternoon was more daring than usual. Pete Kelly established a new record. I beat my old mark by one foot. The sunlight made me sneeze as it bounced off the sidewalk, and beneath me was the familiar noise of sprockets and spokes, the little stressful twangs and creaks of my bike—then the lift and belly thrill of the flight. We didn't go high in the air, but when I landed there was a dense, hard push through my elbows, and my handlebars squeaked down an inch or two. Then the slewing in the dry dirt beyond the walk, and for a moment all the girls' eyes were still upon me.

As Ben came up to take his ritual jump, I said, "Come on, genius." This was a bit like poking a snake, and I didn't say it very loudly. I'll never know if he heard it or not. But I still see him very clearly as he swung his long leg up over his bike. I see his blue sock and a section of white, hairless leg, thin and uniform as a length of two-inch pipe. He pushed off and began to pump hard. His long, limp hair came down over his forehead, and the wind pushed it aside, parted it in the middle. His mouth was set, made into a little slit by effort—the same expression he wore when he was mad at me—and he hunched over those strange handlebars of his that bent down and around like ram's horns. There he went, his chain grinding, and he hit the ramp. I think his tire blew then and his wheel buckled later, when he landed, but others said no, everything went haywire at once.

I saw Ben in the air, swimming, parallel to his bike, and on his face still was that same determined, closed look I always see in my memories of him. Then he and the bike came down together. We got to him pretty quickly; I was proud because I was the first to get there, and we tried to untangle him. It was serious, we knew—no mere scrape case. His head didn't want to come off the handlebars, and we knew enough to leave it alone while the girls' screams brought authority from inside the school.

Dr. Winston was there in ten minutes, and when he and the school nurse removed Ben from his bike, Ben's long hands spread and contracted as though he were rubbing coins between his thumbs and forefingers. They took him off to North-lee to the hospital, and by the next day the janitor had put bleach on the cement where Ben had bled, and a sawhorse over the canted block of sidewalk.

How were we all affected by this? It was shocking enough, but it was only a bicycle accident, I think we felt. That hex nut, for instance, that dented Ben's skull—I'd turned it with a wrench while Ben held the handlebars straight. It was too familiar, not the instrument of the drama we wanted in our lives— not with the shadow of a Corsair in our minds and that huge radial engine still roaring in our ears.

When I met Mr. Caswell on the street a few days after the accident, I asked again—I had called at the house earlier—how Ben was getting along.

"Ben is still very sick, David," he said. "He's very, very sick."

"Is he going to be out of school long?"

"We don't know how long." Mr. Caswell's voice was calm and exact. "He hasn't come to yet, you see."

I think he already knew that the part of Ben's brain that governed consciousness had been damaged. His voice was calm, but his eyes were glittery—not really wet, I thought, but they looked as if they had been polished.

"I hope he gets well soon," I said.

"Thank you. Thank you, David," he said.

I didn't know what to do, so I stared at him for a moment,

not able to share his feelings, though I knew immediately that Ben was in very grave danger and Mr. Caswell was grieving for his son. Already grieving—that I knew. I told him that Mr. Skelton had announced in assembly that Ben would graduate next June with the rest of us, even though he might miss spring term.

"Yes, he told us," Mr. Caswell said. And then a strange thing happened to his mouth. As he drew in a long breath, his teeth clicked together, hard, about ten times. Nothing else happened, except that I suddenly felt his grief behind my own eyes, and my throat hurt badly. For a moment he looked straight at me, seeing what I was embarrassed to be caught at. I thought, it isn't certain that Ben won't get well again. But I knew, and perhaps because it is the healthy trick of a child to blame the inanimate for every accident, I felt myself begin to burn with an indignation inexpressible in any other way.

"It was that lousy bike!" I shouted. "That stupid bike!"

He was surprised. His mouth opened and closed upon the colorless, uniform rows of his dentures. He made a motion with his arm, and I thought he meant to put his mailbag down, so that he could comfort me. I walked away without looking back.

Ben never did regain consciousness. He died of pneumonia three years later, in 1946, while I was stationed at Fort Lawton, Seattle. I suppose I did, finally, have a few moments of glory in that war, although they were all Stateside. But as a veteran, if I'd admitted it, my claims to the war were fraudulent. The war missed me. My reserve enlistment ran out two months before the Korean War. That one missed me, too, so I am quite aware that things do miss, like the little bullet that once followed its blind trajectory so close to my heart.

Today, when Mr. Caswell came to our house, Davy wasn't there to meet him because he'd gone shopping with his mother. I walked down and met him halfway.

"Hi, Dave," he said, and unbuckled the strap from a bundle of letters and bills and junk, as he has now many thousand times.

"Hi, Bill," I said, because we are both grown men now, and I can't call him "Mr. Caswell."

With his gray hand, he gave me a couple of letters and said, sternly, "Where's my assistant today?"

Because he said it in an apparently serious way, he took me a little by surprise. I was caught, staring, while he waited for me to get the joke. I soon understood how he meant his stern voice to be taken, but he had put me off balance, and for a moment I felt the beat of my heart. "Went shopping with his mother," I said.

"Well, now," he said, and looked at me for a moment or two longer.

As I've said, we had never spoken of Ben, in all those years, and I found that I couldn't, even now, though I would have liked to, if only to try to exorcise those memories of a time so full of fierce expectation. I might have told Mr. Caswell of the power that Ben still seems to hold over me—Ben, who still seems strong, unbeaten by time and reality. But what would that have meant to him? We were, both of us, merely survivors, who felt, I suppose, the irrational guilt that all survivors feel. Mr. Caswell didn't say anything further to me. We stood there in a kind of deadlock, looking at each other. Then, with tolerance and complicity, we slid our soft glances apart.

Horned Pout Are Evil

HORNED POUT are evil, and it is only upon those evenings when one's dark star is in the ascendance that the urge to catch them comes. They are the slimy fish with bodies like biceps. They grunt at you, and they are poison to the touch in a darkly magic way, because if you hold them in just the right way they can't harm you. But they are slippery, and when you probe for the hook they grind down on your fingers with their sharp but shallow teeth. You know that no matter how careful you are, at least one spine will get you, and these spines are covered with a highly irritating scum that keeps the wound sore for days. You go for horned pout in the darkest part of the night, by lantern light on doubtful, tarnlike water. They never die; in the morning they still lie bug-eyed in your bucket, smacking their wet lips and twitching their black barbels. Every horrible, necessary thing you do to them is done while they live. You skin them while they twitch and complain, and their pink meat quivers upon the board, quivers again in the salted batter, and then you eat them.

The Japanese favor a fish that is deadly poisonous, and expert butchers cut the meat close enough to the center of poison to give the meat some of its flavor, but not too close to kill—most of the time. A kind of culinary Russian roulette. While I've never heard of anyone being killed by a horned pout, I do suggest some similarity here. The fascination of the abomination, as Conrad said. The closer we get to nature, the less we tend to sentimentalize it, and the more we recognize ourselves as part of its infinite patience, its cruelty and beauty. Without the knowledge of danger, how can we aspire to be alive? We must keep our senses quivering.

One warm night in August the urge for horned pout came—or, more properly, it came first to my son, Peter, who was then nine. The night was moonless and dark blue, and the stars were hazy. We were at our cabin on the mountain, and the bug season was mostly over. Trout fishing was in the doldrums, and neither of us had felt that tapping message from what is wild for a long time.

After Pete suggested it, and the idea began to take hold, we naturally began to think of Ozzie Huckins. One reason was, he'd be hurt if we didn't at least ask him, even though his wife might not let him go, and others were that he lived down on the flats where there were mudworms and night crawlers, and he had a boat and a Jeep pickup. I had a boat, too, but it was down on the lake. We could have fished in the lake, in the delta where the Fowler River comes into it, but the horned pout ran quite small there. Ozzie would know of some pond deep in the woods or swamps, accessible only to his Jeep. Also there was Ozzie's hard cider, which is nearly too beautiful to drink out of ordinary tumblers. The current batch, I knew, had aged two years in used Newburyport rum barrels before being bottled. It was nearly colorless, clear except for a few tiny flakes, like those in Goldwasser, and not quite as grossly carbonated as champagne. Some of these qualities were caused by Ozzie's hanging a cheesecloth bag of raw hamburger in each barrel during the aging process. Someday I'm going to find out why, but until I do I'll savor this paradox along with all the others.

Anyway, we gathered our fly rods, clippers, flashlights, pliers, bait cans, and a five-gallon bucket. I filled my Coleman lantern and oiled its pump, and under the disapproving eye of my wife and daughter, Pete and I took off down the mountain. If Ozzie couldn't go, we'd hunt night crawlers on his lawn and go in our boat.

As we approached Ozzie's farm, I had the usual twinge of hesitation. Ozzie's wife, Gisela, was a strange and formidable girl. He married her when he was forty and she was twenty-six, thinking, he told me, that he was getting "about the nearest thing to a good squaw I could find hereabouts." "Some squaw," I'd said then. She was a very pretty girl. She came from a large, poor family, and he figured she'd be a good, quiet, hardworking type. Alas for poor Ozzie; what he got in that gamble was a good, hardworking, ambitious, intense, explosive girl who wanted to come up in the world and drag old Ozzie along with her. She disapproved of idle hands, and idle hands were what Ozzie had cultivated most of his life. Before his marriage he worked occasionally in the woods and did odd jobs—just enough to pay the taxes on his farm and make payments on his Jeep. Now he commuted by car pool to the ball-bearing factory in Sommerslee and was making payments on a Ford, a new kitchen complete with dispose-all, a new septic system, a vacuum cleaner, a living-room set, a drilled well, a forced-hot-air furnace, a TV, and other things. Once he listed them all to me, his voice growing smaller and smaller under the enormity of these commitments.

She couldn't keep him from going hunting and fishing, but she had the power to make him sad, and when Ozzie was sad, no one was sadder. He was a big, pale man with large ropy muscles full of knots, green eyes, and very even, horn-yellow teeth. He always wore the standard green workman's uniform and an old checked hunting cap.

Gisela, who met us at the door, was still a very handsome woman, narrow-waisted and small-boned, with soft black hair and sharp blue eyes. She smiled pleasantly until she divined our purpose from our clothes, and then her smile turned frozen—a smile of her inner sense of the inevitability of sloth, decadence, and innate worthlessness. In spite of this she let us into her clean and shining kitchen.

Ozzie sat there at the Formica dinette set looking out of place, trying to smile. I nervously suggested horned pouting.

"I don't know," he said furtively, and at that moment we both hated ourselves. Gisela, still smiling that inside-out smile, went to the sink and carefully wiped a Teflon frypan. Pete stood carefully near the door.

"Well," I said, "we'd like to hunt a few night crawlers on your lawn, anyway. Pete and I'd like to catch a few fish—maybe down on the Fowler River."

"No size to 'em there," Ozzie said. "I could show you a place they run to a pound or better." A quick look toward Gisela, and his face turned blank, stunned. "Goddammit," he muttered.

"Well," I said soothingly, "we'll pick up a few night crawlers, if you don't mind. Good night, Gisela." She didn't turn, but I did. Pete was already outside the door.

Night crawlers are quick and wary beasts, and even though we held red cellophane over our flashlight lenses (they aren't supposed to be sensitive to red light), it took a lot of concentration to get them. These were nice, muscular worms running to about six inches, and we seldom found one with his whole length out of the ground. The important thing was to figure out which end was anchored, and grab him at the right end before he snapped back into his hole. We'd picked up twenty or thirty by the time we heard the barn doors slide open and the Jeep start. Ozzie drove out with the boat in the truck bed, and we quickly transferred our gear to the Jeep. Without a word we were off.

"Jesus H. Christ," Ozzie said, finally, and added, "Oh, pardon me, Pete."

"That's okay," Pete said.

Ozzie was sad, and we didn't say much, even when we left the gravel road and groaned through the transfer box up a brushy tote road. Ozzie was very gentle with machines, and we took the rocks and sloughs in low-low for about a mile.

"There," he said finally, although I could see nothing but leaves in the headlights. "Down there's Pickle Pond." We descended, then, into a bowl surrounded on three sides by steep cliffs. At the shore the black water was silent, and a long shaft of ledge ran down at a steep angle into darkness. "Deep," Ozzie said. I lit the Coleman lantern, and its hissing white light made us a room in the darkness. We got the boat into the water and put our gear in it. He'd thought, of course, to bring the cooler and a few bottles of cider, and I put our beer and ginger ale in it with the cider. Ozzie had a huge can of night crawlers he'd gathered surreptitiously a few nights before, so we had plenty of bait. As we shoved out toward the middle of the pond, he sighed and said, "Fish now, pay later."

My hands were trembling as I strung my rod with sinking line and short leader. I said we used fly rods for horned pout, which might cause some purists to blink. My feeling about the fly rod, however, is that it has evolved not merely as a tool to catch fish, but as an excruciatingly sensitive instrument made to communicate the wild energy of a fish straight to your quivering brain—an extension, in fact, of your very nerves. This magnified return is desired as much for its own sake as for the help it gives in making a proper strike, so why not experience horned pout this way too?

Ozzie anchored out in the pond in about ten feet of water, and we lowered our angry worms down into the black until they touched bottom, then raised them a little, each according to his own mysterious calculations. We waited, while the lantern hissed and moths danced across the smooth water. The lantern's whiter light set us out as though we were suspended in space. The water was as black as the night, but if we looked very carefully across to the cliffs and woods we could pick out the muted glimmer of a branch, or a damp slab of ledge. In between was nothing except the miracle of our suspension and the bright moths dancing past on surface tension.

Pete said, "I got a bite!" in a hushed voice. "See? See?" His rod tip bent, came back, bent again—a motion not caused by anything human. Something down there worried his hook, something alive down there near the bottom. "He's eating it!" Pete said, and struck, not too hard. Then his rod bent again, and shivered.

"By God, he's got one!" Ozzie said happily. "Old Pete got the first one!"

"Don't yank him, now," I said, unable to keep my mouth shut. Pete tended to resent such advice. He reeled him in and carefully lifted him over the gunwale. He was a nice size—not a pound by any means, but a good horned pout about ten inches long. They're nearly all head, but this one would have some good meat on him. He grunted—a sort of dull, clicking, gutty sound—and Pete stuck his fingers into the wide mouth. With the black barbels hanging down, the horned pout looked like a dark, piscine Fu Manchu. "Look at him bite me," Pete said proudly. This is something I'm a little squeamish about, but Pete doesn't seem to be. The beady eyes gleamed while Pete worked the hook out, and a drop of blood came to the lips before Pete dropped him into the bucket. "See?" Pete said, and showed us where the skin of his knuckles was slightly chewed. I use a pliers, myself, explaining that it's hard enough to hold the fish without getting impaled by one of the three barbs. Actually, I don't quite like to stick my naked fingers into any wild mouth.

After that they began to hit, and we all brought them in. In a lull we broke out the cider, and a ginger ale for Pete. Pretty soon the cider was gone and we'd started on the beer. Time doesn't seem to pass at night on horned pout water, it is gone as soon as you think about it. We'd nearly filled the big bucket with fish, we were covered with slime, bits of worm, and fish blood, and suddenly it was one o'clock. We didn't have our limits—that would have meant 120 fish among us—but we had plenty. Ozzie was laughing and carrying on. "I goochy geechee geechee goochy *gotcha!*" he'd say, and strike a fish he'd divined as having just sucked the hook in far enough. "Oh, man! What a mess of fish we got!"

But as he rowed back toward the Jeep he grew morose again. Fish now, pay later. There is something indefensible, at best, about a man slightly woozy from hard cider, covered with blood and stinking slime, who carries a bucket of gasping fish into an immaculate kitchen. He didn't say much as we drove back to his farm, but he insisted that we come in and he'd show us how easy it was to skin horned pout.

"She'll be in bed, don't worry," he said. "Maybe she won't be asleep, but she'll be in bed. She don't like horned pout in any way, shape, manner, or form."

When I tried to get out of coming in, he said, "Don't worry! I ain't going to use you as no lightning rod. But if a man can't clean a mess of horned pout in his own goddam kitchen, what the hell good is it?"

So we went in with the bucket. Ozzie got out his folding knife and grabbed the first unlucky horned pout, who quivered and flicked his tail—just the tail sticking out hopelessly below Ozzie's big hand.

"Now watch," he said, and an expression of grim pleasure

and determination held his pale face firm. The other horned pout seemed to watch from the bucket. He used the barbs for leverage, his fingers firmly around them below their points, and cut the tough skin all around the head just above the dorsal barb. The fish quivered and complained. "Now!" Ozzie said fiercely, and with firm strength inserted the blade under the dorsal barb and peeled it and all the black skin down to the tail. The flayed horned pout flopped some more, and still flopped as Ozzie cut off the head and flicked out the bared guts with a thumbnail. "Done! Simple as pie!"

But it wasn't simple. Pete and I poked and peeled and dropped fish on the floor while Ozzie efficiently dealt with ten to our one.

"You got to be firm with 'em," he said, intensely proud of his skill. "When you get the knack, it's easy. I never even got stuck once." As he said this he gathered heads, skin, and guts together on the drainboard and pushed them into a garbage bag.

"Let us help you clean up," I said, but he waved the offer away. Then we all glanced toward the door to the dining room, thinking of Gisela, that force. Ozzie may have blanched a little.

"Never mind," he said, and with the garbage bag full, he went to shape it, somehow—a gesture anyone will make with any unshapely package—patting it together. Kipling once wrote that there is one wound that will make any grown man cry—a bullet through the palm of the hand. One of those disembodied heads, in any case, proved at that moment what a horned pout's spines are for. Ozzie didn't cry, but he did nothing but breathe for a while.

Finally he straightened up and grinned. "Ain't it the way, though," he said. "No matter how careful you are, by God, one's going to get you good. I never seen it fail." In his voice was great affection for those barbs. He sucked reflexively on his palm for a moment longer, and then we all began without argument to clean up the rest of the mess.

Soon Pete and I left. We stank of fish, too, and in my bones, at least, was that sated weariness caused by perhaps too much slaughter in the getting of our meat. At least we wouldn't have to go through that process in the morning. Our fish lay neatly bare in a plastic bag, ready for the seasoned flour. I had the

feeling that after a shower and a long sleep I'd meet the demands of civilization a little differently—perhaps with a little
more respect. Slaughter as therapy? I wondered if Pete felt
something of this, or if, in his natural state—a kind of brave
acceptance of everything—it was something he hadn't yet had
to discover about us all.

The Snows of Minnesota

THE FIRST snow came on a warm gray evening—little balls of snow the size of pinheads, at first. Jimmy Paulson held out his palms to them, and they bounced, stuck, and each with a tiny sting melted away into a point of moisture no bigger than a bead of mist. The air was full, right up past the houses and the bare, silent maple trees, full of these quick, floating little balls of snow, and Jimmy was suddenly happy, as he had always been at the first snow when he was at home. Then he remembered that he was not home anymore, but in Leah, New Hampshire, in the yard of this strange old house more than a thousand miles away from Duluth, from his friends, Harold Johnson and Paul Krause, even away from himself as he really was, the person he had once earned the right to be. Was it snowing in Duluth? Did this same gentle storm cover the lake, and Park Point, and the North Shore where the dark woods came down to the lake? No, probably not. He knew better—that in between this dense sky and the sky of Minnesota were clear, empty spaces impossible for him to cross.

He knew that his family had left their home and come across to this place of old houses and fat trees because his father had been transferred—a word that seemed dishonorable, even dangerous. It had been explained to him that this had really been a promotion for his father, and that the family could now afford this big, dark house on a quiet street. A dead-end street, his mother had said with happiness in her voice; a safe street. But still, "transferred," this action done upon them all, seemed totally without their consent, and made them all smaller and tenderer, diminished in the world. Where was the lake, the fresh, blue water of Lake Superior? They told him the Atlantic Ocean was not far away, and they would drive over to see it sometime. But that would be an old salt sea, briny and green, not the great lake he desired. It was as if he needed the lake in order to breathe, and ever since he had moved to New Hampshire he felt that something was wrong with his body. He was short of breath, and didn't want to eat. Once he had vomited for no reason, and cried for no reason.

In school, his classmates talked with hard, dry voices, and said words like "modren" for "modern," and "idear" for "idea." They put r's where none belonged and left them off where they should have been, and had strange, stiff ways of moving, as though they were being watched by enemies. The school playground was nothing but hard dirt and worn tree roots that came to the surface and froze, helpless under the grinding feet of the children. No one spoke, or could know how to speak, in the close and funny language of his friends, Harold and Paul, who perhaps right now walked through another snow, and jumped over barberry bushes now powdering in the soft Duluth evening. Those brave and funny cavaliers. This was to have been the winter of the fifth grade, when their ages changed from one digit to two, and they would become the princes of boyhood. Ten. "Ten," he said out loud, and the word was lost in the dark street where the snow, now changing into soft flakes, seemed against the bulk of his family's new, but old, old house to be a snow that had happened back in history sometime, long before he was born.

He went into his house quietly, hearing his mother in the kitchen, and went up to his room, where most of his things still sat in boxes. Some were toys, like Mr. Machine, now much too young for him. Arranged around the room in odd piles were his books, now stacked more by size than subject matter, so that a book on tunnels was on top of *The Wind in the Willows*, and his dictionary lay on a Sears, Roebuck catalogue. His best airplane models had suffered minor damage, and he could have fixed them easily, yet a bent landing gear or a broken tail now seemed a fatal injury, as though it had been a disaster of flight, and the plane had crashed. His paper wasp nest was partly squashed, and lay next to a plastic globe of the world that was smudged at the point of Lake Superior, where his finger had so many times pressed against Duluth. Again the sickish tiredness came over him, and he sat on his bed staring at the striped wallpaper, his eyes sliding quickly out of focus, wishing to be where he could not be.

His father's new car came down the street and turned into the driveway, muffled by the snow, and the garage door rumbled down and locked with a thump before his father's heavy steps came into the kitchen.

Harry and Ruth Paulson had noticed the change in their son, and had worried about it, and talked it over. It was a difficult adjustment for him, they agreed. Harry went to hang his coat in the hall closet, and came back into the kitchen. "Is he home yet?" he asked hopefully. They both hoped Jimmy would find a friend and come home late for supper one of these nights, the way he frequently had back in Duluth.

"I don't know," Ruth said. She missed Duluth, too, and her friends there, but she'd been so busy fixing up the new house she hadn't had much time to think about it. What people she'd met seemed quite friendly. Everybody moved these days; she'd read that one out of three American families moved every year. But that, she thought, did not alter the fact of her son's sadness. She would try to make this house into a home for him. She would scrape it, and paint it, and buy pretty curtains for the windows. They would all sit in the long living room, on the new furniture, and look at the fire. She had a lot to do, but she would do it. And when the house was perfect, then they would all begin to live in it.

"He'll snap out of it. You'll see," Harry said.

"I think he's home," Ruth said.

Harry went upstairs to see, and found his son sitting on the bed, his coat still on.

"Jimmy," he said.

"Yeah, Dad."

"You feel all right?"

"Sure."

"I mean, I know how hard it is to . . ." To what? Harry thought. "To adjust to a new place." He could almost hear the word through his son's ears: *adjust*. It seemed a bad thing to have to do.

"Dad?"

"What?"

"Do you think it's snowing in Duluth?"

Actually, Harry had worked like hell in Duluth, especially in the last five years, and the town might just as well have been Des Moines or Atlanta, for all the time he'd had to think about it. He had grown up in Duluth, though, and for just one moment he did feel his son's homesickness, just a flash of it, and then it faded and was gone. It must have been a memory of some time in his childhood, a memory of a memory. What he could see was that Jimmy was listless and unhappy—that was plain enough.

"Do you think it's snowing in Duluth?" Jimmy asked again, his thin face turned toward the window.

"It might be, but I don't think it would be the same storm."

"No, I guess not." Jimmy's hands, still in his mittens, lay palms up in his lap.

His arms seemed so listless that Harry could believe he'd lost the power to raise them, and moved by Jimmy's sadness he began again to feel that wisp of memory of his own childhood. They had lived on Park Point, between the bay and the lake, on the bay side of the narrow point of sand. In the winter, the snow sometimes drifted as high as the trolley wires, and the house creaked and moved in the blizzards that roared in from the lake and tried to push them into the bay. He'd lie in bed, just on the edge of real fear, and try to hold the house down on its precarious foundation. Now, just for a flash, just for the smallest instant, he was filled with the unbearable pleasure of memory. "You'd better get ready for dinner," he said.

Jimmy nodded, and began, slowly and weakly, to pull his mittens off. At supper, he was almost too polite, and ate very little. After supper he went right to his room, and Harry and Ruth remained silent at the table.

*   *   *

All that night it snowed. The snow drifted softly over the house, sometimes ticking lightly against the windows. Down through the bare trees it came, to fill up the lawn and cover over the street. On the spruce and pine at the end of the street, it stopped, then sifted down through the dark branches that seemed almost unbelievably green where the streetlight touched them. Jimmy stood at his window, wrapped in a blanket. He'd awakened at four in the morning and smelled the snow, somehow—or maybe it was the hard dryness of his radiator, which was too hot to touch. Then he heard the softness of the snow. At first there was his happiness about the first snow of the year, and then it seemed too cruel that he was far from home in this foreign place, like the dream in which it is your father standing in the dark, and you are so relieved until he turns and it is not your father at all.

The snowplow trucks had long been out; he heard on other streets their muffled boom and scrape, and after a while one came slowly down his street, snow streaming across its dim headlights, its weight felt in the timbers of the house, and shoved its great wave of seething snow into the trees at the dead end; then it backed, turned, and pushed back up the street. The snow still whirled down, invisible until it fell below the streetlight, where it turned white and glided into the pureness of the ground. In a few minutes, the street was as smooth as it had been before.

Jimmy went back to bed, but lay awake, and later the great truck came back down the street. He must have slept, although the night seemed very long, and each time the plow rumbled and boomed he half waked. In the morning, as he lay unrested in the warm bed, he wondered if he had heard the plow three times or a hundred times. With the sheet over his eyes, so close his eyelashes touched it, he stared into whiteness. What if the snow had come up like this over his windows, over the house, pure and white and soft as blindness? The street would have to be a tunnel, then, and the whole town subterranean. He pulled the sheet away from his eyes and looked; the snow still fell past his window. A toilet flushed, and then his parents spoke softly in the hall as they moved past his door. It was Saturday, and they didn't want to wake him because he had looked thin and tired. He knew they were worried about him, and he was

vaguely sorry about that, but ever since they all had been transferred away from home, his parents' authority, even the
strength of his concern for them, seemed to have lost importance. It was as if they were all merely puppets, moved by
someone else's hand.

Late in the morning, he got up and went downstairs in his
pajamas and bathrobe. The dry air in his room had made him
thirsty, and he had a glass of milk. His mother wanted to make
him scrambled eggs, which he usually liked, but he didn't want
any. She seemed upset by this, and even in his own mind, as he
examined the vision of a plate of scrambled eggs, yellow folds
steaming, he wondered how they could seem chalky and
strange—too strange to eat.

"Isn't the snow nice?" his mother asked. "You love the
snow."

"Yeah," he said, but this was not his snow. It had come
unhoped-for, with neither his joy nor his permission.

All Saturday it snowed, and the plow returned several
times. Instead of their shoveling the driveway, as he and his
father had done on their steep street in Duluth, a jeep came
and plowed them out. That evening the jeep had to come again,
and with a great many backings and turnings did a mammoth
but sloppy job on the driveway. When the town plow came
back, it pushed everything down into the trees. After supper, a
big yellow loader came, and with its scoop piled the snow higher
against the evergreens, until their tops were like Christmas trees
growing on a white hill. The pile was at least fifteen feet high.

On Sunday morning, the TV said New Hampshire had
received twenty-five inches of snow, and though it had begun to
taper off, there would be no school in many towns on Monday.
Later, the local radio station said Leah was one of those towns;
the school buses would not be able to get through to the out-
lying roads of the school district for at least another day.

That morning, Jimmy felt tired. His arms almost ached—
seemed just on the verge of pain whenever he moved them. He
sat watching television, and afterward couldn't remember what
he'd seen. His mother asked him why he didn't unpack his
things and arrange his room—it was so much nicer than the
little room he'd had back in Duluth. He said he might, but
merely went upstairs and sat on his bed for a while. When he

stood up he looked out the window at the huge pile of snow the loader had made; he had never seen so much snow piled so high in one heap—a mountain of snow. He thought of the buried trees descending like elevators down into the white, deep into a kind of blankness, where all was pure and new. A little shiver of excitement startled him, because he wasn't sure what had caused it. That pureness, like a piece of white paper to draw on, where you alone run the pencil that carves out the world from the flatness of it. But why should he care, all of a sudden? He knew only that in the deep pile existed possibilities for him, perhaps a way to change his weakness back into some kind of action, and so he put on his long underwear and ski pants, then went downstairs and took his rubber boots from the hall closet into the kitchen. He knew his mother was happy to see him want to go outside—she made sure that he had his mackinaw buttoned, tucked his scarf in around his neck, and didn't ask him where he was going.

He remembered having seen something on the back wall of the garage that had not been too interesting, but now he went out to look at it more closely. It was a little folding shovel, and he knew from television that in the Army it was called an entrenching tool, used by soldiers to dig foxholes. It even had a green canvas scabbard he could, with some bending of the wire clasps, hitch on his belt. Some previous tenant of the house had hung it on the wall and left it—he knew it didn't belong to his father—and so without asking he took it for his own.

He approached the snow pile circumspectly; he wondered about this, too, for he had every right to examine it, and no other children lived on the street. Slowly he pushed through the light snow, waist-high in places, around the back of the garage, through the trees, so that he came onto the pile from the rear. The snow wall, much harder than the snow that had merely fallen of its own weight, rose up before him, laced by green branches. At the base of a pine tree, the branches had caused a natural tunnel, and he got down on his knees to look into it. The light came through the walls, softly, and all around him the snow breathed clean cold onto his face. After a few feet, the tunnel came to nothing; he crawled inside, on his knees on the pine needles sifted over with light snow, and he couldn't even turn around. He began digging merely to make the tunnel big enough so he wouldn't have to back into it in order to see the opening from the inside, but the snow cleaved off so easily and the wall he began to carve with the green blade of his shovel was so much his own smooth creation he kept on until he had nowhere to put the snow. It would take too long to kick it out the door, and he'd get snow up his waist, so he struggled out into the daylight again, in his nose the smell of snow, like cold water. He needed other tools—a cardboard box to put the snow in, and he could slide it out easily; plenty of boxes were in the basement, left over from moving.

He didn't want to have to go back to the house—there was even some reluctance to make his trail plain, as though he might be followed or observed. But he needed the box, and he did go back, successfully unseen—his mother was upstairs— and found a good box, narrow and long, and not too high. This he carried back above the snow, so as not to leave an imprint of its smoothness or squareness anywhere, and he felt relief when the branches closed over him again. Farther inside the tunnel he felt even more safe, and with each carving stroke of his shovel his safety seemed to increase: the room grew in volume. Bluish light came down through the arched ceiling, and as he moved the end wall past the tree, the room grew lighter. By four o'clock, as the light began to fade, his room was five feet wide, and nearly five feet high at the top of the arch. Carefully he cleaned the floor and sharpened the corners, then pushed the box outside along its smooth worn track, to empty it again. As the last light faded, he returned to sit in his snow room; quietly the cold moved out of the walls and surrounded him, yet he was not cold. Before he left, he put the shovel and the box inside, and carefully covered the entrance with blocks of snow.

That evening his father asked him what he'd done all day, and he said he'd watched television, and then played in the snow for a while. As he lay in bed that night waiting for sleep, he seemed to be in the snow room again, and it was huge as a cavern. He could look up the wall, higher than houses, and see the smooth strokes carved by his shovel. The great strokes had smoothed a wall high as a palisade.

In the morning, he woke at the first light. His hands and arms were sore, yet seemed stronger, and a sense of urgency, not happy but at least purposeful, made him get out of bed immediately. He gathered his clothes as quietly as possible and went down to the kitchen to dress. Though he wasn't hungry, he decided to eat a bowl of cereal; he must leave evidence that he had eaten, and also he knew that his body needed the food. This was a strange idea he had never worked upon himself before—he had been forced to eat things that were good for him, carrots and cauliflower and other things that seemed to grow in the mouth, but now by his own choice he ate without hunger, so that he could go to his snow room without being followed, and have the strength to work. This deliberate treatment of his body, without the simple desire of appetite, was so new it seemed dangerous, and he shivered for a moment with a fear like the tingle of falling.

As another precaution he tore a piece of paper from the grocery list pad and wrote a note:

Dear Mother and Dad,
     I have gone out to play in the snow.
          love,
          Jimmy Paulson

Later, Harry and Ruth examined the note. "That's a good sign, I'd say," Harry said.

"I wish he had a friend," Ruth said. "I wish some other children lived on the street. Do you have to go to work this morning? You could do something with him—play with him or something. Go skating."

"There's no skating with this snow. Anyway, it hasn't been cold long enough to freeze the rink."

"You could do something with him."

"You know I have to go to work," Harry said, with some of his impatience showing. He felt guilty—a little—and it seemed mostly Ruth's fault. "I'm responsible for the whole plant now. You know that. Things no one else can do."

"You go away on Saturdays, on Sundays. You go down there. When does he get to see you?"

"Ruth, I have to. I simply have to, now. Later on, I'll get things organized, but now there are so many things."

"We could have stayed in Duluth!" she said, and began to cry.

He wanted to tell her the facts of life—that when a man is offered a promotion and refuses, or even hesitates, he is through. They couldn't have stayed in Duluth. That was absolutely impossible. But he'd told her all this before, in calmer circumstances. He went to work leaving everything like that.

Jimmy began to carve a door upon the rear wall of his room. He made the lintel, then the sides, carefully cutting a sharp edge all around, even where the plow had folded some sand into the snow, and then shaved down the center of the door until it stood upon the wall with the authority of its squareness. It seemed a door he might simply open, if he knew how, and then he might walk through it into that perfect uncreated world beyond.

When he pushed the box full of snow out into the sunlight, he was blinded, and couldn't keep his eyes open. Then, when he pushed the box ahead of him back into the hole, it was almost too dark to see, and his new door seemed just too primitive—only some marks upon the wall. He would have to have light, and immediately he remembered the red candles that had been stored so near a radiator they had melted over upon themselves into jointed-looking shapes. They were somewhere in the basement, in a shoe box; they would never be used, yet never thrown away, and he knew he could have them.

He would need the light, because he felt certain he was going beyond the carved door, deep into the interior of that place he almost knew already. Why was he sure, for instance, that the door entered immediately upon a passage, and not another room? And at the end of the passage, another door led to a vast place of light, where he could breathe freely again and not be sick.

He knelt in the dim cave tasting the bitter dye of his mitten; he wanted only to pass into that place, but he had to wonder about himself, and for the last time to speculate upon his belief in such childish magic. No, it was there, and therefore true; how could he not believe it? The world was there, waiting to be defined by his own hands. Now he would have to get to work; he needed the candles, so he must go out into the sunlight of the unhappy town, and go back to the big house for a while. He would have to take time out for lunch, too, because of his mother. He wasn't worried that she would come out to see what he was doing, because she wasn't the kind of person who ever left the sidewalk to go out into the snow. She wouldn't even have the right kind of boots for that. Then, after that delay, he could come back to this real work.

When Harry Paulson got home from work that evening, Ruth opened the kitchen door before he could put his hand on the knob, and stood there dramatically, her hands flickering across her face.

"It's dark, and he's still out there by himself! What can he be doing in the dark?"

"I'm sure he's all right," Harry said, but he turned to go and see. In the garage, he met Jimmy coming in, and pretended to look for something in the car. Then, because he had falsified his intentions, he couldn't ask Jimmy what he'd been doing. Ruth did, though.

"I'm building something," Jimmy said. To Harry he seemed not so much evasive as simply bored by their interest.

"What are you building?" Ruth asked.

"Sort of a fort. You know," Jimmy said wearily.

"You're all wet!"

"Now, Ruth," Harry said. "Naturally he's going to get wet in the snow."

"But he hasn't been feeling well!"

"I feel fine," Jimmy said.

"He doesn't look fine. He looks pale, and he doesn't eat enough. I made him a sandwich for lunch and I found most of it in the garbage can."

"I ate the meat out of it," Jimmy said.

"You've got to eat more. You've got to go to school tomorrow, and you look so tired and thin!" Ruth's voice quavered.

Harry stood by, helpless. He felt that he should be the one to understand his own son. He'd always seemed to before. But now this strangeness came up in front of him—this and other things—and they seemed beyond understanding.

Jimmy sat down on the kitchen floor and began to pull off his boots, and Harry could at least help with that. As he pulled at Jimmy's boots, the little boy seemed as light as cloth, and Harry had to hold him by his skinny knee with one hand and pull a boot off with the other. Jimmy lay back passively and let this be done.

"You'll have a hot bath before supper," Ruth said. "Look at his feet. They're practically blue!"

"That's only stain from my socks," Jimmy said.

He was calm, and went upstairs in his underwear, slowly for him. He actually walked. Harry could not remember seeing Jimmy walk up the stairs before, and he was not so old himself he couldn't remember the time when he never walked up the stairs, but always took them at a run. When did it happen, that great change in him? It seemed such an important point in his life that he felt he should remember the exact set of stairs, and the very hour in which he had lost that easy lightness in his body.

After getting in the tub, Jimmy lay back in the hot water that burned quickly at his skin and then was merely thick and warm. The back of the tub seared his shoulders with ice, and that changed, too, so that in a moment he lay suspended in warmth so benevolent the water seemed part of him, as though it moved easily through the pores of his skin. He thought of a reptile sunning on a rock, having to be no more than the extension of the temperature of the world, and when the world cooled, he cooled, and still felt nothing, no more than the rock itself felt its changes and retractions.

He went to sleep, and woke soon after in slightly cooler water. This he knew, but he seemed to feel no heat, no cold. He thought of all the things he knew. He knew so many things. Why up was the same as down, how he lived on a planet smaller than a mote of dust, all alone in indifferent space so wide that in the reaches of his mind, when he tried to conceive of it, his imagination slid over the smooth edge of eternity and fell forever. Yet came back, somehow *was* back inside his head, fragile and illusive.

He dreamed of cloud walls all around him that turned and were cleaved, and he moved down a long passage his mind projected as if it were a light sharp as blades. Soon the walls ended in folds and misty geysers that shot away violently and disappeared, and there was the dark, warm city, at Christmas, with the snow drifting off the lake. He descended at his will, down into Lester Park among the tall pines, the three boys coming home late, wet, warm, cheering the snow, planning labyrinths, invincible in their understanding. Their laughter turned visible, like sparks and flames in the falling snow. Blue, red, green—the colors of Christmas. *Yay!* he heard them yell, faintly as they crossed the bridge over the river that splashed in the dark down toward the lake. As their yells and laughter faded homeward across the park, his heart turned inside out with love.

During the next few days, Harry began to worry about what, exactly, it was that kept Jimmy out until suppertime each night. He'd come right home from school, change his clothes, and work on whatever it was, out there, on into the dark. He looked exhausted, yet he spent all of his after-school time out there in the snow. All he would say was that he was building a fort of some kind.

On Friday morning, Harry went to the plant with a slightly queasy feeling because he had to fire two men. One was a maintenance man, a carpenter. He took it as if he had expected it all the time, but the other man was an assistant in purchasing, who said in a surprised, shocked voice that he had never "got let go" before from any job. Harry told him that it wasn't a matter of his competence but one of organization. This was not exactly true, and after the man had left his office his head began to throb, and he felt vaguely nauseated. He told his secretary he'd be back after lunch, and went home.

"I don't want to be sneaky," he said to Ruth, "but I've got to see what Jimmy's doing out there. He won't tell me anything."

"I'm so worried about him," Ruth said. "He used to be such a normal boy. He used to be so happy with us."

Harry put on a pair of old pants, a mackinaw, and boots. He didn't intend to tell Jimmy he'd gone to look, if he could get away with it, and again he had the queasy feeling that came from deception. Had there ever been a time in his life when he lived simply, and never had to tell anything but the truth? He couldn't remember, but there must have been such an innocent time—a time before it had become necessary to manipulate, to be devious. Was it in his childhood? No, he could not honestly say that; there had always been secrets to be kept. And yet he had a twinge of yearning for such a time—also a moment of fear, as though he had gone out just too far on thin ice, and yearned for the shore.

Jimmy's path led around back of the garage into the trees. Its bottom was smooth and hard, and he didn't have to worry about leaving tracks; he needn't have changed his clothes, he thought, and began to make little of his spying. He'd just look, turn around, and come back. But at the end of the path he found only unorganized piles of snow around the main pile made by the plows. Nothing. Then he saw that certain tracks, or more permanent depressions, seemed to lead to one place, though an attempt had been to disguise this. Two big disks of snow hid the door, and as Harry moved them carefully aside, knowing that he would remember exactly how they had been placed, his guilt came back; this place was really meant to be a secret. Now he could never talk to Jimmy about it.

He got down on his hands and knees and looked inside. Dim light came from above, bluish white. The interior seemed very large, and across the room an arched doorway led into sheer blackness. He would be required to do more than just look, and he was a little afraid. This place could be physically dangerous to Jimmy, he supposed, but that wasn't what occupied him now, or caused any of his fear. As he crawled inside, the blue surrounded him—this strange room created by his son; in a brutal way he seemed to be entering his son's mind, that protected place that had always seemed so large in proportion to the little boy's mere body. His knees made dents upon the floor. On each side of the room, red candles stood in niches carved from the walls, and in a long cardboard box he found the entrenching tool that used to hang on the rear wall of the garage. He remembered the half-melted candles now. And the entrenching tool—he had never missed it at all, and this seemed not only a dereliction of his observation, but a dereliction of his love.

In order to see past the arched doorway, he had to take one of the candles and light it. The walls turned warmly white, and he saw how carefully they had been smoothed and made square.

He couldn't go down the farther passage because the sill was raised, and his weight would squash the whole floor down. But he could look down that hallway to its end, which was obviously unfinished. Where would it go? Where did Jimmy want to go down there? God, it was a marvelous and scary place, this sculptured cave, and how proud a boy would be of it! But Jimmy had done it all alone, for his own lonely purposes, and Harry felt awe for his son's determination. Kids just didn't stick to anything this long, or work so hard. Then he had, again, the hollow, painful feeling that he could now see what he would never be told. This dark cave. Yes, it was a marvelous cave, but he knew Jimmy never intended to show it to him.

He put the candle back, and blew it out, then tried to erase all the signs of his intrusion. With his fists he beat out the impressions his knees had made in the floor, and when he came out into daylight again he took a long time to hide the entrance exactly as Jimmy had.

"It's a snow cave, sort of," he said to Ruth when he returned to the house. "You won't mention to Jimmy that I've seen it."

"All right."

"I mean this, Ruth. Can you possibly keep your mouth shut about it?" He heard the hard edge of his voice, and saw it strike her. She was hurt, but he meant to impress her. He had to make sure, and again he felt brutal. "It's important he doesn't know. Do you understand?"

"I don't understand anything!" she said, and her eyes became glossy.

"I don't either," he said. "Jesus Christ, I don't either."

"I thought when I made the house right," Ruth said. "When I fixed the house, we could all be happy again. Remember when Jimmy was a baby?" She put her hand on his arm. "We had more time for everything then, didn't we?"

"We had less money," he said.

"That's right. You didn't have to work so hard."

"It's not that, Ruth. I don't think I work harder than I did then. I've just got less time left over."

"We used to go skating."

"Yes, we did," he said, and he remembered the gliding, the showing off, the time when everything he did had been a kind of friendly competition. He remembered that time, sadly, but without a real sense of loss.

That night when Jimmy came in from his cave, he coughed, and it sounded like the blat of a sheep. Harry watched him try to keep from coughing. His eyes were dark, desperate, and his arms shook inside his jacket sleeves. Ruth heard the cough, and came running.

"It's all right," Jimmy said. "I feel fine."

"Get the thermometer!" Ruth cried. "It's in the bathroom cabinet upstairs!"

When Harry came back with the thermometer, Ruth had Jimmy's wet clothes off, and they hustled him upstairs, with the thermometer sticking out of his mouth, and wrapped him, scowling and muttering, in a blanket. His temperature was 104.

"I don't care!" he yelled. "I feel fine!" Promptly he went into a kind of fit. He kicked the blanket off him entirely, and started to get up. Harry had to hold him down, and it was like holding a fluttering bird. Jimmy was so weakly violent, and the way he moved his arms and legs seemed as strange as the movements of a bird—as though the joints and muscles were not made to move the way a human's did. Harry was so surprised at this behavior he lost his breath, and couldn't speak. He just held Jimmy down on the bed. Ruth called the doctor, and as they waited for him they tried to soothe Jimmy, but nothing worked. First he froze and then he burned, and when he stopped fighting them it was only because of exhaustion.

The doctor was a heavy old man who wheezed after climbing the stairs. He examined Jimmy, who glared at him silently. "He's going to be in bed for a while," the doctor said. "If he keeps fighting you, you'll have to take his temperature rectally."

"But what is it he's got?" Ruth asked.

The doctor shook his head. "Who knows what's going around? Might as well call it flu as anything. Just keep an eye on him, and if he don't improve, let me know." He said he'd call in a prescription to the pharmacy and Harry could pick it up. "I've got ten other cases in town just like this. It'll last three, four days, and then, when the fever goes, he'll be weak as a dishcloth for a few days. Give him aspirin. Make him take liquids. Keep him in bed." The doctor packed his satchel and left.

Jimmy glared and shivered; he seemed only to be waiting for his strength to come back.

"Jimmy," Harry said, "will you stay in bed?" Jimmy's teeth clicked, and Harry saw hatred in his face. Why did he deserve that? "Jimmy," he said, "we want to help you get well." The boy's pale face, pale as paper, turned ugly. For a moment Harry couldn't recognize him, as though he could read there no person at all, just pure obstinacy and hatred. Harry's anger rose in him icily, like the pulse of a wave, and receded, leaving him weak and empty. "But will you stay in bed like we ask?"

"Yes," Jimmy said, and turned his face away.

To Jimmy it was not the days that passed but the undulations of his fever. His stomach ached, his bones ached; he sweated and then lay in icy water. Only when he began to get well did his real desperation return, and he feared for the secrecy of his cave. He knew what would happen to it if someone found it. What did you do when you found a thing made of snow? You destroyed it, because it was only snow. He could see himself jumping on the roof, and bringing the arched ceiling down into meaningless rubble. Even now some boy might be having that instinctive fun.

One night he woke in the dark, feeling that he had crossed that indefinable point where, no matter what happens, the body has won, and is mending. His bones no longer ached; he was merely weak. He heard himself whimper, and decided that he couldn't live, actually could not continue to live, without knowing if his cave had been discovered. He got out of bed, and stood balancing himself in the dark. His feet had become so sensitive that the rug stung them as he sneaked down the stairs. In the hall closet he found his outdoor clothes by touch, and put them on over his pajamas. He cried silently when he couldn't, at first, find his other boot, and cried again when he had too much trouble pulling it on, but he made no sound. He had no fear of the dark of the middle of the night, and this seemed a kind of illness itself, and proved to him that his desperation was real. On the way out through the garage, he stopped and took the flashlight from the dashboard of the car, and then went out on his path.

The cave had been found. The door was uncovered and partly broken, as though someone had stood up too soon on the way out. The bent candles were all strewn around in the packed snow in front, where strange feet had scuffled and stamped.

The cardboard box had been taken outside and squashed, and the entrenching tool was not in it.

He looked inside the doorway, and saw where careless shoulders had crunched into his walls and ruined them. With their knowledge of his cave they had killed it; he would never go inside again. He heard his own voice crying, and the sound was so undeserved, had been caused by such brutal unfairness, that he began to rage, and threw himself against the door. They would never enter it again, either. With all his strength he climbed up and jumped upon the cave, breaking it into chunks and slabs, filling up the floor. He could still hear himself crying.

Harry woke up in a sweat; either he was coming down with Jimmy's flu, or he'd forgotten to turn down the thermostat before coming to bed. It was four in the morning, the unprotected time when all disasters, all regrets and failures, are poised upon the exposed surface of the mind like water spiders on surface tension—on nothing, really, but a kind of delicate force. Ruth slept on, and at the end of each of her long breaths of sleep she slightly voiced a sigh, as though she were having a sad dream. When he raised the blankets, cold reached out of the heat of the room and laid an icy hand on his chest. He decided to move; any sort of action was better than lying here in the power of his thoughts. He'd check the thermostat and take some aspirin.

On the way, he looked in on Jimmy and found him missing. He wasn't in the bathroom. No lights seemed to be on downstairs; careful not to wake Ruth, he went down to see. Jimmy's outdoor clothes and boots were gone, and he quickly got into his own, putting his overshoes on over his bare feet. The car door was open and the flashlight was gone, but it was a clear night, and the stars themselves seemed to give him light as he followed Jimmy's path toward the cave.

At first he thought Jimmy was in a fight. He heard thrashing and crying, and the flashlight beam swung wildly against the trees and across the snow. He came on the run, and grabbed Jimmy up in his arms. Jimmy struggled violently, and again Harry thought of the feeble violence of a bird.

"Get away! Leave me alone!" Jimmy cried.

"Jim," Harry said. "Jim—"

"It's ruined!" Jimmy cried. He struggled, trying to bend Harry's fingers back so he could get loose. "Get out of here! Leave me alone!" He sobbed and hiccupped; his teeth clicked in anger, and his only purpose was to get loose, to get away.

"Listen, Jim! Listen!" Harry said, and shook him, but Jimmy only struggled harder.

"God damn you!" Jimmy yelled, and Harry let him go. At first Jimmy turned toward his cave, then ran back along his worn path toward the house. Harry picked up the flashlight, shone it once across the tumbled wreckage of Jimmy's marvelous cave, and then followed him back to the house.

Ruth was up, and they put Jimmy back to bed. He was tired, sad, and lay there moving his head slowly from side to side.

"You do feel better, don't you, Jimmy?" Ruth said.

Jimmy nodded, yet his large dark eyes were blank, and his mouth was set. He didn't reply when they turned out his light and said good night.

When they were back in bed, Ruth moved toward Harry and put her hand on his chest. "Is he going to be all right?" she asked.

"Somebody found his snow house and ruined it," Harry said, "but I suppose that was inevitable."

"It's a shame," she said. "What was it like?"

"Very elaborate. He'd done a remarkable job for a boy."

"Why do you think he did it—worked so hard on it?" Ruth asked.

The radiator hissed and ticked; he'd forgotten to check the thermostat, and now he'd have to get up and do it. He lay there for a moment with her hand like a weight on his chest. There had been a time in his childhood, too, before his friends had grown old and tame, when the great lake rose in the winter, terrible and magic, into walls of blue ice, and the snow drifted high as the houses. Lying in bed, he saw himself as a child amid the wonder of those snow-clad houses, and he felt a sudden stab of envy toward that child, who lived in a world he never had to make. Now, he thought, he understood what his son was trying to do out there in the snow. "He was trying to make Duluth," he said.

Paranoia

MY NAME is Aaron Benham, and I am a writer of fiction, a college professor, and an unwilling collector of paranoiacs. Perhaps I am no more surrounded by paranoiacs than anyone else, but sometimes I wonder. Like those who fear dogs only to excite in all dogs an immediate, aggressive affection, I seem doomed to be the chosen confessor of those who have systematized their delusions. I wonder if they know how much they frighten me.

Long ago I used to try to explain to them that the world was mainly plotless, chaotic, random. I used to have that warmth and time. In spite of their eyes that are always bright beyond mere alertness, as bright beyond the tender depths of protoplasm as polished gemstones, I once, in my surfeit of time, brought them home for a drink and tried to explain. That was before I knew how short life was, how long it takes to learn the craft I am apprenticed to.

This morning I have just finished reading a short novel written by G., a student. At three this afternoon, in my office at school, we will have a conference. I ought immediately to tell him that he has no ear for dialogue, that his few metaphors consistently violate his intent, and finally that his chief motive for writing, so clearly revealed in his novel, is not the creation of art but an attempt to create legitimate targets for vengeance. His villains are carefully prepared and set up for their deserved reward, and his hero is armed and ready. Armed, in this case, with a weapon G. actually carries himself; he once proudly showed me the knife he carries in his boot—a vicious little dagger he calls an "Arkansas toothpick."

In the last conference I had with G. a week ago, he chose not to discuss the short story he had written, but to tell me about the universal cheating in courses where multiple-choice tests are given. At other times he has revealed to me the blatant callousness, cynicism, laziness, senility, dope addiction, and suspected perversions of my colleagues. In his revelatory stance he is more than a little threatening. He leans his shoulders toward me smiling the bitter yet triumphant smile of one who knows all, and demands that I enter his world. I, too, should find in the discovery of evil the joy that keeps his eyes so icy bright.

You can see why I'm not looking forward to the three-o'clock conference with G. His intimidating attitude causes me to be dishonest with him, and in that sense he is right; his psychosis is not all fantasy. It is the encompassing magnitude of his "delusional system" that disheartens me, that diminishes my soul and makes me evade my responsibilities toward him. He excludes the world until there is only he and I, and in that small cold cell I am lonely and apprehensive. So I nod, or shake my head in feigned wonder, and wait for the hour to pass.

And while I wait rather tensely here in my study for the hour when I'll have to go to my office and meet G., I remember other confrontations with delusion. Perhaps there is an order to them, not in time but in another way. In fiction one plays a strange game with ugliness and fear.

F., an occasional handyman and jack-of-all-trades in our town, came up to me in the general store and told me that he had been seeing several deer, including a large buck that would go at least eight points and two hundred pounds, in the orchard behind his house. The deer nearly always came into the orchard at dusk, he said, and why didn't I come out and see if I could "connect"?

F. was a rugged, dark little man, about thirty-five years old. He always wore the laborer's uniform of our region, which in all seasons is, basically, green chino work pants and shirt, and leather boots. At this time, since it was November and getting cold, he had added to this basic outfit a greasy red wool hunting cap with his hunting license pinned to the crown, and a faded red sweatshirt. He had been sitting with the others on the benches in front of the store in the mild morning sun when I came to get the Sunday papers, and I was surprised when he followed me into the store, touched my arm, and offered me a chance at his deer. I hadn't shot a deer for two years in a row, and the offer excited me perhaps beyond my better judgment, because I knew that F. was a tense and unusual character, a man involved in many complicated, interlocking local feuds. Some of these involved work that he had contracted to do and never finished, some were over damages he had claimed for one reason or another, some were with the selectmen and road agent concerning the plowing or grading of the gravel road that led to his place. He was quite a verbally clever man, and his voice was heard often in town meeting. He was generally considered to be a good workman, too—if you could get him to do the work. He could blast ledge, fix nearly anything mechanical, paint, paper, shingle, glaze, wire, do stonemasonry that was widely admired by other professionals, and so on. At times, however, he wouldn't do anything for months on end except sit on the benches of the general store, or drive around in his old pickup truck drinking beer and tossing the empty cans with an expert backhand flip out of the window of the cab into the truck bed. Or he wouldn't be seen at all for weeks.

His hand, still on my arm, was a cracked red instrument of scars and calluses, the ridged brown fingernails packed smoothly with hardened black.

"You git your gun and come on out 'bout three-thirty— 'bout an hour 'fore dark. You know the way."

I thanked him for the chance at the deer, and said that I knew approximately where he lived, but I'd never been there and wasn't sure I could find the place after I left the blacktop.

He feigned surprise—or I thought he did; all of F.'s publicly displayed emotions seemed exaggerated, meant for effect. Then he laughed loudly, his hard little eyes, as always, watching through the mask, and gave me closer directions.

"You familiar with the back road to Cascom?" he said, and

continued with the directions, smiling as if the whole thing were a needless hypocrisy and of course I knew the way exactly. At the time, partly, I suppose, because of my greed for venison, I took this to be only another of F.'s peculiarities. The reason for the gift, I thought, was that I had recently published a book. This event had been mentioned in our local newspaper, and I thought F.'s gesture was a manifestation of the intense interest that even the smallest amount of celebrity seems to evoke.

That afternoon at three-thirty I found F.'s place, a run-down farm typical of our region. The small unpainted house was fairly level upon its foundations, but the barn sagged, a wooden silo had spun down upon itself like pickup sticks, and the connecting outbuildings and sheds had all begun to lean heavily upon one another, doors sprung, roofs mostly stripped by wind and ice of their ancient tar paper.

Nailed to a tree in the ragged front yard was a sign, uneven black letters on a white-painted board:

THELMA'S BEAUTY SHOP

The house had been well banked with sawdust, but the sawdust was old, reddened by age, probably put there winters ago and left by someone who didn't care enough that the house would rot at its footings.

I didn't see F.'s truck anywhere, but thought it might be around in back or in one of the leaning sheds. The front door to the house was obviously never used; it seemed as permanently fused into its frame as the gray subsurface of an old wound in a tree. I left my rifle in the car and followed the worn track to the kitchen door, feeling that I was being observed. I knocked, and after a suitable amount of time the door was opened by a young woman in her late twenties. She seemed frightened, but asked me without the usual belligerence that emotion causes what I wanted. I said F. had asked me to come out this afternoon to see if the deer would come into the orchard.

"You mean he asked you to come here?" she said.

"Yes."

She seemed puzzled and cautious. After some worried thought she asked me to come in and sit down. I sat at the table in the large, crowded kitchen. The implements of the beauty shop stood among the domestic paraphernalia like a double exposure, dominated by what I took to be a hair dryer, a huge, battered chromed bell on a stand.

"You're Thelma?" I asked, and she nodded, smiling quickly. She knew who I was; she told me that her cousin had been a student of mine several years before, and that the cousin had pointed me out to her once.

"I don't get to town much, though," she added. She wanted to be friendly, but it was so obvious her friendliness was undercut by fear. I watched her as she prepared coffee, thinking even then how one might document this unfortunate woman, who seemed in her unhappiness typical, common, yet sharply her own living self. Her hair was a dull, lusterless brown that no surface beautification would ever bring to life, her face was smooth and well-boned, yet dark, wasted by the forces of poverty and unhappiness. That look, which is common among oppressed children and women, had deeper causes than poor diet and a lack of sunlight. She seemed a woman of another kind of shadow, a prisoner of this prideless house. It took a startled second look to see that she was pretty, that beneath her faded print dress she still carried her light burden of woman's flesh with grace. When we smiled at each other, we both grew tense and shy, as if appalled by a vague and secret understanding.

F. came in then, banging the door open. He stood in the doorway, arms akimbo, a look of mock anger on his face. "Well!" he said fiercely, looking from Thelma to me, then back to Thelma. "So you come after all!" He laughed, to indicate that his fierceness was only put on, but we were not all that reassured. "Come on," he said, and took his Winchester from a wall rack made of cocked deer hooves.

Until dark, F. and I sat beside a granite boulder where we could overlook the small orchard, but the deer didn't come that evening. Their one great talent is, of course, survival. When it became so dark we couldn't see our front sights, F. got up, saying, "Tomorrow. Sure as hell they'll be coming back one of these nights. Let's give her a try tomorrow."

We walked back to the house in the dark, coming upon its warm window lights. In the kitchen we sat at the table and had a cup of the coffee Thelma had made earlier.

F. sat across from me, grinning like a wise cat. "I don't know what's going on these days up to the college," he said, his expression belaying his words. "Some of them coeds, they wear their skirts any higher they going to have two new cheeks to powder!"

Thelma was over at the oil stove, her back to us, and F. pretended that she couldn't hear. His hand rose to the side of his mouth—one of the strange devices he used to superpose his own artifices upon reality. "It must git you all hot and bothered, having to look at it all day long." He laughed and pounded the table. When this timed paroxysm was over, he wiped his eyes. "And you a writer, too," he added, shaking his head.

I grew weary at the thought of trying to plead anything before the court of F.'s prejudices. "Sometimes it's not easy," I said.

" 'Course I suppose you get caught with your eyeballs hanging out they'd throw your ass out of there."

"No," I said recklessly. "We can look all we want."

He seemed taken aback. "That so?" He expressed exaggerated surprise. Even his thick black hair seemed to stiffen as his eyes stared at me. "Well, you never know!"

I began to wonder just what I'd said to cause such a reaction, but of course it mattered little what I'd said; F.'s drama coexisted with real life. Finally he did drop this subject and we talked for a while of the deer—a subject as rigidly classical in its turns and counterturns as Oriental theater. When I left, I promised to come back the next afternoon.

Again when I arrived at the small farmhouse, F. wasn't there, but a rusted-out Chevrolet was parked next to the kitchen. Thelma opened the door for me without my having to knock. I saw immediately that she had prettied herself up. She wore red lipstick, and her hair was fluffed out. She had just finished with a customer, a pale woman in her forties who, below the convolutions of her freshly baked hair, wore a man's old mackinaw over a polka-dot dress, her milk-white legs descended into unbuckled galoshes.

As Thelma explained carefully that I had come to hunt with F., the woman's steady eyes judged this information upon its own merits.

After the woman left, Thelma was busy putting away the various objects of her profession. In the air, competing with the domestic odors of the kitchen, was the odor that always reminds me of burnt feathers, or burnt glue—the chemical that sets the hair. As I watched her putting away the jars of goo, the racks of curlers and other torture devices that women think powerful enough to do magic, I knew by the delicacy of Thelma's movements that she knew I watched her. For me she kept her back straight, calculated the cant of her pelvis as she knelt to a cupboard, the profile of her breasts as she rose on tiptoe to reach another. It was all innocent and pretty, and I felt considerably more than pity for her.

Now, I am a man whose mere daydreams do not excite guilt. In my fiction I am constantly haunted by adultery, murder, cruelty, and betrayal, but that is another world, and in it I will enter any darkness, leaving whatever loyalties I have back in the real world. So if I begin to consider then, even in the most vivid detail, how I would take F.'s young wife to a motel on the highway to the city, ease her of all the sickness of her ugly marriage (in bed, she trembles as I gently touch her pink, childless nipple, etc., etc.)—I felt no guilt. Thoughts are merely thoughts.

And I was here to kill a deer. A knife at my belt, my accurate Marlin in the car, I was prepared only for that kind of reality.

F. came in then. He stood in the open doorway looking at us, not speaking. Toward him Thelma turned the wasted look of apprehension.

"My!" he began in a high falsetto. "Ain't we all gussied up! What's the occasion, as if I didn't know." He turned to me. "Ain't she something, though? You kind of like her sweet little ass, don't you, Professor."

He strode forward and hit her in the mouth. She nearly fell down, but held on to the counter, one hand over the lower part of her face.

"Hey!" I said.

He turned to me, his hands held low in front of him, as though he expected, or welcomed, an attack.

"You think I'm so bone-dumb I don't know what's going on? I knowed for a long time." Without looking at her he hit her with the back of his hand, and her head hit the cabinet like a piece of wood. A canister set rattled on the counter. Quickly he took his rifle from the deer-hoof rack and levered a shell into the chamber. The rifle pointed at my belly, where I felt its ghostly power in the form of ice. "You want to stay and watch," he said, "or you want to get the hell out of here?"

I heard Thelma bawling as I left. At first I was going to call the police, and I drove fast down the gravel road in the cool light of dusk. But by the time I got back to town I had gone through in my imagination what that summons would entail in this world, where actions beget actions. I considered my wife, my family, but mostly my work, the symmetries and balances I pursue, and my dwindling reservoir of imagination and time.

I don't have to look for trouble in this world; it comes to me. For instance, there is a little man I've seen three times over the last few years. I find him waiting for me in the hall in front of my office door. I don't remember his name, but I remember him so well that after not seeing him for a year or more I am aware of the increasing gray in his brush-cut black hair. He is wiry, big-handed, a factory worker, as quick in his movements as a squirrel that finds itself a little too far from the nearest tree. As I come up to my office door I see him, and keep my eyes away from his as I unlock the door. After I've entered the office he stands in the doorway peering at my name in the little card slot on the door, then at me with alert, avaricious eyes. He asks if I am Professor Benham, and during our subsequent interview makes absolutely no reference to ever having seen me before.

Something is wrong, he says, with what's going on in the White House, and he needs my advice.

Should I agree that things are going wrong? Things are going wrong indeed, and I could go on intemperately for an hour, for two hours, for a marathon, a filibuster, a teach-in. The difference between his delusional system and mine is that mine is not encapsulated, and my despair at the vain and vicious actions of men can be documented at all levels. Something is going wrong in the White House, in the Kremlin, in Peking, in Cairo, in Athens, in Tel Aviv, in the Vatican, in your living room and mine. Something is going wrong and it always has the symptoms of the incurable psychosis he has brought to me with such excitement that I know he believes it to be a precious gift.

He has a letter from the Office of the President, an answer to a letter he has previously sent. He has studied this answer very carefully, as you can imagine, and in its bland, perfectly trite, noncommittal platitudes he has found a code in the form of an anagram. If you take the first letter of the first word, the second letter of the second word, the third letter of the third word (at this point his smile is sure and hard, for even the most skeptical dolt would have to be convinced by now), you will see that these letters, slightly rearranged (according to an arithmetical formula he won't go into now), spell DEATH U.S. The President is surrounded by Communists, but how to let the President know? And there is one other little problem—he wants to be rewarded for submitting this vital information to the President. He wants to be paid, and paid well.

I am not a snake-poker. I am afraid of this man and of the multitudes he represents. The things I might tell him, however, rush through my mind like the horrible thoughts one can't thrust away at four in the morning.

I might close the door and turn toward him slowly, a grim smile on my face, and say, "So you know. It is very unfortunate for you, sir, that you have such an inquiring mind. But you haven't gone quite far enough, and I can tell you this because you will never get out of this building alive: the President is in no danger, *for he is one of us!*"

I think with awe of the perfect ecstasy these words would evoke in him. What glorious, heroic justification! How terrible it is of me to deprive him of this gift.

But of course I don't want to enter his system in such an active role; he has already enlisted me in the secret armies of his fantasy, and I want to resign my commission, please, thank you. I do not want to be caught again. So in order to get away I must lie with great subtlety, treat his madness with respect and even sympathy, yet beg to disagree with certain of his conclusions— when all the time my violent apprehension screams from below: *Kill him, don't let him get out of this building alive.*

I look around me and observe how reality and our common paranoid tendencies reinforce each other. For instance, I believe that H., a radical student, was framed on a marijuana charge by the police in a nearby town. He is a militant who has a pure, messianic contempt for drugs, alcohol, or any other distraction that might lessen his usefulness to the cause he so fanatically serves. I have known him for three years, and at first we were quite close. Now, I no longer question to his face the elaborate system he has devised in order to find, over and over again, evidence that there is a deep, revolutionary alliance between his faction and the great masses of the exploited workers of America. I wonder how much longer he will even speak to me.

He may be mad, dangerously infected by one idea, but he did not keep marijuana in the bottle marked "oregano" on the shelf above his stove. In their raid upon his apartment the police triumphantly confiscated his posters of Che Guevara and Mao Tse-tung, and also informed the newspapers that "human excrement" was found on his floors. He and his wife had recently adopted an un-house-trained puppy.

Where does delusion end and reality begin as our various delusions start to mesh? The connection is made, and madness, as always, seems dominant.

And now another incident comes to mind, one that happened many years ago, when I was a young soldier. In Phenix City, Alabama, was a second-story beer joint frequented by paratroopers from nearby Fort Benning, Georgia. Perhaps Phenix City has changed, and the second-story place, along with all the other squalid clip joints, has disappeared, but in those days the town, with its air of small-time graft, was a study in degradation, in which the varied possibilities of humanity seemed to have been reduced to nothing but a vicious strut.

The second-story bar was called Club Geronimo, after the fierce Apache chief whose name had been adopted by the Airborne as its battle cry. One entered the place by way of a wooden outside staircase. Inside the club were mismatched wooden and metal tables, chairs, a linoleum floor always damp with spilled beer and booze, and several young but used-looking waitresses who changed off during any evening because of accepted propositions or the results of slugging the dregs of too many drinks. On the musty, wallpapered walls were calendar pictures of streamlined blondes in shorts and halters. Hamburgers and other simple foods were served, but these were not highly recommended.

If a paratrooper left Club Geronimo with a girl, it was proper for him to use the stairs, but otherwise he had to jump off the balcony—a descent of some twelve feet—onto the hard dirt alley below. Because of previous broken ankles, collarbones, and wrists, this practice was frowned upon by the MPs, and if they caught you at it you would receive "company punishment" for two weeks. But the punishment by the members of your company for breaking tradition was rather harsh too. So, while drinking in Club Geronimo, you always had ahead of you this scary little choice of exit. Somehow this awaiting test made the atmosphere of the club a little more edgy than it ordinarily would have been even among paratroopers, who had already, by volunteering for such duty, indicated their physical narcissism.

But this is a story of madness in the context of madness, about the actions of Corporal E., who couldn't seem to leave me alone. He came from Pennsylvania, where he had grown up on a farm. Though he was solidly built, I always thought of his broad muscles as lacking in tone, like an animal raised too quickly for slaughter, transformed at the end into its proper increments of protein and fat, something less than animal. He carried no extra fat, of course, but to me his strength seemed dumb, badly organized. He was always ordering me to do push-ups, and because he was cadre I had to do them. It seemed to perplex him that I did push-ups as easily as I did, and I could see in his eyes a deep yearning for some more satisfying way to utilize me. At the time, surrounded as I was by the Army's irrationality, I didn't consider his constant need of me to indicate any nameable psychosis, but now I think I can put a name to it, and the name is erotic delusion. He was always winking at me, and bumping into me, his expression indicating collusion between us. It was only after my usual cold or exasperated response that he would have me do the push-ups.

This night, he'd been watching me for a while, and when I was coming back from the head he deliberately bumped me into a table. When I didn't respond the way his delusion predicted, he pointed to the wet linoleum and told me to get down there and give him twenty. I examined the cruddy floor and my clean, creased chinos and told him to go fuck himself.

I won't reproduce the usual ceremonial posturings and banal insults that followed. Suffice to say that at a certain point he hit me on the left cheek hard enough to hurt like hell and cause me to taste blood. I won't indulge here in the usual modest protestations of inadequacy, either. What happened next was that I hurt Corporal E. very badly—so badly, evidently, that he was reduced to a strange, childish panic. He managed to grab my left hand and clamp his teeth over my bent forefinger. Once his jaws were set, the rest of him turned passive and still. In considerable pain, I found myself standing there with the corporal more or less on the end of my left arm.

A strange feeling. His eyes were open, and seemed to stare into mine. I requested that he let go. When he didn't comply, I made the mistake of hitting him in the nose. The pain became unbearable, as if the blow had turned the bolt in a lock. He didn't even blink, and blood from his nose mixed with blood from my finger. I had to get away from him. I felt that I was becoming my own finger, as though he had all of me in his jaws. I continued to argue with his unwavering gaze.

"Let go or I'll have to hit you with this bottle," I said reasonably, pressing a beer bottle tentatively along his head above his ear. "Let go and I won't hit you anymore, okay?"

Maybe he had won after all, I thought. I couldn't believe, had never known before, how one small member of my body could generate so much pain. I became afraid of all wounds, as tender as a child. Even the twelve-foot jump from the balcony now loomed before me like an impossible cliff. The pain was so intense I couldn't hit him with the bottle for fear of causing such pain in him.

My friends had gathered around us. They argued with him too, and offered me helpful suggestions I could barely hear through the vibrating pain. They told me to hit him, to gouge out his eyes. One tried to pry open the jaws with a spoon, another by pressing the joints of the jawbone with his thumbs, another by strangulation. Nothing worked. I began to faint, and had to put my head down for a moment until the drab colors of the linoleum resumed their proper tones. I tapped his head with the bottle, a tender, tentative little blow that failed to register in his bright eyes. The others discussed where on his head would be the best spot to sap him. No one wanted to kill him, really, but all could see that the situation was intolerable. Corporal E.'s right canine, in particular, was half sunk into my

finger, surely grating upon white bone. "Maybe they got a crow-
bar," I heard someone say.

The pain flowed up my forearm and scorched my elbow,
played about with my upper arm, sometimes on the surface,
then again like the thrust of a huge needle down into the clefts
between the muscles themselves. My arm felt flayed, then
drawn, as though it were being stripped, layer by gleaming
layer. I had no idea what was going on in the Club Geronimo
then, I just spoke to the corporal's steadfast madness. I had a
steel table fork at his throat, the dull tines pressing into the
complications of his neck. "I'll kill you," I told him. "I'll have to.
I'm going to shove this fork clean through your neck. I'll twist
it. Let go. Listen, do you hear me? I can't stand this. I'll have to
kill you. Let go. Let go of my finger. Let go."

My earnestness had reduced me to plain language. I called
him no names, accused him and his mother of no perversions.
It was as though we were alone, made one by this terrible connection, bone to bone. When I touched the fork to his neck the
pain thrust my own consciousness askew. It was just his head
that had me, like the severed head of a snapping turtle clenched
upon a stick, the stick you hold out, dreamlike, as a substitute
for your hand.

The pain increased. It never reached a plateau where I
might confront it, know it, and negotiate some kind of treaty
with it. But it was the sight of his teeth deep in my flesh, and the
fear of amputation, that finally made me act. I took the bottle
again, and began to tap above his ear. With each small blow my
whole left side was seared by fire. I felt like a man having to
amputate his own limb. Still operating, I think, was a deep rule
against murder, but this was true desperation and I began to
tap his head harder, faster, the soft ring of the bottle on his
skull growing harder until the tympanic hollows below his bones
answered, and finally his black pupils widened. With a slow,
even, peaceful elevation of his gaze the pigmented parts of his
eyes moved up into his forehead. His jaws slowly opened upon
a gush of my blood and I was free, singular; it was like being
born again.

A human bite is considered dangerous, and my crushed
and torn finger was treated by the medics in radical fashion.
After the novocaine, the cleaning, the stitches, the tetanus and

penicillin shots, I felt as I know Corporal E. did the next morning—that something much more climactic than a saloon fight had occurred. Within a week he had arranged to have himself transferred out of the regiment.

Soon I will have to go to my office to have the conference with G. about his frightening novel, and I find myself in anxiety, yearning again for that sudden clear freedom, the clamped homunculus gone from my flesh forever.

Did I say that one of the fictional objects G. has set up for vengeance is a college professor whose open, rather shy demeanor hides the most calculating, malicious intent, and whose initials are the same as mine? This character in G.'s novel is called Albert Bamberger, and in the end, when Bamberger is found out, degraded and subjected to public contumely, G.'s lack of narrative and descriptive talent is transcended by a kind of gleeful energy. At the most dramatic point, Albert Bamberger, attempting to escape, is brought down by a knife thrown by the hero.

Am I right in believing that Albert Bamberger, who gets the "Arkansas toothpick" between his shoulder blades, is me, or am I just another madly alert animal in a world of imagined conspiracy? G. will no doubt watch me slyly as we discuss his novel, because I won't bring this matter of identification into the open. That is what he will be waiting for, but I won't do it. I know he wants me to admit it, to have to feel that fictional blade, that ghostly steel, in my back.

We use each other, the materials of reality, our experiences, everything at all in our "encapsulated delusional systems." Even in my apprehension I sense my kinship with G., and cannot wholly condemn his mad attempt to make his own satisfying order out of chaos. I, too, am driven by a similar *horror vacui.* Though I would call my work by another name, I will use G. and all the rest for my own purposes, use them coldly and without mercy, more coldly than their own warm needful selves could ever understand.

The Buck in Trotevale's

I watch my son pursue an apple across the floor. He is seven months old. He grabs the shiny globe with both hands and puts it to his mouth: *squeak, squeak,* he gums it. There it goes, rolling bumpily beneath a chair, while he gravely watches. Onward! He'll corner the damned thing. Someday he'll get his teeth into such promising fruit. Meanwhile, he tries. And tries again—he won't give up. I am sure that I was never so determined. Although his eyes are mirror images of mine, I am uncomfortably aware of an alien deepness there, as if even now he were governed by a discipline I have never known. He works at his apple as he does at his world, single-mindedly, until it either accommodates him or shows itself to be impervious. Now the apple has escaped him again, and he watches it until it stops rolling, marks it well before arranging himself for the long crawl toward it. He rarely cries . . . and I wonder, knowing that they will always be mine, at the injustice of this stranger's inevitable wounds. . . .

When I was fourteen, coping with that world of benevolent rulers—coping with an instinctive directness much like my son's—Mr. Brown rented our furnished room. Now, I believe

Mr. Brown to have been a kind of Yankee, although I didn't at first because he came from the South—from Massachusetts, where all those Massachusetts hunters come from, the ones who park in the middle of the road and shoot heifers for deer, not knowing the difference; proudly (it is said every year) bearing their pied trophies through Leah Town Square on the fenders of their Buicks, deer tags fluttering from bovine ears. I never saw this, myself, but at fourteen, New Hampshire boys are careful license-plate watchers. *Massachusetts.* I still hear some disapproval echoing in my older voice.

I didn't know Mr. Brown very well at first. He was quiet, and had a talent for missing squeaky boards and squeaky stairs. I'd see him in the upstairs hall once in a while, between his room and the bathroom. He'd come home from work, wash, and change his clothes before walking downtown to the Welkum Diner for his supper. I can see him walking down Maple Street—tall, superbly balanced, each foot reaching the sidewalk as if searching carefully for purchase. His heels rose lightly before each step, and I believed that if the sidewalk had suddenly tipped right up on its side, Mr. Brown would have been ready for it. He was in his late sixties, I suppose—an almost too handsome man with his tanned face and thick white hair, his straight shoulders—and yet I like to think of him as being in his seventies. Seventy-seven makes me think of him, the two numerals spare and lean as the man, trim as most men are who grow old and active. He walked a lot. He even skied, and on winter Sundays we would see him on Pike Hill doing his graceful old-fashioned christies on the unbroken snow, each long ski under control, his ski clothes fresh and dry. In the summer he hired a high school boy and a motorboat and water-skied on Lake Cascom. His age was a little more apparent when he wore bathing trunks, of course. His belly bulged out. But even then, seeing that taut little pot, you knew that it contained only enough innards to run the lean body. There was no surplus about Mr. Brown.

He hunted, too. His shotgun was a Purdey. He let me see it in its oak-and-leather case, luminous as if a fire burned beneath the French walnut stock, the metal covered with delicate English scrollwork. His deer rifle was almost too beautiful for my young eyes, and I have never seen another like it. It was made in Austria, between the wars, and had two barrels, over and under, like a shotgun, but with a high carved comb to the stock to bring Mr. Brown's eye up to an iron sight. I held this masterpiece, a prince among our common Winchesters and Marlins.

"I have it because, in its own way, it's almost as beautiful as a deer," he said. "I'm sure the deer couldn't care less, but I do."

But precious as it was, I would have chosen my father's Winchester. With that familiar weapon in my hand, my vision of myself as a Yankee boy, thin-lipped and taciturn, was complete. Such foreign beauties as the over-and-under could not seduce me from the common dream.

One conforms, of course, without knowing it—and not only to the common dream, for I was skillfully eased into my after-school job at Trotevale's without once questioning the justice of this sentence. Collusion it was, I know now, between my parents and *their* dream of Education. Mr. Brown was Trotevale's shoe clerk, and that was how I got to know him a little better.

Every day after school, and on the long Saturdays, I found myself a clerk among the socks and shirts, with a button on the cash register sacred to my hesitant finger. Hair combed, white shirt and bow tie, I hid down the long aisles of glass-fronted, varnished counters, pretending to be a customer.

I couldn't find anything. I couldn't tie a knot on a parcel. I counted change too many times before reluctantly giving it up to a customer. "Where are the handkerchiefs?" I would desperately ask a passing clerk. "Where are the boys' blue denim pants sizes three or four, and what does that mean—age, or inches?" All day I trotted back and forth between customer and source of information, and by the end of the first long Saturday I was amazed and a little frightened by the number of things there were to know, just to being a clerk. Having exhausted everyone else's patience (how could they remember how many times I'd asked the same question?), I had taken to asking Mr. Brown everything. He never chided me for my profound lack of interest; he had an extremely dependable fund of gentle patience.

"Don't you have a family?" I asked him once. "Why do you live in our furnished room? Are you going to live here forever?"

"No, I don't have a family," he said, no obvious opinion of

families in his voice. "No mother, no father, no wife, no children. And most likely I won't stay here or anyplace else forever.
And that's not such an uncommon way to be." He smiled that
private smile of experience. "I'm what you might call an old
bastard. Nobody claims me but myself."

I know now that this is not so terribly uncommon. There
are many nomadic old bastards come to Leah and pass through,
not all of them bums or lumberjacks with a quick eye for a
bottle. Many are short-order cooks, those skinny food-haters;
you can see their bones, their silver identification bracelets,
tattoos, and spatulas in any diner, their sunken faces framed by
the exhaust fan. There are other kinds: awning-menders, em-
balmers, one-shot salesmen fleeing some private suburban
nightmare—and clerks, like Mr. Brown. They stay a year or two
and head around the circuit once again: Rhode Island, Massachusetts, New Hampshire, Maine, Vermont. Old men, mostly,
pretty set in their ways, they almost have to be single. The jobs
pay little, but there's always a job somewhere.

Trotevale's store is no longer on Leah's square. A couple of
years ago the Cascom Savings Bank, next door, took over both
buildings, and now the two look like one. Built in 1854 of wood,
modernized by a sheathing of red brick in 1907, they are now
modernized again, rather gaudily, in three-colored cathedral
stone which seems to be held together by chrome strips, like a
modern automobile. You hardly notice the disappearance.
Trotevale's sign was black, framed by gilt paint, and the raised
gilt letters said TROTEVALE's. That's all. Two counters ran down
the middle of the store, piled with sweaters, shirts, gloves, and
other kinds of "good" clothes. Work clothes were in the basement, piled on plain tables. On the left side of the main floor,
shoe boxes filled the wall from front to back, and Mr. Brown, if
there were no customers, sat composedly in one of the four
wooden armchairs. On the right, glass-fronted cases reached to
the ceiling, and every ten feet or so a pair of long-handled
tweezers, long enough to reach the highest five-dollar Dobbs,
leaned against the cabinets. Ladies' undisplayables were upstairs, along with the office and the tailor's room, on a wide
balcony that went all the way around, close below the stamped-
metal ceiling. The balustrade was carved orange cypress: balls,
flutes, grapes, Corinthian capitals, and Roman arches. The

whole store was fine, consistent 1907, except for the surface of the main floor, which had been covered with plastic tile in wide green and white squares. Upon this miraculous surface the old mahogany counters, the cast-iron adjustable tie racks, the jig-sawed buttresses and varnished legs all seemed to float, as in a painting by Dali, an inch or so above the floor. It was Trote-vale's first concession to those two-page magazine ads (before and after), and of course it wasn't enough. All it did was knock the pins out from under 1907.

Each day after school I'd go home, change my clothes, and go to Trotevale's for the two hours until closing time. On Saturday I came in at eight-thirty in the morning. Eleven and a half hours! And those long, dusty afternoons were rarely broken by anything amusing. I watched the second hand of the white-faced clock at the back of the store, and sometimes it stopped dead for what seemed like whole seconds. Long ones they were, too. Sometimes I looked at myself, back, front, and sides, in the tricky fitting mirrors, not caring at all for my profile. Better the front view, and I could practice my frigid Yankee stare—that bright aggressive look I found legitimate upon the faces of my friends—the one that declares equality and asks: *What kind of a damn fool are you?*

At other times, in that mirror, I could wish upon my face bones the crisp dignity of Mr. Brown's straight nose, the regal depth of those blue eyes. Old man that he was, I began to pay him the compliment of imitation. When he spoke—while showing me how to tie the string around a package without having to let go of one end to tie the knot, without asking the customer for the use of a finger—he emitted a low, rather kindly humming sound. "Mmmm," he would croon for "Yes," or for "Oh, is that so?" or for mere wordless sympathy. I believe he meant to let you know that he was listening, or that he understood exactly how you felt, and this nonword was the least interrupting of all assents. I don't know. Perhaps it led to a certain distance between himself and the person he communicated with, as meaningful words would not. But I'd hear it, deep in his chest somewhere, a kind of cellolike vibrato, as hard to locate as a partridge drumming in the deep woods.

I began doing this myself, and found that Mr. Brown's idiosyncrasies and his *presence,* in a way, were noted. "Listen!"

my father said at supper. "He's doing *that,* like Mr. Brown!" Strangely, I was pleased, rather than embarrassed. But of course I stopped doing it. I developed, instead, a slow smile— one that took several seconds to mature, like Mr. Brown's. My mother's comment was less pleasing: "If I didn't know how old you were, I'd say you were filling your pants."

Bessie Sleeper was the secretary and bookkeeper for Old Man Trotevale, who had shingles and rarely came to the store. Bessie weighed two hundred pounds, but had tiny feet. In the back of the store an open-shaft service elevator ran from the basement to the office on the balcony, and this was known, not to Bessie, as Bessie's Hoist. It creaked as she stepped upon it and pulled the rope which started huge flywheels in the basement. *Clang* went the collapsible gate that somehow never caught your fingers in its disappearing parallelograms, and Bessie rose. She walked as if she carried a bucket of water in each hand, her face bitterly clenched with effort, her tiny blue eyes stabbing about for a place to sit her burden down. She was always very nice to me. She loved Mr. Brown.

Her feet were truly perfect, he said, and nearly every week she bought a pair of shoes. I can see her, wedged into one of the old wooden armchairs, a spot of molten thrill somewhere deep, deep—certainly not showing—as Mr. Brown, cool in his white shirt and black arm garters, held her foot in his strong, dry hand.

If any one person, in the continuing absence of Old Man Trotevale, ran the store, it was Mr. Hummington, a busy little middle-aged man who wore rimless octagonal glasses the color of an old photograph. You could see his eyes way down in there in the mauve twilight, moving around. They didn't seem to have any whites. He had black hair that seemed to grow all on one side of his head, form a rigid slab across the top, and end rootlessly above the opposite ear. I knew his secret: I saw him bend too far over one time, behind the overcoats, and as one expects something to follow when a cover flies open, I half expected his brains to fall out. He was always busy arranging things, changing things—the plastic floor was his project— marking prices and code upon labels: an expert, a dynamo. It was he who totaled up the cash register and told jokes in a high and businesslike voice. I remember him best in a series of gestures: he breaks a roll of pennies over his finger (it didn't hurt), spills them into a little rubber capsule, slaps the capsule into its carriage, and snaps the handle which shoots it on a wire up to Bessie's balcony cash register.

"Was a clerk. Young feller. No longer with us." (Snicker.) "Put a mouse in the tube and sent it up to Bessie!" All this in a tone as smooth as steel, with a look half warning, half prediction. Should I have laughed? Perhaps I tried one of Mr. Brown's slow smiles.

There were other clerks, pale, retail creatures who fade quickly from memory. One was Randall Perkins, whose father owned the Leah Paper Mill. His father, having evidently assessed his son's talents, had arranged the job for him in the restful atmosphere of Trotevale's. I see him, a tall, vacant boy, standing with a suit of long winter underwear in limp hands, the virile red wool, the functional flaps in interesting contrast to his ennui.

All this while there have been rumblings from above—a permanent, threatening overtone. In his little enclosure on the balcony my personal ogre was at work, his sewing machine ripping off machine-gun bursts. Oaths and maledictions! I dreaded Mr. Halperin, the tailor. He cursed in odd languages, he sat like a malignant toad and blamed me for the pants I brought him. His wet gray eyes glared across ridges of brown flesh. His head was large, bald, and thrust itself forward from shoulders hardly wider than his neck. His behind was as wide as a woman's, and hid his stool completely, as if its legs went up and stuck right into meat. He always wore a complete black suit, and on the top of his head a black skullcap which I thought to be a mask, like an eye patch, covering some horrible concavity.

"In Berlin I am a tailor! I do not make with such *dreck!*"

I was unused to such foreign behavior. My Yankee family, had it come to such screaming, would have found itself wading in fresh blood. Occasionally I came close to crying under Mr. Halperin's barrages, and I dreaded Mr. Hummington's purposeful approach, suit folded over his arm: "Take this up to the Jew."

"I can't stand it," I said to Mr. Brown. "He *yells* at me."

"Mr. Halperin is a very good tailor," Mr. Brown said.

"Why doesn't he tailor, then, and not yell at me?" To my shame, tears of injustice did come to my eyes.

"Now, now. He doesn't mean anything by it. Mr. Halperin's had a hard life and he's angry about it."

"I don't like him," I said. "I don't like him one little bit." With a bitter look toward the balcony, I retired to my hiding place behind the overcoat racks. Above, the machine rattled viciously.

I held it against Mr. Brown that he and the tailor were friendly. The tailor never screamed at Mr. Brown, nor was he sullen, as he was with Mr. Trotevale and Mr. Hummington. A strange pair they were on the cozy, elm-lined streets of Leah. One was far too handsome, the other far too ugly: both were deformed, I'm sure, in Leah's eyes. They were watched and snickered after as they walked, one tall and too smoothly graceful; the other on thick legs, humping along to keep up.

One evening at our house Mr. Brown came downstairs and stood in the living-room archway, wearing a long silk smoking jacket. My mother and father immediately stood up, then sat down, embarrassed by their instinctive gesture of respect.

"I came to ask," Mr. Brown said formally, "if it would be all right if Mr. Halperin visited me in my room. We'll play chess, which is a very quiet game, although by nature Mr. Halperin is not always quiet." He smiled.

"Oh, fine! Perfectly all right! Sure!" came from my mother and father at the same time. I'm sure they had hardly heard a word. An exquisite orange-and-gold dragon climbed about Mr. Brown's chest and breathed scarlet fire over his breast pocket. We were all stunned by this animal.

And so, a few days later, Mr. Brown introduced the old tailor to my mother and father. Mr. Halperin bowed, called my mother something German, and shook hands too much. After the introducing was done there was a short, deep silence while everyone's eyes shifted here and there, and then Mr. Brown took the tailor upstairs.

I didn't consider myself especially sneaky. But there were two of me, and separation was sometimes hard to mark. Blame could be shifted. And in that constant pursuit of personality I would have done away with one. The other I called Tabber, a sort of north-of-Boston Simon Templar, a creature of the erotic or violent night, a cool customer. The window of Mr. Brown's room opened onto the front-porch roof, and so did the window of mine.

Of course I expected to see, in that familiar room, nothing more horrifying than two old men playing chess. But Tabber, a dark blanket wrapped about his shoulders, eased himself along the shingles to his observation post beneath the whicking leaves of the black maple. He was not afraid of the dark. I was, occasionally. He was entirely fascinated by the Abomination. I was afraid of it. In my half-innocent mind the canon of sin was infinitely long: Demonology, Sex, the Elders of Zion, Werewolves, Toads with Jewels in Their Heads, Warts at a Touch, Step on a Crack and Break Your Mother's Back! I didn't believe any of it. Tabber depended upon his Winchester, I upon a skepticism that was too much a protest against the ghoulish residue of childhood.

We crouched there in the cool September night, deliciously illegal, hidden from the neighbors by the tree and from Mr. Brown and Mr. Halperin by the photonic qualities of the window screen. My mother had lent Mr. Brown her card table, and there sat the two men. I looked directly over Mr. Brown's square shoulder at the tailor's thick scowl. Two empty beer bottles stood on the dresser, and beside Mr. Brown's walnut chessboard were the two glass steins he had bought for the occasion. Both men smoked pipes, the tailor's a hornlike meerschaum that rested against the knot of his tie, Mr. Brown's a thin briar. Streamers of smoke passed slowly through the window screen and past my face without changing shape, like ghosts passing through a wall.

I watched them for a long time as they played. They hardly spoke. When the tailor drank he didn't take his pipe out of his mouth, just shoved it around to the side with his stein.

"Well?" the tailor said.

Mr. Brown didn't answer for a second or two, then the white head began to nod. I could tell by his ears that he smiled.

"Well done," he said. "Very well done. I didn't know it had happened to me until just now."

"Four moves," the tailor said.

Mr. Brown kept on nodding. "You are very good, Mr. Halperin."

"From you? A compliment." Somehow the tailor managed to look pleased while still scowling. You are not bad, Mr. Brown."

"I know that, but I'm nowhere near as good as you."

"It is good that you say it!" The tailor may have tried to smile beneath the rolls of his cheeks. "I knew you would be good, of course," he said.

"You did!"

"Of course I did!"

From some unaccountable reason the tailor was becoming angry. His gray eyes glittered, his baggy lids quivered. Tabber may have reached for his Winchester, but I was glad that the capable back of Mr. Brown screened me, even as little as it did, from the sight of the tailor's anger.

My admiration for Mr. Brown increased, too, because he remained perfectly calm. I could almost hear his basal hum—his sympathetic, yet impersonal purr.

"Tell me why, Mr. Halperin," he said soothingly.

The tailor got up, jarring the card table and teetering the chessmen, and stamped around the room for a while. He began to breathe short, explosive little gasps, and finally he turned toward Mr. Brown. With an ominously quick hand he pulled out his wallet and extracted a photograph in a plastic cover.

"Look at this! Look at it! And tell me if there is no resemblance!"

Mr. Brown took the photograph. Over his shoulder I saw the two men in the picture, one short and one tall. They wore bathing suits with funny tops, like summer underwear, and that was all I could see.

"It is my favorite picture. Why? Because next to me he is Adonis. Such a toad as me!" the tailor said proudly. "He was the same, like you. There are persons who are naturally beautiful, naturally graceful. It is my theory! They are good at everything."

Mr. Brown had been watching the tailor, not the picture, and he said, "Who was he, then?"

The tailor scowled worse than ever, ground his teeth, and began to make a high, whining noise, as if he were in terrible pain. He put his hands over his ears and his head began to sway from side to side. "He was my brother. My brother Hy . . ." (My face ached from unconscious imitation, as if I too were bound to speak.) "My brother *Hyman!*" And tears poured, a solid faucet-stream of tears poured down his face. "I am sorry! So stupid! Forgive me!" he said in a voice that seemed to come bubbling up from under water.

Mr. Brown seemed completely unaffected. He gravely studied the photograph. The tailor wiped his face and blew his nose, emerging from this process unscathed, his face exactly as it had been before. Mr. Brown finally looked up.

"Yes, there is a resemblance," he said at last, and handed the picture back with a steady hand. I could see his other hand beneath the table, kneading his thigh.

Beneath my blanket, kneeling on the mossy shingles, I watched and recovered with the tailor. Tabber had returned to his simpler world of bang-you're-dead, and I was alone. I had never seen a man cry. I, myself, hadn't really *cried* for a long time—maybe a whole year. And why were the sloppy tears of this old man, whom I disliked, so catching? I was absolutely disgusted with myself, and with whatever undependable lever had pulled those tears out of me. I felt tricked, unfairly manipulated by the tailor. "God damn you," I whispered, "God damn you old bastard!" and wiped the traitorous tears into my blanket.

The tailor, completely recovered, began to set up the chessboard again, but Mr. Brown said that he was too tired. I retreated into the leaves until they left the room. When Mr. Brown came back, the tailor then walking lumpily beneath the streetlight on his way home, I came back to the window. Mr. Brown sat down in his easy chair, motionless for a moment, his face tight and unhappy. Then he raised his hands to the level of his eyes. They were shaking. I watched him for a while, but he just sat there, so I left him.

In the afternoons that followed Mr. Halperin's outbreak and on the long Saturdays, he became, as I watched, overly friendly toward Mr. Brown. The tall man was as precisely friendly as before, but the tailor would rush downstairs to talk excitedly, his hands dangerously wild among the racks and stacks of the main floor. He was making Mr. Brown a suit, and to the barely perceptible annoyance of Mr. Brown descended upon him even when he was waiting on a customer, looped a tape about his chest, the thick arms roughly pushing, the ugly face brushing Mr. Brown's ear. Then he whipped the tape off and brought it close to his eyes.

"Forty! Thirty-two!" he roared for everyone in the store to hear. "Magnificent! It is for such men suits should fit!" Humming, nodding, grunting, waving his yellow tape, he rushed back upstairs to his shop.

At times he came to argue, especially when Chief Atmon stopped by to talk to Mr. Brown about guns. The tailor did not like uniforms, and our Chief of Police did little to reassure him. To Chief Atmon, the tailor was a living joke, and the sight of him was enough to bring on a ponderous merriment. "Gay cock off in yawm," he would suggest to the infuriated tailor.

"If you are going to speak Yiddish, why don't you correct yourself?" the tailor said.

"I learned it in the Army," Chief Atmon explained.

Mr. Brown would not join the Cascom River Fish and Game Club, but he did listen—he had little choice—to Atmon's hunting stories. Atmon was a big man, as big as anyone in Leah. His blue uniform fitted tightly as the bark of a tree around his great legs and torso. He was an excellent pistol shot, and it was always surprising to see the loud man so steady, so suddenly cool and precise, as he fired on the Cascom River range, then bursting again in the vacuum of a crushing bang, breathing the fumes of his smokeless powder, looking for the hole he always found in the black.

When he hunted he cursed the animal he pursued. "There goes the son of a bitch! Kill the bastard!" he would yell as a deer slipped away through the alders. And when he killed: "I got the son of a bitch right in the boiler room! Right in the goddam boiler room!"

He was a successful hunter, hunted legally, and got his deer through study and marksmanship. The boys of Leah admired him for this, and we grinned painfully but sincerely as our clavicles unbent after one of his whacks on the back. The big man was fierce and loud, but friendly—there was no doubt about that. He even wanted Mr. Halperin to like him—you could see the little eyes up there in the open red face, searching nervously for signs of affection.

"A murderer," Mr. Halperin said, staring at Chief Atmon's

departing back and at the huge Colt .44 that Atmon carried tight and black against his hip.

Mr. Brown considered this. "No. But maybe he could be."

"He hates the animals," Mr. Halperin said. "He kills out of hate. He carries proudly his pistol. He plays with it."

"Chief Atmon isn't a bad man, though," Mr. Brown said slowly. "Look how he loves his little beagle. . . ."

"Of course! He is a sentimental slob. The worst kind of murderer. I've seen such swine crying over their dogs while men died. And what is this beagle? A murder dog, meant to break the backs of rabbits!"

"No. A fine little dog, doing what he is meant to do. But Chief Atmon, now," Mr. Brown said thoughtfully, "he loves his little dog. You see, it doesn't run away from him. I suppose he believes the little dog loves him." He smiled. "Don't ever run away from him, Mr. Halperin."

"I have run away from worse than that punchinello," Mr. Halperin said.

"I neither like him nor dislike him," Mr. Brown said. "I don't hunt with him."

"Yes, you hunt, don't you," Mr. Halperin said disgustedly. "How can you? Do you gloat over the red blood you spill?"

"Do you think I do?"

"I cannot think of a reason for murder."

"If you think it is murder I can't begin to explain it to you," Mr. Brown said tolerantly.

"But why? But why?" The tailor waved his hands in Mr. Brown's face. "Look at it! Here is a beautiful deer, a fine animal; he eats only the little grasses, the little twigs from the trees. He hurts nobody. All he asks is to live, to grow tall and beautiful. You sneak to wound him, shoot big balls of lead through his living body. What did he do to you? He has pain! He falls!" The tailor's eyes were full of tears.

"Mr. Halperin," Mr. Brown said calmly (but from my inconspicuous distance I remembered his shaking hands). "A buck is not a man. He is better-equipped than a man. If you want to make a man out of him, the man you make will be an unpleasant one. He is murderous in the rut. He lets his does go first across any dangerous ground. He is completely disloyal, completely selfish. I don't make a man out of him, and I don't judge him. He is beautiful and correct for what he is. We've driven off most of his natural enemies, like the wolf, because we thought they threatened us. And now he has two major enemies left, Mr. Halperin. Neither is man. One is starvation, and none of his fine talents gives him a chance against that horror. Another is the breeding of the defective among him, which will make him small, ugly, and stupid and even wipe him out. Hunting man is the only enemy left that he is equipped to overcome. And if the slow and the feeble among him are not killed, he will no longer be the most beautiful animal on earth."

Mr. Halperin looked away, his head bent, his hands held out, palms up. "I have heard such theories before, in Germany," he said.

"You're talking about people, Mr. Halperin. I'm talking about deer. . . ."

"So there's a difference?" the tailor said, and abruptly turned away.

I had never heard such beautiful theories, but in the town of Leah, where hunting is part of life, where school is for girls when deer season opens on the first of November and the paper mill is closed, we never thought too much about *killing* deer. You *got* a deer, and he was yours. From the wild flash and flag of him, the noise of his canny rush for escape, he changed. He became your own, to touch, to show, and finally to eat. I retreated to my coatrack hideaway, gloating over Mr. Brown's victorious argument. I went to the fitting mirrors and practiced him, ignoring my pointy profile.

Mr. Halperin didn't speak about hunting again, but if anything, his demonstrative affection for Mr. Brown increased. The swoops to measure him, the constant cornerings and contacts, began to tell. Once I saw Mr. Brown avoid him—saw him turn and go back to the basement when he saw that Mr. Halperin was waiting for him by the shoe-fitting chairs. The tailor would come up often and put his hand on Mr. Brown's shoulder—a shoulder held rigid. Finally Mr. Brown turned to him, and said, in a clear, cold voice, "Don't *lean* on me, Mr. Halperin."

The tailor jumped back, his hand still in the air at the height of Mr. Brown's shoulder. "What? What?" he asked.

Mr. Brown ignored him, and continued to wait on Bessie,

who was stolidly buying a pair of shoes—her impersonal foot caress at the hands of Mr. Brown.

At the foot of the stairs the tailor turned around. His eyes were wet again, and he smiled a twisty little smile. "So!" he said to me. "So we know! When didn't it? Look! He waits on that fat pig who has the soul of a garbage can, the mouth like a hemorrhoid!" He shook his head. "Ah, he is so just like! So cold!"

When he had the time he still worked on Mr. Brown's suit, still made the necessary measurements—but formally now, with prior permission. Most of the time he sat in his little room, firing off bursts of stitches, waiting to cuss me out.

. . . Until that morning in November. Leah Town Square was sere, hardened by a morning frost; the tall elms were creaky in the cold sunlight, and I was hardened and hopeless at the beginning of another endless Saturday. I crossed the green but dying grass, passed the empty benches that would soon be taken in. It was the first day of hunting season and I must wear a necktie and white shirt, hear the sporadic shots echoing down from the dark hills of Leah. The deer, jumped by hunters, would be moving nervously through the quiet spruce, leaping past the bright beeches into darkness. And I must wait on people who didn't care enough—who didn't care at all.

From a distance I had seen Bessie and Mr. Brown standing in front of Trotevale's, but the frosty wind made my eyes water, and I kept them down, not bothering to wonder why the two didn't go straight inside on a cold morning. As I came nearer I saw that Bessie was in a state of unrest. Something jiggled the mass, made her stamp her precious feet and open and shut her soundless mouth. Mr. Brown stood next to her, and they both peered in through the big window to the right of the front door. When I came up to them it was a terrible and delicious shock to me, too: the big window was only half there. Slabs and splinters of glass glittered upon the sidewalk; wide sheets of it and millions of jagged darts of it had crushed Mr. Hummington's window display of ties and hats.

"Something moving *around* in there!" Bessie whined. Through the unnatural hole we heard bumpings from the rear, thumps and breaking glass.

The rest of the clerks and Mr. Halperin had come by the time Mr. Hummington arrived at a run, his key foremost.

"Late! Late!" he explained, as if his lateness were something so odd it must be proclaimed. Then he saw the broken window, and with military precision he stabbed the Yale lock with his key and overran it, nearly shattering the glass of the door with his forehead. We cautiously followed him inside—all except Bessie, who remained outside uttering complaining little squeaks.

The glass case that had contained men's jewelry—tiepins and cufflinks of coated brass, little arrows meant to look as if they pierced your necktie, springlike instruments to skewer collars down, personalized buckles and their heaps of interchangeable letters in plastic mother-of-pearl—this case was smashed and trampled, and shoddy brightwork spewed down the aisle. Stray neckties were everywhere, brightly coiling and dangling like tropical snakes in a zoo. The coatracks at the rear were all tipped over, and piles of blue and brown material lay heaped in rows, a plowed field sown with buttons.

We advanced, Mr. Hummington in the lead, silent except for the crunch of glass beneath our feet. No sound came from the dark areas at the rear of the store, and we all had the feeling of being watched.

"Got to call Mr. Trotevale," Mr. Hummington whispered.

"We ought to get out of here," Randall Perkins suggested. Though far in the rear, he had armed himself with or was merely carrying an empty tie rack. Bessie had moved through the door and scared us badly by screaming, "Are you all right?"

Mr. Hummington turned wrathfully, but before he could say anything the ominous presence we had all been conscious of, the author of this terrible derangement, rose before us, gathered itself before Mr. Hummington: a great buck with bone-white antlers, thick neck, and deep, wild eyes. Mr. Hummington must have been close enough to feel the sharp explosions of wind from the buck's black nostrils.

With his hands slack at his sides and his mouth open, Mr. Hummington stared. All his famous energy had left him, drawn out at a look as awed sighs were drawn from us. The buck's brawny neck trembled with inhuman energy, his black eyes struck away what little nerve we had. In the sudden presence of his fierce strength we were all at once aware of our weakness. The coward's swift insight froze our shy bodies. I, for one, knew in my belly the force of those bony antlers, the power of those sharp hoofs. And the awesome dignity of the huge animal was not dispelled at all by the cheap neckties that flapped from his antlers, gaudy but unfunny: they might have been our own dangling guts.

After the long moment of fear, the deer rose on its hind legs to turn in the narrow aisle. Mr. Hummington fell solidly to the floor and scuttled, with swimming motions, back toward us on the slippery plastic. His head thumped against my shin, and he looked up, without his glasses, astounded at my unmoving presence. His eyes were metallic little beads deep under his forehead. None of the rest of us had run because the deer had—one smooth leap had taken him directly into the banister of the basement stairs. He took the heavy wood downstairs with him as easily as if it had been a spiderweb across a trail. From the basement we heard a clatter and a thump, then nothing. We had been hearing, but not caring about, Bessie's screams for help. She stood blocking the front door, importuning the town of Leah and the police. Eventually both came.

With the deer more or less safely in the basement, Mr. Hummington took charge. Bessie was led to the elevator and installed in her office on the balcony, Mr. Halperin was sent to his shop, and the rest of us were directed to begin cleaning up. The shoe department hadn't been damaged, and we didn't miss Mr. Brown. While we were sweeping up the jewelry he had been in the basement.

"He's back in the corner by the work shirts," Mr. Brown said. "I'm afraid he'll hurt himself."

"Hurt himself! *Hurt* himself!" Mr. Hummington said.

"He may break a leg if we scare him too badly."

"He may break his goddam neck! Look at this place! Look at the hoof marks in my new floor! Look at the glass!" Mr. Hummington yelled.

Mr. Brown looked gravely down at him, a certain amount of contempt detectable in his calmness. Mr. Hummington turned away.

"What's Mr. Trotevale going to say? We can't get any new glass until Monday, and he has the shingles again. We'll have to borrow a mattress box from the furniture store and put it over the hole and it'll look just goddam awful!" Some of this was private moan.

People had begun to gather on the sidewalk, and they stood two deep, staring in, steaming the good window so that they had to keep wiping to see. They all seemed to be waving at us. The front door had been locked, but this didn't stop Chief Atmon, who jumped crushingly through the broken window, scattering hats and glass over the floor I'd just swept.

"Where is he?" Atmon yelled, his big hands held open and forward like a wrestler's.

"He's down in the basement and he's as big as a horse," Mr. Hummington said.

"Hah!"

"He's bigger'n you, Harold," Mr. Hummington said. "You're not going to wrestle him out of there."

Atmon looked questioningly at Mr. Brown.

"Three hundred pounds. Ten points," Mr. Brown said.

"Wow!" Atmon's hand dropped tentatively to the butt of his big revolver. On his face was an expression of fierce anticipation.

"Goddam, Harold! You shoot him and you'll ruin half the work clothes. Blood all over the place!" Mr. Hummington cried. "You can't do that! All those chinos! You can't do it!"

"I can drop him in his tracks. One shot. No splatter. Right in the goddam boiler room."

"No! No! You've got to lasso him. Tie him up!"

"I ain't no cowboy," Atmon said. "What about you, Brown?"

"You might tie him up, but by the time you do he'll have wrecked everything down there, and hurt himself," Mr. Brown said.

"Shoot him!" Atmon said. "Only thing *to* do."

"Why don't we just let him go?" Mr. Brown said.

An immediate, wondering silence. We all looked at Mr. Brown as if at a stranger, and from that point on he lost force; he seemed to fade before our eyes, and the more he said, the less his opinion counted. Aside from considerations of retribution for the damage done to the store, and especially the damage done to our equilibrium, the idea was impossible. The deer would have to come back upstairs and leave the store at street level. Then he would have to find his way back to the woods, a matter of a half-mile in the best direction. Such gaunt majesty as his would be too alone, too terrible upon the quiet streets of Leah. He'd be sure to get into more trouble somewhere along the line.

"He got in here by himself," Mr. Brown said. "If he isn't driven crazy he might be able to find his way back where he belongs."

"He don't belong *here*," Mr. Hummington said.

"Belongs in my freezer-locker, that's where he belongs," Chief Atmon said.

"Listen," Mr. Brown said, "he isn't stupid. He's big and he's old, and you don't get that way by being stupid."

"So who says he was?" Atmon said.

"He just doesn't belong here. You can't shoot him here. It's too strange for him. Out in the woods he'd make us all look like fools."

"So who says he wouldn't? Only he ain't out in the woods, by God!" Atmon said, grinning. "He ain't *out* in the woods."

"Why'd he have to come to town, anyway?" Mr. Hummington asked plaintively.

"I'll tell you why," Mr. Brown said. "Because so many brave hunters were out with jack lights last night. I never heard so many shots in the middle of the night. It's a wonder everybody in this town hasn't got his deer all tagged and hung up already. Somebody stampeded this buck. It's not his fault he ran into town."

"So whose fault is it? It ain't mine, but I got to get him out of here," Atmon said.

"How about the game warden?" Mr. Hummington asked hopefully.

"He's out with his thermometer testing to find them deer was jacked last night," Atmon said. "Who could find him?"

Chief Atmon had been edging impatiently toward the basement stairs; Mr. Hummington, who wanted a promise of no bloodshed, was backing away in front. Mr. Brown walked back to his shoe department, turned, and stood motionless, watching.

And at that moment, without having to look behind him, Mr. Hummington *knew*. With barely a creak of stairs the buck appeared, whole and majestic. Quick as a squirrel on a tree, Mr. Hummington scrambled around in back of the Chief of Police.

Tall and proud, the buck stood over us all, his head high, the magnificent rack of antlers gleaming. He looked from one side of the store to the other, seeming to calculate a mighty leap that would easily clear our heads. His muzzle was dark, yet a silvery fringe of white hairs showed his age. His neck was as thick as a man's waist—a trunk of rigid muscle to carry great antlers. He held our eyes again—held them absolutely—an invincible magnetism in that wild beauty.

Atmon himself was struck silent for a long time. Then he had his Colt in his hand, and we all heard three cold clicks as he pulled back the long hammer.

"MURDERER!"

For a moment I thought this tearing sound was the expected shot, and then in the shocked silence after this astounding word we saw the tailor on the balcony, his squat legs spread, his stubby hands gripping the rail. His face was black with blood, his eyes burned down upon the startled Chief of Police.

"MURDERER! MURDERER! Mr. Brown! Do you see what he is doing? *What are you doing about it?*"

Like the buck itself, Mr. Brown did not move during this outburst. He stood quietly by his wall of shoe boxes, his eyes still, as if he were blind, or in hiding.

The tailor watched him for a second, and then began to stamp his feet, to shriek in German, the words torn by great sobs and sneezes as he hit his disintegrated face with his fists.

The deer took this moment to make his try for freedom, catching us all with our eyes upon the bawling tailor. Chief Atmon's reaction was swift, and had been predicted. He fired, stunning us all, breaking the buck's long back in midair as he made his first arching leap toward the front of the store. He came down upon rigid forelegs, his hindquarters useless, and slid to the feet of Mr. Brown.

"Got him!" Chief Atmon yelled triumphantly. It had been a tremendous, classic shot from a handgun, yet we were silent, still. The buck still lived. Propped upon his forelegs, his rack still held high, he looked straight at Chief Atmon, waiting. Mr. Brown watched too. "I got him! I got him! I got him!"

"Not quite in the boiler room," Mr. Brown said quietly.

"God damn you! I got him, so shut your lousy mouth!" Chief Atmon screamed. A long sigh from the rest of us, and

Chief Atmon whirled around. He seemed to look right at me. *This is what I am good at,* his eyes implored. *And wasn't that a beautiful shot?*

The deer's calm eyes were black and deep. His nostrils flared at each even breath. His rump lay broken behind him, the long, silky-haired legs splayed across the shiny plastic squares. Atmon came up, his revolver cocked.

"Get the hell out of the way. I'm going to finish him off." Mr. Brown moved away, carefully, quietly. The deer glanced at him once and then turned to watch Chief Atmon and the black gun that was pointed at his neck. He didn't try to move, but held his head as high as the good forelegs could hold it, waiting, breathing steadily, his ears erect and still as if he meant to hear, as well as see, the final explosion. . . . Which came. Chief Atmon was right: there was very little blood from either wound. The big slug broke the buck's neck and killed him. With a little sigh he dropped his head. An antler rang against the wall and he was very little quieter than he had been alive. His eyes were open, still luminous—but not so deep: those dark wells had silted up.

In the terrible vacuum of Chief Atmon's victory we watched Mr. Brown pace down the squares toward the cloak rack. Each foot precise upon a square, he hit no cracks. His handsome face was as unchangeable as if it were made of wax— the stern, expressionless mourning of waxwork nobility upon a tumbrel. He would look at none of us: whether it was disdain, or the wily ploy of a camouflaged animal afraid its eyes might shine, I didn't know. At the cloak rack he unhurriedly put on his coat and hat, then as proudly, or as carefully casual in the face of danger, he turned around and walked out.

The tailor's long wail of mourning grew above us, its waves and intensifications strangely formal and rhythmical, as if it were a rite of sorrow perfected by the legions of the bereaved.

Bessie, her heavy face no longer under the protection of her habit of determination, stood at the rail and wept.

Later in the morning, when Mr. Hummington's energy had restored the order of our existence, I found myself with a pair of pants in my hand, making the usual climb to the tailor's shop.

The bursts of his sewing machine were as abrupt as always,

and this time he heard my step upon the stairs and turned toward me, dropping a stiff lapel upon his table.

"He is gone?" he asked, gray eyes popping miserably from the brown lids. And without waiting for my reply he asked again, "He is gone?"

"He didn't even say goodbye," I said, echoing in the words of Mr. Hummington a disapproval I didn't feel.

"Goodbye?" the tailor yelled, bringing his fist down upon the rubber bulb of his chalk marker. "Goodbye?"

A cloud of blue dust rose above the scarred table. Blue chalk hung between us like a mist, and the tailor's eyes began to fill with rage and tears. I backed toward the stairs, feeling for the carved railing, a solid thing to follow back.

"Did you want him to say goodbye? Are you still foolish? Do you cry because of this?" the tailor demanded, bringing his fist down on the table so hard the lapel jumped.

I *hadn't* cried. In spite of the tears I'd seen, I hadn't caught them, and I considered this a terrible insult—an unforgivable insult; considered this and suddenly burst out bawling, enraged by the underhanded trick.

"God damn you son of a bitch!" I yelled.

"Ah! That's better," the tailor said calmly, as if my tears had released and strengthened him. "Do you think I don't know you, my funny little one? It is *his* nature to try to escape. He does not know how *we* survive, eh? Never mind! *We* are the slobs who make the world." He motioned with his hand. "Now give me the pants you got in your hand and go back to work. Go on!"

I left him, seeing that shrewd and twisted smile as I fled to my hiding place behind the overcoats, to my private ceremony; the tearful funeral of that thin-lipped version of myself as Tabber, as a Yankee boy of ice and few swift words. I heard again the tailor's long wail as it had grown over the deer's death and Mr. Brown's escape, and now I found the doleful music apt, as if it were part of a ritual some memory of my flesh found anything but alien and strange.

. . . Not so long ago, though Trotevale's and the things of Trotevale's are scattered to the rag bags and the antique shops of Leah.

My son fixes me to here and now, the only place and time there is: he has cornered his apple by the stairs, and found that he can break the skin by smashing it against the edge of the bottom step. He sits quietly, his little tongue busy on the split, his eyes darkly watchful. He reminds me of an animal—a young raccoon in some quiet corner of the deep woods—self-sufficient, aware. "You little bastard," I say admiringly, with perhaps too much affection in my voice. "You little bastard . . ." Gently, because he is soft and young. And with fear, for I do not really know what I should hope for him.

The Orphan's Wife

MICHAEL STORY, at sixty-one, contemplated his possible retirement, although nothing, as far as he knew, loomed in the near future to cause him to have to retire. It was an idea that came and went—came in off moments, sometimes moments of irritation or of fatigue, though not that often, really. The idea was occasionally fascinating, that was all. Sometimes, contemplating retirement, he recognized a feeling he'd had in his twenties, that a life was out there to choose, and that he had the power, if he wanted to use it, to choose that new life. Choice was the thing.

There were two directions in which imagination and hope could go—forward, into the land of unknown possibilities, and backward, into the land of choices taken, where the alternatives were as mysterious as the future ever was. He could never know whether the choices he had made in his life had been good ones or bad. After each choice was the memory of the former life, and memories of the life before earlier choices, and earlier ones. Memories of memories.

But suppose the man he had been at thirty could suddenly look out of these older eyes, not knowing what had happened in between, having only the evidence here in this room. What sort of wondering evaluation would he make? Michael had no blood relatives to judge his life or his performance. No one had looked at him that way, judging or praising.

And what would that young man see right now, to guess at a life by? He'd be observant enough to look at the small desk calendar and see that more than thirty years had passed, that he was more than thirty years on, into his future. Then he would look around, at the room and at the window. Beyond the small panes of the big window was a white field, apple trees, tall pines, and a set of distant wintery hills. Within the warm room was a fieldstone fireplace containing a silent fire of applewood and oak. Over the mantel was a large black-and-white print, a lithograph of two reclining women, one blond and one dark-haired; the young man would recognize this as the work of Yasuo Kuniyoshi. In the room were bookcases full of books, shredded dust jackets peeling here and there across their backs, and a city scene in oil by Aaron Bohrod. Yes, he'd see that.

Thirty years! The young man would guess that he was in New England. New Hampshire? He, himself, could not remember wanting, at the age of thirty, to go back to Leah, New Hampshire. That came later—another choice among all the choices taken or not taken. All those choices. No, instead of having the young man come here, he would go back. One could go back, as well as forward: each way was a fantasy in part, and memory itself tended to weave its own cohesion. In Paris there was the right bank and the left, but in which direction was the pale spring sun? In Des Moines, Iowa, were the generous houses of the well-off, each built as a version of happiness and perfection. But was a thing (a couch, a window, a radio) on the right or on the left? Memory cared less about such technicalities than one thought it did. What it really cared about were those tones and flashes of the sensual—tastes, odors, colors—that by their vividness kept the past from being totally lost. Now, memory . . .

The car hummed contentedly, the sun was climbing in a dusky fresh day, and beside him a beautiful girl drowsed in the morning light, her fresh yellow hair as clean and somehow as unanimal as corn silk. On either side of the straight highway the corn, in thick yet graceful ranks, seemed to breathe heavy life into the air. It was Iowa in August, and the sense, the feel, of growing was so thick he wondered how anything could matter anywhere but here. It was as though he had come, finally, to the center of life itself. Come as an alien, though.

Phyllis certainly hadn't come as an alien. He had to glance down at her smooth long legs that were so clean and perfect they were hard to believe. Her strong hand lay open on the seat, and in its openness, its quietness, life moved without the jangling of nerves or the sweat of emotion. It seemed to him that the lovely hand lived with a natural economy and rightness, as did Phyllis. All she needed was food and water, and her skin glowed, her eyes stayed pure and blue, and her blood moved smoothly through her healthy flesh. He liked to drive with her drowsing beside him, with the clean smell of her in his nose.

Because, awake, Phyllis was constantly active. Always her mind grappled with something or other; there was always some paradox or some injustice toward which she directed herself. Idleness to her was not a sin, it was something which didn't exist. She read, she listened, she went to things like lectures and plays and rallies; and she was the first girl he had ever known whose schedule hadn't perceptibly changed under his influence.

She was, he couldn't help thinking, not his type at all. His girls had always been in tune, somehow. Intellectual types, basically passive under the casual force of his desires, careful to get the joke, to have heard of everything, to act as comrade as well as lover. Those poor girls. Phyllis would despise their obeisance to his male ironies. If Phyllis didn't really think something was funny, she didn't laugh.

She woke up.

"Where are we?" She yawned and stretched her long muscles, and he was startled, as usual, by the quick chemical change in him whenever he saw her move her body like that. It was sharp, and almost hurt.

"We're in Iowa at last," he said.

"Oh? Where?" She sat forward and looked around at the green banks of corn as though, being a native after all, she might be able to tell at a glance.

"Somewhere west of Davenport," he said.

A sign came by: Clabber Girl Baking Powder.

"I've always wondered what 'Clabber' meant," Phyllis said. "I've always meant to ask somebody or look it up but I never have. Isn't it funny? You have these little questions and you never ask them?"

"I know what it means," he said, and she turned toward him delightedly, took hold of his arm, and smiled as though it were really a great treasure he had to give to her.

"Really? Michael!"

"Yes, I know what it means."

"Tell me! Tell me!"

"It means curds, like in cottage cheese, or butter. Maybe the clabber girl churned the stuff. You know, the girl on the farm who made the clabber."

"Wonderful! I *know* that's right, Michael. But how did you know? You've never lived on a farm." She was still delightedly squeezing his arm.

"You know my peculiar memory," he said. "Once, God knows why, I signed up for a course in Irish. The word comes from the Irish."

"You remember everything, Michael. I honestly believe you do. It's so wonderful! You know it makes me feel more valuable? You never forget anything so nothing's lost, and I've got everything right here beside me. No, I don't mean valuable—me being, that is. No, wait a minute. Yes, I do. Do you remember everything about me?" She blushed and looked away, grinning happily at the highway and the endless green and blue outside.

"Every little thing," he said.

"Oh, my goodness!" she said. "Oh my goodness!"

"Is that why you want to marry me?" he asked. "Because I'm just a kind of permanent record? An encyclopedia?"

She looked at him, suddenly thoughtful, and her words seemed to come out automatically. "I want to marry you be-cause I love you."

But she still smiled at the countryside. She didn't ask him why he wanted to marry her. This was a question he had to ask himself. And he asked that question again, getting no straight answer.

Perry had asked him, in Paris, why he had suddenly decided to go home. His answer then was "Because I'm twenty-five and I discover that I have piles." So he'd gone back home, finished law school, and now (it seemed more or less part of the same plan) he was headed toward marriage with this girl from Iowa. Headed toward it at sixty-five miles an hour on a concrete causeway that held them above the deep black earth. He would meet Phyllis's mother and father, in Des Moines.

The memory again. Perry had been on Dexedrine for a few days, and Michael and MacGregor were waiting for him to drop so they could carry him across rue Cujas and deposit him in his room. Perry was heavy as hell, too. "Piles?" Perry said. *"Piles?"* And Michael had explained that somehow his image of himself as a youth was in the process of disintegration. "Piles," he said, imitating Perry's British accent, "are not, somehow, compatible with my present life. Farewell." "Rot!" Perry said. "Exactly," Michael had explained. It had begun to seem to him that all his orifices were closing up; he couldn't smile as wide, or laugh as loud, for instance. That was four years ago. Now he was twenty-nine, and a lawyer. His specialty was patents and copyrights, and already he had been relieved of the usual, mechanical tasks of the apprentice; it was his amazing memory again. He found his work at least as fascinating as bridge or chess.

Phyllis was a senior at Sarah Lawrence, and she was twenty-two. They had known each other less than a year. "Carnally," she said once, "we have known each other only six months."

He grinned himself, now, as the highway made a ninety-degree right turn (a corrected section line, he supposed, and in a certain number of yards it would make a ninety-degree left turn and continue straight west), but in his grin he felt some self-consciousness; there was just a little fear mixed in with his amusement. Yes, there was, and he liked that fear, because it made him feel alive. In a few hours he would have occasion for another fear, too, and he looked forward to it. Phyllis would present him to her parents, and that would be interesting.

William and Hannah Krause would not be shocked by his appearance, because he looked as conventionally Anglo-Saxon as anybody. He was even blond. But there was something about him, he knew, that would give the Krauses pause. It always happened. Some turn of phrase or turn of mouth would, he was afraid, turn the father's thoughts to darkness. He'd seen it happen before; it was as though he suddenly became a Negro in the sight of fathers. Their little daughters—they had a hard time facing up to it.

And the daughters, how they seemed to rub it in. Strange, because girls had always wanted to bring him home to show their parents, and he thought one reason was his conventional appearance, as though they wanted to show their worried parents what a clean, nice young man they had, so their parents wouldn't worry about them. But it never seemed to work out that way. What usually happened was that the father seemed to grow more bouncy on his feet, and a little caustic in his remarks. Well, he would see.

Michael was born in Leah, New Hampshire, and lived there until fourth grade, when he was nine. His parents died in an automobile accident that year, 1936, and he'd had to leave New Hampshire to go to New York City, to the house of his grandmother and grandfather, a brownstone on Tenth Street with the sidewalk in front and in back a dusty little garden with a broken fountain and a fig tree that was in a state of suspended animation. The garden there, compared to this rich Iowa earth, was such that the plants were always dirty to the touch. In that house nothing much was kept from him or given to him; because of his youth and his grandparents' age he did what he wanted and made his own rules. When he was old enough he was sent to boarding school, and after that there was the Army and college. His grandfather was still alive, but Michael went to that house only as a visitor; the old man's memory wasn't too good, and most of the time he considered Michael to be his son rather than his grandson. It was disconcerting to act as the impersonator of a father he hadn't known too well anyway. Michael's grandmother was dead, and with her had gone all the remembered evidence of family and relatives—cousins and second cousins, ancestors and aunts. When his grandfather died he would in effect have no family, and so it was as a kind of singleton he traveled through Iowa with this warm girl.

"I wonder what you'll think of them," Phyllis said.

"I wonder what they'll think of me."

She was honest; she wouldn't ever lie. "Yes, I wonder," she said, looking at him speculatively.

"Can you look out of your mother's eyes and see me?" he said.

"That's a funny idea."

"Sort of incestuous."

"Well," she said, "I wouldn't stay inside her *too* long." She thought for a moment, then added, "My God! Poor old Daddy. He's such a dear ass."

"I'll tell him you said so."

"He'll be very impressed by you—lawyer and all that. Don't be too hard on him. Tell him how much money you make—I'm sure he makes three times as much."

"You think he's a good man, don't you?"

She cocked her head and thought. It was as if she had never before considered this. "Well, he's a *good* man," she said.

"You mean he's stupid."

"Not exactly," she said.

"Sort of vaguely," he said, and she punched him playfully on the arm. It hurt, though. Somehow she'd found the exact place, and it hurt like hell.

In a couple of hours they came to Iowa City, where they had decided to stop and eat, and as they came down a surprisingly steep hill into the town he was impressed by the large trees and the look of permanence and grace in some of the houses.

"Well, it's a college town," Phyllis said.

"What college?"

"The State University of Iowa," Phyllis said.

"I thought that was in Ames."

"No, that's Iowa State."

"Oh. That figures."

"Listen," Phyllis said. "If you think you can patronize Iowa, wait till you meet Mother. She can do it better, and she's lived here all her life."

They stopped at a diner, and as they sat down in a booth the waitress came so quickly and cheerfully, with such an excited and really friendly smile, Michael was certain she must be an old friend of Phyllis's.

"Hello!" the waitress said, and Phyllis smiled back, as friendly as the waitress. How they seemed to love each other! The waitress, whose blond hair and perfect teeth were quite similar to Phyllis's, handed them menus and asked if they'd had a good trip. "All the way from New York?" She had seen their license plate.

"We stopped over twice," Phyllis said. "Once in Ohio and once in Moline."

"Moline's a nice town," the waitress said. "Have you got much farther to go?"

"My folks live in Des Moines," Phyllis said.

"Oh, that's nice. I like Des Moines. Well, you've got over a hundred miles to go. You'll make it for supper, I bet."

"They're expecting us, anyway," Phyllis said.

"That's nice. They'll be so happy to see you again."

They did order, finally, and after they'd eaten, the waitress came to the door with them and asked them to drive carefully.

"Goodbye!"

"Goodbye! Goodbye!"

In the car again, he asked Phyllis if she had known the girl. She just looked at him. "Know her? No, of course not. Oh. I see what you mean. No, that's something you'll get used to out here."

"Well, I gave her a good tip."

Now Phyllis was startled. "But you didn't have to at all! She wasn't being friendly for tips. In fact, there's a law against tipping in Iowa. Did you know that? You only tip in sin places, like nightclubs and bars."

"These strange foreign customs!" he said.

"And of course the bars only serve beer," Phyllis said.

They drove on through the town and over a rich brown river, then up again into the inevitable tall corn, where the highway again was a white corridor through all that fuming green life. The sky was wider than he had ever seen it—wider than on a ship—and bluer. And in the sky was the sun, a deliberate part of this system of growth. Symbiosis, he thought; everything is making and reproducing, waxing big. The sun was a huge ball of heat that gave and at the same time drew; it sucked out moisture, and yet the air was full of moisture. Everything was growing. He felt like the one cool piece of matter, the one constant, steady thing in this moiling place. As cool, almost, as a piece of ice.

After he had driven for a while, Phyllis became fidgety; she went through the dash compartment looking for something, anything, to read, and he suggested that she drive. She liked this. She loved to drive, and she was very good at it. She'd even taken driving in high school. So he stopped the car and they changed places. The thick corn seemed to tremble, not so much from the mild wind as from growth itself, and as he looked closely at the black earth it seemed unnatural that there were so few weeds around the bases of the stalks, that they stood too cleanly in the rich black.

With Phyllis driving he lay back in the seat, not wanting to make her self-conscious by looking at her or at the road. But he found it hard not to look at this woman he was going to marry. Those hips were to be his, in a way; the smooth insides of those adequate thighs his forever. And with the lively body all the other things about her. Her fantastic energy, her commitment to everything in the world. Once she had said to him, "I warn you, Michael. If there are any rallies, or sit-ins, or anything like that, you know me, I'll be there too. I'll be right in it up to my neck." She would be, too.

He wondered why causes had never appealed to him, why his sympathies, though clear enough, never roused him to action. It was as if he lacked some essential quality of optimism, or excitement—as if he had in a rather un-American way never developed hope of controlling the future.

So why should he marry this American? Again the little shiver of fear, undeniably painful, undeniably pleasant. Risky, bittersweet. Once before he had thought he was in love, in Paris, and the girl's name was Eva. She was from Lyon, and was going to Beaux-Arts. She made a little extra money sketching portraits in bars, and she'd been so pretty in her dark, complicated little way—she looked so pale and interesting—he let her sketch him once, in the Capoulade, and soon they were together most of the time.

His memory, even in this humid Iowa August, brought back that early spring in Paris. He and Eva walked together in the Luxembourg Gardens. It was in that first tentative, almost cruel part of spring, bitterly cold except in the sun, when the people came out from their damp rooms into the Gardens, carefully turning themselves in the sun. It was a time of delicate balance between warmth and cold. When a cloud came over everyone turned cold and shivery, and for a long moment it would be winter again. The sun was always a little warmer when the cloud had passed, and the wind a little colder.

They had been holding hands and running. They walked, out of breath, across the early grass to the pond and statue, and he remembered feeling as if he were coming out of hibernation—tremendously tense and hungry, yet not irritable.

"You're all of a piece," he said in English, then laughed—as if the laugh itself could do for a translation.

"What did you say?" she asked seriously. She wanted to learn how to laugh with him, and quite seriously she asked questions.

He picked her up, his face sifting through her dark hair, and pretended to throw her into the pond. Her arm around his neck was confident, and she smiled.

"You seem so young—much younger than the French boys. Are all Americans so young?"

"I'm five years older than you!" he said.

"You must keep on saying that. 'How *old* I am!' And then you run through the Luxembourg Gardens!"

"You little twirp," he said in English, and kissed her. He remembered that first time with such clarity that he could actually see Eva and himself—their faces firm, clear ivory in the sun. He remembered even that their teeth had touched once, lightly, and he could still feel, even hear, that solid little click. She seemed perfectly happy to be held. She would wait, confident of him, yet ready to be released, anticipating his movements by a period of time so precisely minute that it seemed to have nothing to do with the mechanisms of consciousness. Unless she meant it to happen, she never moved against him—they never matched strength. Often they would be at Jewell's nightclub listening to the jazz or trying to hear MacGregor's sentimental piano over the talk, and Perry or Jewell would be sitting with them admiring such nice love. Fat black Jewell, who liked to see them together so much, who kept watch over them as though they were her little white pets she was mating, who fed them Southern Fried Chicken, the specialty of the house. But that was all gone by.

Nearly a year later, when his GI Bill ran out and he decided to go home, he said goodbye to Eva. It seemed so inevitable that he must leave—simply fate, implacable and remorseless—that he'd said goodbye to Eva as he might have said goodbye to any friend. She had never suffered in his presence, and he thought she realized that there were many Michaels in the world, as well as many Evas; he was terribly unhappy and helpless when she cried and cried. But how could he comfort her when he'd already received a check from home to buy his passage? She refused to believe that he considered himself merely one of thousands; she refused to believe that he was interchangeable. While he was in law school and she back home in Lyon they wrote to each other perhaps twice a year until she was married.

"Des Moines!" Phyllis said.

"What does it mean?" Michael asked her.

"My God! I was born here, and I don't know! It's the name of the river, but I don't know what it means!" She was really troubled. "I don't think I ever knew. I don't think anybody ever told me."

"Maybe nobody knows," Michael said.

"I must find out. I've got to. You remind me to look it up the minute we get home."

Home, he thought. This medium-sized city, with no particular distinguishing marks except for the greenness of its green wherever there was grass, was home. There was a river, a long bridge, those business buildings and blocks that might have been imported from New Jersey or anywhere in America, the same gleaming automobiles.

It was late afternoon, and Phyllis had driven very fast for a hundred miles, but she didn't seem at all tired.

"Should we bring a present?" he asked. "A bottle of wine or something?"

"Oh, no. No, I don't think so. I don't think that would be right. Dad will want to give *us* everything. He won't want to get a present. Besides, you need a little book to get liquor. You have to go to a state liquor store, you know, and buy a little book, and they write down in it everything you buy."

"For Christ's sake."

"Well, don't worry. There'll be plenty of liquor around," Phyllis said.

They left the neighborhood of gas stations and stores, drove past the neat little cottage-houses of wood or stucco, each with its luxuriant little lawn and hedge, and then came to a neighborhood where the trees, maples and oaks and elms, were taller and thicker in their trunks, where the houses were set back away from the street, and farther apart, each in its own park of rich green. And then suddenly they were turning into a long driveway, and it was a pleasant little shock to him that they were here, and would now have to stop and get out in front of the house. He saw it, long, brown, and low. He shivered. It had a certain grace to it, this big house, and it belonged where it was among its carefully tended trees. A sprinkler made a huge diaphanous bell of mist beside the driveway, and a gray Cadillac sat on the smooth damp asphalt as if it belonged there. The house itself was made of some kind of brown stone, and in its long spaces unbroken by windows, its tall, recessed windows, and its dark overhangs he recognized the spatial generosity that money can buy.

But they were there, and a tall woman and a tall, pink man were coming at them, running at them, great smiles and cries of love filling the air.

He woke at two in the morning, sober. He knew where he was—in a guest room, because the bed was high and too soft, and everything was so clean it squeaked. Phyllis was there beside the bed, shaking him.

"Michael!" she whispered. "Wake up for a minute!" The moon was bright enough so that he could see his watch.

"I hate you for looking at your watch," she whispered as she slid in beside him. He turned toward her, his arm sliding across her smooth, firm belly, his nose aching at the bridge it was so full of her, and he sneezed violently into her shoulder. "I love you," she said, and she grabbed him so hard it hurt. Just before he was into her, into that surprising dark violence in a girl so fresh and young, he had the idea that he must try to teach her to be more gentle, more feminine, more passive somehow in her embraces. It was he who should work upon her—she shouldn't try to grab everything herself. He thought this before she melted and got what she wanted, until, it always seemed to him, she turned to butter like the tiger in "Little Black Sambo."

Later they smoked, lying side by side in the narrow bed. With two in it they had to balance themselves, really; it was like floating in water. Phyllis put out her cigarette and snuggled down beside him.

"You'd better not go to sleep," he said.

"I won't. They know anyway, though," she said.

"You mean you told them?" He knew she was impossibly honest, but not, he hoped, that honest.

"No. I don't want to hurt them. But you know damn well they knew the minute they laid eyes on you."

"I always thought I looked like a nice boy," he said.

"You look like a nice boy *superficially*," she said. "Anyway, I think they like you. I don't think Dad would like you if you didn't seem to be a man. Once I brought a boy home and Dad *sneered* at him. Really. He was a nice boy, but sort of a sissy, and Dad knew right away."

He found it hard to visualize a sneer on William Krause's face. When they'd got out of the car there was the big pink hand in his, and on the man's face the most straightforward grin of delight. He was a fairly fat man, whose skin was almost indelicately pink. He looked a little translucent, as though he were not full of blood but were pink as ham clean through. What hair he had left was blond, and each hair was as thick as a toothbrush bristle. His eyes were pale, pale blue. He wore a white shirt open at the neck, and with the low, nearly horizontal sun coming across the lawn and hitting him he seemed brighter and bigger than life. Michael had to blink.

"Come on, Mike!" William Krause said. "After that drive you need a drink!" He took Michael's arm and started off with him.

Phyllis had to reach out and pull him back in order to introduce him to her mother. Hannah Krause was a tall, well-built woman with a good square chin and open eyes, nearly as tall as her husband, but not so husky. Michael could see Phyllis at that age. *You are tall, like your mother,* he thought—the words of a song MacGregor used to sing. And now, seeing this older version of Phyllis, he saw why she had always seemed, in the weirdest way, familiar, as though he'd known her somewhere before, in his childhood, or at least before the war, or in school long ago. It was that girl of the nineties—or was it the tens and teens of this century—the Gibson Girl. Both she and her mother had that same clean, almost masculine yet delicate face.

Hannah took his hand in her firm one, and in spite of some embarrassment over her husband's behavior, smiled and welcomed him. Really, he thought, they were nice people, and in the next few days he got to know both of them better than he had expected to under the circumstances of his being their daughter's suitor. He liked them both, their liveliness, their excitements, their conventional, and he thought typical, civilization. But still he was an alien, an orphan from another city, a man seven years older than their sweet daughter, a man with a seedy past, too, if they only knew, a past that included some dangerous experiments with ugliness, and too much indifference to the coldness and cruelty of the world.

And so it seemed to him each night when Phyllis slipped tender and naked into his bed that he was doing these people dirt, defiling their clean, hopeful lives.

Six months later he and Phyllis sat at the Capoulade, in Paris, and he turned in the wire chair and spoke to her. "You see that one there by the kiosk, Phyllis? He's looking at *Paris Match*. No, he's looking at *Ladies' Home Journal*. The one with the beard and spats and all that goes with spats. You met him yesterday. The Indian—the bloody Oxford Indian. We used to call him Kris Le Barbus."

"He's very attractive," Phyllis said.

He looked again, startled, at the Indian.

"We called him 'the Armpit,' among other things. And he spent most of his time scheming for blondes."

"Well, what's wrong with that, if you like blondes?" Phyllis said. "Didn't you scheme a little for me?"

"Not for sociological reasons, I don't think."

"How do you know?" Phyllis asked seriously. "You imply that he wants blondes because he's fairly black, but maybe you want them (me, that is, I hope) because you're blond yourself—maybe that's just as sick." She turned her wide blue Iowa eyes on him, and he admired their precision and purity; he thought of fresh vegetables and cornflakes.

"A sort of inbreeding?" he said.

She smiled at him. "I never think of anything like that—I mean like genetics—when I think of a man. You, that is," she said, and moved her hand down his arm.

He loved her—good God, he had married her!—but she never quite agreed with him about anything, and sitting here in the Capoulade, where he'd sat so many times with another girl, he had to make comparisons. The other girl was Eva, and he decided that after breakfast he would take a sentimental little walk in the Luxembourg Gardens.

"It's late," Phyllis said. "I told Mother and Dad I'd meet them at ten!"

"It's not much of a walk."

"You don't want to come?" She was really disappointed, and as she stared straight at him he leaned toward her and kissed her. She pushed her lips firmly back at his, and then began to gather her things from the table.

"I promised Jean and Jewell I'd see them this morning," he said, and Phyllis looked at once tortured and guilty. She wanted so much to do the right thing, to help people and to give sympathy to them. Suddenly he shivered, seeing again the vision of Henri Varniol dead, Jewell, his fat black wife sobbing, at the heartrending, shoddy *pompe funèbre* yesterday in Montreuil. Phyllis had been brave, near to tears, and now she felt guilty because she didn't want to see Jewell again in such sorrow. God knew it had been horrible—the ghastly wax flowers that had seen too many poor corpses, the fly-blown horses slipping on the cobbles and grunting, soon enough to be on their own way to the *boucherie chevalline*.

So many things had changed since he'd left Paris. Henri was dead of cancer. MacGregor was dead of TB and alcohol. Jewell had told him that, her huge moony mammy's face broken and sorrowful. Nothing was good—no news was good of the years he had been away. Jewell had even lost the permit for her club, and the French were not so tolerant now that the quarter contained so many Negroes.

He put his icy glass along his cheek and smelled the Cognac. MacGregor used to call the drink a finalobe, and had died probably without knowing exactly what had killed him, certainly not caring very much. He wasn't an alcoholic, that was the funny part. No more than a suicide by gas is addicted to gas.

"Do you think I ought to come?" Phyllis asked.

"No, you promised your folks," he said. He smiled at her for her dutifulness, and she understood. She would have come if he'd asked her, he knew. Her careful hair, the color of honey, moved softly against her ear as she shook her head.

Outside the glass partition the boulevard was wet, the magazines in the kiosk wilted in their brackets. A cold wind came along the sidewalk, through the crack below the partition, and touched his ankles, swirled damply over the table, and made waves across the liquid blue flames of the overhead gas heaters. She took a Kleenex out of her handbag and carefully pressed the coffee from her lips.

"I don't know where we're going after the Flea Market, but will you remember five o'clock at the Cujas? We'll meet there for a drink. They want to take us out to dinner *so* badly."

"I'm looking forward to it," he said. She didn't believe him, and she was only partly right. The fact was that he did like her parents, but nobody else could quite believe it.

"It's something we have to do," she said, and he saw a grave thought pass across her clear face as she remembered her own dereliction of duty.

"It's all right, Phyllis," he said. Another thing that bothered her in some moral way was that this off-season trip to Paris was a wedding present from her parents. She didn't like to be beholden to them, and yet she loved them.

He saw her watching herself as she left, walking towards herself all the way to the wall mirror, then making a sharp turn out the door. And what could she see but a clean and pretty girl, most likely the prettiest in sight at anytime, and that smooth, athletic body that moved with such natural authority? She was pregnant, but it wasn't noticeable yet. There was a lump inside her belly, though, and she was always making him put his hand on it, to feel it.

He put his glass down on the round table. It was still full and the ice had melted. He couldn't drink at breakfast anymore, and this was another indication that things had changed. He was healthier, probably, than he had been back in those days, but something was missing. They all used to drink before breakfast then and never care. They'd talk themselves sober, run upstairs, get into an argument or a fight, take off to anywhere with a twenty-dollar traveler's check and a sleeping bag. A headache was a trophy then, not a symptom of decay.

Those were the days of his exuberance, before Pinay overevaluated the franc, before the GI Bill ran out. The ones who were left seemed to have exact and prissy little schedules, like old maids—certain restaurants, certain fresh croissants, certain hours for everything. Most had gone back, as he had, to their own countries, where they could earn money.

Perry had gone back to England. Plump and affable Perry, who was sometimes broke and sometimes not frowned upon at Barclays Bank. Once they had gone off to Germany, he and Torgy and MacGregor, and left Perry broke. They'd asked Perry if he wanted to come, and hadn't thought about Perry's being a Jew. Nothing could have made Perry go to Germany. When they'd come back they found Perry shivering in his room. He'd sold his overcoat and was about to be thrown out for lack of rent—actually starving. He'd lost fifteen pounds. They half-carried him to the Vietnamese restaurant on rue M. Le Prince and fed him fifteen egg rolls and a bottle of wine. Perry said:

"Those who have crossed
With direct eyes, to death's other Kingdom
Remember us—if at all—not as lost
Violent souls, but only
As the hollow men
The stuffed men."

With that he belched and forgave them.

MacGregor had played the piano, then, at Jewell's night-club. Nobody listened. And now Perry had gone back to England for good. Jewell had told him that. Jean the Czech had told him that, too, and that Torgy, the Dane, had borrowed a typewriter and sold it three times before going back to Denmark. Then he took the typewriter with him.

Michael rapped his key against the glass, and the waiter came with a fat wallet to give him tattered change.

He walked, remembering, across the boulevard to the Luxembourg Gardens, then to the Italianate little statue by the goldfish pond. The stone girl lay on her side, beautiful, ideal, still able to cause in him a sad, delightful shiver. Some son of a bitch had thrown a hot dog into the shallow pool, and it floated near its bread, surrounded by an obscene, scummy haze. The fat gold carp ignored it.

The stone girl wore dead leaves; one had landed on her cheek, another lightly touched her breast. It started to rain again, slowly, mistily, as it had on and off for days. The old people on the benches drew their coats a little tighter, but did not get up to go.

He left the Gardens and walked down the long hill to the Seine. The plane trees had been pruned to the bolls and looked like crooked clubs. The buildings leaned backward in the rain, as cold inside as they were out. In the cafés the girls' ankles were bluish with the cold, and the floors were all damp stone, wet tile, as chilling as the street but not so clean.

He remembered that he used to dream at night. He had had happy dreams, victorious dreams. He had quite often been happy for no reason at all. He remembered walking with Eva along the river, running, suddenly jumping up on top of the wall along the river, running, jumping down and over benches, cracking his heels in the air.

He stopped and bought a package of Gauloise Bleus. He used to inhale the smoke that seemed to have particles as big as grains of sand in it, it was so strong. Torgy, who was a sailor, said once that they could always tell when they were approaching the coast of France: they could smell the piss and Gauloises. He pulled one of the lumpy cigarettes out and lit it. It was like trying to inhale something solid, like a golf ball. One more segment of his appetite had gone.

At the bottom of Boul' Mich' he turned toward rue Galande, where Jean the Czech lived. The narrow, crooked little alley of a street dripped and echoed. The concierge was quite impressed by his expensive clothes, and she let him in with no questions. He climbed the last flight to Jean's door in that dark—the timed hall light was always too quick to go out.

Jean let him in and smiled politely. The top button of his shirt was unbuttoned, but he would button it and tighten his tie before he went outside. He always wore a complete set of clothes—vest, tie, hat, coat, everything neatly in place, yet grimy. He buttoned his shirt and tightened the hard knot of his tie.

"You'll come with me," he said. "Some of us are going to Jewell's Club."

"She's not open. . . ."

"No, but she's going to be there. She has the radio. It's disgusting, but we're going to hear the latest excuses from Moscow." Jean's face was bitter, and his long, pointed nose seemed to quiver. Surprisingly, he poured two glasses of white wine.

Michael looked closely at his face and saw the unmistakable signs of too much alcohol—thin red veins in the whites of his eyes, and beneath his eyes, incipient little softenings, he looked a little more like a Frenchman.

"So you drink now," Michael said.

"Why not?" Jean said recklessly.

"You never used to."

"What good is it not to? I am now a Neutralist. Neutralists always drink too much." He sat at his desk and snapped the bottle with his fingernail. "It's not even decent wine."

"It's all right. I used to drink worse."

Jean examined Michael's clothes.

"By the looks of you, you don't now," he said.

"No, I've got some money now."

Jean tossed off the rest of his wine. The reckless gesture did not suit him. Michael had always been aware of Jean's envy in matters such as this. The young Americans usually had an air. They could dress like bums and still not be treated like bums. The police looked at them differently. Jean without his suit, without his tie, without his careful respectability, would be lost among the rest of the Cold War's tidewrack, as inconsequential as one of the cats in Les Halles.

His room was bare, his books were stacked neatly beside his desk. Another icon of his former faith had disappeared: Picasso's dove had come down from the yellow walls.

"Do you remember Eva?" Jean asked.

"Yes. She is in Lyon. . . ."

"Married to a disgusting middle-class who owns a hotel. She now takes money from the *poules* and cleans the bidets."

"It's too bad," Michael said.

"But it's security."

"I'd rather be insecure and not have to clean the bidets," Michael said, although he wondered if this was really true.

"It's easy for an American to say that!" Jean said angrily, then slumped down as if he had just remembered that he was a Neutralist. "I would rather have seen you marry her and take her to America. Why didn't you?"

He thought of Eva, smooth as the stone girl in the Luxembourg Gardens, and lost to him. Her complicated, yet submissive little face, her dark hair—all seemed to be in shadow.

"But you are married," Jean said.

"Oh, yes. I'm married all right. I'm goddam well married."

"I hated you then. I think I still do. Have some more wine and we'll go to Jewell's. She always liked you, God knows why."

"We're both Americans," Michael said. "And besides, she never really believed all that crap you used to have to believe about the Sunday lynchings in Central Park."

"She's a Negro!" Jean said.

"Look, we come from the same town. She just lived farther uptown than I did." Then Michael decided not to do this to Jean. "She always did like me, that's true. She told my fortune once. She doesn't do that for everybody."

A Communist fortune-teller is the only kind, he told her once, who can tell the future according to scientific principles. This did not amuse her. It was one superstition she would not give up.

Jewell liked Eva. It pleased Jewell to see them together—another non-Marxian rudiment like the fortune-telling. Jewell wanted them to be together, and once told him, "Michael, that girl belongs to you, hear? She's a sweet woman, Michael!" And then the huge laugh, and with it the level large eyes, serious, observant, and kind. She often invited them to stay after hours to hear the jam sessions and drink the free liquor.

Jewell's Club was the rage then, and the French and the tourists came to hear the jazz and eat Southern Fried Chicken. Sidney Bechet came to play his soprano sax, and it was popular with Le Jazz Club de France.

"Jewell is broke," Jean said. "Her landlord is kicking her out of the building. They'll probably kick her out of France." He looked hopelessly out the window, where the rain sifted down. "Will they take her back in America?"

"Didn't she give up her citizenship?"

Jean stared at him fiercely. "Yes, but she's no longer a Communist. Oh, don't tell me! You know what they'll do with Jewell? They'll take her out to the middle of the Atlantic and push her overboard. She's drinking now, too," he added.

"All Neutralists drink too much," Michael said.

"You aren't drinking very much."

"I don't know what I am yet."

"You're a lousy American, that's what you are," Jean said.

They walked up Boul' Mich' on the way to Jewell's. The

rain had turned into a fine mist, and Jean had to stop every once in a while to wipe his glasses. Michael waited for him, and then they'd continue.

He remembered one time at Jewell's. Eva had come to live with him just a little while before, and they were always together. She had loved him so damned much. He thought then that he would never tire of such self-effacement, such constant, undemanding love. She would stand behind him even at poker games, never saying a word, one hand lightly on his shoulder—always lightly—as if she didn't quite dare to hold him. And she went to Jewell's with him. Even MacGregor had stayed that night after the jam session. Perry was there, too. All three of them were apolitical, but Jewell liked them. She liked to see Perry eat.

This night after the jam session they listened—Jean, Kris Le Barbus, Jewell, and the rest, to the English-language broadcast from the Warsaw Peace Conference. This was in 1950 or 1951. Henri Varniol was there, too, cleaning up behind the bar. He didn't speak English, and occasionally Jewell would translate for him. Henri had fought in Spain.

The voices of the Americans came across the Iron Curtain, across the battlegrounds, all the way from Warsaw in the distance. He would never forget those honest Midwestern voices. The passion, the belief, the love. . . . Jewell cried silently. *"Humanity!"* the voices cried. *"Love one another!"*

Jewell's big black hand crept to her face, and tears made her wide cheeks shine. She *loved.* The word "humanity" alone could make her cry. They all loved Jewell and she protected them; Jean stared fiercely into the air, killing fascists and klansmen by the hundreds in his mind.

Michael, Perry, and MacGregor were embarrassed for Jewell. They smiled painfully at each other. He remembered the smiles vividly. It was unbearable.

The voices pleaded, "Peace, peace . . ."—voices out of time past, out of the thirties, refusing to give up the dream. One said, "Comrades! Comrades of all lands! I have here in my hand some dirt. It is good dirt, good soil. I smell it, I crumble it in my hand and see that it is good soil. But it is more than soil! It has been anointed by the blood of thousands of men and women who died for freedom! It is the soil of Stalingrad! Soil of the city named for our great leader, where the Red Army fought the Nazis and turned them back, where the spirit of these men will never be forgotten! Our leader will never forget! Our Stalin will lead us on to greater victories! Our comrade Stalin!"

And the music, the hymns to Stalin, until MacGregor could stand it no longer. He jumped out in front of the radio, his awkward, skeletal arms raised, the deadly flush of the tubercular like spots of makeup on his cheeks.

"Jewell!" he yelled. "Look!" And for Henri and Jean he said in his bad French, *"J'ai ici une petite morceau de merde! C'est bonne merde! C'est merde délicieuse! Je mange! C'est la merde de Staline!"*

Henri threw him out into the street. Perry, Michael, and Eva took him home. Jewell hired him back a week later, when he came to her hungry, coughing, already having had one small hemorrhage. Jewell was happy then and forgave everyone.

Jean had stopped again to wipe his glasses.

"When Stalin died, and all that business came out, it was bad enough, but after Hungary she went into mourning," he said. "She wasn't a red-hot mama anymore."

Jewell let them in herself. She had gone all to fat and looked old and tired, her back flat above the buttocks, her belly beyond the help of girdles.

"Michael," she said. "Well, now, boy. How you doin'? Come into my nightclub, Michael." She patted his cheek—a flash of soft, pink palm. Her voice was deep and husky, and she seemed a little drunk. The bar was littered with cigarette ashes and dirty glasses, and the huge clean-up light in the ceiling made naked the small cracks and smudges along the walls, fingerprints and evidences of spilled drinks. The twisted dead neon tubes along the ceiling, that had given cool blue light, looked in the glare of the great bulb like dirty plumbing. The room was much smaller than he remembered it to be.

Kris Le Barbus came up behind, Jewell's glass in his hand. His spats shone.

"I say, old chap, your wife is smashing! Not half I say!" Coming from the depths of his black beard, where his moist red lips hid, the precise little voice seemed quite innocent.

Jewell took her glass away from him.

"Go turn on the radio," she said. Her voice was like coal

rumbling down a chute. "Michael, have a drink on the house. Have some scotch, man. The beer's flatter'n you know what. Kris, turn that radio on." She still wore her funeral dress, now wrinkled and salt-white around the armpits. They took their drinks to a table.

"That's some wife you got there, Michael." Her expression told him nothing at all.

"I guess so," he said.

"Li'l Eva's down to Lyon, I tell you that?"

"Yeah, Jewell, I know."

"Li'l Eva, she married a big spender, Michael. He come in here once last year, she walkin' slightly behind. Shocked, man! Wicked nightlife! Little bourgeois tightwad. He run a short-time joint down there, man. You know—they always got plenty hot water. Somebody told me. You happy, Michael?"

"Not to see you like this, Jewell."

"Don't you never mind Jewell. Kris! Bring me some ice, boy."

From the radio a strident voice said something about counterrevolutionary bandits.

"I don't dig that jazz no more, Michael."

"I never did, Jewell."

"You never got with it, Michael," she said, smiling.

Kris brought a bowl of ice cubes.

"I really must go, Jewell," Kris said. "Perhaps I can come back later on."

"Don't ever try to fool me, Kris. I don't give a damn," Jewell said. Kris looked a little shocked, patted her on the shoulder, and left.

"I dig that Hindu the most," Jewell said. She watched the scotch flow down the ice cubes in her glass, and Michael watched too; her concentrated expression pulled his eyes to the ice as though it were a crystal ball she was examining.

"You happy, Michael? You love your wife?"

"Jewell . . ."

"Now, don't git your water hot, Michael. We been friends a long time. What I mean, not like Jean and MacGregor. Never did care for no apron strings, man. I always liked you 'cause you never needed no *care*. Never had to wipe no puke off your vest, nor listen to you cry, nor put you to bed, thasall."

"That's true, come to think of it," he said.

"Drink up, man!"

The radio voice had changed, had become French. Static came in waves. Jean fiddled with the knobs and the voice faded, then came in clearly: "Capitalism withers . . . a world free from fear, from war . . . *L'humanité* . . ."

Jewell listened for a moment, her face implacable and mean, her big hands clasped together.

"Weasel words, weasel words," she said. "They got a *nerve!* You can take the lousy French, too."

"Where are you going to go, Jewell?"

She looked up at him and smiled. "That's the tough one, Michael. I'm a woman without a country, Michael, singin' those fat, black, homesick blues." She took a little sip of her drink with her big lips, and went on, looking at him and away, then back to him, somewhat apologetically, he thought, as though she knew it was not her role to confide or to confess. "The only Frenchman I ever liked, I loved him. That was Hank Varniol. I come over here in 'forty-seven, I was married to a lieutenant in the U.S. of A. Army, and that prissy, brownnose *loo*-tenant and me, we wasn't compatible. He's more interested in being a captain than he was a man."

Suddenly she drank up the rest of her drink and squeezed an ice cube back into her glass.

"You never was in love with li'l Eva."

"I guess not really."

"Well, man, you sure married yourself a piece of blue eyes and hygiene, Michael. She about sweet enough to eat."

"Did you like her, Jewell?"

"That don't make no never mind."

"You think I should have married Eva? You said so once."

"Look, Michael, I ain't no fortune-teller. I ain't no gypsy palm reader. I been known to been wrong. And when I'm wrong, I'm in *error*. Alls I know is you marry what you want, not what wants you—not if you're a man, anyways. You dint want li'l Eva's all I know. She could been a radiant angel come down from Paradise, it wouldn't of made no difference. I guess you wanted a piece of angle food cake!" She laughed, her head thrown back and her big smooth hands flat on the table.

Jean was still fiddling with the radio, and his head, bent toward the temperamental machine, was bony and sharp on his

stiff neck. There had always been something angular and unforgiving about Jean, but now, without his rigid belief to hold
him together, he no longer seemed all one piece, as though he
had been put together out of children's blocks.

Not so with Jewell. She had taken on her new cynicism with
a good deal of authority, even though it made her unhappy.
She had always played the role of the experienced one who was
willing to tell the facts of life to poor little white boys and girls,
and in this there had always been proper cynicism. But she had
never acted out those principles of self-interest she ascribed to
the world. She had been truly generous and magnanimous.
Impulsively he put his hands across the table upon her big
warm ones. Her eyes opened wide and she stared at his white
hands covering hers.

"Jewell," he said, "how can I help you?"

"You would, too," she said.

"You need money?"

"Git me a passport to Seventh Avenue, Michael. Now with
Hank dead and gone I got no call to stay in France." She began
to inhale sharply, in little gasps that were cut off as if by her
teeth. "No," she said, "I ain't going to cry no more. Cried all last
night and I ain't going to cry no more."

He wrote down the address of his law firm and gave it to
her. "You can reach me there," he said.

He countersigned five twenty-dollar traveler's checks and
gave them to her.

"Michael, honey," she said. "You do mean it, don't you?"

"I never was very impulsive, Jewell. You know that. You
know damned well I mean it."

"Yeah, man. I never thought you could swing."

Then she smiled at him, and as she smiled she turned her
big hands palms up and they enclosed his, so dark and warm
they seemed to enclose his arms all the way to his elbows. He
couldn't follow her. He didn't know what she meant; but she
smiled and smiled, and it was her long white teeth, in the dark
moving expanse of face, that he remembered—fixed landmarks
in that wide, warm darkness.

After he left Jewell he wandered around to old places. He
ate lunch at the Vietnamese restaurant where they'd fed poor
starving Perry, looked into the black hole of a hotel where he'd

lived for a while once, bought the *Paris Review* and tried to read it while sitting at a small *café tabac* in a side street where he might avoid people he had known. But he could not forget Jewell's face. There were the white teeth, and he saw them clearly, but there, also, were the eyes, and they said something bad about him. They judged. As for Jewell, she would find something else to believe in, someone else to love, because she was full of life. She hadn't been thinking about herself, she had been looking straight at Michael, and it was as if she looked upon a dead man.

He was not afraid; he was not even afraid not to be afraid. He had never loved Eva; that was something as wishful upon Jewell's part as her crazy Stalinism, and she knew it. When he had played lover and happy clown, had played nervous, had played mooncalf, always there was inside him something like despair, which is death. And he thought, now, Yes, I know it. There is no meaning to anything. That I poked Phyllis and knocked her up—is that supposed to mean something?

At a quarter to five he walked back toward the Cujas, and arrived on time. They were there. They'd been to the Flea Market, to the top of the Eiffel Tower, to Napoleon's Tomb and other such places. The day before they'd been to the Louvre. Mrs. Krause did all this sightseeing with an interesting combination of attitudes—half dutifully, half apologetically. She knew a lot about things; at home in Des Moines she was the cultural attaché of all her clubs. She also belonged to things like the League of Women Voters. Michael had admired her from the start, although she would insist upon talking to him in a language her husband couldn't follow. Not in French, but in something that might have been called Cultural. "The Existentialists," she would say. "The Existentialists: . . ." (He was always seeing colons in her sentences.) "How does Camus change the meaning of Existentialism? Meurseault and Dr. Rieux: if Dr. Rieux is an Existentialist 'saint,' what is Meurseault?" And so on. She was willing to quote Sartre, too. As far as William Krause was concerned, the word "existential" did not exist. He didn't hear it at all, and when his wife began to speak of such things she might as well have been speaking French. Actually she couldn't speak French; she apologized for this, saying that she'd had Spanish in school (Cornell College, Mount Vernon, Iowa) instead.

When he came into the Cujas the three of them were sitting at a booth in back. Hannah Krause couldn't see it, but her husband had his shoes off, and M. Claude, the *patron,* was amused by this. All three looked a little tired in spite of their fresh clothes and clean faces. When Phyllis looked around and saw him he had to admit to a distinct little shiver of pleasure. Her fur coat was off her shoulders. She wore a beige dress, and her fine shoulders were so straight beneath the cloth, her arms so lithe and well defined.

How pleased William Krause was to see another man he could talk to! He loved his women, but he didn't really talk to them.

"Hey, Mike!" he said, smiling and shoving over, his feet on top of his shoes—they slid over, too. He was drinking beer, while the women were having *apéritifs.* "Have a seat," he said. "What're you having?" He pointed to the *apéritifs.* "It's beer for me. If I had any of that stuff I'd be snockered before the meat course!"

Michael said hello to everybody and sat down next to him, then shook hands with M. Claude, who had come over.

"Doo bear?" William Krause suggested to M. Claude, holding two big fingers up as a help in translation, and at the same time raising his nearly invisible eyebrows at Michael. And he was right, beer was what Michael wanted. A small matter, but in a way a clue to the man's nature; one had to know him for a while before one gave him credit for being right so consistently in small things.

He was a good businessman and, as far as Michael could tell, an honest one. He owned a contracting "outfit," as he called it, and some real estate, including farms in the rich land of central Iowa. He liked to build houses, but especially he liked to build barns. "God, I love barns!" he would say. "I'm just nuts about barns!" Once, on Michael's first visit to Iowa, William Krause had taken him out to one of his tenants' farms. The occasion came about because a horse had sleeping sickness, and the tenant had called, desperate for men to help lift the horse up so that it could be slung upright in its stall. They drove fast, on the narrow Iowa highway, in William Krause's Cadillac, and when they reached the farm four other men, the tenant's neighbors, were there, and the veterinarian. In the dark stall, beneath a single light bulb shaded somewhat by cobwebs, a big brown horse slept upon its knees. The men were trying to put a rope from a block and tackle beneath its brisket, and the only sounds were breath and the voice of the tenant, who kept saying, "Good girl. Come on, girl. Wake up, girl. Get on your feet, girl." William Krause went immediately to the horse and put his hands upon it, the men moving just out of his way. He stepped carefully toward its head, his rich overcoat brushing the brown hair and black mane, lifted the head and felt the horse's eyes.

"She ain't going to get up by herself, Jim," he said to the tenant. "I got another block and tackle in the trunk of my car. You got a canvas tarp? We got to have one at least twelve-ounce."

"Got a eight-by-twelve fifteen-ounce tarp in my pickup," one of the neighbors said, and went out to get it. William Krause tossed his car keys to Michael; by this time he was getting the rope under the brisket. When Michael came back with the surprisingly heavy blocks and rope, back from the night air into the humid, hay- and horse-smelling barn, the vet was putting a huge syringe back into his gladstone bag, and the front part of the horse had been raised a few inches from the sawdust.

Eventually they got the horse off the ground, but it took all their strength, and all their clothes were sweat through before the fifteen-ounce tarp had been slung beneath the horse's belly and over the sides of the stall. Michael's most vivid memory of that night was the picture of William Krause, his overcoat and jacket off, his hands beneath and around the horse's hind legs, her behind pressed against his white shirt and her black tail draped like a cloak over his straining neck and shoulders. The face was red, now, with great effort, and its fat had suddenly changed into hard muscle.

Then it was over, and the horse nodded, its sleepy, running eyes half open, one forefoot doubled over. But it was more or less upon its feet. They all went into the bright, clean milk house, where the tenant, a quiet man about thirty years old, had a bottle of Canadian Club in the milk cooler.

They drank out of white enameled cups, and sat quietly, speaking gently like people in a hospital: "Bill, what's your wife going to say when she sees all that on your nice white shirt?"

"I'll tell her it was a damn fine lady I was helping out, Jim."

"You can say that again."

"What d'you say, Doc?"

"Hard to tell at this stage."

But really they were very happy, and their calm words hummed with it; the fact was simply that they were helping each other, and this happiness, not the ritual drink, was the real payment for all their effort.

Now, in the brightly lighted bar, Michael turned to William Krause and reminded him of that time.

"Did the horse live, Bill?" he asked.

William Krause's face turned genuinely sad for a moment. "No," he said. "About a week later she died."

The Krauses wanted to take them to the Tour d'Argent, a place Michael had of course never visited under the GI Bill, and they began walking down Boul' Mich' toward the Seine. Just before they came to Boulevard Saint-Germain they were coming up behind a little gendarme ("Ain't the cops *small* here!" William Krause murmured to Michael), and just then from around the corner came an Arab boy about fifteen years old—a peanut vendor. Before the boy knew it he was straight up against the gendarme, and Michael had never seen such total fear on any face; suddenly the small, brown, rather withered-looking young face writhed with terror, the eyes bulging and the brownish teeth visible. The gendarme did something like a slow pirouette to the left, and with his white stick pressed the boy against the side of the building. And kept pressing, shoving the end of the stick into the boy's sternum and leaning on it. All this in silence. They could see the boy's tongue.

Michael was not going to stop, but Hannah and William Krause already had, and Phyllis with them. The gendarme sensed their presence and looked around.

"Eh?" he said, his brows rising. Then he looked up at William Krause and said ominously, "*Doucement, doucement, Monsieur.*"

Hannah Krause said in her most blaring tone of voice, "What are you doing to that boy?"

The gendarme smiled, his eyes half closed, and said, "Madame, it is none of your business." Not quite like that; as he said the words he punctuated each with a fierce little shove upon his stick, where it still pinned the boy to the wall. "Madame. Eet. Eeze. None. Of. Your. Beeze *Ness!*" The boy's open, terrified face, like a frieze against the gray stone, never moved.

"We've got to report him," Hannah Krause said, ignoring the gendarme's poisonous look. She added in a practical voice, "Look for a number on him, Bill. Has he got a number on him?"

"My God!" Phyllis said. "Why is he doing that?"

As if in answer the small gendarme, using his club with great speed, suddenly beat the boy down to the pavement. There were sounds like the beating of a carpet. Head, side, back, anywhere. Harder and harder he beat upon the boy, smashing him down and as out of shape as a bundle of old clothes.

"Oh, no!" Phyllis screamed. "He's killing him! He's killing him! Stop it! *Stop it!*" Hannah, too, was crying out loud and moaning, and Michael had to hold Phyllis back. He looked down into her desperate face and saw there horror of himself for holding her back. "Let me go!" she screamed at him. "What's the matter with you?"

He turned, and the gendarme was gone. Only now, of course, could he kneel and look at the bundle on the sidewalk. As in a nightmare he half expected to find there only a bundle of clothes, no flesh inside at all. But as he knelt, two men pushed him aside, picked up the boy and his peanut tray without a sound, without a word, and carried him off. On the sidewalk there was nothing, not a spilled peanut, not a drop of blood. No one else had stopped to watch, although many must have seen it. And now it might never have happened at all.

Only the look in Phyllis's eyes was there.

They moved on, their faces dreamy with horror.

"Cops!" William Krause said finally, and Michael could tell by his voice that he knew of the inadequacy of what he was about to say. "Cops. Big cops, little cops. Mike, did you see that kid's face there? Looked like a bunch of angleworms! By God, I'll tell you one thing, and I ain't just clacking my gums. If I saw that happen in Des Moines I'd *doucement* that son of a bitch, one way or the other."

"But it does happen in Des Moines!" Hannah said. "We've got a report on it, Bill. The League has a report on it."

"Yeah, but they don't do it on the main drag at seven o'clock in the evening, Hannah. They know it ain't the thing to do."

Michael could not get Phyllis to look at him. As they walked down toward the Seine she kept in step with him, but let him know by her quietness and the precision of her steps that she considered herself to be alone.

They found the Tour d'Argent, and rode up the slow elevator to the dining room. Hannah Krause, too, was not satisfied by the way her husband had handled the gendarme, and neither was she satisfied by his complacency about the police of Des Moines. She tried to overlook these things, but Michael could sense her irritation.

After they had looked out of the big windows at the Île they ordered wine and food, then endured with good grace a little lecture by the waiter, who told them that parties who dined at Tour d'Agent did not order four separate entrées. They took his suggestion to have pressed duck.

"It must be goin' slow tonight," William Krause said, and laughed. He was still trying to make them forget what they had seen on the street. His wife and the waiter gave him hard looks.

But Hannah Krause had to say something when William Krause referred to Jewell as a "darky."

"You found that friend of yours, Mike? Who lost her husband? Phyl says she's a darky."

"William Krause," Hannah Krause said evenly.

"What?"

"If you don't know . . ."

"Know what, for God's sake, Hannah? You look like you smelled something bad."

"You don't use that word when you talk about members of the Negro race."

"Hell," he said, smiling at Michael and then looking seriously back at his wife. "You *told* me, Hannah, that there wasn't no Negro race, only the human race."

"*Dad, it's not funny!*" Phyllis said, and they all looked at her quickly because her voice was almost ugly.

William Krause was immediately contrite. "Mike, I never meant to joke about your friend, you know? I didn't mean anything by that word. It's just that I never know when they're going to jump on me with both feet, goddammit!"

From then on he was subdued, although he drank a great deal of wine. Afterwards he insisted that he and Michael take the women back to the hotel and then go have a drink. "I want to have a man-to-man talk with my son-in-law," he said. He was more than a little drunk, and the women decided they had to humor him.

Before they left the women off in the hotel lobby, Michael took Phyllis aside to try to reassure her.

"I'll take care of him," he said. "I'll get him back as soon as possible."

She stared at him, a reevaluating look, cold and intelligent.

"What difference does it make to you?" she said.

"Phyllis," he whispered, and tried to put his arms around her, but she stood rigidly, her arms wrapped around her body so that she was nothing to him but a bulky bundle of fur. She shuddered as he touched her.

"I'll take care to get him back," he said.

"Don't bother," Phyllis said calmly. "Really don't bother yourself."

"Come on, Mike!" William Krause said, and they left the women and walked back across the river and up Boul' Mich'. "Women!" William Krause said. "Women! You can't live with 'em and you can't live without 'em." He strode a little unevenly up the boulevard, and when they came to rue Cujas he found it familiar, so they went into the Cujas and sat at the same booth they'd had earlier.

M. Claude came over, and they shook hands. Michael did an impulsive thing.

"*Deux finalobes*," he said.

"*Finalobe?*" Then M. Claude remembered, and he said, "*Oui! Monsieur MacGregor!*" He smiled sadly. "*Un homme très gentil.*" He shook his head sadly as he went to get the drinks.

"What's that about?" William Krause said.

"A friend of mine used to order brandy and water that way, and Claude remembers. The guy's dead now."

"I'm sorry, Mike."

So was Michael; it seemed such a trite, sentimental thing to have done.

But he did wish himself back there again, back in time. He would, at least, not find himself in the wrong with a woman. Why had Phyllis suddenly turned rigid? It was not only unfair, it was boring, a pain in the ass. Now if it were only four or five years ago he might be sitting in this same booth, the redheaded MacGregor coughing into his sauce, fat Perry doing most of the talking. Eva would be sitting next to Michael, not saying a word, but with her hand lightly upon his thigh beneath the table. He would have no explanations to make to Eva. She was there, so soft, so agreeable, so passive, in whom his manhood never found resistance, in whom he was the only agent of force. Later they would go to Jewell's to hear the Dixieland, that crazy imitation of joy, and to observe Jewell's dangerous political euphoria, half wanting to believe it. (Did he? That was a surprising thought.) Or they might listen to those voices from Warsaw, those eternal American innocents.

"Women!" William Krause said. "I don't envy you, Mike. She's just like her mother, hard-nosed. Half the time Hannah treats me like a goddam imbecile." He looked at Michael, and he was much drunker than Michael had thought. His forehead's translucent skin was pale now, and shiny, and his pale eyes were filmed over, the whites now pink as his cheeks, so that the irises looked as though they were pasted right on skin. "I mean she wants to *improve* me, for Christ's sake, Mike!"

To Michael's embarrassment there were tears in the man's eyes.

"I love that woman, Mike. I love that woman."

That woman, Michael thought. He could see that valuable, dangerous woman's face—both of their faces—and he felt his anger rising. After all, there was absolutely nothing he could have done to protect that Arab boy from the cop. Nothing. If he'd tried to interfere the cop would have beat the boy all the harder, just to show his power. Couldn't Phyllis realize that? He could explain it to her. Explain that he *knew* what the end result of any such interference would be, that he had seen that the human race was made that way and there was nothing the Des Moines Chapter of the League of Women Voters could do to change it. He would explain this to her; he would present this case with all his skill, using the fantastic precision and breadth of his memory for precedents. It was suddenly more important than anything that he win this one case; it was the only case he had ever really cared about.

And yet as he looked across the table at the sad, big man, he was also angry. He had never been in this kind of trouble before; if anything of the sort had ever developed—that a woman, or anyone, claimed worry from him—he had always gone on to somewhere else, to another country, to another kingdom. He could not make himself owe justification to anyone. But now he seemed to be in a trap, and he was frightened because he knew that he had to go back to Phyllis. But not like this; where would he find the energy for it? How could William Krause bring *his* manhood back, intact, to the tall woman who waited to judge him?

"I guess we'd better go home, Mike," William Krause said.

Michael thought: But why should I have to? I will find Eva (with her sleeves rolled up, scouring a chipped bidet in a room of mildewed wallpaper). I will find another Eva, then; there are plenty of Evas around.

"Come on, Mike. Show me the way to go home."

"Okay, Bill," Michael said.

"I'm tired and I want to go to bed," William Krause said, half-singing the words, his eyebrows raised sadly but humorously. "Us old married men got to face the music."

Suddenly Michael despised the man, and as he spoke his voice took on a hard sound he hadn't heard in it for years. "Face the music," he said. Did he see a change in the dull eyes across the table? Yes, maybe there was a glint of answer, hard and wary. But he thought, So what? If the man wants to be a rug, a worm . . . He went on, probing a little: "So we'll crawl back."

But William Krause was not too easily made angry. He said, "I hope we don't have to crawl, Mike. I can still walk, I think." Trying to be funny.

Michael could feel the slightest part of a sneer on his own face—a tightness in his nostrils.

"Have another drink, then," William Krause said, "but I'm afraid I've had it for tonight."

"You've had it," Michael said, and when he looked up at the big man it was like that dream in which you are looking at a painting, a portrait, and suddenly your bowels turn cold because the painted eyes are not really paint, they are deep and real.

"Listen to me, boy," William Krause said in a clear, steady voice. "Don't try to shit on me in any way. You ain't big enough yet." He looked steadily at Michael for a moment, observing him without any worry or fear at all, and Michael knew it. "I ain't crawling back to my wife, but I would if I had to, and it wouldn't make me small."

Suddenly he laughed out loud, reached across the table, and hit Michael playfully on the shoulder. "Mike, let's have another drink! Christ, you can carry me home!"

Michael wanted to answer the man's forgiveness, to recognize his friendship, but he was in that frozen state, compounded of meanness and embarrassment, where he didn't know how to say the words he knew he should say. And it didn't help to know that William Krause knew it all, saw him clear through and pretended that the words of recognition had been spoken.

They did have another drink, paid, and left the Cujas. The air was still damp and cold, and as they started down toward the river William Krause put his big arm around Michael's shoulder for a moment and said, "Hell, Mike. Don't you think she knows why you can't hit a cop?"

"I don't know, Bill."

William Krause laughed. "God bless 'em!" he said, and now he seemed very happy to be going back. He hummed as he walked along, his overcoat open. "Goddam, look at that pot!" he said, patting his middle. "I've plainly got to lose some weight."

"I could never explain it to her," Michael said.

"Sure, sure. You can't explain *nothing* to a woman, Mike. If it gets to the point where you have to explain, you're licked."

When they reached the hotel the elevator had been turned off for the night, and they walked up the narrow stairs, William Krause ahead, his powerful haunches slowly but surely moving, his broad back solid, his brown overcoat hooked over his shoulder by a finger, as a boy does it.

They came to William Krause's door. "Goddam, look at that key," he said, taking the big brass key from his pocket. "It's a deadly weapon. It's a goddam blunt instrument."

"Good night, Bill," Michael said.

"Good luck, Mike." William Krause grinned as he felt around for the keyhole, and Michael went on alone down the dark hall toward his own room, where she would be waiting.

At the door he stopped. By the transom he could see that the light was on, and why should he have to prove himself? Did he really have a case after all? There was the quiet light above the door, waiting, and he must go in. But he paused, and he was afraid. It was as though he were about to be admitted to a mystery he had long postponed, and it would be terribly painful at first. The first plunge, the first breath. He unlocked the door and went in.

There had been the soft implosion of a car door's closing, than a stirring elsewhere in the house. The scene at the window had gone to darkness, though the snow was still so white in the mind's eye that it seemed phosphorescent, the apple trees and the pines soft black upon its diminished glow.

In his memory were the ranks of the dead or of the lost to him—Eva, Jewell, Jean the Czech, Bill and Hannah Krause, his own parents and grandparents. Even his children, because they were no longer children, and lived elsewhere.

He had decided once, long ago, that only in Leah, where he was born, he might find a sense of continuance—as if place could ever work that way. That had been a choice. One always had choices—like the choice of so many of his generation, and the next, and the next, to divorce and move on.

Soon a woman would enter the paneled doorway there, to the right of the fireplace column. What woman would it be, Michael? If his younger half were here, that creature of his blood, what sort of woman would he expect to see in the doorway? He might not be surprised that she would have upon her graceful bones the slight, sure indications of age. He might, however, think it somewhat strange that, given their temperaments, they were still together, the orphan and his wife.

All Trades, Their Tackle and Trim

"Suppose you get shot?" she said.

He just grinned and sat there picking little brownish pieces of Kleenex out of his rifle, from the silvery place where it slid open. It looked clean enough to her, but the Kleenex kept turning brown.

"I should have got some patches, dammit. Hell of a note—Kleenex on a rifle."

"I mean, suppose you get killed?"

"So I get killed. You get the insurance."

"What insurance? Ten thousand dollars? I'm supposed to put your child through college, not to mention grammar and high school, on that?"

"It'll take care of my funeral, anyway," he said.

"If it weren't a GI policy you probably wouldn't have any at all." She knew this wasn't true; somehow he always made her exaggerate, and then he had the advantage.

"Lucky you," he said. *Splick, splack,* went the rifle bolt. "Now I put some clean dirt back on. Cold tomorrow, so I've got to use powdered graphite." His big fingers delicately tapped some black dust out of a little plastic tube.

"I don't care what you use."

"If I used oil the cold might gum it up."

"I hope it does," she said.

He just grinned some more and went on feeling the black metal, smoothing down the barrel with his hands. Then he threw the rifle to his shoulder, sighted, his whole body suddenly tight, and pulled the trigger. *"Blam!"* he said, and she jumped a little bit. Just a slight little jump in her chair, but she knew he saw it.

"I'm using the hundred-and-ten-grain bullet," he said. "It's very light for the thirty-ought-six, so it goes three thousand, four hundred and twenty feet per second, muzzle velocity, which means that in one second it's gone nearly two-thirds of a mile."

"Why should I listen?" she asked.

"Hell, you've got a great imagination. I thought you'd be interested."

"I told you I wasn't," she said. She ought to get up and leave, but she hadn't anyplace to go. She might go up to the bedroom, but what could she do there?

"So I should get mad?" he said.

"You're completely irresponsible," she said. She had the sinking feeling that she'd said this no more than a minute ago. And of course it never worked with him, anyway.

"I just thought you ought to know what'll happen tomorrow when I pull the trigger."

He leaned back in his chair, hefted his rifle with one hand, and looked at it with a satisfied, almost gloating expression. "Mannlicher-Schoenauer—what a little beauty! Sometimes I wonder how it can be so accurate with only a twenty-inch barrel." He was examining a small blemish on its stock. He took the gun up in both hands and rubbed the stock alongside his nose. "You'd be surprised how much good oil you've got on the side of your nose," he said, and she could see where the grain of the stock shone a little brighter.

"Ugh," she said, and he just smiled and went on feeling his rifle. Tomorrow's equipment lay on the table between them— his dark cartridge belt with the leather pouches and loops for shells, his bone-handled knife he so often and so lovingly sharpened on his oilstone, his pistol in its thick leather holster; everything had been smoothed down and softened by his hands.

She felt sometimes that all the things of his life were too perfect and satisfying. All of his possessions had to be of the best quality, and he treated each one with such loving care. With this thought she had a pang of jealousy, which changed at once into anger. She was better than he. She could conceive of what was true and good; yet she could never organize the truth so that it would strike him.

"Kill, kill, kill," she said bitterly.

"I've been known to miss," he said, and this was one of his infuriating tricks—that his ironic modesty disorganized all her plans.

It wasn't that she was alone; among their social equals he was in the minority, with his murderous knives and guns. His main companions were the high school janitor and the mechanic who fixed the machines in the Laundromat, and when they came to the house they were either coming or going, and sat in the kitchen having drinks like bourbon and ginger ale in juice glasses, with their slimy fish or dead birds oozing on the drainboard of the sink. Once they'd brought back a live mallard and put it on the table, where it stood swaying. They said they thought it might live, and it stood there, its beautiful green head calm, its intelligent brown eyes watching. Somewhere beneath its smooth feathers a shotgun pellet had cut some string, some nerve of flight. She'd watched it in horror; with its duck's head, its flat bill, and gaudy color it should have seemed alien, but it did not. It seemed the perfection of intelligence and dignity, and it watched her with unspeakable knowledge. In a few minutes it settled quietly to the table and died. "Oh, that's too bad," he'd said as he stroked the smooth feathers. "What a beautiful bird."

He put his rifle carefully across two place mats and picked his knife out of its sheath. "All I want tomorrow is one tender little buck," he said. "Old Billy can have his big rack he's always talking about. That one I got two years ago, remember? You couldn't cut the gravy."

"I'd think you'd had enough of killing, by now," she said.

"Nope, not yet."

"Why do you want to do it? You must know how it feels to be shot. You've got that ugly little hole in your leg."

"Oh, hell," he said, smiling. "That's nothing. That was a

military bullet. Also, it was pretty well spent. A sporting bullet like this . . ." He undid a pouch on the belt and pushed a shiny brass-and-copper-colored shell out of its loop. "This little copper thing here is the bullet. This little mother would've taken my leg off like a cleaver."

She wondered where she could go not to hear this any longer, but she couldn't think of a place she wanted to go. She'd married him when she was eighteen, and now, at twenty-six, she had begun to think about the world. He didn't seem to mind her League of Women Voters nights, her discussion groups; but why, back then, when she had been so young and vain, had he seemed so perfect, so much more than adequate? He was sandy-colored, strong and big. He was as clean and warm as a great piece of toast. Mild, yet always knowing how to get what he wanted—and that seemed so important in a man.

"A military bullet isn't meant to kill outright," he said. "It's solid, and makes a nice, clean hole. Of course, a certain amount of hydraulic rupture occurs if it's going anywhere near muzzle velocity. But a wounded man's a lot more bother to the enemy than a dead man. It's only logic. You take this bullet, though . . ." He held the shiny brass-and-copper thing upright, and pinched the copper tip as he pointed it at her. "It's meant to kill, so it's quite complicated inside. See this little bit of lead bared at the tip? And see these little splits down the sides, here? These cause it to expand nearly as big as a quarter, and when it does! They developed these things experimenting on gelatin and flesh . . ."

"Oh, God," she said. "Why do you do this?"

"Do what? If you're going to talk about my getting shot, or possibly shooting somebody, you ought to know something about it."

"Oh, you know so much!" she said. "That's what we got when the Mamoulians and the Wilsons were here."

He laughed, and his laugh seemed so innocent she wondered for a moment if it really weren't.

"The Reverend got sort of shook, didn't he?" he said.

She felt her useless anger again. The Reverend Mamoulian, that good man, had turned nervous and pale. For a frightening moment she had been able to see each stub of a whisker on his thin face, and he spilled a little of his martini onto his clean, white fingers. They had been talking in doleful voices about the violence, the dark and hateful side of our society, and the bill to prohibit the sale of mail-order guns, so that no psychotic like Oswald could get hold of one, and *he*'d said that Oswald had used the wrong bullet, and if *he*'d been Oswald he would have got Connally, too, and of course he wouldn't have needed that third shot. That head shot was just goddam lucky.

George Mamoulian had just come back from Arlington, Virginia, where he'd participated in a voter registration drive, and he told them about it in a slightly tremulous voice, as though, right here in her house, he was in the presence of enemies. A man had followed him for blocks, calling him "nigger lover" and every filthy thing. But even as he told them this he was unsure of himself, as though he expected the wrong response. It was a terrible evening, and all because of *him*. He'd sat there, alert and interested, but somehow bigger and firmer and redder than all the rest of them, so that they all felt frail, and their hopes felt frail, too. He'd insisted upon telling them about the fifty million rifles left over from World War II, and how modern ammunition could stay fresh for decades. That law was ridiculous, he'd told them; maybe they ought to work for a law against the Marine Corps; that was where Oswald learned to point a rifle. He didn't seem to mind at all when they were silent, or when Maude Wilson got terribly upset and called his hunting "atavistic." "That's right!" he'd said, pleased. Though she wasn't certain he knew the meaning of the word.

The Mamoulians and the Wilsons left early, and she'd been so sick and angry she didn't speak to him at all that night. He hadn't seemed to notice.

He put his knife back into the sheath and grinned at her. She had married this man. Somehow she had married him, and what could she say? He had never been any different.

He looked at his watch. "Early up tomorrow," he said. "I've got a date at dawn with a husky little buck. Let's go to bed."

"It's only eight-thirty," she said. When she looked up he was grinning at her, and as he came around the table she saw reflected in his straightforward gaze the beauty and value she must once have wanted him to see.

"I'm not your toy," she said as coldly as she could. "I'm not a thing. I've got a mind!"

"You don't think I'd have married an idiot, do you?" he said, and at her waist she felt, even before he reached for her, the warm prints of his admiring hands.

Voices

ON A whim, Richard Adgate's wife, Nora, bought a cordless telephone, which you could supposedly carry seven hundred feet away from its base station inside the house. The idea was that you could take it to the garden, or to the bathroom, or out to the mailbox, and if someone called, there you were.

It hung upon a little white box when it was recharging, with a muted green indicator to say that all was well. But it often made strange yelps and squeaks. "Quippy quippy quippy," it would say all by itself in the dark room. "Queep, queep." When it legitimately rang, it was not a ring at all, but a soft yowl, like a cat one could hear behind the brash, simultaneous ringing of the other two phones in the house—one in the kitchen and one in the bedroom upstairs. Sometimes, when it muttered to itself and he picked it up, he could hear voices that seemed to come from far away: a woman's calm voice saying, "Well, I don't know. Maybe Thursday if the alternator thing gets fixed. Of course Charlie can't because of Lillian." Or another woman, her excited happiness plain: "Isn't it nice? We're going to Rumling, after all these years!" He wanted to ask where Rumling was, and why it was so marvelous, but he couldn't break into the mysterious ordinary flow of those other lives.

After a while they exchanged that phone for another with a different wavelength; the new one only queeped once in a while, and had no other voices. It was on the new one that he received a call from Sun City, Arizona, from one of his mother's nurse's aides, who said that his mother could no longer make out checks for her nursing care. Actually the rules of the Garden Residential Hotel, where she lived, forbade invalids who needed such care, but Joyce, the manager, was kind, and knew his mother's resistance to the idea of a nursing home.

They knew she had broken her leg, and had been in the hospital, and was now back at the Garden, because she had called and told them these things, sounding on the telephone whatever way she decided that she wanted to sound, and evidently she had wanted to sound competent and in control. They didn't know that her fingers no longer had the strength to write, and that the money left her by her husband was quickly running out. The nursing care alone was costing more than a thousand dollars a week.

Richard remembered when his grandmother died, because of his father's silence. Richard had been six or seven years old. He thought his own mother was there, but what he remembered most was darkness on the street in front of the Horton *Herald*. His father's silence that was like darkness. Someone, maybe the Linotype operator, had received the call, and came out to tell his father on the sidewalk before they went into the building. His father and mother owned and edited the *Herald*, a weekly newspaper in what was then a small town just south of the Twin Cities, on the Mississippi River.

There were facts of history, as well as a son's feelings, in his father's great emotion. Her maiden name was Addie Rosetta Doolittle, and she had raised her six children after her husband, Richard's grandfather, Richard Abner Adgate, disappeared in 1914.

Addie, Richard's father said in his obituary notice in the *Herald*, was a small woman, weighing about a hundred pounds. She died at seventy-four on that Mother's Day in 1943 from "heart failure aggravated by whooping cough." A week later, in the next edition of the paper, he wrote a longer piece about her, how she had raised the six children alone. He made no mention of his father's disappearance, saying only that they had "lost" their father in 1914. In his concluding paragraph he wrote, "Humbly I say that her going leaves me with a deeper duty than ever to be worthy of her, to live as she would have me live. May I, despite all mortal weakness, approach somewhat to her fine faith, her quiet gentility, her sincere affection and her unfailing goodness. To be privileged to remember such a mother is in itself a holy treasure. —Dick A. Adgate."

Richard's name was also Richard Abner Adgate, so there were three of them. There was the deserter (or possibly the murdered), the gentle one who was his father, and himself.

Richard's father married Charlotte Clara Clifford in Duluth on February 2, 1936. Richard was born in Duluth that November. His mother's father, John Walter Clifford, was a lawyer, a bitter, difficult man in some ways because he had lost a fortune in real estate by selling too soon. Of course, these things happened before his own memory began to flicker on, noting the blue skies and the white clouds that never appeared in the old photographs, and he couldn't be certain of them because he was told of them by his mother, whose strange way with even the simplest sort of information had always been part of his life.

"Are you going out there?" Nora asked. Of course he had to go to Arizona, and he tried to define the meaning of Nora's question. What was her mood, and why did she ask? Was she being kind or unkind? On the phone with Joyce, the manager, he'd learned that a local retired minister sometimes acted as a "conservator," taking on power of attorney in such cases and writing checks. That might have been possible; his own schedule was frantic and would be for a month or so. But when he called his mother and suggested this arrangement to her she went into a rage. "Keep that *person* away from me!" Richard had witnessed this sort of rage before—the scorched-earth rage that destroyed its host or the world, whichever was possible.

"I don't see how I can not go out there," he said to Nora. "You know I have to go out there."

"I'll make your reservations," Nora said. She didn't like his mother at all, perhaps for good reasons, but she believed in duty. That he didn't want to go, to get on an airplane he couldn't trust or control, she knew, but she would approve of his having to do it. It was his mother, the subject of her, that could not be brought up without tension between them. This was the sympathy, he supposed, of those married for over a quarter of a century, where everything was known, and known again.

The airport limousine was driven too fast—seventy and eighty on the interstate—by a woman driver in a blue uniform. No doubt this speed was planned, part of its scheduling, though illegal. Everyone in the long limousine seemed dazed, as tight with apprehension as he was. On the airplane the narrow seats in narrow rows enclosed them all, and the familiar unnerving engine-surges and the thumps of the landing gear projected his devalued center of consciousness into the anxious stratosphere. He hadn't smoked for two years, but he'd bought a pack of cigarettes in the airport and he smoked, so even that one bit of pride had been frightened out of him.

In Phoenix, after hours of demeaning attention to height and small variations in the plane's engine noises, too many cigarettes and the booze dispensed as anesthesia, he rented a Ford Escort in grayish heat unnatural to September.

In Sun City, or a suburb of it—or perhaps this retirement city was all suburbs with curving, neatly landscaped residential streets—he found the Garden Residential Hotel, a modern building of two stories with no architectural frills. After a short, hot, but not oppressive walk from his air-conditioned car to the Garden's double entrance—an air lock—was the air-conditioned lobby, a breezeless chill where rows of old people, sitting in arranged chairs, watched a giant television screen. Joyce, at her desk, knew who he must be. She was middle-aged, like him, so they were different from the others, and conscious of it—members of a race, or clan, that had a sharper edge of participation in this world. She was crinkly about her bright eyes, with tinted hair.

"She's been overexcited. She thought you'd be here earlier," Joyce said. The hotel had two floors, and he took the elevator up. In the hall, a Mexican-looking janitor said to a maid, laughing, "Now, there's a strong one we could use!" They all smiled, being younger than the citizens of this old, old country.

A heavy, bent woman in the hall leaned on a cane, the kind that had a wrist cuff, resting, looking beyond him.

His mother's door was open, and he went in to find a

plump young woman in white sitting in a chair beside her bed. His mother was not just thin, she had changed into a bird, her nose a beak, her face all beak and black eyes. Brown bruises were on her arms, the empty, discolored skin hanging below the bones. She could not sit up, but her face in its intensity followed him. It was a long time before this new face of hers became at all familiar to him. While she stared, her mouth opening and closing, the plump younger woman said, "I'm Maria. She's been hyperventilating. She thought you'd be here earlier. We told her and told her when your flight was, but we couldn't change her mind." He understood; Maria seemed a little amused by it.

"Dick!" his mother finally said. He kissed a bone on her face and moved back. The room was dark except for a bedside table lamp, the opaque curtains drawn against the day outside.

"She won't look out the window anymore," Maria said.

The world had become this room.

"I've lived long enough," his mother said. She began to try to cough up something, but didn't have the strength. Maria, with a strong brown arm, lifted her up a little and took what she could get in a Kleenex.

Her leg hadn't mended, and the plastic splint didn't fit properly because she'd lost so much weight. A raw sore covered the back of her leg above the ankle.

A thin man in his seventies, chipper but not well shaved beneath the chin, came in and introduced himself as Frank Weeks. "I was a freshie when Charlotte was a senior, at Macalester. But we all knew who Charlotte was!" he said, sitting on the couch and smiling. "I was a philosophy major, so what good did that do me in the world?"

He was going to go on, but the dark dry voice from the bed said, "Frank!" Meaning that he should go, that there was no room here for his prattle about himself. He got up quickly and said, "Oh, I'm sorry, Charlotte. Sorry!" and left.

Joyce came in then, and his mother said, "What do you think of my son?" While Joyce smiled at this unanswerable question, he was reminded of his childhood. It seemed familiar that poor Frank would not be allowed to say his piece, and that she would show off her only son. *Oh, puh! to Frank,* he could hear her say. *He always says the same thing to anybody new.*

Joyce smiled some more, and said, "It's good to see you so

happy, Charlotte." She gave him a quick, serious look that meant, Come and talk to me, and left.

"Joyce *adores* me," his mother said.

With a spoon Maria fed her some of the liquid food supplement that was all she would eat, and gave her a pill about as big as a BB, washed down with a sip of Pepsi-Cola. She couldn't take larger pills because she said they were too big for her to swallow.

While his mother went into an uneasy sleep, and Maria went down to the dining room to eat lunch, he sat in the dim room looking at a worn copy of the *Chippewa,* the 1933 yearbook of Macalester College. All the young faces seemed set in youth forever, though certain other photographs gave him a chill much like remembrance and loss. One was a winter scene of Macalester Avenue, with bare elms and the dead-white sky of all the old photographs. About four inches of snow had fallen, and the street and lawns were white, a single car's wheel tracks faintly seen in the unplowed snow of the broad avenue. To the left, through the trees, was a brick institutional building with tall windows; to the right were white houses with curtained windows through which he seemed to detect warmth and life. A single woman, in a long coat, could be seen walking down the snowy sidewalk half a block away. Beneath the picture were the words "Where we tread, 'tis hallowed ground."

Underneath his mother's senior portrait was the motto "Oh, what is man that thou art mindful of him!" She looked to the left, and had dark short hair and a long neck, though she wasn't tall. She was even-featured and good-looking as all the Cliffords were. In college she was sometimes called "Cliffie." "Here's to Cliffie," wrote one of her classmates, "may she always be as happy as she has always appeared to be. —Pearl Murray." "Charlotte, the girl who always keeps quiet (?). —Harold Hand." "Where there is life there is hope, and you have the life all right. —Kenny Davis." "You little man hater!! Oh, yes. —Velva B. Minty." "A girl of surprises who surprised me into liking her, much against my will. —Meryl." "Charlotte: with all your faults and freckles—I like you. —Hazel Joe."

A critical, or at least ambivalent, note seemed to be intruding into these comments. "I heard a lot about you before I saw you, Cliffie! —Helen." "Dear Charlotte: I am sorry to say you are still on probation. —Ruth."

In the "Senior Alphabet": "C for Clifford who's fond of the boys;/But those who play football make all the big noise." Even if one read between the lines, the jokes, the cartoons, there was an air of invincible innocence and seriousness about the *Chippewa*. One girl could sign her own photograph with this advice: "Remember old Ethics days in Prof. Andy's room. May you always follow his ethical teaching. —Helen May."

When Maria came back, his mother still asleep, he left the dark room with a feeling of relief. From Joyce's desk in the lobby he called the orthopedic doctor. "Her bones are oatmeal," the doctor said. Of course the doctor wouldn't come there to look at the ill-fitting splint; she'd have to go to the hospital, or to his office, in an ambulance, which Joyce told him his mother refused to do. His surge of anger kept him from saying anything more to the orthopedist. He called her other doctor, who said, "There's nothing wrong with her, you know. She has no illness." Because of this she could no longer stay in the hospital on Medicare.

In her mail was a bill for a computed tomography of the upper body, from a corporation run by two doctors who evidently owned the CAT scan. "Sure," Joyce said. "They go through the hospital, find an old woman with a broken tibia, and convince her to sign away a thousand dollars to see if she's got anything wrong with her lungs. That's how they make a living, I guess." Then Joyce looked unhappy, or worried, about what she would have to say next. "It's about funeral arrangements," she said. "I know you'll have to go back East pretty soon. . . ."

He was glad to assure her that the idea didn't throw him. The idea of death. She recommended two funeral homes nearby.

He first went to the hospital to get her wedding rings, cameo locket, and diamond wristwatch, which had been left in the safe there, and saw the Home Care Services nurse who would visit her at the Garden. At the Thunderbird Bank, the officer who was familiar with her financial affairs estimated that she had about three weeks of available money left, at the rate she was spending it. But she would not leave the Garden and go to a nursing home. She liked Maria, and one other nurse's aide who spelled Maria. There was another one she couldn't stand, but who was the only other one available. No, she'd stay at the

Garden, where she knew people, and where Joyce was. "Joyce *adores* me." But actually Joyce was a kind person, kind enough to bend the rules; his mother would accept adoration, but not kindness.

In front of the Tradition Funeral Home, three large young morticians in suits and ties, at 105 degrees Fahrenheit, tried to open the window of his rented Ford Escort, its keys locked inside. The window was open about an inch because he'd found that the air conditioning worked better that way, and a coat hanger, the modern equivalent of haywire, was the tool over which the three pranced and pushed, each with a perfect theory. Richard had his own theories, too, but hesitated to butt in because they liked what they were doing so much.

The object was to reach the window crank and, if it could be cranked, figure out which way it should be cranked. One of the young morticians wanted to try to pluck the keys from the ignition, and was dampened in his spirits when it was pointed out to him that in Ford Escorts a knob on the steering column had to be pulled in order to release the keys. Why, in the name of automobile design, was this so? No one else, in the clamor of his own ideas, would discuss this with the key-theorist, but even he was not unhappy for long. It was a sort of dance they performed, each given a certain amount of time to do his solo with the wire before he had to relinquish it to the next. Meanwhile all three, surely for the first time on that hot, slow day upon a recognizable American street on the edge of the desert, felt useful and excited.

The architectural style of the Tradition Funeral Home was, as near as Richard could define it, Spanish-modern-romantic, a sort of brown, textured adobe with arches, glass panels, and Palladian windows. Inside, it was somber and dignified, with oil paintings of, for instance, Venice, done in the learn-to-paint-on-television style—motel paintings, elaborately framed, quite similar to those in the lobby and halls of the Garden Residential Hotel. And yet the pictures were lively, and did make your eyes move into created worlds with their own depths. He could acknowledge this, although with a kind of aesthetic guilt. In the deep-carpeted, dark-paneled interiors of the building were no obvious religious symbols.

He had spoken earlier with Les, one of the three young

morticians, about his mother's cremation. Her will, which he'd
found among her papers, stated, ". . . no ceremony, no residue." Just like that, in spite of the religiosity she had proclaimed
throughout her life. She had once even published a book of
"family devotions." But toward the end, where she now was, she
made no mention at all of Christ, or of God. So Richard had
conducted his business with Les, learning that there would be a
special box, costing five hundred dollars, a sort of one-time
crucible, among other charges. Since her will stated "no residue," her ashes would be scattered somewhere at their conve-
nience, in the desert, somewhere.

Now, however, at the ceremony of the window crank—it
had been an hour, at least, of discredited theories—Les had an
idea; a coat hanger was too frail for the job at hand, so he went
into the Tradition and returned with one of those conical flower
holders made of wire of a thicker stock, and a pliers, with which
he fashioned an instrument which worked. There were cheers,
triumphant feelings all around. Richard supposed he'd locked
the keys in the car because he was nervous about having to
arrange his mother's disposal, since she was at that moment, he
would find, ordering Joyce and Maria to call the Thunderbird
Bank, the hospital, and the state and local police to find out
where he'd been for so long. Of course, they didn't make those
calls.

When he got back to the Garden, he tried to explain why
he was late from the bank and the hospital, an explanation
containing the necessary lie, but she was exhausted now. "Diamond," she whispered, raising her hand an inch or so before it
fell back. He put the rings on the thin, bluish finger.

The nurse's aide she didn't like was now on duty, a dumb,
kindly woman from Kentucky who worried about the raw sore
on her leg.

"Let's us see it, now," she said in baby talk. Her name was
Anna. "You be a good girl, now, and do what I say, or we'll have
to spank 'ums, won't we?"

A voice from a dry place near death, with something of
that terminal power: "*What? What* did you say?" It seemed to
come right out of unconsciousness, fiercely aware and aimed at
the fool, who in this case ignored it. His mother's power had
waned, now, and her anger dissolved in exhaustion. She let

herself be turned on her side, while sympathy pains flickered over the skin of his legs. She sighed in pain. From the sore? From the cracked eggshell of bone? Oatmeal!

She groaned, and groaning fell into a kind of sleep. He received a glimpse of the sore, which was red and alive, as if it were an organism stronger than its host.

He leaned away, and looked elsewhere in the room. There was the high school graduation photograph of his daughter, smiling too broadly and thus unlike her, her blond hair to her shoulders. And a photograph of his son, whose hair was long then too—another discarded fashion. Now both of them were in their own lives, needing little from him or from Nora.

He remembered hitchhiking with his mother to the Twin Cities—a first hint that she was acting without his father's knowledge. After the Horton *Herald* went broke, she worked for another newspaper. A man where she worked kept saying to her, "Hey, beautiful." "Hey, beautiful," in a way Richard recognized at the age of seven or eight, and she seemed nothing but pleased and flirtatious.

Much later Richard found that she was not the first wife to leave his father, that he had been married just after high school, for about a year, had sent his wife to art school somewhere, and that she never returned.

When he looked through his father's old photographs, few with any information written on their backs, he thought he could pick out this girl, whose name was Jean. A pretty, dark-haired girl with a strong chin, in a sailor blouse, she looked at the camera while his father looked down at her. His chin and jaw were lithe and young, and the way he looked at her, his face seemed almost skinned.

His mother left his father to go to New York with a visiting politician, a candidate for city councilman who was also a professor of political science at a college on Staten Island.

On Richard's first arrival in New York, by train (a man from Travelers' Aid helped him change trains in Chicago), he had with him from Minnesota a large painted turtle in an odoriferous cardboard box. Childhood seemed full of such errors, abetted by adults.

On Sixth Avenue a man parked his car diagonally to the

curb, got out, and took a leak in the gutter. "No one knows him, so why not?" his mother said. "New York's a big town."

It was his mother's idea to drop the turtle off the Staten Island ferry. That was water down there, wasn't it? He knew the difference between salt and fresh water, even though this was the first salt water he'd ever seen, so at ten he was an accomplice in the turtle's death. It fell turning, like a plate.

The Manhattan skyline and the Statue of Liberty looked more or less like their pictures; more vivid was the water's dull green and all the pale condoms limply floating just beneath the surface.

They lived in a ground-floor apartment in a small house, on a street of small houses. Beyond the end of the street was an area of depressed-looking hay and brush, and a burned-out brick building that had evidently been a paint factory; powdered pigments of all colors were in troughs, tubs, vats and in piles all through the long, broken building, where he and his new acquaintances climbed and crawled.

N. P. Carter, "Dr. Carter," because he had a Ph.D., spent most nights with his mother.

"Who's that?" a friend would ask.

"Dr. Carter."

"Is your mother sick?"

A child of convention, as all children are, he was embarrassed, and couldn't get around it because at ten he had no way, no words, to make less of their relationship. Once, at night, seeing the shadow of N. P. Carter's hat passing a window, Richard was half dreaming, and terrified.

N. P. Carter could not speak directly to Richard at all, not a word, but made jokes associated with his embarrassment— sexual insinuations that Richard recognized and didn't think funny. He wondered if N. P. Carter thought he ought to think them funny. A short, prematurely bald man, seven years younger than Richard's mother, he was an unsuccessful professor who would, a few years later, be chosen by his family to rescue the family lumber business in New Hampshire from near-bankruptcy.

She and N. P. Carter often argued and even threw things like plates and glasses, shouting unforgivable things at each other. He listened; nothing like that had happened between his mother and father, so each time seemed a final end to this relationship, and worth his fear. Later, in Leah, New Hampshire, he found a book of N. P. Carter's he'd evidently taken to heart, concerning how a young man should deal with women. Underlined was the advice to marry a woman older than you, because she would always be grateful, faithful, and treat you like a prince. Other advice was on masturbation, in which it said that you only had a certain supply of sperm and prostatic fluid, so you shouldn't waste it. The book was published in 1930.

It was in the small brown living room of the apartment on Staten Island that she told him that she and his father were getting divorced. There was that hollow consideration, hollow as despair, and then the wonder that she could prefer N. P. Carter, a small, humorless, and often violent man, to his calm father, who could smile without irony, and talk to children. He asked her why she preferred N. P. Carter, and she said that he was satisfying. "He's so *satisfying*," she said.

After the election, in which N. P. Carter lost, she taught at a private school in Manhattan. He saw a note written to her by a fellow teacher: *You promised me you'd never mention the World Fellowship business, ever, and then you blabbed it to Davis. You are a lying, backstabbing bitch!* Reading these words, he had a strong twinge of loyalty to his mother, and yet he also understood; in spite of the urge to share thoughts with her, because she was always friendly and receptive, he hadn't told her very much for a long time. She didn't understand about promises not to say things. Even as a child, and in spite of his anger when she betrayed his secrets, he'd begun to think of her as suffering from something beyond judgment, like a defect, or a sickness.

And then, shortly after he'd begun high school, circumstances allowed his abduction to Leah, New Hampshire, a prisoner half willing, half hopeful, aware of the irrational powers of adulthood. N. P. Carter and his mother were married, and they left for New Hampshire in a 1949 Ford, which N. P. Carter drove at eighty-five and ninety miles an hour. Richard sat in the backseat among suitcases, tremendously alert, ready to dive to the floor before the accident. This was before he learned to drive, but he recognized pathology. When near-accidents occurred, his mother would suck in her breath with a hiss, and

N. P. Carter thought this amusing, so he would deliberately steer toward other cars, just enough to evoke the hiss.

The town of Leah with its square and elm trees and white churches, if viewed from certain angles, was as pretty as a scene from Currier and Ives.

The next year, at fifteen, he had an after-school job in Trotevale's clothing store and had saved enough money to at least buy a bus ticket to Minnesota, but he never quite made that decision. His father wrote to him that he was going to school to become a high school teacher, and was pretty hard up, but that if he wanted to come, maybe he could get a job after school and they would do all right. He could read duty in his father's words, and much pain.

When he was sixteen and his mother was working in New Hampshire for the New York *Herald Tribune* Fresh Air Fund, she told him that she'd met a man a lot like his father. "He's so much like Dick it's amazing," she said. She had to tell someone of her adventures, her symptoms, her periods, her aches and ecstasies. "He's tall and sort of shy, like Dick, and he's got Dick's dumb sense of humor."

He thought of N. P. Carter's book, which advised one to marry an older woman.

Leah High School seemed to him an anarchy ruled by the strong and the stupid. Teachers and principals left, were replaced, left again. Certain types of students, in this vacuum, ruled the hallways and the yards. For the three adolescent years he was there, he paid great attention to the terrain ahead and behind him. His mother would sign any excuse he made for not attending, so he skipped school as much as he attended. There were certain advantages in having the sort of mother he had. At seventeen, with her written permission and his great relief, he joined the Navy.

He came back to Leah at the same time N. P. Carter killed himself in the automobile accident that had been inevitable, Richard thought, for all the years. He and a local lawyer took N. P. Carter's portfolio of stocks and bonds to the lawyer's office and a copy of *The New York Times,* added up the quotations, and found that Charlotte Clifford Carter was a comparatively wealthy woman. Until that moment no one had known how well N. P. Carter had done in the lumber business.

Richard went to college, and his mother, at fifty, began a life of affluence, travel, and the buying and selling of houses and apartments in places like Manhattan, Washington, D.C., northern California, New Hampshire, Maryland, Arizona—she lost money on most of them because she sold cheaply when she got the urge to move on, but she seemed to have enough money to lead this sort of life.

When Richard and Nora Barnes, a girl he'd met in college, were married and had children, his mother brought presents, sent presents such as expensive furniture they hadn't room for, arrived always without notice, and soon aggravated Nora beyond her usual pragmatic equanimity. "She won't give me *time* to invite her," Nora said. "Does she own us?" His mother brought to Leah, where they now lived, a young man she'd met at an Arthur Murray Dance Studio, a dance instructor named Stavros whose arms were raw from the abrading operations necessary to remove the tattoos he had decorated himself with in an earlier, less classy life. She had given Stavros a Cadillac convertible, in which they arrived, unannounced, as usual.

When her brother, Joe, visiting, picked up the baby and it gurgled at him, his mother cried a long and soft "Noooooo," which meant that it was wrong, all wrong, because the baby should gurgle and smile only at her. Richard recognized it as the primal long call of jealousy, or more than jealousy. What if she had all the power in the world? With her, every emotion was close to the skin, and always uttered and acted upon.

He tried to reassure Nora by explaining that he understood his mother, or thought he did, and that she was no threat to either of them. His mother didn't own them, couldn't buy them; it was that she believed she controlled the world, and could operate it by charm or by the lies that were her natural language. But Nora would not transmute this smiling dangerous woman into a psychological syndrome, didn't trust her for a minute with a child, and suffered much guilt because of her own chilly behavior.

What his mother did upon arrival was to pick a chair in the living room and surround it with her needs and possessions—Kleenex, pocketbook, pillboxes, discarded pieces of clothing, wrappers—and in this chair she would receive, and give, and watch. She wanted laughter and good feeling, to be the star but also to flatter everyone present and to be flattered back. Any promise, any contract, any moral principle, would be sacrificed for this moment.

He could never, by saying anything about his mother, ease Nora's mind. "She lent us money," Nora said, "so she really does think she owns us."

"No," he said, trying to explain. "She really does think she owns everyone, not just us. She thinks she owns Stavros, too. Well, maybe she does own Stavros."

She'd bought Stavros a business he'd been interested in, a series of ancient popcorn vending machines, the kind with a bare light bulb to keep the popcorn warm, in run-down Washington, D.C., movie houses. The problem was crickets, which liked popcorn and invaded the machines. It was disconcerting to patrons when they felt the frantic soft bodies of crickets in their hands, or mouths.

Stavros soon departed, or was dismissed, and she sold the last house she'd bought and redecorated, and she was off to India, and South America, and Europe, and Hong Kong, and Taiwan. She liked to take passage on Chinese freighters because the crews were so respectful and solicitous.

And she came back, bearing strange gifts; did she think Nora would wear a necklace of polished green stones that weighed, or seemed to weigh, five pounds? The children simply put in their orders for what they wanted, without benefit of Nora's advice or consent. He tried to talk to his mother; it seemed to him normal to try to straighten things out as much as possible. But though he could, by his criticism, make his mother cry and fight back, he could never define for her what Nora couldn't stand. It was impossible, truly. The things she did that were the most aggravating seemed not choices on her part at all, but the inevitable motions of the center of her being. Both children understood this quickly and by themselves; their affection for her was tolerant and slightly wary.

Now while his mother slept, or was dulled by pain and drugs, he went through her papers and bills, trying to put them in order. That evening he left her asleep, with Maria in charge, and found himself in a cheap motel just outside the limits of Sun City, across a broad avenue lined with amazingly tall palm trees. His hanger-on motel didn't have telephones in its rooms, which might or might not have been the reason he didn't call Nora that night.

What if no one ever heard from him again?

The next day his mother was "up," receiving visitors to whom she could show off her son, her faithful son who'd flown all the way from the East to see her. Even the banished Frank Weeks was welcome, provided he didn't try to start a conversation on the side. Four old men and one thin old woman stood around her bed. Their voices seemed young, Midwestern, and hopeful. His mother, whose new bird-face, beaked-face, Richard was becoming used to, gleamed her pleasure at them all. They really did like her. She had the talent, as she'd always had, to make her guests feel the benevolent and exciting importance of her recognitions.

"Well, now, we're going to have a game of bridge," one man said meaningfully to Richard. "But you've got to be sixty or over!" The man, whose name Richard had immediately forgotten, was heavy, and waxy-pale gray in skin and hair and eyes. But his voice had spoken to the world with authority and humor for a lifetime.

His mother begged off from the bridge game, and finally they left, chattering about their leisure, their game, like children going to play.

He thought they seemed nice people, and said so to his mother. But he shouldn't have. "They're idiots," she said. "They're a bunch of children."

Christmases had been particularly horrible, all of them over the years when his mother came and a frigid tension belied the soft colors of the lighted tree, the quiet New Hampshire snow falling past the windows. He hated both women for their irrational female hatred of each other. Their sour looks, their silences painful to him as bellyaches, their taut voices—both, of course, put-upon—were obscene to him, alien to any life of his. It was not his disposition or his fate or his vision of his home and family; it was all wrong, foreign, a story not his own.

There must have been some grave mistake.

It was generally accepted, in his father's family, that the first Richard Abner Adgate had been a deserter, not a victim. If so, something had caused him to run away. He would have been forty-four or forty-five, a relatively young man. No one had ever hinted at another woman. She'd have had to be someone from what was then a fairly small town, and everyone would have known. No, if he ran away, as Richard now wanted to run away from this room, this whole history, he probably ran away unencumbered by the cause of another imprisonment. He just ran.

His mother groaned, and in spite of what he saw, and knew, he couldn't help wonder if she was lying, groaning for witnesses. She said she wanted to die, but had she ever told the truth? It had become his nature to be wary.

Look, he thought in self-disgust, this is an old, old woman near death (probably). No, get away from skepticism unseemly beside this bed of pain. Stop such thoughts. She was a creature worn out by the years, cursed by the real knowledge, perhaps for the first time in her life, that she had little power left. Always the judgments came. He didn't respect her; did he even like her? He should feel the pity and sympathy his deepest beliefs told him any dying animal deserved.

He had an appointment to see a lawyer, one recommended to him by the man at the bank. In order to sign checks for her he would have to have power of attorney, and of course there was her will, and probate, and all that to be taken care of eventually.

When she slept, having been given more of the BB-sized pills, he got out of there, though he was an hour early for his appointment with the lawyer. A form of desertion. He'd have to guide her hand when she came to sign the power of attorney—a strange sort of forgery, the weak hand holding the pen, the hand itself held and powered. Right now, however, he had to get out. Sensitive him.

He stopped first at his motel, and called Nora from the pay phone outside.

"Well, when you didn't call last night," Nora said judgmentally, "I wondered."

"Wondered what?" he said. He didn't want to identify his sudden emotion as self-pity, not at his age.

"This phone's been peeping and chirping like the other one, and I think it's affecting the other phones. I can hear voices sometimes. How's your mother?"

"Not very good."

She was silent, nearly thirty years' worth of dialogue on this subject expressed.

"I'm going to tell her I can only stay until Friday," he said, which would be a lie. Nora, of course, would never have told such a lie no matter the circumstances. This was known. "She's running out of money," he said.

"You know we promised to help Sarah in graduate school."

He had calculated, taking into consideration rent at the Garden, nurse's aides, doctors, drugs, vs. social security and a mortgage she still held on one of her former houses, that in three weeks he would have to start paying out two thousand dollars a month. He would have to sell that mortgage of hers. Actually, he expected her to live another ten years. One of these days she would start eating again, the leg would heal, and so on. Such recoveries had happened to her in the past, and he had no precedent of death. It would mean that his plans to retire early, at sixty, were out the window, as well as his daughter Sarah's projected late entrance to graduate school, which he had actually forgotten about until now.

"I'll just pack her off, pissing and moaning, to the Country Farm," he said. This conversation was becoming irredeemable. This often happened on the telephone, which seemed to bring out the worst in both of them. They both sighed, Nora in a sort of resigned disgust. There were other voices, too, talking away below their sighs. "Yes, of course," he heard clearly, and a music of clear small notes, a distant, atonal xylophone. Then, "Just a second, I'll put him on." Such friendliness. "Hello?"

When he returned from the lawyer's office, with the lawyer's secretary as a witness, and signed with his mother's forceless hand the power of attorney forms, she was "up" again, and fairly cheerful about her hand's weakness.

Richard had to get her and N. P. Carter's social security numbers, and the correct names of her mother and father, for Les at the Tradition. "Your father's name was John Walter Clifford?" he said.

"Yes. John Walter," his mother said proudly, as if John Walter were a character to reckon with. "He was six-foot-three and all legs."

He could pretend that he needed the names and the social security numbers for the power of attorney. He could lie so easily. "And Grandmother's name was Mary Fanny, right?"

"Mary Fanny Lathrop. She was so small and petite. I took after her. The Lathrops were an old, old family. The Reverend Joshua Lathrop came to the Plymouth Colony in 1659. The Adgates, on the other hand, never amounted to much, and your father was such a failure I don't know why I ever married him. He was handsome enough and good at sports, but he just never had any gumption. He got fired from his job with the State of Minnesota. He said his boss didn't like him. Huh!" As Maria settled her leg back down, she gave a dry groan and tried to cough up some mucus. She hadn't the strength to get it up, and her streamlined bird's face poked and pecked, as if she tried to drink the air. Maria helped her sit up, and the recalcitrant mucus was an imagined presence, loopy and grainy in the room.

His father had never said anything critical of her, at least never to him, as if it would not be good for a child to hear anything bad about its mother. That was no doubt what his father thought, and acted upon. He'd died at seventy-one, of an initial and massive heart attack after swimming thirty laps in a YMCA pool, leaving a wife and two other sons, who grieved for him, as did his colleagues and the citizens of the town. Richard had flown out to Minnesota for the services, and the fondness for his father was manifest everywhere. Not grave respect, but fondness.

That evening Joyce had a tray sent up for him and for Maria—another kindness. Before they had their suppers, Maria fed his mother a few spoonfuls of the liquid food supplement, material she took with no interest and then lapsed back into something like sleep. Maria, whom he'd thought so young, was a grandmother. Her husband had a mariachi band, full-time. Her last name was Rodriguez, he found out by asking—no one in Arizona seemed to use last names. It was "Joyce of the Gardens," "Les of the Tradition," "Jerri of Home Care." Except for the doctors, who had only last names. On the medication book on the night table Joyce had written, *If Charlotte should expire, don't call the paramedics, call me and then call Les at the Tradition.*

Expire: she said she wanted to die. It was shameful to think of the expense of her living on, but he did. This was inside, unheard, a lie only in its lack of expression. She, on the other hand, had always said everything that came into her mind, it seemed to him, though everything was twisted by a prior design. In that voice that went back to his infancy, so familiar its character could not be defined except that it contained the warmth of its self-confidence, she had always spoken. What power that voice must have had when she was young, when youth's svelte tensions caused everything to be forgiven. Maybe that was why his father had married her, one of the reasons. He must have had at least some intimation that she, like his first wife, Jean, was not quite a person of "fine faith, quiet gentility, and unfailing goodness." Maybe Addie Rosetta was like that, really. Maybe that was possible. But it seemed to him that what we do in youth, given external beauty, is to mistakenly create the rest. We want a companion, but we need an exotic, our opposite, a mystery, perhaps because it was our common peril and our fate to be born of woman, suckled and wiped and reassured by a woman.

Her bird's head turned to the right, to the left, only the nose having kept its weight of flesh.

"Ah, she's in pain," Maria said, "but I'm not supposed to give her another one for an hour."

The beaked face turned left and right, left and right. "If I had one in my hand I'd give it to her now," he said, and Maria immediately got one out of the drawer.

"You said it, not me," she said, putting the pill into his hand. He gave it to his mother, pushing it into her lips, with a sip of Pepsi-Cola from a paper cup, and they watched her in complicity until she settled down in sleep.

Soon after that he said, "I guess I'd better go. I'll be back in the morning." Maria looked at him and nodded, still in complicity, forgiving his sensitivity, or discomfort, or cowardice— some weakness or other to be forgiven of men.

At his motel he poured himself an inch of bourbon in a bathroom glass, and smoked a cigarette. He supposed this was a lie, too, a lie to his future. He began to formulate the details of the conference on sales, or on something, which he would use as an excuse to go back to New Hampshire. Surrounded by uncomforting lies, he could hear his own voice plausibly explaining to everyone his reasons for leaving. Business, you know. Business, my dears.

In the morning Joyce said, "You know what Maria said to me? She said, 'They *like* each other! He ought to take her home with him.'"

In a special ambulance airplane? They smiled, knowing all the ramifications, a sort of cabal of relative youth.

He told Joyce he'd have to leave tomorrow, wondering if she understood all about that, too. After a silence she said that she would have all of his mother's possessions sent to him . . . afterwards. . . . There were also several cartons in the basement, in storage.

"I'm grateful, for everything," he said.

"Oh, I know how it is," she said. "My mother was in a nursing home. How she hated it! She couldn't afford . . . we couldn't afford . . . we both worked and couldn't care for her."

It was as if Joyce, with her natural sympathy, considered him one of her kind, one of those people who cared without thought, without selfish reservations. He believed there were such natural people in the world—a society from which he was by nature excluded. Not that he didn't do, in the end, whatever had to be done. But it was not natural to him. He was a creature of fears—of flying on commercial airplanes, of disagreements, of heights, of being trapped in small places, of the wounds of others. He was not enough separate from his mother's pain and death, or from any wrong thing she might do. He was afraid of others making fools of themselves, or disgracing themselves. With him it was all fearful duty, but now he had done what, technically, had to be done here, and he would leave this place tomorrow.

He sat at his mother's bedside throughout the day. She had a sister and brother-in-law who had retired to Sun City, but when he suggested that he ought to call them, or see them, her rage was as simple as it had been at the idea of the "conservator," or at her old acquaintance from Macalester. This was her younger sister who, she believed, had looked up to her as a child, and had betrayed her, as Nora had, by not properly adoring her. In her weakness her sudden anger, like the sore on her leg, seemed to have a life more vibrant than her own.

Because he was her only child he had an authority over her he considered fraudulent. "My son," she called him to everyone, and assigned to him superior qualities because of this. He had always been the only one who could tell her to cut it out, that she was wrong, that they were not going to do whatever outrageous thing she wanted everyone to do. He'd told Nora so many times that if you couldn't say no to her you couldn't stay in the same room with her. But Nora could never assume that right.

He made out checks on her checkbook to her doctors, to the morally doubtful CAT scan outfit, to the Garden Residential Hotel, to her nurse's aides, to a pharmacy for drugs and the useless splint—thousands of dollars of the few thousand left from N. P. Carter's fortune.

His mother watched him make out checks for the assorted bills. "If he knew what I've done with his money I'd be in real trouble," she said. She couldn't smile but she could give a quick laugh, more a cough. Maria had gone down to the dining room for her lunch, so they were alone.

"But you married a saint," she said, a hint, a twist in tone implying what she thought of saints. Pretty boring. The "but" implied an alternative—who else but Charlotte Clara Clifford? He heard those ancient voices, forever young: "Where there is life there is hope, and you have the life all right. —Kenny Davis." "Here's to 'Cliffie,' may she always be as happy as she has always appeared to be. —Pearl Murray." Those voices from the thirties, in their twenties. He saw again the ancient photographs of her youth, she smiling a smile collusive with life, willing all possibilities.

"At first Nora liked you a lot," he said. "She thought you were a fascinating woman." Why bring all that up? Wouldn't he ever learn?

"Puh!" she said. If she'd been able to she would have raised her arms and stroked her jewelry, implying superiority over and boredom with that other woman's opinions. He seemed to hear all the voices that had ever asked, minds boggled, *How can you do that? How can you say that?*

He told her that because of a business meeting, an important conference, and so on, he would have to leave tomorrow.

"I want to die," she said, her black eyes on him. "I've lived long enough. It would be best if I died now."

In spite of their long history it seemed strange not to believe such a statement.

For the rest of the day and evening she was partly asleep, then in pain, then asleep again.

When he came the next morning she was, with Anna's help, trying to cope with mucus, and had no time for anything else. There was just not enough force in her percussions of breath. When he said that it was time for him to drive to Phoenix, to the car rental place where they would shuttle him to the airport, he kissed a place beside her fleshy beak and tried to say something to make his desertion more or less official and all right. "Things happen," he said. "Go on going on, you know. To take care of things. . . ."

He thought she signified goodbye. After all, no one could forbid his going. The two figures of the women were occupied as he left, and then, to them, he was of course gone.

Joyce was not at her desk. In the arranged chairs the old people silently watched large movements upon the grainy surface of the oversized television screen.

At the airport in Phoenix he waited an hour and a half for his plane, and on the flight he was more edgy than usual, his anxiety a mix of guilt and superstition somehow based upon ironic justice. The wing of the 727 did its hydraulic metamorphosis for takeoff, and then solidified again for flight. Why did the engine noises change? Why should there be such turbulent shaking of the long tube in a clear desert sky? In place of anxiety he chose real danger—the dry cigarettes left in the squashed pack.

The 727 landed at dusk at Logan Airport, in Boston, and he'd survived.

The next day he called his mother across the time zones. Maria answered, and must have held the phone for her. "Keep those letters coming!" his mother said in a hearty voice. "Did you know my son visited me?"

Maria took the phone and said with some embarrassment, "She's a little confused this morning. Her lungs seem to be clearing up, though, and she took some real food."

"That's a good sign," he said. She would, with the force of life she'd been blessed or cursed with, live forever, beyond sanctions or boundaries, as always. Below their voices, in a wind of faint human syllables, was the xylophonic music of distance.

Two days later Maria called him to say that his mother had "passed away." It had happened on her shift, at 10:20 A.M., mountain time. Maria was so genuinely sorry she seemed, like Joyce, to want to elevate him into the society of the caring.

His relief did not surprise him, only the purity of it. "Thank you, Maria. Thank you for calling," he said in imitation of her sadness, in honor of her feelings.

In the next few days, Les of the Tradition did his work, and the lawyer began his. Joyce called and told him how much the sending on of her possessions would cost, payable to UPS. In the dark room the cordless telephone occasionally queeped. One night he dreamed he answered it. "Dick," his mother said, not strangely, because he knew that tone of worry or of her wanting something. "Dick, I don't know where I *am!*"

If he made any answer to her, to the images of his mother called up by her unchanging voice—youth to middle age, to the final beaked face in the dark room—it was beyond the space the dream allotted.

It was that predawn time when the only light was the faint ghastly blue from the digital clock. His arm was over Nora, her woman's solidity and softness as familiar and as strange as the fact that they had slept in the same bed for over a quarter of a century—he, a man and thus simple to himself, and this other creature in whose life he figured so astoundingly.

Something had been lost long ago, something singular and pure. He lay awake for a long time, until the outer light grew behind the curtains and he knew Nora was awake. She was the only one there, in their bed, in the house where his mother would never again impose herself, to tell about the dream.

"I knew she was dead, but it didn't seem all that strange—you know how dreams are. I just had time to wonder where she was, myself, as if all that energy and ego had to exist somewhere." He meant to make the dream sound curious, and interesting.

"You should have stayed with her," Nora said. "A few more days wouldn't have hurt you that much."

How the truth could betray a mood.

Nora knew that she had startled and hurt him. The circuits between them were manifold, and as alive as nerves. So she turned toward him and offered the comfort of her arms.

There might or might not have been a time when he was singular, and pure, and brave. Perhaps that was the one nostalgia he and his father, unlike their rapscallion namesake, had never acted upon. They knew their very dreams were defined, in ways beyond understanding, by the voices of women.

The Fisherman Who Got Away

RICHARD ADGATE was at Romeo LaVigne's fishing camp on Baie Felicité, Lake Chibougamau, Quebec, with two friends. They were three Americans of middle age, husbands away from their wives and families.

His wife had been unhappy about his coming on this trip, but he'd been working hard, and how often had he ever done anything like go off fishing for a week? He'd asked her this with a defensive stridency she'd of course detected. She, the woman he'd lived with for more than a quarter of a century. He could feel what she felt. She couldn't understand why on earth he'd ever want to escape her, who considered herself fair-minded and good to him. That he wanted to go away with two friends—pretty good friends—why? The children were grown and gone now, and she could easily have come, but she hadn't been asked. How would he like not being asked?

And so it was like that, not something he thought about every minute, but there was an edge, an incompleteness, that made him just slightly oversurprised when on the broad lake a series of ponderous golden boulders as big as houses suddenly appeared beneath his keel when he thought he was in deep water. He didn't want to look down, to have the other world rise up like that to within an arm's reach.

He'd gone out by himself this afternoon in one of Romeo LaVigne's rental boats, a seventeen-foot aluminum square-ended canoe with a rock in the bow for ballast, and a four-horse Evinrude motor. Pete Wallner's boat was a little crowded with three in it, and Joe Porter was getting a divorce and needed conversation, reassurance, or whatever; that was no good with three, either. It seemed unfishermanlike, Joe's constant preoccupation with his problem. Or perhaps it was that a real getting away, a forever getting away, was antithetical to the furlough of a fishing trip. "She" was the word constantly on Joe's lips. "She." Her name was Lois, but it was always "she," and in spite of the immediate unpleasantness, Joe was about to be free of her after all the years. There was a perverse sort of envy in his listeners, too, and Richard could only wonder what it would be like if there were no "she" to make him return, no tether of loyalty and pity and partnership.

In any case, here he was, Richard Adgate, a man no better and no worse in his frailties than other men, he thought, forty-nine years old and quite alone in the suffering of his wife's disapprobation. Her name, empowered by the years, was Nora.

He'd been trolling around a small island a mile or two from Romeo LaVigne's rather shabby log cabins, the only man-caused things in sight except for the Indian camp a couple of hundred yards away from the cabins—log frames with bright red and blue plastic tarps over them. Pete, who had a Lowrance sonar, had told him that the depth dropped to forty feet about fifty yards out from the island, and then to ninety feet ten to twenty yards farther out, so he trolled a medium silver Mooselook Wobbler on lead-core line, with about six colors out, hoping to find that small plateau and not get hung up too often.

The July day was blue, clouds forming always to the southwest, growing, looking dark but not amounting to a rainstorm. The little island was covered by the narrow spruce, virgin spruce less than a foot in diameter, that was the dominant tree everywhere, and so thick you couldn't push your way through them. There were a few birch and a few aspen. Mountain ash was a bush this far north. So far he'd seen a scruffy-looking red fox, a beaver, a sharp-tailed grouse with five or six chicks (the first he'd ever seen), a vole, ravens, unidentified ducks, a kill-deer. This was the boreal forest, chilled and stuntcd most of the year by the polar winds. But in July the air was mild. The lake was warm on the surface, but a foot down it was forty degrees, and the lake trout (*grise* to the French) wcre not very deep.

After a while, no fish taking the silver wobbler, he reeled in, shut off the idling motor, and let the mild wind and little waves tilt him and move him slowly to the northeast, toward a distant, spruce-black shore.

He got his map from his pack and opened it along its folds to where he was, feeling the familiar small shock caused by a map's ideal, formulated authority, its precision reflecting the wide, moving actuality of the lake and the distant, oddly shaped hills. Magnetic north was nearly twenty degrees west of true north here, a knife-sharpening angle. He balanced on his spine in the delicately balanced canoe, above the depths of another inhabited world.

Some of the hills were steep as stairs, cut flat on top; others were rounded like normal hills. None were more than a few hundred feet high, according to his map, yet they had an un-inhabited authority and bulk. In a certain light, like the mild sunlight of this afternoon, a superficial glance made this lake any of the lakes at home, before he noticed that there were no houses, no roads. From certain places outside the bay a buff-colored mine building could be seen, miles to the south, a nar-row tower at least a hundred feet high, though it was difficult to tell at such a distance. On the way in they'd driven through the modern mining and lumbering town of Chibougamau, an is-land itself of neat houses and stores, familiar gas stations, mu-nicipal buildings and even parks, an outpost set in the forest that ran north to tundra and Hudson Bay. Of course, the win-ter here would be like iron, and seem to last forever; no wonder the little town seemed so defensively maintained and civilized. Even Romeo LaVigne, old *voyageur* that he was, and a friend of the Cree, moved back into town when winter came.

To the east, according to his map, was a narrow northward extension of the lake, a passage five or six miles long which opened into a large bay with many islands, where a good-sized river entered, with the symbol for rapids. Lake trout were fine, beautiful fish, but most of his life he'd been a brook trout fisherman, and only occasionally a troller. For him the fish most familiar to his hand, least alien to touch, was the squaretail, the brookie, here called speckled trout or *moucheté*.

There were supposed to be large brook trout in the rivers hereabouts, especially in rapids. But up that long passage, into a place where no one else would be, miles away from anyone— did he really want to go there? Wouldn't those islands loom strangely, and the bottom rise up to startle him? The far bay had a name, Baie Borne; and the river, Rivière Tâche—he didn't know what they meant in French.

Along with his rods and tackle box he had, in his pack, a sandwich, some chocolate, two bottles of Laurentide Ale, and all of the usual outdoors stuff, such as a compass, Band-Aids, nylon line, aspirin, binoculars, safety pins, toilet paper, bug stuff—things gathered over the years. He didn't consider himself fussy or overcautious in these matters. When he went out in a boat he wore a life vest, and when it might rain he wore a broad-brimmed felt hat and took along raingear. It was stupid to suffer the lack of any little thing. On his belt he wore his sheath knife and a pair of Sargent wire-cutter pliers.

He was drifting toward the entrance to the northern passage. He had a full three-gallon tank of gas. Why not go there? Because he was here in northern Quebec in some ridiculous way without permission, and because, for all his years and his knowledge of the water and the woods, there was still within him a small child afraid of the deep and the dark.

In his life he'd never jumped into new things, dangerous things; he'd crept in, somehow, slowly and cautiously, and got to the danger all the same. Not that there could be a real danger here, unless a storm came up, and even then he'd be in no mortal danger. He could always run to shore and wait it out, no matter how long the storm lasted. Even if his motor conked out, broken beyond his ability to fix it, he had a paddle. It would be only time that he could lose. So his friends might worry about him—so what? But it did worry him that they might worry—a small threat of anxiety, a small twinge of that psychic nausea. It all seemed so demeaning he decided he would have to go to the strange bay and the river. He liked to be alone. He did. He was always saying that he did. He started the motor and swung northeast, looking for the passage. Of course, he might go in, and he might not.

The entrance to the passage toward Baie Borne was narrow, full of boulders and with a definite current. He could see that the passage beyond widened and deepened quickly, however, so he throttled down and just made headway as he left the broad lake. He thought of those who explored caves—spelunkers (where did that word come from?) who sometimes crawled into holes so narrow they'd have to bet upon a larger space ahead because they couldn't crawl out backwards. A cowardly thought on a bluebird day. But he got through without touching and went on, at least for now, with dark hills rising on each side.

He didn't know how deep the water might be, but since he edged into this passage at trolling speed he let out the silver wobbler, its long leader, and a couple of colors. One swath on the western hills had been logged, and the greener brush was a wash of light. On top, some birches had been left, their tall trunks against the sky like African trees—a view of Kenya that slowly passed. A small bay opened on his left, and, yes, the map was disconcertingly true again. As he passed the bay's entrance it silently let him by, its farther regions secret, not caring, set for eternity. A heavy cloud to the north, moving away, made his pathway dark.

His rod quivered—a snag or a hit. A fish, he knew as he picked it up, because it moved a little to the side, undulant, like a heartbeat, a small spasm of opinion. He shut off the motor and checked the star drag as he reeled, feeling the caught thing, the line alive between them. A pull from below answered the question of size; it was small, probably a lake trout. It came up against all of its will, no match for his eight-pound leader, the silver three-pronged hook in its flesh somewhere. He would see it soon.

The fish was dark and narrow—a small pike about fourteen inches, hardly a keeper. The brown eyes in the slanted skull saw him. The way to grab a large pike, he'd been told, was to put your thumb and middle finger into its eye sockets, squashing the eyes into the skull: this was supposed to stop their thrashing. He reached down and grabbed this one behind its head, the smooth body a muscle, and forced the tines of the hook down and out, a fragment of white cartilage, broken by a barb, flowing half-loose. His too-strong hands let the small pike go back down. As he let it go he felt a little magnanimous, slightly closer to the vision all fishermen would like to have of themselves someday—a distinguished older man with well-patched waders and a split-bamboo rod, Yeats's fisherman, a "wise and simple man," the paragon of dignified age who is usually observed in the middle distance as he performs each ceremonial fishing rite with understated skill. He always catches a fine brown trout and of course releases it, his sparse gray hackle glowing in the falling light, a tiny hatch, like reversed snow, haloing his old felt hat. Oh, yes, the classic fisherman, his aesthetics honed to the finest moral patina. With age was supposed to come wisdom that was not detachment, mastery that was not boredom, experience that never bred despair.

His canoe moved steadily north through the dark water. He hoped the northern cloud would soon pass and the water would turn a less forbidding blue again. Was he really going to go all the way to the river and its indicated rapids, or not? Looking back, he saw the entrance from the lake had disappeared behind God knew how many hills. That the larger bay and its many islands would come up, inevitably, on map and in real distance, had some of the quality of the sudden boulders that had appeared beneath him in the broad lake.

The motor plugged on smoothly; the long bow moved ahead exactly where he had it go. He might troll, but decided not to because of apprehension about what he might catch. No, not apprehension but because to catch something here might delay him too much. He would catch a Silkie, a monster half fish, half woman, both natures writhing with hatred as they died. He could see in the deep the golden scales on the thighs, the fishbelly-pale shoulders, the inward-turning teeth of a pike. If he trolled he would be mixing exploration, which was perhaps neutral with the gods, with the intent to do harm.

He leaned forward and hefted the gas tank; of course it was still heavy. He could go ten times the map distance with that much gas, and he knew it. If he were at home he would be safe, though deprived of the opportunity to make this lovely, lonely choice. Of course, his wife was home right now, her unhappiness a distant and unsettling power.

Rivière Tâche must be a mile or so farther, with rapids at its mouth, and in some wonderment at his deliberate progress he steered on toward it. Rocks here and there caused tan blushes near the surface of the water, between deep places where to look down was to see, hopefully, nothing but the dark water-gray of depth.

Baie Borne: perhaps *borne* was a cognate—". . . from which no traveler returns." A border? Another land? Across its wide blue he moved, now over sand with patches of weeds here and there, water lilies of some kind with floating round leaves, and then into the positive current from the river. The spruce came nearer on each side, and ahead were rocks and some white water. The southeast wind was at his back, so he shut off the motor, the wind holding him against the current, and got his fly rod out of its tube. In his reel was a sinking line, an old leader, and a tippet he was too lazy or impatient to change. He was always nervous as he strung the leader through the eyelets, but he got the line correctly strung and chose for a fly a medium-sized Gray Ghost. His fingers trembled as he tied his knot and clipped off the tag end. The water was five or six feet deep, the rocks below darker. denser-looking than the boulders out in the bay. His canoe turned in the wind and current, and he tilted the motor up before casting. He would begin here and then go up toward the frothings of white water.

After the first cast, which was only a half-decent cast, in fact a lousy cast, with the leader dropping in a messy coil not ten yards away, he began to strip in his line, worrying only about getting a knot in his leader and not at all about a fish. But the line jerked out straight and his supple pole bent. "My God!" he said. "It's a fish!" He wasn't ready at all, and there was a sense of wrong, of bad timing, as though he'd rather not have a strong fish on just yet, after such a stupid mess of a cast. But the fish was there, whatever it was. He should have changed the tippet; surely more than three pounds had already stretched it out. His nerves went down to the invisible tippet as he let out line, let it out and recovered it. Careful, now! The fish ran up-current, then held for a moment before running down along the far bank, not quite to a snag angled into the water—a complicated dead spruce. He just managed to decrease by tender force the radius of the fish's run down that bank. Then it stopped, and he kept what he hoped was a permissible pressure on it, and then just a little bit more, but he couldn't move it. He was afraid of the sudden emptiness of no connection. "Don't happen," he said. "Don't happen."

He didn't know what kind of fish it was, only that it was big and strong. If it was a brook trout it would be the biggest one he'd ever seen, he was sure of it, a salmon-sized brook trout. It might be a pike, or a large walleye, or a lake whitefish—what else was there here? With one hand he freed his boat net from the paddle: presumptuous to think of netting a fish he couldn't even move. But then the fish came in a little, maybe just a foot or so; the canoe was moving, so it was impossible to tell. But the fish didn't like that, and pulled so hard, so suddenly, he knew the tippet had to break, and for a moment thought it had, a hollow moment, but the fish had come toward him, and now it veered away upstream, the line cutting the surface. He must keep the fish from winding the leader around a rock—just to the limit of what he could do with a three-pound tippet, which was probably good for at least five pounds, except that it was old, so God knew what strength it had. He mustn't get used to its holding.

He had to see this fish. He wanted to own it, to have it. What a will it had, what strength! But the long minutes with his rod quivering, line in and out in desperation, might be too worrying for him. He'd deliberately put himself into a situation in which he felt anxiety. Why had he done that?

Beneath the water the cold muscles fought for life against this fragile extension of his touch. How sickening it must be to be pulled by the invisible—like having a fit, epilepsy, a brain spasm. What did the fish think pulled him so hard, and what part of him said no? He must know the fly itself was too small to have such power; everything he'd ever hunted and eaten told him that, but some force wanted to haul him away from the dark rocks to the ceiling of his world and out of it. Everything smaller than he that moved in his world was food, yet now this small thing he'd tried to eat was overpowering him, little by little, with a constant pressure that felt like death. What else must he know in his neurons, in his lateral canals, and in all the circuits of his perfect body, when he'd lived a life of caution, too, hunter and hunted both?

The wild thing deep in the current was so tenuously bound to him by his skill and desire. . . . By what skill? He was a nervous wreck, trembling and sighing. His line looped at his feet, a coil of it encircling the shank of the paddle. If the fish ran now it would be all over, so he held the rod high and reached down to free the line. The bunched collar of his jacket pushed his hat forward, and because he hadn't thought to fasten the chin strap a gust blew his hat overboard. He reached for it and nearly shipped water, came upright again, and noticed that his tackle box, weighted by the open tray, had dumped lures and eyelets and split shot and all kinds of necessary little objects into the bilge. His hat floated away; the coil of line was still around the paddle. He saw but didn't feel on his line the fish as it came to the surface of the water in a quick, inturning swirl. It was black on its back, deep in the body, spotted, with a flash of orange at the fins; every memory, every known subtlety of shape and behavior, said trout, said eight to ten pounds, the fish of his life that would make this moment, for better or for worse, forever a brilliant window of memory.

He did clear the line from the paddle, and miraculously the fish was still on. He hauled in line as the fish came straight at him. He'd meant to get a multiplying reel and make it left-handed, so he could reel all this line in—why hadn't he done that? Why hadn't he done that long ago, as Ray Bergman had suggested in his book? The stripped line slopped half in and half out of the boat, some of it among his spilled lures so that he'd probably have a bloody Christmas tree of ornaments on it when it came up again.

Something shoved him hard in the back—a mean, hurtful sort of shove; the canoe had drifted into the bank, and it was a dead spruce stub that wanted to push him onto his face. The fish moved upstream again, well out from the bank, thank God. If he could just get hold of the paddle, or even that nasty stub, and push himself away from the bank. He couldn't see why the fish was still on. It could just run away if it wanted—take out his line and all his backing and easily snap the tippet. Of course, the next thing the wise and skillful fisherman would do would be to capsize the boat.

Where was his hat? Over by a sandbar, beached by the wind. He could get it later, if there was going to be a later. His arms seemed to be pushing as well as pulling—pushing against his tendency to pull too hard—and were getting tired. He must keep the fish working against the pitifully small pressure he dared use. He knew he was never going to possess this fish, because it was too good, too beautiful, for the stupid, incompetent likes of Richard Adgate.

For a long time the fish hung into the current. He managed to reach the paddle and to push away from the hostile bank—at least for the moment, though the canoe turned perversely in the current and wind as if it, too, had an opinion about the outcome.

He had time to think that he was not enjoying any of this. His hopes were ridiculous; whatever gods of luck there were had chosen him for their sport.

Yet the fish fought for its life, and did Richard Adgate want to kill to have? He *had* to kill in order to have—a soft hesitation immediately gone banished as too stupid to consider. Just a sickish little echo of a feeling was left, and what did it matter anyway? If only he hadn't been so impatient, and had put on a new leader, maybe six to eight pounds; this was no little midsummer trout brook in New Hampshire. What all this showed was a major flaw in his character, the story of his life. *Unprepared* was his motto.

But the fish stayed on. The wind had been coming up, blowing the canoe up into the current, but at least near the center of the river. Though he'd been turning and turning, he began to see a pattern in the fish's runs; it liked a certain oval area of water and never went to either bank or to the dead spruce. Maybe bigger monsters lurked there and kept it away, although what of its own element might frighten a fish this large he didn't want to think about. Maybe the fish was as stupid as he was, but you didn't get that large by being stupid.

Time passed, and passed, his arms aching, his nervousness institutionalized, or solidified, a sort of seismic temblor in the seat of pain. He had a vaguely hopeful theory that the longer he kept the fish from its fish-business, the weaker it would have to become. Sure, just think of salmonids as weaklings.

He found himself guiding, turning, touching the living fish but thinking of other things. He wondered if he would ever be brave enough to camp out alone here, say on one of the small islands in this bay, alone in the dark night. Could he endure the blackness of that night, the silence of it, when even in broad daylight he was unnerved by the strange coves of a small bay seen in passing?

A rose-white slab glinted over there on the surface—a large fish rolled, and it was his fish, on its side for a moment, its tail giving a tired-looking scull or two before it sank down again.

Then there were a few pulls, weaker shakes of the head, weak though irritated: what *is* this thing pulling on me all the time? And he thought all at once that he might actually bring the fish to the side of the canoe. Maybe. It had been on more than half an hour, now, probably because of his caution, or his cowardice.

The fish came, slowly. When it first saw the canoe, it ran, but not far, and he gently snubbed its run and turned it again. If he startled it too much it would simply run away from him, because it was not really as weak as it seemed. Nothing was as it seemed. With the rod in his left hand, the line snubbed with his fingers, he sneakily got the big boat net handy, then went back to his gentle urging, turning, and soon the fish was next to the canoe. With desperate strength he took the net and scooped it up and into the canoe amidst all the spilled and tangled gear and line and who cared what? He was on his knees, his hands over the net and his fish. What teeth it had! It was a brook trout all right, but changed by size into something oceanic, jaws like forearms, gill covers like saucers.

The Gray Ghost was deep in its tongue, the tippet not even in existence any longer. His metal stringer was in the mess in the bottom of the boat, and he clipped one hanger through the trout's lower jaw and another around a thwart into the chain—of course he would never trust it in the water. As if it understood, the trout wrestled itself out of his grasp, into the air, then came down thrashing on the mess of lures, eyelets, spoons, net, line, sinkers, flies, reel-grease tubes, spinners, hooks, split rings—all the picky little toys and trinkets a fisherman collects.

And it was all right. He could sit back, drift where he would, and look at the sky, which he did for a while. Then he paddled over to the sandbar and retrieved his hat, his good old felt Digger hat that had protected him from so many storms. Good old hat!

He took his De-liar from his fly-fishing vest and measured the fish: twenty-eight inches, eight and a half pounds. The beautiful great fish trembled, dying as it must, as it must. And with that flicker of sadness, "as cold and passionate as the dawn," the world changed for him. It was seven o'clock on this subarctic afternoon, a crisp southeast wind raising a few whitecaps on Baie Borne, the bluest of waters. He pulled the canoe up on the sand and carefully cleaned everything up, put everything away, sponged out all water and slime, made everything shipshape and Bristol fashion.

On his way back through the long passage he headed into the wind, his bow pounding across the larger waves, a Laurentide Ale in his hand. There lay the trout, monstrous, outsized, beyond dreaming of. Who cared that it was nothing he deserved, that because of his clownish errors he should have lost it six times? The knowledge of his fear and awkwardness would only heighten memory. All the rest of his life he would see the pure and desolate bay and the pulse of incoming river, its turbulence meeting the blue water. The black density of the spruce, on island and hill, grew vividly into the past.

But what if he'd lost this fish? Would the shadows fall across these hills in tones of lead? Maybe, but the great fish hadn't got away. That alternate fate was past and gone, as were so many alternates, large and small, to the course of his own life. No matter now; he was brought back, for better or for worse, along a line as sure and fragile as his own.

The Old Dancers

THE YOUNG couples always saw them dancing at the Blue Moon—Wilma and Harvey Lake. She was in her late forties and he was at least sixty. They seemed to enjoy themselves so much. That was what the young couples said: "How they enjoy themselves!" They'd say this fondly, as though Wilma and Harvey, who dressed so carefully in fashions a little too young for them, were somehow old, precocious children, who imitated pleasures not rightly theirs. Wilma's dark hair was dyed, of course, but she groomed herself so well. She'd had only one child by her first husband, and so her figure wasn't bad for her age.

"Why shouldn't they have their fling?" the young couples said; but "fling" was not the right word. Even in their pride the young people knew it wasn't quite the word; the old dancers skimmed across the floor, their faces serene.

Harvey had started as a butcher for Swift & Co., although he was now in business for himself, and Wilma was still the secretary, bookkeeper, and receptionist at the Public Service Co. After they were married she sold her house, and they lived in Harvey's house on School Street. The house was a little too big for just the two of them, but in the storage loft above the garage, in the long attic, and in the unused bedrooms were the

225

dusty remains of their former marriages. Boxes of photographs, sheaves of old fuel bills, children's dolls, model airplanes with broken empennages, high chairs with spoon-chipped trays, bureaus with drawers full of folded clothes, sleds whose runners bore the rust of years ago—they left these relics alone. Each had lived too long in a house of shouting and tears, and now they were careful of each other, careful about such things as nakedness, and the shutting of doors.

"Wilma," Harvey said to the woman who sat beside him in the dim light. It was intermission, and they had walked out on the moving boards to the bench on the floating end of the boat dock. Rowboats nudged each other with wooden sounds, and voices came over the water from the Blue Moon.

"Harvey," she answered.

"Are you chilly?"

"No. It's too warm a night," she said.

"Let me put my jacket over your shoulders."

"No, dear. My scarf is enough." She arranged her blue chiffon scarf, a wisp as insubstantial as breath. He smoothed it across her shoulders, over the crisp fabric of her dress, feeling the slight roundness of age. It flashed across his mind only as security for him. She was so much younger than he; sometimes he didn't want her to be as beautiful as she was.

When he had first become aware of her as a woman, rather than as someone's child, he was an old buck of thirty, dragged down by payments and three children and a wife whose red hands never left the terrible labor of housework. One Saturday night he went with a friend who was interested in basketball to the high school game, and he sat again in the stands, a place he hadn't seen in more than ten years. The kids who yelled and sighed at the progress of the game seemed shadows of himself; he sat with due bills in his wallet, and in his mind the weight of his family in a house down the street, where his wife stood over her ironing board.

Wilma was a cheerleader, and when she jumped her T-shirt rose three or four inches above the waistband of her skirt, exposing just for a moment at the height of her leap white skin so smooth he had to shiver. He had to acknowledge her beauty then, her soft black hair and green eyes, and the way she moved as though she could never tire. Throughout the game he watched her, the delicate way she smoothed her skirt as she turned after a cheer, then sat so lightly on the cheerleaders' bench, her whole body so weightless, yet charged with expectation as she followed the game.

But he had never been so foolish as to fall in love with the unattainable, or even the difficult to obtain. His life had been a series of practical decisions, most of which seemed shortly afterward to have been wrong.

He did not forget her; he followed her life without ever having to ask a question. How she married at nineteen and had a child a few months later. He knew that it was not really his business.

At home he would respond in kind to his wife's complaints. That they were legitimate made them unbearable. He took to buying a six-pack or two every night, or a pint, and once in a rage threw all the living-room furniture out onto the front lawn. When he was forty he stopped drinking, but his wife and daughters had by then given him up entirely, and treated him with all the care they might have shown a grenade: if he was quiet, they were satisfied.

His daughters married as soon as they could, and one February his wife developed a fever of 106 degrees. He took her to Northlee Hospital, and she died that same night. No part of her, they told him, was not full of infection. It was a general septicemia. They couldn't reduce her fever in time, and she burned out like a match. He rarely saw his daughters after that.

When Swift & Co. closed down the plant in Leah, he rented the building and started his own freezer-locker service. In four years he owned the building, and sold not only meat but home freezers, refrigerators, stoves, and washing machines. He did little but work, and when he was fifty-five he found almost to his surprise that he was fairly well off. That was the year Wilma's husband, drunk at ten o'clock on a Sunday morning, drove his car straight into the side of a moving Boston & Maine streamliner at the foot of Water Street and was killed.

In their relationship that was the year when it all began. They loved to remember how it all started with them, how shy and yet direct they could afford to be with each other.

Now, with the floating dock moving beneath them, they looked across Cascom Lake to the eastern shore, a mile away, where cabin lights shone out through the black woods.

Wilma laughed. "Do you remember?" she said.

Of course he remembered; whatever it was made her so happy could not have happened more than five years ago. It pleased him to hear her make gentle fun of him, to tell him how she had waited and waited for him to change the subject of their conversations. He had taken to stopping in at the lobby of the Public Service Co., at first only when he paid his electric bills, then often, to talk about her son in the Navy, or anything else he could think of beforehand, and she'd answered him as though she liked to talk to him. One time it was near her lunch hour, and she invited him to lunch with her at the Leah Inn. It was a fancy place, a dressy place.

She was one of those women who, even though they've married a ne'er-do-well, keep themselves up. She had always been the main support of her home, had kept up the house and dressed her son. When her husband worked, he kept his money back from her, and finally she never bothered to ask for any of it. It was actually her car, paid for by her, he'd wrecked when he killed himself. To see her at her desk at the Public Service Co., so neatly dressed, so cheerfully civilized, no one would have suspected that at home she was often afraid for her life, and that her attempts to have a living room with some effect of graciousness, with pictures on the walls, nice lamps and end tables, and a piano, quite often ended in broken glass and splintered wood. Like Harvey's daughters, her son had escaped as soon as he found a way.

"I'd always watched you with half an eye," Harvey said. "I remember everything because I wasn't doing anything else but work."

"Remember when I invited you to the inn?" she said.

"I'd never been a customer there," he said. "They were always *my* customer."

When she brought him in from the hard sunlight of the street, into the darkness of the inn, it struck him as magic to be suddenly in the intimate dark where their voices could be heard only by each other, though they were in a wide room. Right at noon, in the middle of Leah, a door opened and closed and it was night.

"You had a chicken-salad sandwich," he said. "I didn't know what to have."

"You were very distinguished-looking," she said.

"You told me that then, and when I went home that night, I looked in the bathroom mirror."

"You became positively vain."

He laughed, and then said, taking hold of her hand, "Your hand's cold. The intermission's nearly over. Should we go in?"

They got up and walked, holding hands as they crossed the tippy boards, back toward the Blue Moon. The band had already started to play a fast number—a gallo. They didn't care; sometimes they sat out the fast ones. At the entrance to the ballroom they were not asked to show proof they had paid. All the others had to put their hand under the black light, to show the luminescent stamp of admission, but Wilma and Harvey were always remembered.

After the gallo the little five-piece band played an old fox-trot, "Sweet Eloise," and Harvey took Wilma lightly by the waist. From the revolving globe suspended in the center of the ballroom, steady little flecks of light, in all colors, turned across the dancers, across the walls, and back up through their orbits, where they were lost, found, lost across the high roof rafters. So smoothly they danced. She was there before him, yet was never there in the space into which he moved. He hadn't been a natural dancer, and she had taught him everything. It was a duty that had changed, as he learned, into a terribly precarious pleasure, as though he danced along a tightrope a hundred feet above the ground. He had always thought of his body as a dull thing, heavy and stodgy, although he had admired lightness and grace in others.

"Can you make a plow horse into a trotter?" he'd asked her once. This was in the year of their courtship. He had wanted to take her out, but didn't know where to take her.

"I love to dance," she said. "At home I dance by myself."

He snorted, and laughed ruefully. "I never even danced in school! Sometimes I went to dances, but I just sat there like a lump."

She asked him to dinner at her house, and after dinner she put some records on her phonograph, and began to teach him to dance. It was so strange for him; he thought there must be something wrong, something sinful and ridiculous for Harvey Lake, a rigid old man with false teeth and heavy shoes, to be holding this bright, soft woman in his arms. Her fragrance. His

memories of her as a lovely child; the police should come and
lead him away.

His dead wife had never been so feminine and full of color.
He had married her because it was easy, and because she was
nice enough. He had never been led to expect frivolity or en-
chantment from a woman—that was the stuff of movies, not of
his life. He did remember with mild sadness that his wife once
had smooth arms and was young. She seemed persecuted, always persecuted, used up in menial service until her arms, her
face, her clothes—everything about her turned darker. If it was
his fault, the solution had been so far beyond his understanding
he could not find himself guilty. He would come home and cry
out to his family that he had worked. "I worked all day! I
earned money! I worked!" The faces of his daughters and the
face of his wife became one face, impoverished and secretive.

After the set of fox-trots, Wilma suggested that they sit out
the next set, which would be more modern and violent. So they
walked down onto the dock again, and sat on the farthest bench,
with the black water rising in little mounds against the sides of
the moored rowboats, yet never staining their white strakes.

"I felt awfully tired all of a sudden," she said.

He put his hands on hers and felt her tremble.

"Are you all right? Are you cold?"

"No, no, dear. I'm fine. It's so warm tonight."

"Maybe you're coming down with something. I ought to
take you home and put you to bed." Her hands had stopped
trembling, but his worry died slowly.

"The water must be so warm," she said. "The wind's so
warm coming across the lake."

"Look at all the stars," he said. As he looked up, the stars
were so clearly separate from one another he had the sense of
space, knowing there was no down or up out there in that
magnitude, and he might fall straight up out of the world forever, through the vast indifference of the universe.

"The water seems so deep," she said. "It seems as deep as
forever. It's like a coverlet. You can't see into it, but you can feel
it, so deep."

His first inclination was to reassure her, to tell her that the
water wasn't all that deep right here, maybe only about three
feet. But he was wiser than that, and didn't say it.

*   *   *

After they had seen much of each other for six months, and he had been sure she was seeing no one else, he had asked her if she would consider marriage. He was aware that she had spoken all around this question, as though her words were little scissors that had snipped away each possible doubt in his mind as to her answer. Even so, when her answer came, nothing had been taken from its force, and he was full of joy and gratitude. It was like a stab in his chest. An old man, he kept thinking then. An old man with rust on the back of his hands, to be given that answer.

His house was in a quieter part of town, so they sold her house and used part of the money to redecorate. Two things he gave her, a small upright piano that cost two thousand dollars, and what he considered his best inspiration: a large bathroom and dressing room just for her, with indirect lighting and real tile, plenty of storage space and deep cabinets. He wanted no traffic jams in those places where they must go to repair, where they must deal alone with the ugly things. At his work he sometimes helped with the butchering, although he had a butcher and a salesman working for him, and he had to come home sometimes in soiled clothes, with blood under his fingernails. At work he peeled meat from bone; at home he treated his aging body with lotions and ointments. And so did Wilma. Being a woman, she tried to hold on to her youth more than he ever thought of doing. She needed more time and privacy than he.

The moon was about to rise from behind the hills across the dark lake. From the casino came the diminished, short blares of horns, the high pings of the vibraharp, and the stamp of a foot that was louder than all the other noises. A girl laughed suddenly on the balcony, and the parts of her laughter seemed to fly out over their heads like night birds that had called and then flown silently over.

Wilma trembled so much, all at once, that she couldn't pretend to him that it was nothing.

"I'm not cold," she said.

"But you had an ague. I could feel it!"

"Yes. I don't know what it was."

She was lying, and it frightened him.

"You're coming down with something, and I'm going to

take you home." As he stood up, the dock moved sluggishly, and water sloshed, with a metal noise, inside one of the floating drums. She was so much younger than he, he hadn't thought of her ever being in real danger, but at that moment he remembered his wife's death, and for the first time thought of Wilma in that context. It was true that they were both women, and mortal, and that what he needed could be taken away from him as easily as what he hadn't seemed to need.

With Wilma's hand on his arm they walked down the dock and stepped to the sand, where, if she didn't step light on her toes, her tiny heels would sink out of sight. She laughed for no apparent reason, and squeezed his arm.

"It's nothing," she said. "You're so concerned."

He wouldn't be put out of his seriousness. "You wait here, and I'll get the car." He didn't want her to have to step over the beer cans in the parking lot, or to hear the coarse laughter. Once they had heard a girl crying in the backseat of an old car, and the brutal purr of a man.

He drove the big car down the boat-launching road to where she waited, then got out and went around to open the door for her. This ritual of the door was one he had initiated, and they both smiled at it. They had so many little formalities that gave them pleasure; their lives passed in little gifts and rituals. What they had never done before in their lives they invented, or imitated from the movies—her straightening his tie before they went out, his hand beneath her elbow at a step.

They drove home in their big black Chrysler Imperial, the radio playing softly from both speakers, the powerful headlights making the road ahead brighter than daylight, as though the trees and turns were painted white. Below the windshield, behind glass so clear it seemed not to be there, the great orb of dials glowed.

He wanted to make plans for putting her to bed, with something hot to drink; he tried to remember what his wife had done when her children might have been coming down with something, but he had never really joined in that activity. His wife had done it all. Before he had time to think of something, they were home. Wilma got out quickly and went into the kitchen. He closed the garage doors and went inside, expecting to find her; she wasn't there, or in the dining room or living room. She must have gone straight upstairs, but he heard no water running in the pipes.

She wasn't in any of the bedrooms, yet he heard no noise from her bathroom, and saw no light beneath the door. He had been turning on all the lights; he didn't want to call her, hoping that nothing was strange. He tapped on her bathroom door, then tried the handle, and it was locked.

"Wilma?" he said into the smooth surface of the door. No answer.

"Wilma?"

"Oh, oh," she said from within.

She was in there, in the dark. He couldn't understand, and tried to keep himself from theories. He did not want to go inside. His palms were wet because of the strangeness of it, and his pulse knocked dryly in his throat. He had chosen the locking knobs for the door, and knew how to open them; in the center of the outer knob was a little hole, and he needed something like a nail, or a big pin, or an ice pick to insert into the hole. Desperately he looked around the room. He didn't want to take the time to go down to the kitchen, where he would be sure to find something suitable. But then he remembered that often, in the morning, he would see on Wilma's pillow little black metal things as long as a kitchen match. Little bobby pins, made of crimped metal with their tips dipped in plastic. He found several in the drawer of her night table, took one, and bent it apart as he came back to the door. It worked; a little click and the knob turned. He brushed on the silent light switch as he went inside. Black into soft color, blues of towels, orange-buff garter snaps hung from a clothes bar. Wilma sat at her dressing table, still in her dancing dress, and he saw her back and the back of her black head, yet at the same time her face, open, white; green eyes stared back from the mirror, the green growing wider in her eyes as her pupils shrank into dots.

"What's the matter? What's the matter?"

She didn't answer him. Her face was surrounded by black hair, as though she looked out of darkness.

"Wilma?"

"I've got something wrong with me," she said.

He had nothing to say. He was all dry inside, in his mouth

and in his throat. Finally he heard his own harsh voice: "Where?"

Wilma just shook her head, as if to say, What does it matter? "I'm probably dying," she said.

"Why do you say that?" He stepped forward as though to touch her, and she drew back from him. She was trembling all over. Her shoulders shook, then stopped shaking, then shook again.

"How do you know?" he said. "Have you been to the doctor? Have you had an examination?"

"Oh, I know, I know," she said.

"Wilma!"

She shook her head.

"What do you think is wrong with you?"

"What do you think?" She tried to smile. "The worst thing there is."

"That isn't something you can tell by yourself."

"At our age," she said. "The symptoms. I have a list."

"We'll go to the doctor," he said.

"No!" She really meant it.

"You've got to go to the doctor to find out."

"No. I won't be examined. I won't be looked at. I don't have to."

"How will you ever find out for certain?"

"It doesn't matter. There's nothing they can do anyway."

"Symptoms can be for anything," he said. "What symptoms? You can't tell by yourself."

She shook her head. "Inside me," she said in a small voice, and pulled her knees together. "I didn't want to tell you, but sometimes I get scared and I can't stop shaking."

"Tomorrow I'm taking you to a doctor."

She looked at him closely, squinting out of her mirror at him. In her fingers she kneaded a Kleenex—narrow red fingers, with her rings loose and twinkling, and the tissue pulped, with streaks of black mascara on it.

He felt that it would be wrong for him to plead or argue any longer; he couldn't afford to waste the strength of his position by using up his words. Although he could argue with her, and in the arguing feel that he had a point to make, he knew that he must delay his arguments, and go through the terrible fright he could feel waiting in his body. He had to face that while she was not in front of him, and then he could make his plans. He must be careful with her now.

Then things began to go his way; she slipped off her rings and opened a small jar of cream.

"We'll talk after we've changed," he said. She nodded without looking at him.

He shut the door as he left, and stood quietly on the bedroom carpet, listening to see if she would lock the door again. In his pocket he squeezed the slippery bobby pin.

He went to his bathroom, took off his jacket and shirt, and washed himself, his face moving in the mirror but not quite looked at. He never looked at himself very much, and he felt that if she were gone, it would be as if he were no longer seen at all; he would be invisible. He could not help considering the possibility that she might die, and his fear was so great he was nauseated, and his stomach hurt badly. What part of his life would be left without her? His mouth opened and he saw his false gums.

No. She didn't know what was wrong with her.

He put on a fresh shirt and the scarlet smoking jacket she had given him, and went downstairs to wait for her. The possibility of her death was like a lens through which he saw their home. She had done everything. The white drapes across the front windows, the low davenport in a dark pattern flecked with gold, the deep carpet. Her piano. The marble coffee table, the tall, warm lamps on the end tables. The console phonograph with the little ivory Buddha on top of it, next to the ti plant in a terra-cotta bowl. All these things had meaning only because of her, that he see her among them. Without her the lamps would never be turned on, the piano and the phonograph would be forever silent, the ti plant would die of thirst. The very light would grow yellow and dusty, soiled like the lobby of a cheap hotel.

No. He would be strong with her. For her own good he would take over, and make her see a doctor.

When she came downstairs, she had put on a pair of gold-colored slacks and a sweater, and wore a white silk kerchief around her neck, its flossy ends gaily floating over her shoulder. She came over to him and kissed him.

"I don't want you to worry. It's all in my mind," she said. "Let's forget it." And so they didn't mention it again. They played honeymoon bridge while the phonograph played a stack of records, and his remembering of it came in waves, faded out so that he was happy, then came back with a force that twisted in his stomach. He hadn't lost his resolve. He would make her go to the doctor.

On Sunday they didn't mention it, but on Monday he made an appointment for her to see a doctor. When he picked her up after work, he told her he had made the appointment, and that she was to see the doctor in an hour. She didn't answer, so he started the car and drove toward home. He thought, I don't care what she says or what she does, she's going to see the doctor. When they got home, she went upstairs without a word to him, and after fifteen minutes he went up after her.

He spoke to the closed door of her bathroom. "Wilma?"

As if in answer she sloshed some water around in the bathtub. He thought she wouldn't answer, and so he said again, "Wilma?" But as he said it, she said something he didn't catch, and he had to ask her what she'd said. The water splashed.

The water calmed; he thought of a woman's body in a bathtub, suddenly immobile, and the water moving silently up and down her skin as she breathed.

"You already made the appointment," she said. Her voice was hard because of echoes, and cold. "You're forcing me to go."

"Yes," he said. The water began to run out of the tub. "It won't do any harm to find out," he said, louder, so she would hear it over the sounds of water.

"You knew I'd have to go."

"I knew you wouldn't break the appointment," he said. "Not keep it after it was made."

"Don't be too sure," she said in a voice he wasn't sure of—did she mean she would go this time, or not?

"I'm not sure of anything," he said. "Wilma?"

"What?"

"I'm scared, that's why I had to do it. I'm scared of you being sick. Thinking you've got cancer. You probably haven't got it. I was reading in *Reader's Digest* . . ."

"I read that."

"Well?" he said. Then she came out, wrapped in a bright robe, and put her hand along his face just for a second. Sweet, humid air enveloped him. She went to a closet for a dress.

"I'll be down in a few minutes," she said, and he went back downstairs to wait for her.

When she came down, they went to the car without a word. He took her to the doctor's office and sat alone in the waiting room while she was inside. He thought, Now what will I have to do? She has gone to the doctor. He tried to look at magazines, but they all seemed to be for children, or they were thick as catalogues, and his eyes could never settle anywhere in them, as though he were responsible for turning every single page.

After a long time Wilma came out. She seemed not to see him; her face was disorganized, abstracted. Her eyes were deep—they seemed to have receded into her eye hollows, so that he noticed wrinkles and brown skin. The white collar of her dress was just slightly askew. When he touched her arm, she pulled away from him, and when he looked straight into her face it seemed full of cracks, like cracks in a mirror.

"Come on home," he said.

"Yes," she said.

"Did he find out what's the matter?"

She shivered, skittishly drew her arm away from his hand. "He examined me," she said, her voice growing deep.

At home they had a light supper, which she prepared. She tried not to seem preoccupied with her visit to the doctor, but he read the silences, and after supper he asked again what the doctor had found.

"He said I probably didn't have cancer. That's what he *said*, but what else could he say? He took a smear. They have to look at it in Northlee Hospital. A Pap test. I don't believe anything he said. You remember Norma Walker? She used to have that little beauty parlor in her house? He never told her. Her sister knew, and she told me, but they never told Norma. They don't tell the one that's got it."

She got up from the table and walked quickly into the kitchen, then back. She was trembling, but when he got up to comfort her, she moved away from him, hugging herself with her own arms. He felt old and weak; he could think of nothing to do for her.

"They can't cure it," she said. "They just let the air to it."

"Sometimes they do," he said. "They do cure it. But how do you know that's what you've got? Wait till the test comes back, anyway."

"They can't do anything, really. I don't think they know very much. I've know of cases, and heard about cases. You have to do everything yourself." She looked at him seriously—a shrewd expression, as though she'd just figured it all out. "You can't let them get ahead of you. You have to do everything yourself. Everything."

"Well, suppose you needed a little operation. Could you do it yourself?"

"I'm the one to say I need such a thing, that's what I mean. I'm not an animal! Ugh!" She shuddered again.

"In a way you're an animal," he said, he thought reasonably.

"I don't care about that part of me!" she said. "I've been treated like an animal. Oh, haven't I been treated like an animal! I've been thrown down, and knocked down . . ."

"That's different," he said. "I know about . . ."

But she ran over to him and put her arms around him. "I'm so sorry," she said. "Oh, Harvey! I don't want to think about it. You're so kind to me. I love you so much. Do you love me? I'm talking too much because I'm frightened about everything. In a minute I'll stop talking about it. I don't mind when you touch me—I don't care what you do to me, you're so kind."

"Yes, I love you," he said.

"Did you love your first wife?" she said.

"I don't think so. I don't think I ever did. It was all sort of practical. I don't think I ever even told her I loved her."

"You didn't!"

"No, I don't think so."

"My God! Why did you marry her?"

"I got her pregnant. And besides, I couldn't think of anybody else."

"I loved my husband. I really did, at first. He did terrible things to me."

"We know all this," he said. "Let's not talk about those times."

"Yes. They're ugly. Ugly."

He thought, Yes, they were ugly. He once knocked his wife down on the kitchen floor. It was Harvey Lake, age thirty-eight or so, didn't like something she said and knocked her down flat on her back on the linoleum, right out there in the kitchen, on the linoleum rug that had been peeled up before the new vinyl tile could be laid down.

He led Wilma into the living room and they sat together on the davenport. She let him comfort her.

"Would you like something?" he asked. "Some coffee? Some hot chocolate?"

"There's some wine. Let's have a glass of wine."

He went out to the sideboard and poured two glasses of the white port they drank occasionally, and later they watched television—one of the few shows they enjoyed, *The Arthur Murray Party,* where the people danced and were happy. When they saw a new step they tried it, too, along with the graceful dancers on the television.

The next morning, after he let Wilma off at the Public Service Co., he called the doctor.

"I don't think it's much," the doctor said. "We'll know more when the Pap test is back, of course. But to me it looks like a cystocele. That's a hernia of the bladder. Not too much to fix. The bladder herniates into the vagina, which gives a certain amount of discomfort."

The doctor was young; his voice was brash and know-it-all. Wilma probably didn't like him. Harvey, too, was a little shocked by his matter-of-factness. As though he were talking about a machine.

"She needs an operation?" he asked.

"Ought to have it fixed," the doctor said. "A week, ten days in the hospital at the most." The doctor was probably busy; he seemed impatient. "I told your wife all this yesterday."

"Thank you, Doctor," Harvey said.

That evening while Wilma was getting supper, the phone rang, and Harvey answered it. It was the young doctor, and he said, "I thought you'd want to know the test was negative. There's just the repair that ought to be done. Now, I can schedule her at Northlee next week. Say Tuesday?"

"You'd better let me talk to my wife," Harvey said. "Can I call you back?"

"Not tonight. Call me tomorrow morning." The doctor seemed slightly disgusted at such unreasonable delay.

"All right. Thank you, Doctor."

He went out to the kitchen, came up behind Wilma, and put his arms around her. His hands were shaking.

"That was the doctor. The test was negative. You don't have cancer," he said.

She jumped, and put her hands over her face. Then she retrieved her paring knife and the potato she had dropped into the sink. She said in a cool voice, "But I have to have an operation."

"Yes," he said eagerly. "A week or ten days in the hospital at the most. A little repair is all. That's what he said."

"Repair," she said thoughtfully.

"Well, it's nothing too serious. You've been in the hospital before."

"Only when I had my baby."

"You've been lucky. Anyway, he wants to schedule you for next Tuesday. I'm to call him in the morning."

"I'll have to think about it," she said.

"What's there to think about? It's not really a serious thing."

"I'll have to think about it. Don't force me again."

She hadn't turned to look at him, and he decided not to press her. She knew the facts; what more could he do? What could he tell her now? He had trouble getting a breath, and he stood there helpless, fascinated by her skill with the paring knife. She delicately peeled the potato in a spiral, so that the skin descended into the sink unbroken, like a little spring.

That night he lay in the dark, his lips slippery and loose over his empty gums. He had never been a man to risk very much. He had never even played poker, and for the talent of risk he had substituted hard work and an honesty that was uncommon, even somewhat cowardly, that had at times lost him money. He had been eager to let the facts speak for themselves.

For the rest of the week Wilma was moody, and he could understand that. One meal she'd eat too much, and the next, nothing but a mouthful. Sometimes she looked as though she'd been crying, but he never saw her cry. He'd catch her staring off into a corner, or at something a mile away through the wall. And the next moment she would be happy again, as though she had forgotten all about it.

On Saturday she wanted to go dancing, as they usually did, and he thought it a good idea, if she was up to it; it would take her mind off what she must decide.

"How do you feel?" he asked her.

"Fine, really," she said, but a shadow crossed her face.

That night she wore an orange dress made of crisp, luminescent material, and he wore a sport jacket with a loud check in it, and a black bow tie. They always conferred about what they would wear. She sat close to him as they cruised toward the lake in the big car, and he wished the lake were a hundred miles away through the warm night, on smooth, deserted roads through tall pines. But soon they would arrive at the Blue Moon, where they would debark and be seen, and again he would dance as lightly as he could, using all his skill to smooth the way for her. How he worked to be adequate for her! Each step was a danger, but each step would also be a triumph.

They were welcomed, though not spoken to; the manager of the Blue Moon smiled at them and didn't stamp their wrists with fluorescent ink as he did all the others. The young couples noticed them, too, with expressions almost like ownership.

The band played a waltz as they came in, perhaps just for them, and they swung together around the floor in time with the revolving crystal globe, so that for moments the same diamond of blue light touched Wilma's hair, then moved on to be replaced by other colors. She was smiling, and he felt like a magician who must, by wiles almost beyond his powers, protect her forgetfulness.

As the dance ended, an ugly sound came from one corner of the ballroom. Hardly definable, it was half thump, half breath, and the room grew tense all at once. Everyone turned to look into the dark corner, and Wilma's fingers tightened on Harvey's arm. It was a fight, now stopped, but two young men still postured, one held back by others. A girl walked too quickly through the dancers, her hips awkward, fright causing her heels to strike the floor.

The manager came to the band's microphone and said gaily, "Folks, there's going to be a dividend! You're such a nice crowd! A Paul Jones!" There was something heroic in his false smile; like most managers who want to please, he was despised. Yet he was obeyed with tolerant humor. The band drowned out his last words, leaving him to bob his head, his mouth open.

The circle formed and began to rotate, men clockwise, women counterclockwise, hand to hand, dip and smile. Through Harvey's hand passed the cold and warm hands of women and girls, and each face noted, with stolidity or apprehension, his age and condition. When the music stopped and began again, his partner was a solid young woman who grasped him firmly around the neck and wanted to lead, as though she had danced before only with girls or young brothers. Her smooth white neck was strong, and the movements of her back or hips had nothing to do with him; he could never modify her moves by any pressure or direction. He felt frail and brittle, and he made constant missteps that embarrassed him, and made him feel like a fool. The muscular young woman never seemed to notice. When the music stopped again, he left the circle and stepped into the darkness in order to wipe his face with his handkerchief. His mouth was dry and gritty, as if sand had blown into it.

He had assumed that Wilma was dancing, and at first didn't mind that he couldn't see her orange dress turning on the dance floor. But when she didn't appear right away, he began to wonder if she, too, had left the circle, and he looked carefully all around the room for her, as far as he could see into the dark corners where there were benches. No, she was not there. And she was not out on the balcony, getting a breath of fresh air. She must have gone to the ladies' room. Of course; yet he felt deserted, left alone with all the young animals as strong and ruthless as the one he had danced with, who had no words for him.

He looked once more, to be certain, walking awkwardly around the edges of the whirling dancers, trying to keep out of their way. He felt that if they touched him they would knock him down and break his bones. Wilma was not there, and so he went back to wait near the door to the ladies' room.

She did not come out. The door opened and swung shut, but never to reveal the warm orange of her dress. Other women went in and out, and girls who seemed too young even to be out dancing, and all of them worthless to him. When he grew desperate he stopped one of them.

"Pardon me," he said as quickly as he could, "did you see my wife in there? An orange dress. She's wearing an orange dress."

"Huh?" the girl said, and he saw with despair that she hadn't understood a word, not a word of his question.

"A bright orange dress. My wife." He pointed toward the ladies' room. "Did you see her in there?"

The girl shook her head and moved away.

Wilma might have gone to the car. Perhaps she hadn't felt well, all of a sudden, and had gone to the car. He walked quickly down the stairs and out into the cool air, yearning to see a flash of orange; he would open the car door, and he planned to find her there. But the car was empty.

From the ballroom above him came the shuffle of feet, and the music that seemed discordant, disorganized. The noise of the dancing came down to him through the soft bundles of the pines, into the dark where he stood. He began to walk around the casino, looking into corners and shadows, and once he thought he saw her, but it was a girl in a darker-colored dress, leaning against the wall being sick. She looked at him with dull eyes, and moved deeper into the shadows.

As he came around again to the main entrance he looked down to the dark lake and was struck by fear. He ran across the gravel and through the soft sand, to the wet sand that was harder, then stumbled as he reached the boat dock. He caught himself before he fell, but the desperate exertion caused him sharp pain in his chest. The boards moved beneath his thin shoes, and because he was dizzy and had trouble getting his breath he walked carefully down the center of the dock.

She was there; he saw orange out in the dark, just a gleam of it. For a moment he thought the orange darker, redder than her dress. He walked and walked—the dock seemed miles long; she had never come out here alone before.

She sat quietly on the wooden bench as though nothing strange had happened. They might have had an appointment to meet there, she was so still. He had been terribly frightened, and now that he had found her he felt in himself the possibility of anger. He sat down heavily beside her, trying to keep his harsh breath silent.

After a while she said, "I'm sorry."

His anger moved inside him with the promise of uncontrolled pleasure and release.

"The water's so deep," she said.

She had frightened him half to death, and it was all so ridiculous and unnecessary. He could turn to her and show her the face of anger, tell her the water was about three feet deep at the most, and not to be a goddam fool. Maybe her irrationality needed something like a fist, not this sissified tactfulness, Harvey Lake dressed like a gigolo, a Fancy Dan in a bow tie, smelling of a woman's perfume. It was all unmanly, a dream from which you awakened in shame.

But even though it wasn't deep, the lake was dark enough, the moored boats nudging each other like indifferent animals.

Carefully he arranged his voice. "Do you feel like dancing?" he asked.

Ancient Furies

CHARLIE JOHNSON, newly promoted to associate professor of English, with tenure, sat among his murmurous colleagues in the small modern auditorium. It was late May, and except for certain rituals, this faculty meeting one of them, the academic year was over. Charlie had come in late, but not so late as Felix Tuolemi, who appeared at the side door where everyone could see him, all thick and musty-looking, in a brown suit, an old man of sixty with patchy fringes of gray hair. The dean had already brought the meeting to order, the minutes of the last meeting had been accepted and passed, and the dean now called upon Professor Stone (History), who made the yearly motion recommending the graduating seniors for their appropriate degrees, provided all requirements had been met. The motion was seconded and passed while Felix, staring angrily through his glasses, searched for and found Charlie. He came over and sat down ponderously into a plush seat, little moist sighs and creaks coming from him here and there as if he were some sort of ancient, leaky engine. He smelled a little sour, like old leather.

"You must come to my office after. I have something to show you," Felix whispered.

Charlie didn't know Felix very well. He'd played chess with him three times, once in the faculty lounge and twice in the living room at Felix's lodging house, never winning. But lately Felix had conferred upon Charlie, perhaps because of his promotion, more power than Charlie wanted. Felix taught Russian, though he wasn't Russian, he was some kind of a Balt— Lithuanian, with an Estonian (or was it Polish?) mother, and he'd been in Poland during the Second World War. Charlie hadn't tried very hard to get it all straight. What he did have to know was that Felix hated the new chairman, or chairperson as they were now called, of German and Russian, a German with a name hard to visualize in print, a one-syllable name that contained eight letters and sounded like a collision—Brautsch. Dr. Jurgen Brautsch had been brought into the college by the dean, who had presumably consulted with the other members of Felix's department, but not with Felix, who was in any case untenured and probably not even on "tenure track." Felix had taught at the university for three years, though he didn't have a doctorate or its equivalent in publications.

The meeting was soon over, nearly everyone smiling with relief and the self-critical academic irony Charlie always thought a little fraudulent. The two hundred or so members of the faculty of Liberal Arts who had come to the meeting began to leave the subterranean, or at least windowless, room with its long slant of soft orange seats. This was one of the modern parts of the campus, so different from the plain painted spaces of the old English and Languages building. Administrators worked in buildings of this decor, dating from the boom of the sixties. Here all was acoustics, soft fabrics and bright colors, polished aluminum statues one was not supposed to find representational, and Silex coffee machines with Styrofoam cups and Swedish stainless-steel spoons. By contrast, Moorhouse, the English and Languages building, was built in 1923, and during much of the long winters the terrazzo floors were damp with tracked-in slush in which students' dogs trotted about stiff-legged, with worried expressions, smelling everyone at the knee.

"Well?" Felix said. There was a little V in his W, but Charlie couldn't say exactly what Felix's accent was. Its foreignness seemed to come less from its taint of other languages than from other times.

As they got up to leave, Felix half-lunged forward and stopped, keeping Charlie back with an elbow. "There he is!" he very audibly whispered.

Dr. Jurgen Brautsch was with one of his department members, a young German who was so blond he seemed a little transparent. Brautsch himself was about Felix's age, but tall and lean, carefully dressed according to a code Charlie found unfamiliar but authoritative. Charlie affected Gokey boots and corduroy dungarees, and to him Brautsch's cuticles and linen always seemed too immaculate. German, in his mind, meant this sort of cleanliness. He had never been to Germany, but all the Germans he'd met seemed wealthy, groomed, a little intimidating, as if they were always prepared for some high ceremonial moment.

Then there was Felix, also European, whose tarnished skin seemed swollen and battered. To look at his face was like picking out an expression in a stone, or on the head of a cabbage—there was the mouth, there was the nose, and then the whole face. Not quite that disorganized, but tufts of hair had been missed in deep cracks, and gray mesh screened each nostril. " 'The Hun,' " Felix said, " 'is either at your throat or at your feet.' Said by Winston Churchill."

When Brautsch and his colleague had left the auditorium, Felix went ahead. For a moment Charlie thought of fading off in another direction, but instead he followed Felix across the campus, where the new grass and yellow-green leaves spoke of summer freedom. For the month of June, until summer school began, he, Margie, and Charlie Jr. would have her parents' cabin on Cascom Lake, tall pines all around and waves splashing the polished stones. Margie was happy there, with a proprietary, maintenance-doing attitude toward her childhood place. She would be busy staining shingles and mowing grass, fixing cracked panes, alert for carpenter ants, collecting the confetti and pellet leavings of white-footed mice. He would fix the dock and roll it on its old iron hayrake wheels into the dark water. From the dock he and Charlie Jr., who was five, would catch perch and bass, even an occasional squaretail trout. The cabin was on the rocky east side of the lake, so the mornings were dark beneath the pines, but the evenings were long and warm, with the sun and its afterlight glancing from the lake like a searchlight up into the heavy trees, turning the old cabin orange and then a long fall through the spectrum into dark.

He could do his work there or here, and though he did enjoy that month, it was Margie who looked forward to it each spring.

When they reached Moorhouse, which was named after a man with white sideburns whose portrait half-smiled across the lobby at the main doors, Felix hurried heavily down a long dim hallway to his office. They saw no one; early summer was at the windows and the building smelled stale and abandoned. Felix ushered him into his office, switched on the fluorescent ceiling bar, and looked up and down the hallway before shutting the door. In the small office, enclosed with the old man and the paranoia that Felix's age made pitiful and perhaps legitimate, Charlie felt claustrophobic. He wanted, at least, to be closer to the door than Felix, but Felix made him sit at the desk while he unlocked his filing cabinet, brought out a gray metal box, unlocked that, and took from it a formal-looking black plastic folder, which he placed carefully and dramatically in front of Charlie.

"Read," he said, and moved back to lean against the door. On the first page the winged swastika was unmistakable, but the words were in German. Ten years before, Charlie had passed, by the skin of his teeth, a reading examination in German. "I'm afraid my German isn't that great," he said.

"See the lightning bolts," Felix said, pointing. The back of his thick hand was shiny and freckled with dark spots. "SS—the German runes. You know what it means, *Schutzstaffel?* See the date."

The date Felix pointed to was August 1944.

"Well, that's the year I was born," Charlie said.

"Oh, my God! I'm telling you, this Brautsch— Look here." Felix turned the page. "Look, the name."

There, among many names in what was a biographical listing of some kind, was J. Brautsch, who had published a scholarly-sounding article about Schopenhauer.

"So?" Charlie said.

"This is published in the journal of the Wewelsburg SS Order Castle, these Nazi lies about Schopenhauer. I have read such *Dreck*. This J. Brautsch was an SS officer, an *Obersturmführer*, and now this same J. Brautsch, this strutting Nazi swine, claims he was merely Oberleutnant Brautsch of the Wehrmacht, just a simple soldier, you understand!"

"Well, even if it was him, Felix. For Christ's sake, it was thirty-five years ago."

"You are old enough to shoot Jews and Poles when you are twenty-five years of age."

"Yeah, but if this is the same Brautsch he must have been cleared and all that, right?"

"Puh! To you, ancient history. To me, yesterday. Do you know what it means or not, SS? *Totenkopfverbande, Einsatzgruppe, Sonderkommando?* I am a citizen of this country now for twenty years, and this SS murderer is placed over me so he can take away my profession!"

"Oh, come on. So some J. Brautsch wrote an article about Schopenhauer."

"You don't know about these SS. You must understand that murder was part of their education, part of the training of their intellects. You believe only a few of these swine murdered nine hundred thousand Russian Jews, three million Polish Jews, innumerable Poles and Russians?" Felix was in a sweat, ferocious yet harmless, a huge, seedy teddy bear. The sharp odor of leathery sweat came across the desk and the black documents. Felix actually shook with rage. He was obviously crazy, obsessed by the idea of instant enlightenment, of pure proof. But no one would take him that seriously. Even his motives were suspect; he could not stay on permanently with his few credentials in an upgraded department. The dean had taken some pride in bringing Brautsch here, and with him funds and exchange scholarships from the West German government. And the dean himself was Jewish.

Charlie didn't doubt that Felix had seen and suffered terrible things long ago. He saw Felix as an old man back then, the vision persisting though he knew Felix must have been a young man; the old seemed always to have been old. Photographs came to mind, of thin gray corpses stacked lightly as pick-up-sticks, and some words—Eichmann, Zyklon B, Himmler, Auschwitz—sickening dark names and deeds, but it was all learned history that had come to him as whole and finished as Shiloh or the Somme—ancient, inoperative, the property of historians. Even Vietnam seemed history now, his remembered battles having taken place in graduate school, the route he'd taken, though he'd gone to Washington twice, and once he'd read in public, by candlelight, from the lists of the dead, in which the names of the soldiers were somehow not as meaningful as the names of their home cities and towns.

After seeing that Charlie was in the deepest way indifferent to his proof, Felix became at least for the moment thoughtful and quiet. It was all very interesting, Charlie told him, meaning that much. Because Felix, after his cautious unlockings and whisperings, seemed vulnerable now, Charlie shut the door behind him as he left, as if to seal Felix and his archaic passion into the small room.

He took a quick glance down the corridor where his own office was, marks posted on the door, but no students were there pondering his judgments. The worst thing about final marks was that they could still be argued, and the few students who might argue were the few he really didn't want to talk to, at all, ever, about anything. So those few final marks that had been given with a feeling of middle-range boredom, indecision, and probably generous oversimplification were the ones that were not totally final, and could cause anger or even tears, pleas, hurt silences—all the open, wounding emotions he spent a good part of his life trying to avoid.

At the front entrance he met George Bertram, a rather jaunty medievalist in his fifties whose office was next to his, and they walked across the campus together. Everyone was contentious about something or other, and George Bertram had his cause: "I simply will not use the term 'chairperson,'" he said. "I'm a professor of English and it is my duty to resist the totalitarian mode. Meanings change, of course, and sometimes that can't be helped, but to declare a word valid or invalid by institutional fiat is against my principles, period." He added, after this practiced outburst, "I saw you go by with Felix Tuolemi. Did he show you his documents?"

Charlie was relieved to hear that someone else had been involved. With only the slightest feeling of betrayal he said, "Is he crazy, or what? Are the Israelis about to do an Eichmann on Brautsch?"

"Poor Felix. God only knows. Of course, he's probably right, in a way, about Brautsch. The man's an unreconstructed bloody fascist. Listen to him for five minutes and it's clear as a bell, but even if it's true that our Brautsch wrote the article, so what? Anyway, I'm glad Felix has found himself a new confidant. I need no more lectures on the SS: *'Ich schwore dir, Adolf Hitler'* and all that. I know quite enough about the twentieth century, thank you."

George Bertram turned off toward Faculty Parking Lot B, and Charlie walked on home, to the small apartment that in spite of partitioning still seemed only an alcove in the flow of a large, dismembered old house. Three other fragments of the house's once generous space were also called apartments.

Charlie Jr., home from kindergarten and forbidden afternoon television, played with a cardboard game whose principle of continuing fascination was a mystery to Charlie. A box rotated by the player emitted, from a slot in its side, cardboard markers of various denominations, and the player with the highest score won. Charlie Jr. played this game by himself, often and very seriously, against what dream fate or bargain with luck Charlie didn't know.

Margie came into the living room with the momentum of someone about to go out. She was upset, but would probably not say why; it would be up to him to figure that out, a test of his sensitivity, a moral exercise. She was tall, dark, mysteriously soft-fleshed, and liked to wear red. He had always admired things that were large and graceful.

"Felix Tuolemi just showed me proof that Brautsch was in the Gestapo or something," he said.

"So that's where you were."

"I was at the last faculty meeting." Granted, attending faculty meetings could hardly be called work, but it was part of his job. He didn't see why he had to prove that he worked. "Isn't there some old guy in Vienna that hunts Nazis?" he said. "Maybe Felix ought to call him in."

"Is there gas in the car?"

"I guess so. Where're you headed?"

The word "headed" was too casual.

"You have no idea, have you?" she said, and left.

He didn't know where she was headed, and examined his guilt as if it were an abstraction he might try to define, but it was not something he could turn around this way and that; it was as insubstantial as a faint touch of nausea.

Charlie Jr. spun his box and muttered impatiently.

"What do you want the game to do?" Charlie asked him. "What do you want to happen?"

"I want it to come out right," his son said without looking up. He spun the box and a marker appeared, evidently a wrong one, and he hit the floor with his small fist.

"Do you know where she was going?" Charlie asked.

"To her class."

"I thought her class was on Wednesday."

"It is Wednesday."

Oh, yes, of course it was Wednesday. When his classes were over he tended to forget the names of days, and it was only luck that had brought him home in time for her to go. Somehow she'd known this immediately, even before he'd given himself away. Her class was at a business college in a town five miles away. He had no objection to her becoming a licensed "Realtor," though she no doubt perceived, and resented, the phantom quotation marks he always placed around the word.

Charlie Jr. pushed his game away. "What'll we do?" he asked.

"Monday we'll go to the lake. How about that?"

"I mean right now."

"Oh, I don't know."

"You never make anything happen," Charlie Jr. said. The child's look was too pure, the eyes too accurate. Charlie was hurt, and felt demeaned because he could let himself be hurt. This five-year-old, forty-pound homunculus, his own flesh, dark-eyed, pale, thin-armed, too "adult" for his age, had hurt him.

"Well, what would you like to do?" he said.

Charlie Jr. gave him a look that said yes, see? Proof again, and rolled under the couch.

The telephone rang.

"Professor Johnson?" said a student, a girl.

"Yes?" he said with dread. She gave her name, which evoked dull, sad eyes in conventional flesh.

"About my mark."

"But you didn't do the work. What did you expect?"

"If I don't get a C I won't graduate."

Because she needed, did she think she deserved?

She said, "I'm sorry about the third paper and the final, but my father killed my mother."

"What?"

"My father shot my mother and himself."

"Your father killed your mother?"

"So I had to go home, and I couldn't study. My father's in the hospital in a coma and I have to take care of my sisters."

His confusion was caused by the difference between the information given and the matter-of-fact way it had been given, but at the end her voice became damaged and she made sounds that weren't words. He said he was sorry, and yes, he would change her mark. He still felt a cool wonder separate from the meaning of his words.

He and Charlie Jr. walked to his office, and he sent a change-of-grade form through campus mail. They came back by way of the business district and had soft vanilla cones decorated with chocolate jimmies.

That night he was still bemused in what he thought a morbid, dreamlike way by what his student had so plainly told him. But if one had to impart that information, certain plain words had to be used. He watched Margie remove her clothes. She saw that he watched, and gave him a short glance that didn't acknowledge anything. Lately she had been wearing skirts and blouses.

He said, "I didn't think until after I'd sent in the change of grade that the whole thing might have been made up. Some joke, huh? Guaranteed to blow away the prof's skepticism."

"Why didn't you find out whether it's true or not?"

"I didn't want to find out."

"In other words, you just don't care—is that it?"

"No," he said. He meant to add that maybe he cared too much, but that wasn't quite true, either.

She took a shower and afterwards studied for her State Certification exams. He was still awake when she came to bed, and touched her. She was not just another person, a unit defined by its peripheral membranes and defenses, but a process of which he was a part. They were one thing, where they not? The idea burned in him, and she must have known, but she settled in for sleep, that quietness and departure.

At breakfast she told them rather formally that she wasn't going to the lake this year. She was going to take her exams in the middle of the month. They could go to the lake if they wanted.

Charlie Jr. looked at his father. "Aren't we going to the lake?" He was upset; his mouth turned down.

"We'll see," Charlie said.

"I don't see why you two can't go," Margie said.

Charlie Jr. looked from one to the other, his mouth and chin shriveled by the knowledge of their arbitrary and unpredictable power.

At one o'clock on Sunday afternoon the procession was forming in the green shade of lindens and maples in front of the library, school by school, department by department. There was a sort of gentlemen's agreement that every other year or so one attended commencement, and Charlie had, after all, been promoted and given tenure this year. It might not have been the greatest triumph in the world, but it was something he deserved and had received, and it gave him pleasure. The dark robes and various colorful hoods of his colleagues were real, and meant something not dishonorable.

"A chairperson," George Bertram said, signifying by his diction that he was uttering a composed statement, "is a small creature who lives in, or under, chairs. A spokesperson is similar and lives in wheels."

Charlie responded with the involuntary, mindless yet polite huff of sound required. Though he knew that in this world no pride or pleasure came unalloyed, he couldn't decide whether or not he was happier, or unhappier, than he ought to be. Was it true that the girl's father had shot his wife and then himself? The reality or unreality of that event had too much to do, at the moment, with his own mental balance. Had it happened, or not?

"Look out," George Bertram said. "Here comes Felix."

Felix wore a heavy black robe over his brown suit, and under an odd academic headpiece that looked like a fat beret, his lumpy face ran with sweat. He stopped abruptly in front of them and said in a conspiratorial and peremptory voice, "Have you seen Brautsch?"

Charlie, hearing and gauging the effect of his own answer before uttering it, was appalled. He'd never been one to poke a snake, to change a mood, but he clearly said to Felix, "Haven't you heard?"

"Heard what?" Felix said.

"The Israelis got him."

As Felix heard the words and understood, he began to burn with a flame of joy so pure that anything could be believed, and was, for that one unflawed moment. But even Felix soon recognized the implausibility of his heart's desire. It had been a joke, that strange, risible alliance between ecstasy and death. He barked once, like a startled dog, and turned away.

The Voyage of the Cosmogon

HOUSES THAT Lenny supposes are only ordinary are here full
of ominous strangers. It has always taken him a long time to
get used to new streets and houses. He knows no one in this
new town, Leah, New Hampshire, where his mother has
brought him right in the middle of eighth grade. The children in his new school are hard and self-sufficient. They don't
need him.

Now, in this house without curtains, evening has faded the
street outside. The sofa bed is on the rugless floor in front of
the television. Voices come from the kitchen.

His mother told him once, "I'll never bring a man home."
When she said it he didn't know what she meant by it, why she
had to promise him she wouldn't. But she lied, or forgot that
she ever said it. She looks washed and painted when this new
man comes; she makes herself bright as a flag, and simpler than
she ever is with him. While he ate his supper their voices seemed
bent by smiles and collusion, the man wanting to go to her room
the way she agrees to, his car parked a block away so it won't be
seen in front of their house. She is thirty-six years old and looks
loose around the eye, too old to have on makeup and make
jokes. Her face is worried, knowing that it knows something its

expression doesn't want to admit, yet she laughs at the dumb jokes.

"Hey, Lou, want a screw?" the man said, dropping a silver-colored wood screw on the kitchen table. She laughed and made a disapproving face, glancing at Lenny. She laughed, but she is the loser. There is no honor in that smirking. Why does she subject herself to this man who is shiny around the lips, with a young potbelly and long hard arms? He will hurt her for her folly. Though he never comes here in his uniform, he is a policeman, and in some remembered sense of order, now invalidated by what he sees and hears, Lenny thinks a policeman should never do what this man does.

But now Lenny is alone in the front room, voices coming from the kitchen, and the television will help stop those sounds. Before its sound rises, though, his mother yelps, or laughs, and a chair scrapes. Then the music of his program rises bravely, its deep space-melody touched by a quick descent into a light but dangerous minor that takes his breath and holds him. Just so nothing from this house will hurt the hour he has here, with the people of the *Cosmogon*.

It is an old situation, he knows. He has read science fiction since he was ten, watched with interest several versions of this same theme on television and in old movies that seem to suggest it in one way or another. The people of the doomed planet have set off bravely into deep space in search of another home, a new green-blue world where they can breathe, feel the wind, let nonacidic rain glisten on their shoulders. They are a valiant people, like their Patriarch, Noama, who stands in his brown robes, stern, gray, and wise, on the bridge of their great ship, the *Cosmogon,* a vessel as large and asymmetrical, with its ribs, booms, and quays, as Manhattan Island. There are internal highways and escalators, hydroponic farms, radar complexes, dormitories, even rows of small outer windows whose warm lights glow endearingly against the black vacuum of space.

Lenny is in awe of the immensity of the people's task. They are clever and intelligent, sometimes silly, sometimes mean or dangerous to each other, sometimes loving and generous, but for all their skills they have a task before them that seems far beyond their powers. Space is too vast, the suns of found planets too unstable or dull, incipient supernovas or red giants brooding slowly over dead worlds. Whole galaxies are barren, poisonous, their planets' atmospheres instantaneous death to men and women.

But the people, who are called the Intuint, have an even more immediate problem. The evil Gruhazk, a race as sophisticated technologically as it is morally deficient, pursue them across time for the very protein of their bodies and for ancient hatreds the Intuint know only through legend. The Gruhazk were once Intuint, like the people, though it is hard to believe, for now the Gruhazk ships stalk the *Cosmogon* from galaxy to galaxy, attacking when they can. The small but maneuverable single-seater Intuint fighterships, called Rainfires, again and again have to fight off Gruhazk raids, at great odds, and after such battles there are empty seats at the pilots' mess.

Now the vast unfamiliar constellations pass, and he enters the *Cosmogon,* among the people. There is Noama, who is ever strong and kind, and Buck Hurtler, the devil-may-care pilot, and Coraina, his girl who loves him. Lenny is in love with her loving him. She is so clean and beautiful it is almost as if he can fall into her blue eyes, and her golden hair is soft unto pain. Lenny would be Buck's wingman, flying his own Rainfire against the dark red ships of the Gruhazk. There is Squadron Leader Starr, a handsome, stalwart black man, brave and true, and the clown, Traypots, who pretends to be lazy and clumsy, and the Council of the Elders, some of whom may not be too trustworthy. There is Buck's friend, Adano, and Adano's dark wife, Mora, and their children, Bren and Farima.

The plot unfolds, a mysterious document of time, each instant revealing danger, though Lenny can fear without real anxiety for his people who are so lost in space. This is a universe of meaning, in which the good must finally prevail. But now the Gruhazk have broken the outer ring of protection, light-minutes from the *Cosmogon.* They have a new masking force, an amber cloud of energy composed of particles not at this moment understood by the Intuint. It is Traypots, the outwardly silly young man who masks his care by his clownishness, who perceives the only chance they have. In his sleek Rainfire he patrols that sector, far from his home ship; one thing the Gruhazk cannot understand is a quick and to them irrational decision borne of love.

Meanwhile the *Cosmogon* on its voyage moves to the laws of mass and momentum, its drive a faint flow of energy against the stars, life against death, life a fragile, gentle nucleus here in the vast of absolute zero.

Buck Hurtler knows what Traypots will do. He has long seen through the clown to the brave man beneath. He runs to his Rainfire, makes a quick instrument check before rolling forward through the pressure lock onto the catapult. He can't reach Traypots yet on the telerad circuits—distance and the strange amber cloud interfere—but he homes in through other telemetry on Traypots's distant, lonely Rainfire, a dot of resistance to the assembling Gruhazk fleet.

Will Buck Hurtler get there in time to solve the problem of the amber cloud, and save Traypots from his brave sacrifice?

There is the lively, inane interruption of a commercial, gaudy in exhortation; Lenny doesn't hear its words, its insane irrelevance. There is the sliding of a chair, and his mother's stressed voice. "Don't be so *rough!* Why do you want to be so *rough?*" Why does she want the man here at all, if that is so? He looks at his own small hands. Sometimes when the man is not here she says she doesn't ever want him here again, but that is not the truth.

Then Traypots hears, scratchily, faintly, "Traypots! Traypots! It's Buck! Hold your position! Hold your position! Code order! Verify! Verify!"

That voice. And Traypots seemingly flippant answer, "Hey, Bucko!"

With the whoop of sirens and the hurried but controlled manning of the long pulse cannons, the *Cosmogon* has gone to full battle stations. Everyone has a useful task, even the children over ten years old, such as Bren and Farima in their helmets and antiflash suits of mirror-cloth.

On the battle bridge of the *Cosmogon,* Squadron Leader Starr confers with gray Noama, Commander of the *Cosmogon* and Patriarch of the Intuint. Noama says, "Until we know what it is, we can't risk a squadron; we are few and they are many. The *Cosmogon* must not be left undefended." Noama's face is sad but strong, his voice deep and fatherly with wisdom.

"But what about Buck and Traypots? We can't just . . ."

"It's your job to fight, my impatient friend," Noama says,

putting a hand on Squadron Leader Starr's shoulder, "but it is mine to ensure the survival of the Intuint."

Suddenly a mussy-looking woman who is meant to be engagingly stupid says directly to Lenny, "I just can't face my face in the morning without my Nu-Kreme!" She turns her head abruptly to what she holds in her hand, a small blue jar two inches from her eyes. He turns down the sound, a mistake, since he hears his mother moan. She and the man have gone into her bedroom off the kitchen. Sometimes he can't tell her cries of pleasure from her cries of dismay. "I'm a yeller," she said to him once. "I can't help it when I'm getting satisfied." She said this as if she were not talking to him at all, but to some person like herself. "Oh, yes my Aunt Fanny," she said. "A long time ago I truly blew it. I blew it with your father and I know what, when, why, and how I blew it. I blued, screwed, and tattooed it!" Her raucous laughter ignored him, who was the only one there. She was a little drunk then.

Adano says, "We have four minutes and fifteen seconds of optimal time; then it's nip and tuck, Noama."

"I'm afraid our strategy is up to Buck and Traypots," Noama says. Then he gives the command: "Rainfires scramble in three minutes." His steady voice penetrates the *Cosmogon,* echoing in every chamber of the great ship.

The theme music rises; the hour has passed and the episode will continue next week. That music, its triumphant hope, its sadness into the minor, says farewell, for a time. Lenny knows the Gruhazk will be outthought and outfought by the brave Intuint. He knows it, but there will be that gray time without their companionship.

He turns off the television, because anything on it is now meaningless, and he hears these sounds: "Jesus, keep it down, will you? My kid's out there!"

He goes to the kitchen to get a glass of milk, or a Coke if there is one. The warped linoleum his mother calls "horseblanket" is worn to the brown beneath table legs and chair legs. His mother and the man are behind one painted door, the narrow stairs to his own room behind another. In his small room, imprisoned behind a dresser, is another door beyond which an old man, the owner of the house, has his apartment. He takes his glass of milk to his room.

That night he dreams that he is in school and his mother comes to get him. There is a whisper throughout the room: *She masticates.* All are looking at him and then at the door, his mother a disorganized presence there in the hall, with strange straps and tubes coming and going in her clothes. The whisper continues: *She masticates.* Lenny knows that "masticates" means only to chew the food in your mouth, but in the dream it means something crude and reprehensible.

In the morning he makes his breakfast of cornflakes and a piece of toast. His mother isn't up; maybe she isn't going to the restaurant today. Maybe she'll lose her job. He has no power in these matters.

On the bus a girl deliberately sits next to him. Her name is Ruth and she is pale, unattractive, and bigger than he is. Because he is new she is trying to be kind to him, he knows. She is not trying to make fun of him or anything; she's too vulnerable herself for that. But for some reason he acts as if he can't understand anything she says. He pretends to be deaf, he doesn't know why. Maybe he thinks it's just a joke, but she is soon embarrassed and silent, and he didn't mean to do that, but it's too late.

Maybe he'll just play deaf all the time. All the subjects in his classes he's already covered in his other school, so he doesn't listen much anyway. And out of class the kids all talk about things he's never paid much attention to, like music; he doesn't care about the noisy singers and bands they admire. He's heard the names and the music, but he hasn't the slightest idea why one should be better than another. They all seem to hate x and admire y. Why?

One day he asked a boy named Walter, who was about as plain as himself, and in whom he thought he saw some sort of kinship, if he liked *The Voyage of the Cosmogon.* Walter said he never watched it. He still feels as if he tried to suck up to Walter, and even worse he did it at the expense of what means more than anything to him. He doesn't really want to share the *Cosmogon* with anyone.

His English teacher, Mrs. Martin, is beginning to look at him with worry, so he gives her some of the deaf treatment too. He can't seem to help it; he's never been like this before, but now he seems willing to throw the whole place away, to act crazy even though he really doesn't think he should. But it's almost a relief to act crazy.

If it could only be Sunday night, at eight.

Mrs. Martin says, "Leonard, are you with us?" She is nice, so why does he want to act crazy? He just looks at her, and it's so easy, knowing his look is odd, sort of wall-eyed, and it feels like wetting his pants or something.

For twenty years, Marsha Martin has been doing all the chores required of a junior high school teacher in Leah, New Hampshire. Her husband, Ray, taught English for twenty-two years in the senior high school. They've had no children, though they've tried. Two years ago last fall, a week into the school year, Ray found that he could no longer enter a class-room. They found him in the small teachers' lounge next to the principal's office smoking cigarettes, something he hadn't done since the Surgeon General's Report of 1964. After twenty-two years he was due a year's sick pay, and his therapy, which is supposed to help him return to teaching, is still being paid for under the group plan, though they have to pay the premiums themselves.

Marsha is forty-two, and things aren't going very well be-tween her and Ray. He doesn't seem to think of ever working again, at anything. He's like a boarder in the house. He's gone to his study, in which he sits all day reading old magazines and sometimes watching sports on the small black-and-white TV set her mother gave them long ago. Now he's begun to sleep there, too. She may be a little overweight, but she's will-ing to diet and do exercises if that will please him. She doesn't know how else to please him. She tries to be nice to him, but then she's always tried to be nice to him. He's depressed, too, because they are living on less than half of what they've been used to. They've had to give up his car, and her old Toyota is rusting out.

Late one afternoon she knocks on his study door. It's the room off the kitchen that was once a big pantry. When they bought the house in 1964 he had so much fun fixing the room up with a desk and bookshelves and a large casement window onto the backyard, where the apple tree, now an unpruned giant, was framed in his view. Now the tree is everywhere, brown angled branches like legs and arms all over the yard and the sky.

"Yes," he says from inside the room.

"It's me. May I come in?" She hears him heave himself off the sofa he now sleeps on. She hears him rustle and stack his magazines, mostly old copies of *Life* and *Esquire*.

"Come in," he says, and opens the door. Against what he once was, the hopeful young writer to whom teaching was a stopgap, is this ruddy, middle-aged, overweight man whose skin seems under pressure from its contents. He wears jeans and a plaid cotton shirt, tails half out, his fringe of reddish hair uncombed, his beard honey-colored now because of all the white in it. Cigarette stink makes the air seem as old as the inside of a moldy trunk. His shame at his present condition is strong in the room, and they never speak of it.

"I thought we'd have frozen entrées or something like that for dinner," she says. "Maybe some soup with it."

He shrugs. He can no longer sit at his desk, at his typewriter, he's told her. Twenty years ago he sold a story to *Yankee*, about a man hunting grouse with his son, the story showing how such sport requires responsibility and a sense of love and honor toward the wilderness and its inhabitants. Its "denizens," he'd called them, but really the grouse were the inhabitants and the hero and his son were the denizens. He used to laugh at that boner of his, saying there really was a difference; look it up in the dictionary.

"I'm sorry," he says. "I know you're tired. You shouldn't have to think about dinner."

"We've got those Stouffer Lasagnas. They're always pretty good. Would you like that?"

"Sure."

She can't make him come out of this funk, or spell, or whatever it is. She's tried, but when he sees her trying, or hears her allude to the future in any way, he goes back in and shuts the door.

One evening, sent by his mother to the store for milk and Coke, Lenny notices that a picture of Noama, Coraina, and Buck Hurtler is on the cover of the new *TV Guide*, so he buys it, and later takes this treasure to his room to look at it more carefully. Noama's face is broad, old in a clean, wrinkled, coppery way, his mouth wide, with a wise and kindly half-smile. He stands above and to the left of the young couple, who are bril liant in their beauty and strength; it is the strength of love and justice, of course, in a dangerous universe. Inside *TV Guide,* where the words about them begin, is another picture, of Squadron Leader Starr, Traypots, Adano and Mora, and Bren and Farima, who are his age. Sometimes he is older, a Rainfire pilot, but sometimes as he enters their world he is their age. Farima is dark, with luminous, lively dark eyes, and small, new breasts. Often he envisions a strangely endless scene in which he and Farima are lying next to each other in the *Cosmogon's* fitness room under the sunlamps. He has on only the skin-tight bikinis worn there, and she the same except for a small bra. And there they are, and remain, next to each other. They don't talk. This scene can go on forever. It is as though she is the sun, and he is the sun, and they are radiant in each other's presence. And nothing, nothing ever has to change.

But there are words connected to the pictures in *TV Guide.* *Will Darryl Grossman's Super Space Opera achieve orbit? Retail outlets report that sales of tie-ins such as T-shirts, toys, and dolls are not going all that well, and network executives are tracking the ratings progress of this potential $20 million bomb with extreme care.*

Toys. Yes, there are toys—Rainfire fighters, Gruhazk fighters, the *Cosmogon* itself. Though his fingers, in an earlier, juvenile way, wanted to hold and poise those toys in the air, he quickly thrust this childish desire away as a form of sacrilege. The plastic dolls with their shiny foreheads disgusted him from the beginning.

"I want to be in the *Cosmogon,*" he says now, out loud, listening to his own yearning voice. He doesn't want to bring some imitation of the *Cosmogon* to this world, he wants to go there, to them. He knows they are all actors, and that the whole thing is staged for the cameras. But if such beauty and honor and symmetry can be created, why can't it *be?* Someone loves it besides him. Maybe they all do, so it must exist, even if only in an imagined universe. It will be there at eight o'clock on Sunday night, and things will happen that he doesn't have to imagine. It will all happen in his eyes that the Intuint will in some heartbreaking way once again temporarily defeat the Gruhazk, and their own selfishness, their imperfections, and their fears.

He has no other base that he can trust. He remembers his

father as a threat to his mother. He took his mother's side only because she was weaker, though she was always louder. They both seemed insane to him, but she was the one who, when struck, fell down, her violent, insulting voice fragmented, finally, into meaningless noises. He believed she was what his father called her, and that she had done what his father said she had done. He has studied her all his life and never shut his eyes or stopped up his ears, powerless as he is. He once asked her why she acted the way she did. "Don't you think I'm pretty?" she asked back. "Do you think I'm ugly or something? Look at that leg—don't you think that's a pretty sensational leg?" Drawing up her skirt so he could see her leg all the way to her pink panties, she gave a saucy lift to her chin and a tilt to her head. It was wrong of her to ask him this, but it was the violation of the meaning of his question, of the logic he asked to be put into consideration, that orphaned him, and made him so apprehensive about the future.

When he reads stories he becomes afraid for those characters into whose minds he can see. When he read *The Wind in the Willows* he knew what Mole truly felt, and he read on fearfully, wondering just when Mole's friend Rat would betray him. Even if Rat never did betray Mole, he was anxious about it all the way through. The world he knows is more like his meanness to the girl, Ruth, who tried to be kind to him on the bus.

He hears his own voice, in a trembly, shameful way near to tears, say,"I'm homesick for the *Cosmogon*."

Whenever Traypots is about to go into combat, when his laser cannons are fully armed, he sings a sad little song:

> Love, I'll sing you
> Of sweet yarrow
> In the valley
> Of the Harrow—"

We never see the faces of the Gruhazk, just their cruel scarlet ships, which are bigger and better armed than the Rainfires, but not as maneuverable. Traypots often looks surprised, as if he's just sat on something he didn't know was there, and his freckles are sometimes shiny with sweat, his red hair spiky and surprised-looking too. On his forehead a fringe of it sticks down like bangs from under his blue helmet. He is not careless, however, and he is not foolhardy. Before any dangerous business begins there is a moment, just a moment, when his eyes are deep with an awareness of honor and of death. And then comes the grin, the daring, the little love song that is sincere, too, a sad little song about something that is lost but might someday be found again. First, however, there is a battle to be fought.

Lenny, too, would die for the Intuint—for Coraina and Buck Hurtler, Bren and Farima. There is no one in his life worth such dedication, but he would fight to the death for them. In the next episode Traypots might be killed because he will try to save Buck Hurtler. Maybe Traypots will attack the leader of the Gruhazk fighters, or even their base ship. Maybe neither he nor Buck will be killed, but if one of them is lost all the Intuint will mourn a brave comrade.

He wakes alone in the winter night, snow at the panes of his bare, luminous window. The snow has in it a soft phosphorescence, diffused and white, a reflection of the streetlights of this strange town. He is a prisoner of where he is.

The man who comes to see his mother, her partner in their folly, always wears a small revolver high on his right hip, beneath his parka. Sometimes he puts it on the kitchen table in its black holster, where it lies as strange on the table as a shoe. Lenny is powerfully curious about the gun, but between him and his curiosity is his disapproval of the man, like a shield; he pretends not even to look at it.

Now, in the cold snow light, he would like to rise, just his self, whatever it is that is his self, out of the peeling barrenness of his room in the rickety house. He would rise through and above the night. There is fantasy in his rising above the town, the state, the Western Hemisphere, the globe of the earth diminishing below him. He doesn't like fantasy; he wants to deserve what he gets, but now he has no ship to take him to far space where the *Cosmogon* journeys between the stars.

Is there anything scientific about the method he must use? He must translate the substance of his body from here to there. And how can he so easily find the *Cosmogon?* He wills it, and thus it is imperfect, all of it, because it is only his creation.

They meet him in the transporter room: "Who are you?" they say. "Where did you come from?" He stands there, embarrassed, in his thin pajamas and bare feet. Then Farima brings him sandals and a dark cloak, which she helps put around his shoulders. Her cool dark arm brushes his cheek.

Again they meet him in the transporter room, a room something like the one in *Star Trek,* created here by Lenny, for Lenny, because he has no ship. This time only Bren and Farima are there. He can't be sure who the others were, in the first scene. Bren, curious and friendly, holds out his hand for a handshake, and so does Farima.

He is some kind of hero, or at least a wonder, because he has appeared here all by himself in deep space. "Where are you from, lad?" Adamo asks in a kind voice.

"From what galaxy, young fellow?" Noama asks.

"The Milky Way," he hears his own voice say. It seems a frivolous thing to call a galaxy, and he wonders if there is a more scientific name for it.

Again, as he becomes visible in the transporter room, only Farima is there. She has a soft blue robe for him to wear, just like her own, and as she helps him into it her cool dark arm brushes his cheek. "Where did you come from—from what far place have you come?" she asks him.

"From the planet Earth," he says.

She looks into his eyes with sympathy and kindness. She takes his hand to lead him somewhere, he hasn't yet thought where.

As he shimmers, becoming visible in the transporter room, Mora, Adamo's wife and the mother of Bren and Farima, has a soft blanket ready to wrap around him. "It must have been a cold journey for a brave boy," she says, and hugs him, blanket and all, to her warmth, which is deep and complicated, as are the soft mounds of her body into which he melts like an infant.

Adamo appears and puts his hand on Lenny's head. "You will live with us in our quarters," he says, "and be a special friend to Bren and Farima."

Lenny, Bren, and Farima are at their battle station, dressed in mirror-cloth uniforms, their flame-damper tanks and nozzle guns worn over their shoulders. They can see from their round window most of the great living breadth and length of the *Cosmogon* as it slowly turns to a new course. Stars slide beneath and then reappear as the great ship turns. But the battle never comes, because he cannot make it happen.

In a wide sky-chamber of the *Cosmogon* are forests where, in moments of peace, the Intuint can walk, and breathe the freshness and the moisture of the trees. He and Farima walk a long green path among evergreens, holding hands. A cool brook flows alongside the path. His love for her causes her dark hair and skin to gleam in all their little spatial curves and turns— nose, cheek, a wavelike whorl of her hair, red highlights in its ebony. They sit down side by side, and her cool arm touches his. There is no need to say anything. She is smooth and her young breasts are like little tangerines, or smooth like hard-boiled eggs. . . . He has no right to know this yet. But by luck he is important, a curiosity, with no history here of shame or embarrassment. It is all so delicate, and no one says anything that doesn't have to be said.

He shivers and is a billion miles away, alone in his room, snow at the window. The *Cosmogon* is a tiny speck far beyond his ken.

But tonight at eight o'clock there will be a renewal, their shapes and colors close to him again. More than vision, there will be action, to move them forward in time. All he wants to do is to be with the Intuint on the *Cosmogon*. That is all he wants to do. He doesn't want to do anything else. There isn't an occupation in the world he's the slightest bit interested in, or a place in the world, or a time in it, or anything that could happen in it that might interest him. He's not interested in NASA, or in the shuttle and its careless accidents. They all saw the *Challenger* blow up, and Mrs. Martin cried. It was all stupid and ugly, and the kind of people responsible for it don't interest him. That kind of people bore him, bore him, and they are everywhere. They are like his mother, like his schoolfellows, like his teachers, like the policeman who comes to drink and leer and make dangerous, unfunny jokes.

Unfunny jokes are dangerous, he would like to tell his mother, because they bully her into false signals of pleasure. Or are they false? He doesn't know.

That day, Monday, Mrs. Martin asks him to stay after school and talk to her.

"You've been acting strange in class," she says. She is sloppy with her smile and breasts and kindness, all of them sort of bouncy and loose, but he doesn't dislike her; how could he? When he first came to this school he made the mistake of putting up his hand and answering a question, so she knows he knows things. She knows, and she talks to him and looks at him in class. She looks hurt when he won't answer her, really hurt, and this makes him feel bad, and stubborn, and dangerous. He hurt the girl Ruth that way too. What a world, in which you hurt those who mean well.

"Are you very unhappy, Leonard?"

What is unhappy? He's always been the way he is, except while he's with the Intuint.

"I know you're bright, and I can't blame you for being bored in class sometimes when we have to go over and over what you already know."

He should be flattered by this, but instead he feels his face begin to turn into the face of a lizard, and he can't stop it.

"When does your mother get home from work?"

"Urk, urk," he says. His throat says this, but his hands decide to try to be helpful, so he signals with six fingers.

"At six?"

His head nods, his eyes cross, and his tongue goes under his upper lip and bulges it out.

"Oh, Leonard," she says softly, disappointed but with affection, and in return he gives her the wall-eyed, deaf look, feeling bad about it and out of control. Just so she doesn't come tonight and disturb *The Voyage of the Cosmogon*. He must keep her away.

"At night *he's* there," he says.

"He? Oh. I'll call her first, of course."

"Not tonight."

"No?"

"Tomorrow."

"All right," she says. The calm straightforwardness of the words shock him; he can't remember ever speaking to an adult who could make a decision based purely upon his unargued preference.

That night at eight o'clock it is announced that this will be the final episode of *The Voyage of the Cosmogon* in this time slot. At least two more episodes have been filmed, but they may or may not be shown some time in the future, at some other hour, under some other sponsorship. The station management apologizes for the unexpected schedule change, which is the responsibility of the network, not of the station.

At first he doesn't quite listen, just as he didn't pay too much attention to what he read in *TV Guide* last week. But now he understands.

When she calls Leonard's mother, a little after six, she hears immediately that the woman isn't very bright. "Yeah, certainly," Lenny's mother says. "Any old time."

Why is it that intelligence can be heard, or not heard, in a phrase? To the eye it's even more obviously there or not there, and when she meets Louise she wonders how she can be Leonard's mother. There is nothing of him there in her eyes, which seem to see very little but the reflection of how she is observed, as if she constantly looks at a moving picture of herself. She is vivacious in crude, gesturing ways, and in her middle thirties she's too worn for her dyed auburn hair, green eyelids, and bright slacks slashed with stylized paintbrush strokes of yellow and pink.

The apartment in the run-down house has an empty, echoey feeling, old paint discolored on floors and walls. The uncurtained front room they sit in has a sofa, a recliner, a metal stand for an ashtray, and a television set.

"Yeah, it's hard on the kid to move so much, but my cousin got me this job, you know? But I didn't like it so I went back to waitressing but anyway here we are, stuck in East Overshoe. I mean, life's like that when you're kind of out of money. You got to go where you got to go," Louise says, shrugging the jaunty, philosophical shrug of experience, of hard knocks. She's bragging. But she's not a cruel or really indifferent woman, it's obvious. Her dullness, however, must be dangerous to a bright and solitary child.

As they talk, Marsha sees that there is nothing she can ask Louise to do.

"He never had no trouble in school before."

"Does he ever bring any friends home?"

"Well, we just got here. He never did bring no little friends home, though, come to think of it. But we always moved a lot. I mean Natick, Lowell, Manchester, a real bad year in Belmont you don't want to hear about, believe me, and now he's stuck here in this godforsaken—excuse me—little burg about halfway to the North Pole, it feels like."

Maybe it isn't time yet to suggest counseling for Leonard,

or maybe she doesn't want to say such a thing to Louise, at all, anytime. She'll try to talk to him, but when that will be, or can be, she just doesn't know. All she can do is try to make friends with him. He isn't the only pupil she has whose consciousness is semi-moribund in school, but he's the smartest one. She knows that he hears not just words, but what she means to say, and this in spite of his facial tics. There is that sub-glow of intelligence in his narrow face, his face that reminds her of a hatchet, his mouth, when pursed up, like a nick in the blade, his narrow eyes always a little swollen.

After half an hour she leaves, after promising, though she wasn't asked, to try to help Leonard as much as she can.

He has lived with the *Cosmogon* and the Intuint for the last time. All through the last episode he watched through a haze of farewell. What happened near the amber cloud was that Buck Hurtler and Traypots went into their "antilogic attack mode." The Gruhazk were strictly logical; everything they did was based upon "best case–worst case" suppositions. Knowing this, Buck and Traypots acted absurdly, according to their sense of humor. First they chased each other's tail, then seemed to shoot at each other, barely missing. And they had some luck, too— why not? Traypots loosed a pulse torpedo into the cloud, just to see what would happen, and by sheer luck destroyed a Gruhazk ship on the far side. It was just pure luck, but all of this information, fed into the Gruhazk battle computer, caused a sort of paralysis of will, and the two Rainfires managed to fight off at least a hundred Gruhazk ships until the Rainfire squadrons arrived. With that, and the loss of eight of their ships, the Gruhazk retreated into far space.

And that is all, forever, as though a Gruhazk torpedo has come sliding in from space and blown the *Cosmogon* and all the Intuint into a brief flash of dust. He can make that end in his mind because he knows they are gone. Even if by chance he gets to see the last, lost episodes, they will just be history, incidents from past lives.

There is loss, like a cold wind through his chest.

The next day, after work, his mother comes clattering in with noisy shopping bags and, squatting, lets them thump out of her arms onto the kitchen table.

"He's coming over around eight," she says. "I asked him not to come anymore 'less he can make up his mind between her and me. He *says* he's going to make up his mind. Ha! Little bears like their honey but I told him he better make up his mind whose honey he likes best. I guess I made myself pretty clear this time."

As she reaches to a cupboard, Lenny looks at her buttocks and shanks. Beneath the cloth, between her legs, sticky-sweet is the honey the policeman craves without love, without even politeness. She could get pregnant, and she could get a disease—even a fatal one. Then he realizes that he doesn't really care. He has no power anyway, except maybe the power to leave. He's going to leave here, why not? There is such a thing as choice.

Marsha asks Leonard to stay after last class. Today he seems farther away than ever, in a sort of waking sleep, and she has to make up her mind about some help for him, from someplace.

He sits at his desk in the third row and doesn't even look at her.

"Leonard?" she says, and then the gray waste of her own helplessness, or maybe incompetence, stifles any further thought she might have had. "Leonard, what's the matter? You don't do anything, you don't say anything. What's the matter?" All she can think of to do is ask that question, and her helplessness makes her want to cry.

He glances at her for a second and she sees, clear as a wink of light, that he has sympathy for her, but emotionally he is so far away his understanding is almost an abstraction, something he has left behind.

The present school counselor is a young woman who seems nice enough, in a way, but after the shuttle blew up in front of the children there was an awful lot of doubtful advice, or melodramatic advice, from that quarter. But who knows? She has never met the psychiatrist in Northlee that Ray sees every other week. Ray thinks he isn't doing much good, trying to cure a wasted life, which is an impossibility anyway.

But you've taught so many students! she cried. How can you say that's a waste? I never wanted to teach, Ray said. And I never did it very well anyway.

"Leonard? I want to help you. You know that, don't you?"

He raises his head and smiles at her, briefly, but the smile is cool, too ancient and understanding to have come from a thirteen-year-old. She has to ask for help for him outside of herself, something she would never have thought of doing a few years ago.

When they've been silent for a while, she lets him go.

That night, alone in the king-sized bed, she is awakened by a percussive crash that is damped by walls and doors but still imperative, its following hush full of apprehension. She goes downstairs to the kitchen, to the door to the pantry room, in the fluorescent kitchen light. She knocks on the door and calls to him, but there is no answer. Light shows beneath the door, but he doesn't answer.

The next day Mrs. Martin is not in school, so they have a substitute teacher. On the bus after school, Ruth tells him in a mean and even gleeful voice that Mrs. Martin's husband blew his brains out. "Did you hear about Mrs. Martin?" she says. "Her husband *blew his brains out!*" She speaks this way for revenge, to startle him, not because she feels glad about it. He doesn't think to have any reaction at all. He just looks at her, and soon she feels so sorry about what happened and how she spoke about it that she looks sick.

Lenny feels nothing about it at first—nothing but the feeling he has when he hears about an accident that happened to strangers, or sees the aftermath on TV, or the way he first felt about the shuttle when it blew up—a sort of thrill mixed with an icky feeling, as if his hands were greasy.

But then he has a closer vision of Mrs. Martin, not as a teacher but as an ordinary person who is soft and pleasant, who cares about what she does. She might have loved her husband. She may be jiggly and a little sloppy, unlike the people of the *Cosmogon,* who are beautiful and clear, but that wouldn't make her feel any less, would it. Maybe even worse.

It has been two days since Marsha found Ray's body. She had to observe that he'd removed the vinyl storm window from the frame and opened the casement window before he did it. He took his shotgun, with which he used to hunt grouse, when that was a joyful thing for a man to do, put the barrel in his mouth, and blew the back of his head out the window into the backyard. It is inescapable that he removed the vinyl frame from its magnetic tape and opened the casement window in order to save her from having to clean up the pieces of his head. And that seems to be his only testament. There is no note, no words for her, so everything is gone, and what she meant to him, if anything, is gone without a word. Then she feels guilty that she has translated his death into her own selfish resentment.

She reads the obituary in the *Leah Free Press:*

Raymond Martin

LEAH—Raymond S. Martin, Jr., 45, of 6 Water St., died at his home Wednesday, March 8, 1986. Born June 17, 1941, the son of Raymond S. and Mary (Hooper) Martin, he grew up in Leah, attended Leah schools and the University of New Hampshire. He taught English and social studies, coached the Debating Team and various sports at Leah Senior High School for twenty-two years.

He is survived by his wife, Marsha.

Memorial services will be held at Balcher's Funeral Home. . . .

There are so many things not there. He was a good teacher once, when he had the energy of his youth and could take the unending hours. But he "burned out." Twenty-two years and he had nothing to look forward to. Not like Christa McAuliffe, with all the smiles and promise, in her baggy space suit. It took longer to kill Ray. Of course, he might have done the other things he wanted to do, but he didn't, and then he found all of this time gone, and he hadn't done what he wanted. But who has? Why do we live? Just to put in the time? No, it can at least feel good to live. Tastes and touches, sights and sounds and smells.

Maybe if she hadn't given him the frozen entrée, and the canned soup . . . But she was tired that day, and all he did was study his damned old magazines.

Her glance falls upon a headline.

Despondent Over TV Cancellation

Hastings, Minnesota (AP)—14-year-old Judson
Paul White, after leaving a note saying that he didn't
"choose to live" after the cancellation of the television
serial *The Voyage of the Cosmogon,* jumped to his death
from a bridge over the frozen Mississippi River.

A ninth-grader. Think of the emptiness of that boy's life.
There must have been nothing at all left for him. Just nothing.

Around ten o'clock Lenny goes down the narrow stairs to
the kitchen. He hasn't heard their voices for a while, so they're
probably in her room. He doesn't know what he wants, whether
he's thirsty or not. He doesn't think there's anything about to
happen, unless it's something he might do himself, that has
caused his breath to leave him like this. He's so anxious he has
trouble breathing, and he can't understand how he can be this
anxious about nothing.

The policeman has left his revolver in its black holster on
the table. It's partly covered by the *Enquirer,* slightly behind an
empty six-pack carton and empty beer bottles, but its heavy
presence is immediately clear. From its darkness comes darkness. It's some kind of a Gruhazk weapon, not that it isn't interesting, and of such power, if he can believe anything he'd
seen and heard, that a finger's worth of pressure can cause
instant oblivion.

It is forbidden to him, but he picks it up. At first he can't
get the revolver out of its black holster, but then he finds that
if he presses a metal pad in the holster, the weighty gun comes
out into his hand. Marcas Registradas, Smith & Wesson, Spring-
field, Mass., it says on the frame. It's like toy pistols he's had,
except for the weight and smooth blue-black finish. The lead
noses of bullets can be seen in the chambers, and brass gleams
at the back of the cylinder. The policeman never before left it
out here when he was in there with her, but from the noises he
heard tonight, and the empty six-packs and nearly empty vodka
bottle, they must have gotten especially drunk. A cigarette has
burned out down to its filter on the Formica tabletop. His mother's green shoes are under a chair, one on its side.

He takes the revolver in his right hand and aims it at the

sink, at the faucet, at the soap dish, at the vodka bottle, at a highball glass smudged with greasy red at its rim. "Blam, blam, blam, blam, blam," he whispers. Then, a little surprised that he does it, he points the revolver at his own head, the cool muzzle at his ear. "Blam," he whispers.

Why not? He can't think of anything else he wants to do. It's sort of a balance. It isn't that he has no friends, for instance, it's that he doesn't want any. And this world is not being run correctly—it's as if the Gruhazk have taken over; all his life he's been told that there's going to be a war, started by men, which will cook everybody's face off and destroy the world. And that "we" are doing this and that, out of greed, to kill everything alive. His breath comes hard, but his hand doesn't tremble, in spite of his anxiety. He could get out of it right now. He pulls the trigger just a little bit, against a spring, then takes the revolver away from his ear and looks at it. The hammer rises as he pulls; he lets it go back down. Pulling the trigger cocks it first, then . . .

Say he does do it. In that case he must imagine what will happen after he's gone. All he would like to do is leave, but he's still got to think of the result. He always thinks of results, like how he hurt Ruth and Mrs. Martin by pretending to be deaf. Why did he do that? Because they aren't as handsome as the Intuint? Because he is just naturally cruel?

Before, when he thought of Farima, he thought of her dark skin naked. He'd saved her from the Gruhazk, and she was grateful, and he was going to do something he shouldn't. But the Intuint are all gone. They are gone and they were all just actors in the first place, so they're doubly gone, and what is left is the embarrassment and shame of his belief.

From his mother's room comes a mumbling, and a sleepy, high complaint, and then the rhythmic plunging of bedsprings. A shot would stop that. They would find him on the floor in a syrup of blood. His mother is weak and scatterbrained, but no matter what she's ever done or not done, she will be hurt and sorry.

He's not worried that they will come out and see him playing with the gun, because he can dematerialize instantly, with the pull of a finger. And what will Ruth say then, and what will Mrs. Martin say? These thoughts are shameful, because enjoyed, almost in the way his sexual thoughts about Farima were shameful. And there has been the one death, of a man he doesn't know except as a dark mist of fascination and horror surrounding Mrs. Martin, who called him *Leonard* in spite of his willful craziness. There is still a balance, but there is also the choice he now wearily makes, to put the revolver away, the black holster accepting it with a cold Gruhazk click, metal to metal.

Marsha is in the room off the kitchen, in the cigarette stink that seems to have entered every texture—books, curtains, rug, walls. She's still looking for a note, a goodbye, anything. There's the tape recorder she gave him for Christmas seven or eight years ago—he had the idea that he could dictate his book to himself, but that didn't work. She finds the recorder on a shelf, uniformly whitened by dust. He used to keep notebooks, but the latest ones she can find are dated more than a year ago, and have to do with his novel—mostly questions to himself. Anything he might have mailed to her would be here by now. They've never made out wills, so they've never had a safe-deposit box. It looks more and more as if he just didn't bother to say anything to her at all, and it makes her seem so worthless.

His life and his despair were on another plane altogether, and she was just furniture. They never even slept together anymore, not for months.

Today a young policeman she doesn't know brought back his shotgun and put it, which was kind of him, in its rack. She didn't want to touch it, although God knows it's innocent enough, a machine that only does what it's told.

She's looking through Ray's old magazines. The oldest is an issue of *Life* from 1963—the year they were married. Maybe he thought that was the last year he was a great young writer, before he got married and settled down to mediocrity, his wife a millstone around his neck. There's Natalie Wood, as a starlet; he used to say she looked like Natalie Wood. Natalie Wood is dead.

On the other hand, she herself probably has another forty years of stumping and squatting through the world, doing little good, filling space with ugly flesh. The question is, why not get it over with? No, really, seriously. How about it? There are three boxes of twelve-gauge shells on the shelf below the gun rack, and she knows how to break the gun, insert a shell in either barrel, close it, and push off the safety. Then it's ready to go. There were always guns around her family's house. Would that be too violent? What's violent when you're dead?

She actually takes two steps toward the gun, her hand actually held out to grasp it, and before she stops she has a feeling of marvelous and dirty freedom. Then she stops.

Well, there's Leonard, who is seriously depressed and needs help, for one thing. Of course, if you're dead you don't care. You don't care if you ate a whole German chocolate Sara Lee layer cake, half thawed, as she did a little while ago, either. But there is Leonard, and they've looked at each other as if through a window intelligence opens only to its own, a small thing among the thoughtless cruelties of the universe.

Certainties

ONCE, WHILE hunting ruffed grouse on our mountain, I came gradually but certainly to the conclusion that I was not where I was. I'd crossed Carr Brook, in a steep little valley, and climbed up through great beech and yellow birch into land which was unfamiliar to me. I'd been through it years before, but each depression, or each large boulder, didn't strike me with the kind of maplike solidity it would have on more familiar land. When I came back down to my brook again, it all seemed new and strange, and I had convinced myself that I was a ridge away, on another brook. I wasn't more than a mile from the cabin, standing at a little pool I'd fished through not more than a couple of months before, and yet I was absolutely certain that I was, in fact, on Brock Brook, a half-mile away.

It is the nature of this certainty that fascinates me. Something happens in the wilderness, where there are no straight lines, where the land is owned and stabilized and changed only by the weather and the trees, that is unsettling and at the same time intensely pleasurable. I remember portaging with my father in the Arrowhead Country of northern Minnesota, when I was nine or ten. I came to the edge of an uninhabited lake and saw a house—windows, roofline, and chimney—made in my selective consciousness out of the random crisscrosses of branches and the trunks of trees. The house was there and yet, as I approached, the branches sorted themselves into wilderness again, and the huge and comforting house vanished. Vanished like smoke, and nothing was left of it—not one sawn board, or shingle, or pane of glass. That hollow feeling, of aloneness, even of abandonment, was the nearest thing to nightmare I'd ever experienced while awake. And yet after that I courted the experience, and looked for more of those houses among the trees, just to see them swirl off into emptiness again, and once again feel that deep pang of loneliness.

My experience on the brook reminded me of this compulsive game I'd played as a child, because when I climbed up out of the brook's gorge I came to a place on the Clark Trail I knew very well. An hour before I'd sat on that rock and smoked a cigarette. There was the apple tree, bent and blasted, yet still alive somehow, hung with its own dead limbs. I'd eaten one of its wild apples, and left the core. There in the damp moss was the butt of the cigarette I (I?) had smoked. But I could believe none of this, because first the world had somehow to jar itself back into place, and my certain knowledge that I could not be there had to fade away into the fragments of hallucination it really was. For a moment I was in a wholly imaginary country— truly lost, nowhere. It wasn't until I had returned to the cabin (was it really there?), and traced my probable route on the geodetic map, that my certainty began to fade out like the memory of a dream. I had to go to the map—wanted to—in order to reassure the civilized part of me that was truly offended by such disorientation. Yet the memory is deep and good.

I think of those primitive maps made by explorers in galleons, who saw whole shores of terra incognita pass by their landward boards—maps strangely certain in their inaccuracies, in the hard, jagged corners of things. Why did the cartographer's hand carve out that imaginary bay, on that imaginary ocean full of carplike fish bigger than ships? I have the feeling that it was more than inaccuracy, even more than fakery. That is the ocean of absolute certainty, and has nothing to do with astrolabes, sextants, or lead lines.

A couple of years ago I had the opportunity to examine such a map, this time made in similar wonder and discovery, of our own mountain, and to test its accuracies against the geodetic map I go by. It was made by a nine-year-old boy, and of course to him—against his certainties—the geodetic map was interesting but confused.

One August morning, around seven o'clock, someone began tapping rather diffidently on the back door of the cabin. The door is big and heavy, made out of two-inch hemlock planks, but my wife heard, and got up to answer. When she opened the door, there were two boys, aged nine and seven, who politely asked how to get to Leah. Now, by road, Leah is about twenty miles, and by the Clark Trail, which runs by our cabin, it's about six miles, over the top of Cascom Mountain. My wife at first assumed that an adult was out on the trail, and the boys had been sent to the door to ask directions. But then she began to suspect that they were alone, and had them come inside. Well, yes, they were lost, they guessed. The older one, whose name was Mark, had that wide, dreamy face I always associate with Finns, or Lapps. They were both pale and blond. Mark introduced his brother, David, and my wife made them some breakfast, while our two children sat and stared quietly at these travelers.

Neither was scratched, or particularly dirty, and yet they'd spent the night alone on the mountain. Their family had camped on the Leah side, near the summit (actually within the township of Northlee), and the boys had been given permission to climb to the fire lookout tower if they'd come right back, because supper would be ready soon. When they got to the summit, which is bald granite, the world, somehow when they weren't looking, turned itself around 180 degrees, and they came down the east side instead of the west. We figured this out from what they told us between mouthfuls. David at one point endeared himself to my wife by changing the subject and saying our cabin was nice. I told Mark that I'd better take them down to the Appalachian Mountain Club lodge so we could telephone their parents.

"Oh, they won't be up this early," he said. "They never get up before nine."

I wonder if I'm right in finding here the peculiar aura of hallucination caused by the wilderness. Mark, it turned out, was very observant. When he came by with his family a couple of weeks later they brought presents for our children that were right for their ages and sexes—although no words had passed between them while they ate their breakfasts. And his descriptions to his father of our cabin, and our car, were very accurate. He was a bright and very thoughtful boy. But they had been in the deep woods, not in civilization. I can't imagine him saying such a thing if, for instance, they had stayed out all night in the city. This was different. His father, I found out later, lost fifteen pounds that night, and I suppose Mark later began to realize that this was possible.

I asked him where they'd slept, and Mark said matter-of-factly that when it grew dark and they couldn't see, they simply lay down and went to sleep. David said, "I slept on my brother's back"—a casual bit of information that still causes emotion in me.

The mountain on this side could be extremely dangerous; there are sheer cliffs, clefts in the granite a boy could slide into and never be found, literally impenetrable islands of dwarf spruce, whose dark passages are deceptively welcoming at first, then turn into interlocking and diminishing traps. All around a small forest called Cathedral Spruce, tall trees have blown down crisscrossed, eight or ten feet deep; they came through that maze, too, by the narrow cut trail which weaves and winds between the piles of trees. But they lay down and went to sleep.

When I got down to the Appalachian Mountain Club, among the excitements of organized search and rescue—wardens, state police, two-way radios, weary hikers who had been searching all night, even a helicopter fluffing its way across the peak of Firescrew—Mark began to realize that something rather enormous had occurred, and he turned quite thoughtful. When I left the boys with the very weary Art Costin, then the manager of the lodge, and the forest warden who would drive them the twenty miles to Leah, Mark sat picking at his second breakfast and staring out the window toward a face of Cascom Mountain that was now steep and bright in the morning sunlight.

It was a couple of weeks later, when the boys came back with their parents, that Mark showed me the elaborate map he had made, which traced in loving detail the landmarks and contours of the strange country that they had traveled through.

"There's where we crossed the second brook," he said, pointing to this document. "And we slept below this cliff, where we heard the bear." There was the bear, its fangs and claws.

"I think that you probably crossed Carr Brook twice," I told him. "Let me show you on the geodetic map."

He looked at it with polite interest for a moment, then turned back to stare dreamily into his own map, at that country of experience whose certainties were deeper than any map of mine.

"I love the woods," he said. "I love to go out in the woods."

To be lost? I wondered. "Weren't you scared up there when it got dark?" I asked him.

"I was scared, all right," Mark said. "Everything was *black*."

"You did the right thing to lie down and try to sleep."

"It was David made me do that," he said. "He just wouldn't move in the dark. He said he wouldn't take one more step."

David was running around, playing with our children, who were, as usual, screaming and yelling with every breath. Mark didn't seem to notice all that racket. He sat at the plank table, quiet, thoughtful, enjoying his fearful memories.

There are few dark places left on our maps, and we need that dark, if only to leave behind us all our rigid, belittling geometries, signs, and boundaries—certainties that diminish us, that tell us by the numbers exactly where we are, and that things are merely what they are, not what they can seem.